MENESTRELLORUM MULTITUDO

Guillotin Le Sautreour

Queen's Psaltery-player, 1298-1319.

(By courtesy of the Public Record Office E101/684/62/3)

MENESTRELLORUM MULTITUDO

MINSTRELS AT A ROYAL FEAST

by

CONSTANCE BULLOCK-DAVIES

CARDIFF
UNIVERSITY OF WALES PRESS
1978

PRINTED IN WALES
BY THE CAMBRIAN NEWS (ABERYSTWYTH) LTD.

ACKNOWLEDGEMENT

The parchment roll which forms the kernel of this piece of research work first attracted my attention on account of its provocative nature. Those who steep themselves in mediaeval literature become all too familiar with ' the minstrel ', a stock figure in romance, faceless and nameless, unless he happened to be a Taillefer, a Tristan or a Blondel. The Payroll, no more than a list of names of authentic minstrels, constituted a challenge. It offered me an opportunity to get nearer to minstrels as human beings, provided I could find means of identifying them.

Searching for references to them in thirteenth and fourteenth century manuscripts entailed many months of reading in the Public Record Office and the British Museum. This part of my work I should never have accomplished without the help of the Leverhulme Trust, to whom I am deeply grateful for the award of an Emeritus Fellowship.

CONTENTS

ABBREVIATIONS

Manuscripts

References prefaced by E101 and C are to the Exchequer records in the Public Record Office. All others, unless otherwise stated, are to the collections in the British Museum.

Printed sources

Bain. *Calendar of Documents relating to Scotland,* ed. Joseph Bain. 4 vols. (Edinburgh 1881-88)

CCR. *Calendars of Close Rolls.*

CFMA. *Classiques français du Moyen Age.*

CLL. *Calendar of Letter-books of the City of London,* A to F.

CPR. *Calendars of Patent Rolls.*

Foedera. Rymer's *Foedera,* Record Commission, 1816-69.

LQG. *Liber Quotidianus Contrarotulatoris Garderobae anno regni regis Edwardi primi vicesimo octavo,* ed. for the Society of Antiquaries by Lort, Gough, Topham and Brand. (Lond. 1787)

PW. *Parliamentary Writs.*

RHS. Royal Historical Society (publications of)

SATF. *Société des Anciens Textes Français.*

INTRODUCTION

1. *Why the feast was held*

The splendid feast which was held on Whitsunday, 22 May 1306, in honour of the knighting of Edward of Carnarvon had its roots in murder. Perhaps it was a prognostication of the grievous fate awaiting him when he became king. The situation in Scotland after the abdication of Balliol in July 1296 was one which was bound to encourage treachery and rebellion. Had the little queen Margaret, Prince Edward's betrothed, survived, much bloodshed and hatred might have been avoided, for the intention of Edward I to unite the two countries by a dynastic marriage was at least politically sound; but fate decreed otherwise. In the thirteenth century a country left without a reigning monarch was considered fair game to any man strong enough to purloin it. Balliol, who had been settled on the throne by arbitration and willing acceptance, had not proved equal to the task of either ruling his kingdom or standing up to the English king in defence of its independence, with the result that his final submission and surrendering of his realm to Edward I left Scotland open to cruel internal strife and restless with burning resentment. William Wallace's head, impaled on London Bridge, was still rotting there when Robert Bruce and John Comyn ' the Red ' of Badenoch were chosen, with others, by Edward I to be ' counsellors ' of Scotland under the newly-appointed Lieutenant, John of Brittany. They were commissioned to draw up a new code of laws, based on the old Scottish ones, and to present it to the king at the end of April 1306. Contrary to all his expectations, every hope of a peaceful settlement in Scotland was shattered, even before Lent had been reached; and by the men in whom he had placed his full trust.

The story of Bruce's assumption of power and kingship needs no repetition here; it is neither necessary nor relevant. What does concern us is the brutal act which proceded his coronation.

Although Bruce and Comyn had long been engaged in plotting to obtain the independence of their country, it seems that they disliked or suspected each other. Comyn had been an active rebel against the English crown for some time before Bruce withdrew his allegiance, yet, by his marriage to Johanna, daughter of William de Valence, earl of Pembroke, he had now become a kinsman of Edward I and therefore potentially suspect in the eyes of many Scottish nobles. On the other hand, Bruce, a legitimate claimant to the throne of Scotland, was also earl of Huntingdon and was both trusted and favoured by Edward I. No one will ever be able to unravel the tortuous sequence of events which led up to Comyn's murder by Bruce. It is a dark and turbulent story within whose many versions the truth will lie forever hidden. Contemporary and later accounts of what happened do not agree one with the other, yet one fact is indisputable. Whatever Bruce's reasons may have been, whether they were innocuous or deceitful, it is certain that he sent a message to Comyn asking him to meet him at Dumfries on 10 February 1306.

According to the *Chronica de Melsa*[1] Bruce had previously sent letters to the earls and barons of Scotland, requesting their attendance at Scone for the purpose of discussing with him business relative to the realm. When they met he put it to them that, if they wanted to elect him king, he would undertake to defend them and the kingdom against not only the king of England but any potential enemy. All consented except John Comyn, who walked out of the meeting. Intensely angered, Bruce and his promoters fixed another day, for a second meeting, this time at Dumfries. Whether this is the correct explanation it is now impossible to ascertain. Only the actual meeting at Dumfries stands unchallenged. From this point on all contemporary accounts of what followed are in substantial agreement as to time, place and attendant circumstances. Bruce, it appears, sent his brothers, Nigel and Thomas, to Comyn, inviting him to meet him on Thursday, 10 February, at Dumfries, ostensibly to talk about some piece of business which affected them both, *super quibusdam negotiis . . . quae tangebant utrosque.* That the invitation was couched in friendly terms seems fairly certain for Comyn, not suspecting foul play, accepted it and arrived at Dumfries accompanied by his uncle, Sir Robert Comyn and a few other attendants.

---

[1] *Chronica Monasterii de Melsa.* ed. E. E. Bond, (Rolls Ser. 1867), II, 275–6.

Among Bruce's companions was his brother-in-law, Christopher Seton.

The rendezvous was the cloister of the church of the Friars Minor. When the two parties met they greeted each other with the kiss of courtesy, ' *sed non pacis* ' adds the chronicler of Guisborough,[2] with dismal hindsight. They talked together for a while, apparently in harmony, but then Bruce's mood seems suddenly to have changed. He began to upbraid Comyn accusing him of treachery, saying that he had vilified him to the king of England to the extent of undermining his place in the king's confidence. Comyn attempted to reply in explanatory and pacifying tones, but Bruce evidently did not want to listen; instead, he kicked him and struck him with his sword— a thrust ' *per medium corpus* ' so the *Chronica de Melsa* states— and then retreated; but his companions followed the wounded Comyn who, in order to get away and also to reach sanctuary, had fled into the church. They caught up with him and struck him down ' *in pavimento altaris* ', that is, on the wide, paved space at the base of the altar steps. Comyn's uncle, Sir Robert, made an effort to beat off the attackers but Christopher Seton killed him instantly by striking him on the head with his sword. No doubt Bruce and his party now believed that Comyn was finished. They left the church.

This flash of fury might not have been quite so culpable if matters had been left to stand as they were. Such rash, personal encounters, flaming tempers and lethal sword-play were commonplace at the time. The life of a man was held cheap provided circumstances could be said to warrant the overlooking of his assassination.

The monks had carried Comyn into the vestry to attend to his wound and to hear his confession. Some evilly-intentioned creatures informed Bruce that he was still alive. On hearing this unwelcome news he gave orders that he should be taken out of the vestry and killed. If the *Chronicle of Guisborough* speaks true, this was the sorry end to the affair. Comyn was dragged out and finally despatched on the steps of the high altar. He may have been trying, once again, to reach the altar for

---

[2] *The Chronicle of Walter of Guisborough*, ed. Harry Rothwell, (*RHS.*, 1957), 366–8.

sanctuary, for he was killed so near it that ' his blood spattered the holy table and even the altar itself.'

Sacrilege had now been added to treachery and murder.

Exactly when the news reached Edward is difficult to determine; it could not have been more than about ten days later. Because John of Brittany had been unable to take up his duties immediately Edward had placed Scotland in the temporary custody of four Commissioners, one of whom was Lamberton, archbishop of St. Andrews. What he did not know was that Bruce had already, in the autumn of 1305,[3] entered into a secret bond of mutual help with Lamberton. In fact, Edward seems to have been completely unaware of the seditious political ferment in Scotland for, on 16 February, six days after Comyn had been murdered, he had renewed the powers of the Commissioners. It is not surprising that, when he did come to know what was happening, he flew into one of his rages. Viewed from his standpoint what had been committed was crude treachery.

By Wednesday, 23 February, part of the truth had reached him. On that day he handed to Sir John de Mowbray[4] the custody of the English lands of ' the late John Comyn of Badenoch ' until his heir should reach his majority. On the following day, exactly a fortnight after the murder, he issued a mandate to his clerk in Scotland to the following effect : ' that, having heard that Sir John Comyn and his uncle, Sir Robert Comyn, had been murdered by some people who were doing their utmost to trouble the peace and quiet of Scotland, he ordered him to keep peace in his district to the best of his ability and to warn people not to have any contact with the enemy.'[5] Was it possible that he did not yet know who the culprits were ?

He had already made seven expeditions into Scotland in an attempt to subdue it. After the execution of Wallace he probably considered that he had succeeded; the wish, at any rate, could have been father to the thought, for he was now in his sixty-seventh year and seriously ill. He could no longer ride his horse without suffering great pain. It is clear from

---

[3] Robert Bruce, G. W. S. Barrow, (Lond. 1965), 206–8.
[4] CPR (1301–7), 417.
[5] Bain, II, 471.

entries in the Patent Rolls that within a week of committing the custody of Comyn's lands to John de Mowbray he had decided to invade Scotland for the eighth time. By 1 March he was at Westminster ordering the sheriffs of London to send 1,000 quarters of 'great salt' to Berwick-on-Tweed 'against the arrival there of the king and his magnates and others of his subjects who are going thither to repress the malice of certain Scots who have lately risen up against him in Scotland'.[6] He had even fixed the date. The salt was to be at Berwick ' at the Ascension next ', that is, 12 May. During the last fortnight in March the sheriffs of the counties were commanded to provide stores of victuals, wine and horse-shoes and nails, to be carried ' with all speed ' to Carlisle and Newcastle-on-Tyne. These and other preparations were being made so that he might contain possible rebellion but three weeks later fresh news arrived which entirely altered the situation. Bruce had had himself crowned King of Scotland. Edward had already sent messengers to the Pope to complain of the sacrilege that Bruce and his companions had committed. This further insult utterly infuriated him and he set himself to conduct a full-scale offensive against not only rebellious vassals and sacrilegious murderers but a man who had, in his eyes, now dared to usurp his royal authority.

Bruce had been crowned at Scone on Friday, 25 March, two days before Palm Sunday. By the Tuesday of Easter week Edward had created two military commands under Aymer de Valence and Henry Percy. The whole of the north of England and parts of lowland Scotland were to be speedily mobilised. Two days later, on Thursday, 7 April, he issued a mandate to these two commanders, granting them power ' to receive into the king's peace, without consulting the king, the mesne men of the land of Scotland who have risen in insurrection but are willing to come in—but not anyone who was at or privy to the murder of John Comyn, or any of the magnates of the land '.[7] From which it can be concluded that his implacable vengeance was going to be directed not against the Scottish people but against the murderers and the nobles and prelates who supported them.

[6] *CCR* (1302–7), 437–8.
[7] *CPR* (1301–7), 426.

Having made what provision he deemed necessary for the mustering and victualling of his troops, Edward now turned to the important problem of increasing the number of his knights, since it was they who would take the brunt of the fighting in open warfare.

Of the fifteen hundred or so knights of the shires who constituted the king's actual war-potential in this class, only about five hundred were available for military service at any one given time. The élite were the bannerets, the king's household knights, usually sons of well-born, well-to-do families. Next came the knights attached to the great baronial households and the feudal fees. It was these who formed the nucleus of the army, but in times of war their number needed to be much augmented, not merely because they were comparatively few but because, under a warlike monarch such as Edward I, there was persistent and considerable wastage among their ranks. At sieges, like the one at Caerlaverock in 1300, the infantry normally took the first shock; the knights followed up with stone-throwing and battering assaults upon the castle walls and gate, but on a field of battle it was the knights who sustained the fierce clash of the melée; the cavalry charge was still the classic ingredient in military tactics. Despite their protective armour they were open to savage carnage and crippling accident; they were by no means invulnerable and their lives and term of service could well be short. What inroads Edward's campaigns in Wales, Gascony, Flanders and Scotland made into his body of knights can be realised by noting how many of them died young, leaving small children as their heirs. It has been estimated that the average number of years during which a knight was engaged on active military service was about ten or twelve. Small wonder that Edward needed more knights for his latest expedition to Scotland. The *Parliamentary Writs* prove that from time to time throughout his reign he would order those of his subjects ' who ought to be knights and are not ' to take up knighthood before a specified date. These were men who held land to the value of £20 to £40 per annum. Men of these moderate means could not afford to keep up all the obligations of knighthood. Equipment was an expensive item; war-chargers more so. Numbers wriggled out of the obligation by either paying a lump sum or by managing to get excused on grounds of physical unfitness. ' Far from knighthood being in Edward's time the exclusive privilege of men of high birth and fortune, ' says Moor, ' the exact opposite was the case; and it might with little exaggeration be affirmed that the honour was almost more difficult to avoid than to obtain '.[8] Nevertheless, avoid it men did in increasing numbers.

For the campaign against Bruce the king needed knights quickly. How he obtained them illustrates his military shrewdness as well as his insight into human nature.

It had long been customary for the king to confer knighthood upon aristocratic young men at the regular festivals celebrated throughout the year, more especially at Christmas, Epiphany, Easter and Whitsun. The aspirants were usually relatives or friends of the royal family or powerful members of the nobility. With these notables a select group of young men, kin and friends, would be dubbed at the same time, sometimes fifteen in number, at others, as many as forty. In 1306 Edward, Prince of Wales, was twenty-two years old and not yet knighted. His father, surely with an old soldier's eye to the mainchance, conceived the idea of holding the customary royal dubbing ceremony with a difference.

On 6 April, the Wednesday of Easter week, he issued mandates to the sheriffs of the counties announcing his intention of conferring knighthood upon the Prince of Wales and commanding them to proclaim that ' all those who are not knights and who would *wish* to be so (not *ought*), ' should come to London this side of Whitsunday next to receive the necessary equipment from the King's Wardrobe and at his gift, so that they might receive knighthood from him on the same day.'[9]

The social impact of this proclamation upon adventurous and ambitious young men, particularly those in the shires, is not hard to imagine. To be dubbed with the king's son, to have rich robes and equipment provided free, to have a holiday in London, to attend the subsequent royal banquet at Westminster, was the opportunity of a lifetime. Here was no curt command, no drab, automatic ' taking up ' of knighthood, which one could ill afford, with the burden of expense upon one's own poor shoulders. It was an invitation, a magnificent

---

[8] *Knights of Edward I*, Rev. Charles Moor, IV, Introd. v.
[9] *Foedera*, I, ii, 983.

royal gesture, although not conceived by Edward in quite the terms used by Ashmole : ' to adorn the splendour of his Court and augment the glory of his intended Expedition into Scotland '.[10] It was more in the nature of a glittering bait dangled by a wily old royal fisherman.

ii. *The preparations and the knighting*

The following weeks showed no diminution in either Edward's energy or the pace of his preparations. He had already ordered provisions for the army, and had sent to the Constable of Bordeaux for 200 tuns (50,400 gallons) of wine, to be shipped to Skinburness ' for the king's use in the fresh rebellion of the Scots '.[1] He had also seen to it that all his archbishops, bishops, abbots, friars and ' all ecclesiastical persons and women ' who owed knight-service were warned to have their service at Carlisle by not later than 9 July, or else go to the Exchequer to pay for their exemptions.[2]

On 5 April he ordered all the sheriffs of England ' to cause to come before the king and his council at Westminster on the morrow of Holy Trinity ' (Monday, 30 May), two knights of their shires, two citizens from every city in them, and one or two burgesses from each borough, according to its size, ' to treat and ordain to make an aid to the king for making Edward, his eldest son, a knight, which he proposes to do at Whitsuntide '. They were also to warn archbishops, bishops, abbots, priors and other men of religion throughout their bailiwicks ' to be there by proctors or attorneys to treat and ordain likewise '.[3] This heterogeneous crowd, the representatives of the country's taxpayers, duly assembled at Westminster on the appointed day and granted, not without some of the usual grumbling, the aids asked for, the counties promising a thirtieth of all their movable goods, the prelates, citizens and burgesses, a twentieth. This done, the financial side of the affair, so far as Edward was concerned, was virtually settled; but this was

---

[10] *The Institutions, Laws and Ceremonies of the Most Noble Order of the Garter,* Elias Ashmole (Lond. 1672). Facsimile edition, Lond. 1971, 37.

[1] *CPR* (1301—7), 417.
[2] *Ibid.,* 437–8.
[3] *CCR* (1302–7), 438.

not the end of the preparations; there was the all-important question of provision in kind to be organised.

Between 14 and 17 April, he issued mandates[4] to all the sheriffs ' to cause to be bought and purveyed in places where it may be done to the king's greatest advantage and to the least grievance of the people ' practically everything that would be needed for both ceremony and banquet. Surrey, Sussex and Kent were called upon to provide each a 100 quarters of wheat and 300 quarters of oats. To Warwickshire, Leicestershire, Bedfordshire and Buckinghamshire was assigned the duty of providing the meat. Between them it amounted to 400 oxen, 800 sheep, 400 pigs and 40 boars. The city of London had to provide 20 lead vessels, other vessels in brass, as well as utensils for the kitchen, all to be delivered at Westminster by Wednesday, 3 May. The Sheriff of Southampton (Hampshire) was ordered ' to cause to be chosen forthwith ' 50 carpenters and to see to it that within three days from the receipt of the order (issued on 17 April) they would be at the palace of Westminster, there to do ' whatever John de Drokenesford, the keeper of the King's Wardrobe, and Robert de la Warde, the steward of the King's Household, or either one of them shall direct '. In addition, Hampshire was to provide 80 pieces of coarse cloth for covering temporary shelters, to be delivered to the King's Wardrobe by the same date. The sheriffs of Bedfordshire and Buckinghamshire were called upon to supply 60 pieces of the same material, ' to be bought in the town of Wycombe and elsewhere '. Other commodities, which formed part of the king's special gift ' to Edward, the king's son, at his knighting on Whitsunday and to those who are taking up the arms of knighthood with him ' included 80 rolls of scarlet and other coloured cloth, 2000 ells (2500 yds.) of linen, 4000 ells (5000 yds.) of canvas, 30 pieces of wax and 20 ' boillones ' (measure unknown) of almonds. Two of the king's clerks, the sheriffs and ' other lieges ' were to buy them at St. Botolph's Fair. The cloth was part of the consignment of material which together with that already existing in the Wardrobe, was going to be distributed among the knights-aspirant for the making of their outfits.

---

4 *Ibid.*, 375, 377, 423.

It now wanted four weeks and four days to Pentecost. This was all the time which was being allowed for the various commissions to the sheriffs to be fulfilled. The 50 carpenters had to be in London a month before the ceremony, so that they could, among other things, start making and erecting shelters, seats and scaffoldings to accommodate the aspirants, their servants, the ladies, visitors and sight-seers. Our recent experience of the preparations for the Investiture of Prince Charles within and outside Caernarvon castle affords an excellent modern parallel to what the streets of London and the palace of Westminster must have looked like in the spring of 1306.

While all the work was going on in London the king and his court remained at Westminster, and no move to London was made until six days before the great event. The itineraries are not in complete agreement about his movements during the week following Ascension. He appears to have set out for London on either the Monday or the Wednesday before Whitsun. What is certain is that on the Wednesday and Thursday nights, 18 and 19 May, he rested at Cobham (Surrey) and arrived at the palace of Westminster on the Friday. It was a journey of only 65 miles but he took so long to cover them because he was travelling not on horseback but in a litter.[5]

London was full to overflowing. Of the dozen odd references to the knighting which have survived in the chronicles of the period only three, those in the *Flores Historiarum*, the *Annales Londoniensis* and Nicholas Trevet's *Annales* contain any details which can be considered usefully informative to us of a much later age. Even these are painfully brief and referential rather than descriptive. Now and again one comes across a sentence which gives a glimpse of what was happening, but sometimes they appear to contradict one another or are so allusive that the information imparted tends to confuse instead of enlighten.

---

[5] '*Post Pacha movit se rex versus Londonias curizando, quia ob infirmitatem quam habuit in tibiis, non potuit equitare*'. Trevet, 408.
A reference to the king's litter occurs in E101/362/20. See p. xxvii. How really ill Edward was can be gathered from the account of his journey to Scotland after the knighting was over. The *Chronicon de Lanercost* draws a sad picture of him making slow, painful progress in his litter: '*Rex autem, propter senectutem et debilitatem lento gradu, factis multis parvis dietis et vectus in lecto supra dorsa equorum, appropinquavit cum regina versus Marchiam Scotiae*'. p. 205.

In order to reconstruct the events of this exciting Whitsun week-end it is necessary to bring together the relevant facts embedded in all the accounts and augment them with stray pieces of information found in the Wardrobe and other records. Unhappily many of the pieces of the jig-saw are lost forever; the picture can never be complete, yet enough of it can be put together to satisfy a little of our curiosity with regard to historical fact and at the same time, if we so desire, to whet our imagination.

How many men accepted the king's generous offer ? In the words of the proclamation the invitation was open to ' all ', but an examination of the extant list of men to whom livery was issued proves that ' all ' seems to have meant what the monk of Westminster, the author of the *Flores Historiarum*, described as ' *quotquot milites tenerentur fieri milites sucessione paterna* '.[6] The majority were sons of knights who would have taken up knighthood as a matter of course. All but a few, such as John le Blound, Mayor of London, belonged to the nobility and the landed gentry. It would be rash to say that all were young. Their ages, where it has been possible to discover or estimate them, ranged from under twenty to fifty plus.

The complete total cannot be accurately determined because the numbers given in the various accounts are all different. The *Flores Historiarum*, the best, put the total at 300, although it is necessary to voice a reservation here, since the words in which the author speaks are capable of more than one interpretation. As it was he who defined the ' all ' of the invitation as those who would take up knighthood by paternal succession, it is not surprising to find that he restricts the classes of aspirants to sons of earls, barons and knights, thus excluding in his computation men like John le Blound. The other London authority, the author of the *Annales Londoniensis*, says that 297, or ' 300 minus 3 ' as he puts it, were knighted on Whitsunday and this number definitely included the Mayor; but he then adds, ' *et in eadem ebdomada facti fuerunt sex milites* '. Up to the present I have discovered no corroboration of this fact in other records. Trevet separates the Prince, the earl Warenne and the earl of Arundel from his total, which he says ' is said

---

[6] Vol. III, 131.

to have exceeded 240 '. The Guisborough chronicler gives the same total as that in the *Annales Londoniensis*, but the Prince of Wales was not included. Peter de Langtoft has 300, the *Annales de Wigornia* ' about 300 ', the *Gesta Edwardi Primi* ' Prince Edward and more than 80 others ', Adam of Murimuth ' about 100 ', Geoffrey le Baker, ' Prince Edward and 100 others ', Rishanger, ' a numerous company of noble young men ', and the French *Chronicle of London*, ' Prince Edward, 92 others and John le Blound, the Mayor '.[7]

Two independent lists from the Wardrobe records of Edward I may be set against these estimates. Ashmole prints what he calls ' a perfect Catalogue ' of the names of the new knights which he found in a Roll of John Drokenesford,[8] at that time in the possession of the King's Remembrancer. It contained 267 names. Shaw, who reprinted this list in his *The Knights of England*,[9] searched for John Drokenesford's roll but could not find it. He also consulted E101/369/4 fragments which may well be part of the missing roll for, as he says, they ' give the names of a small proportion of the knights printed in the text'. He collated them with Ashmole's list but the number, of course, remains the same, namely, 267.

There is another manuscript in the Public Record Office which he did not come across, E101/362/20. It is a list of issues of cloth from the Wardrobe to the aspirants, each one of whom is named. While it cannot be Ashmole's manuscript, for it has 27 fewer names, it does contain at least a dozen additional ones not found in his list. It consists of only two membranes, each of equal length, but there is no heading or title written at the top of the first, so that it may be incomplete. The manuscript is badly rubbed in places, rendering six or more names illegible. Since both Ashmole's list and E101/362/20 are incomplete and, by collating them I have accounted for 282 knights, it would seem as though the numbers given by the

---

[7] John Selden, *Titles of Honour*, (Lond. 1672), mentions a chronicle which he calls 'old annals of Ireland', in which the number was said to have been 400. I have been unable to identify this work.

[8] Modern historians since Tout often refer to him as (John) Droxford, which is the later form of the name of the village in Hampshire (3 miles ENE of Bishop's Waltham), from which he apparently derived his surname; but, for the sake of clarity, I retain the form by which he is always called in the Wardrobe accounts.

[9] Vol. I, 111–22.

two London chronicles are likely to be most nearly correct, that is, 297-300.

Their presence in London, even in 1306, would not have caused any lodging or traffic problems, had the knights come by themselves. A city accustomed to influxes of foreign princes and nobles with their numerous trains would scarcely have noticed the 300 men up for a special knighting at the palace. What caused the congestion were the thousands of others who were not there to be dubbed, the great dignitaries and officers of state, whose presence was either obligatory or desirable; the Patriarch, the archbishops, bishops, abbots, earls and barons, with their countless servants and hangers-on; the knights, with their squires and grooms; the parents of at least some of the aspirants, with their servants, to say nothing of the countesses, ladies, wives, mothers, sisters and younger brothers, with their waiting-men and women, their wafer-makers and personal minstrels; and, to crown all, the swelling mob of sight-seers, itinerant musicians and mountebanks. A hint of the congestion in the city is given by the author of the *Annales Londoniensis*, who says that, according to the estimate of some of the heralds in London at the time, the number of knights alone reached 1000, which, in terms of people, should be interpreted as 3000 or 4000, since every knight had at least one squire, one groom and one minstrel; often many more.

Naturally, accommodation was at a premium. The magnates had their own residences in London; the aristocratic aspirants stayed in either the king's or the prince's households; the vast majority of those who had come only to watch would have sought lodging for themselves and their servants in the houses and inns of the city. For the accommodation of the remainder of the aspirants the king was responsible. They were his guests. How he solved the problem is described by the monk of Westminster. Temporary quarters were set up in the area surrounding the New Temple. Some delightful Thames-side gardens must have been destroyed in the process, for walls were demolished and fruit-trees felled in order that tents and pavilions might be erected, in which ' the aspirants could each robe themselves in their gold-embroidered garments'.

On the Saturday night pandemonium reigned. By order of the king, the Prince, with the élite of the aspirants, such as the young earls of Warenne and Arundel, John Comyn's son and other high-born youths, performed their vigils in the abbey church of Westminster, but it must have been a most distracting time for them, for there was such a din going on outside, of trumpets and high-pitched shouting of people ' *prae gaudio* ', that the monk of Westminster, who has left us this all too brief but still vibrant description, declared that the *Jubilatio* being sung in the convent could not be heard from one side of the choir to the other.

If we substitute more modern popular instruments for the trumpets, the picture he has drawn strikes one as being a very familiar one; that of London in festive mood, with huge, milling crowds packing the streets, deafening noise from un-ceasing laughter and shouting, blatant music in the open air and everywhere a feeling of abandon and excitement. The scene at the New Temple could hardly have been different. It is here that a great proportion of the citizens would have been thronging in the hope of catching sight through the tent-flaps of young gentlemen getting themselves ready for the ceremony, of watching squires carrying the gleaming new arms or grooms currying their masters' horses in readiness for the morning's cavalcade to the Abbey. Something of the universal crush comes through the scanty words of the same chronicler, who had gleaned at second-hand some news of what it was like in the city. Down at the Temple, he says, an aspirant performed his vigil wherever he had been able to seize a place, ' *quotquot poterat capere ille locus* '. The scramble to capture a few square feet of pavement on which to kneel for the night was probably much less decorous than one cares to imagine.

The *apparatus* which the king gave to each aspirant consisted of helmet, hauberk, lance, sword and spurs, together with material for the making of his ceremonial robes and ritual bed. Horse and harness were not included. Since the proclamation issued on 6 April had stated that these things had to be collected from the Wardrobe ' this side of the coming Whitsun ', it is to be understood that the men had to send their servants to London in good time in order that their clothes and beds might be made as soon as possible. The list of issues of cloth already referred to, E101/362/20, brings this part of the prepara-

tion vividly to life. Every candidate is named and the amount
and kind of cloth handed to him stated. It is not a comprehensive list in the sense that materials for the whole outfit are
specified. For that we have to rely on other manuscript evidence. E101/362/20 enumerates only the cloth given for
making the handsome *cointesia* or full-dress mantle and the
ritual mattress and quilt. The young aspirant had to have
other articles of dress besides. There exist in E101/369/4 and
E101/381/11[10] a collection of mandates and receipts for knightly
clothing supplied by the Wardrobe in 1306 and 1325 respectively. Together they provide a full catalogue of the range of
issues made.

When a young gentleman was to have knighthood conferred
upon him the king issued a mandate, in French, to his Clerk
of the Wardrobe, ordering him to supply the said gentleman
with an outfit suitable to his status, ' *une robe convenable pur son
estat*,' which meant that the quality of the livery was not
statutory but could vary in richness according to the social
grade of the recipient. The garments, however, of whatever
materials they were made, were always the same : a *cointesia*,
or elaborate mantle invariably made of some rich cloth (usually
scarlet) and interwoven with gold thread; a *roba* or fur-trimmed
outer dress, similar to a bliault; a *pena*, a kind of cape-like
pelisse made of fur and covered with muslin on the inside and
silk or worsted on the outside; a shirt of linen and breeches
of the same; a *capa* or cloak, made like a poncho, which was
worn during vigil; and a fur-lined *capucium* or hood. The ritual
bed was composed of a canvas pallet, the *matracium*, filled with
straw and covered with linen or richer material, and a *culcitra*
or quilt. The gentleman's squire or other ' attorney ' fetched
them from the Wardrobe. It was the attorney who signed the
receipt and it is in the receipt, in Latin, that the details of the
outfit are recorded. Because E101/369/4 consists only of

---

[10] Unfortunately the E101/369/4 collection relating to the Whitsun knighting
of 1306 are only the French mandates sent by the king to John de Drokenesford. The formula runs: '*Nous vous mandoms que a* (name of aspirant) *qui serra fait
nouveau chevalier en la Compaignie Edward nostre cher filz a ceste procheine feste de
Pentecoste facez auoir auenant attir sicome assiert a son estat*'. The complementary
ones in Latin, which would have contained details of the issues, are missing,
but those quoted from the 1325 group afford adequate information about the
list of garments for which the cloth and fur were intended.

mandates, the following issue, which is a typical Wardrobe receipt has been chosen from the later E101/381/11 : ' let it be known to all by these presents that I, William Beler, have received from Master Thomas de Useflete, Clerk of the Great Wardrobe of the lord King, for the use of Henry le Vavasseur, for making him a new knight, by order of the same lord King, by privy seal : namely, for his *cointesia*, 6 ells of cloth of Tarsus and one *pena* of squirrel-fur of 8 rows.   For his *capa* during vigil, 4 ells of brown-mixed cloth.   For his two *robae* (i.e. a year's livery), 10½ ells of green and 10½ ells of azure blue cloth, 2 furs of ' popple '[11] and 2 furs of squirrel, each of 6 rows; and 2 hoods of marten-fur of 4 rows.   Item, for his bed, that is to say, for his quilt, 2 lengths of cloth of gold in Meseneaux and one piece of worsted (*carda*) ;[12] for his mattress, one piece of worsted. For his issue of linen, 24 ells, and for that of his canvas, 10 ells. In witness whereof I append my seal '.

The ell was 45 ins., so that over 80 yards of material were handed to William, not counting the cloth of gold and the muslin, because the terms of measurements used for these, *pannus* and *pecia* respectively, are ones for which there is no known modern equivalent. The total quantity could not have been much short of 100 yds.

With this in mind we can now appreciate the inadequacy of the list in E101/362/20.   It gives the allocations of stuffs for only the *cointesia, culcitra* and *matracium* (sometimes). There is a choice of materials, all rich and costly : silk embroidered with gold thread, satin and velvet, cloth of Ypres, arista, Meseneaux and *cindon afforciatus*, ' pure silk '.   Two lengths (*panni*) were allowed for each *cointesia* and three for each quilt.   As for the colours of these sumptous fabrics, they bring to mind the brilliant miniatures in our illuminated manuscripts, depicting gold-embroidered mantles of crimson and blue, *robae* of green and azure, scarlet cloaks, brown fur-lined hoods and bed-coverlets of gold-embroidered linen or yellow silk.[13]   Even the

---

[11] This fur is mentioned frequently in the issues. It seems to denote either a mixture of skins or a special fur that was sewn up in wavy lines or which carried a wavy pattern. See *NED.*, s.v. *Popple*. sb. 3 and vb. (b) ; and *Pebble*, vb. 3.

[12] *Carda*, a kind of cloth, possibly similar to worsted, because flags and standards were made of it.

[13] Beautiful contemporary illustrations of both clothing and bedding are to be found in Royal MSS., 14 E, iii, ff. 14ʳ, 32ʳ, 33ᵛ, 77ᵛ, 86ʳ *et seq.*

clerk's prosaic statement of account at the end of the list conjures up a vision of a corner of the king's Great Wardrobe, that huge repository of precious goods of which bales and rolls of materials formed a significant part. The stock of cloth remaining in it from the preceding year, 1305, was fairly small, just over 87 *panni*. Purchases for the current year increased it to 1138 *panni* and 15 ins. What was left after the distribution to the aspirants was a mere ' 23 *panni*, an ell and 1 quarter (5 ins.) '.

On the second membrane, following the long list of liveries, there is another subsidiary issue of silk to sundry persons, including members of the royal family, the king's tailor and some 16 of the aspirants who were being given pieces of silk for their mattresses and quilts. The list seems to be more in the nature of a clerk's note to be entered later in an official account, and since the only material issued was *cindon afforciatus*, it is possible that it is a memorandum for whomsoever was responsible for keeping account of the yardage of specially good silk in stock. The entries are varied and valuable because they add interesting details to knowledge of the occasion. Eleanor de Clare, the king's grand-daughter, was given 3 pieces of red silk to line a quilt made of cloth of Turkey and 16 pieces to make a dorsal curtain for her bed. The little princes, Thomas and Edmund, aged five and four respectively, received 10 pieces of yellow and red silk for their mattresses and a piece and a half for ' garnishing ' their dresses. Geoffrey, the king's tailor, received several issues which indicate that the king's mind was running on other things besides clothes. As well as making a red silk lining for a seat cushion for La Dammoisele de Bar and re-covering the king's pelisse with green silk, he was engaged upon making a green silk housing for the king's litter and twelve silk banners for the army; six of the arms of St. Edmund and St. Edward in blue and yellow silk and 6 of St. George in red and white.

Seven separate issues were made to the Prince, only a moiety of what he must have had, yet they testify to the gorgeousness of his attire and private apartment; 5 pieces of yellow silk for lining a quilt, 1 piece of green for lining his cloak, 10 pieces of various colours for making 2 mattresses, 5 pieces of red for making a dorsal curtain, 5 pieces of green for making another curtain, 6 pieces of red for lining another quilt and 5 pieces, colour unspecified, for lining the quilt of his second bed. One further entry is a reminder of the prime reason for the Pente-cost knighting. Behind all the pomp and festivity lay the murder of John Comyn : ' To Hugo de Bongeye for armature, banners and pennons for the lord Prince for the Scottish war, 43 pieces of silk of different colours.'

It may be safely assumed that by Saturday evening, 21 May, all the aspirants had not only collected their arms and cloth from the Wardrobe but had had their complete outfits made. By late evening each one, clad in fresh linen and his vigil-cloak, would have been in his hard-won place in Church, there to kneel, facing the altar until sunrise. No aspirant was allowed to sit. It would be taken for granted that each one would be addressing himself to prayer and meditation, but it is more than likely that now and again thoughts of the day's excitement and the morrow's coming honour crept into his mind during the long, dark hours of watching. If they did not he would have been more fitted to be a monk than a soldier. At dawn, tired from his arduous vigil, he would return to his room or tent thankfully to stretch his limbs on his pallet for a short rest before being wakened by his squire to rise once more and prepare himself for Mass and the knighting at Westminster. He was bathed, shaved and groomed, his beard (if he had one) being neatly trimmed to a point and his hair curled over his ears as the fashion then was. Finally he donned his *roba*, *pelisse* and handsome *cointesia* and hood.

While the majority were being robed in their pavilions and tents around New Temple, Prince Edward and his companions were being attired in their richer, more expensive garments in the palace. After Mass, King Edward knighted his son; with his own hands he girded him with belt and sword. Henry de Lacy, kinsman of the king and earl of Lincoln, fastened on one gilt spur and Humphrey de Bohun, son-in-law of the king, earl of Hereford and Constable of England, the other. As soon as he had received the accolade from his father and had been formally declared Duke of Aquitaine, the twenty-two year old Prince proceeded, with his entourage, to the Abbey, because it was he who was going to dub all the rest.

Nowadays we are accustomed to seeing royal ceremonial

meticulously organised and faultlessly carried out. This early fourteenth century knighting, while it was no doubt more sumptuous, in terms of flamboyant opulence, than any ceremony of ours today, was, as far as organisation went, a superbly colourful but suffocating, disorderly spectacle.

The Abbey church was packed, the people in it being dangerously overwhelming in the way excitable crowds always are. Immediately in front of the high altar, where the dubbing was taking place, the mob was so dense and pushing that two knights were crushed to death. Several of the aspirants, while they were being led forward to the Prince, fainted in the press, even though each of them had at least three knights escorting and protecting him. The situation of the Prince was equally precarious. He was far from safe in the squeezing, turbulent mass of onlookers. In order to keep himself clear he had to mount the altar steps and stand close to the altar itself. There ' separated from the mob and amid the plunging of fiery war-horses,[14] he girded his companions '.

iii. *The feast*

While the crushing programme of knighting was being carried on in the abbey church the larderers, pantlers and butlers, the cooks, bakers, waferers, turnspits and scullions were hard at work preparing the banquet which was to crown the day's activities. The cauldrons and brass vessels supplied by the city of London were being called into service to boil the ' muttons ' and ' bacons ' sent in by the counties, and to poach the immense quantities of fish purchased by the king's clerks from the London fishmongers. There is no actual record of the game and poultry which must also have been on the menu and the thousands of eggs bought to be turned into sauces, puddings and *doucets* or baked custards, but the Close Rolls provide ample evidence of the numbers which would have been pouring into the kitchens : dozens of swans, peacocks, cranes,

---

[14] The presence of war-horses in the Abbey may seem strange to us, but, during the middle ages nobles and knights rode about indoors as a matter of course, particularly on grand occasions when ceremonies and banquets were held in the immense halls. The Bury chronicler, when describing the wedding feast of Edward I and Margaret of France in 1299, refers to the great number of earls and barons who were riding about in the great hall of the archbishop of Canterbury in which the new queen and her stepson were eating: '*Regina uero et filius regis in magna aula archiepiscopi regalia celebrauerunt conuiuia ubi inter prandendum equitauerunt quam plurimi comites et barones.*' (p. 153).

pheasants and hares, a thousand hens and two thousand eggs
at a time. The twenty *boillones* of almonds, bought at St.
Botolph's fair expressly for the Prince, would have been used
not only for sweetmeats but to make ' milk of almonds ', an
indispensable ingredient in the delicate *blankmangers* or white
meats so popular at the time. As for the hundreds of quarters
of wheat, they would have already been ground into flour for
the waferers and bakers to make into after-dinner wafers and
wastels and *manchets*, the elegant white rolls, ' *plus blans que
n'est lis en este* ',[1] which accompanied all aristocratic repasts.
Wine, as always, would flow like water. It was only half paid
for,[2] but who, except the vintners, cared about that ?

Over six and a half centuries have passed since the king and
his court sat down, with his barons and new knights to partake
of this enormous feast. Splendid though it was, no detailed
account[3] of it has been preserved; probably because banquets

---

[1] 'whiter than marble in summer'. From Jean Renaut's *Galeran de Bretagne* (ed.
Lucien Foulet, Paris 1966, CFMA). Although written in the early part of the
thirteenth century, the scene Renaut draws of the preparations for the wedding
feast of Galeran was very similar to the one witnessed by the London populace
on the eve of the knighting:

> En la ville va emplissant
> La sabmadi avesprissant,
> Y-tant baron et y-tant conte
> Que je n'en sçay nommer le conte
> Et d'autre gent y ra foison;
> Si n'y a loge ne maison
> Qui ne soit de gent toute plaine.
> Et on y aporte et amaine,
> Et sur charretes et sur chars,
> Cerfs et cengliers et autres chars
> Et sur les sommiers lé poissons
> . . . .
> Si a maint cygne et main faisant,
> Et foison de pain beluté   (6775–89)

[2] The city of London had granted, as part of its aid, 2000 marks (about £14000)
for wine for the occasion. It paid half the sum in good time, but somehow or
other, the remainder seemed never to be forthcoming. The king had given a
tally for it to his butler, William Trent, upon whose shoulders then lay the
onus of collecting the cash and seeing that the unfortunate vintners were paid.
The City fathers had bound themselves to pay the remaining 1000 marks by
2 November, but on 17 October 1308, the Prince, now Edward II, was
dunning them, complaining of their remissness and strictly enjoining them to
see that the money still owing 'be forthwith paid'.

[3] Only one detail of the magnificence in Westminster Hall has survived, a note
of the issue of 4 lengths of gold-threaded cloth for hanging on the wall behind
King Edward and the Prince while they sat at the banquet: *Domini Thome de
Bykenore ad extendum per parietes retro dominos Regem et Principem dum sedebunt ad
prandium in festo Pentecostes apud Westmonasterium--iiij panni ad aurum in canabo.*
(C47/3/30).

at Court, particularly during the major festivals of the year, were commonplace occurrences. The counties were quite used to supplying, for example, 100 hares, 6 swans, 2 boars and 6 peacocks each for normal Easter and Whitsun feasts at the palace. This Pentecost one of 1306 was on a larger scale; that was all. The author of the *Annales Londoniensis* dismisses it in one short, laconic sentence : ' *Et eodem die Pentecostes magnum convivium apud Westmonasterium tentum* ', adding, in the nature of an afterthought, ' the Patriarch of Jerusalem, the bishop of Rochester and many earls and barons were there '. To him, at any rate, there was nothing worthy of special remark about it, although he must have been, as one might say, within smell of the kitchens. Peter de Langtoft in faraway Yorkshire, because he had no details to go upon, contented himself with referring to it in conventional fashion :

> *Nule ame se mervale de jeu et joe assez*
> *Ou feste fu ferrue de tele solempnetez.*
> *Unkes en Bretagne puys que Dieu fu nez*
> *N'estoyt tel nobleye en villes n'en citez*
> *Forpris Karlioun en antiquitez*
> *Quant sire Arthur luy reis i fust coronnez.* (Vol. II, p. 369)

Like all generalities this says precisely nothing. For lack of specific information Peter fell back on the chronicler's habit of dragging in the threadbare comparison with the fictitious coronation feast of Arthur fabricated by Geoffrey of Monmouth. The few references to it which occur in other chronicles need to be examined with care and caution. Only three contain any worthwhile mention of the banquet as distinct from the ceremony of knighting. Langtoft's, which constitutes the fourth, is valueless. The other three are contained in the *Annales* of Nicholas Trevet, the *Flores Historiarum* and the *Chronica* of Adam de Murimuth. For the sake of convenient reference they are quoted and translated here :

Trevet : ' *Eodem die cum sedisset rex in mensa, novis militibus circumdatus, ingressa menestrellorum multitudo, portantium multiplici ornatu amictus, ut milites praecipue novos invitarent et inducerent ad vovendum factum armorum aliquod coram signo. Vovit et imprimis rex ipse, quod vindictam accipiet de contemptu illato Deo et ecclesiae per Robertum de Brus; et hoc expleto nunquam contra Christianos arma portaret, sed in Terram Sanctam sine reditu dirigeret iter suus. Vovit autem regis filius quod nunquam duas noctes in uno loco moraretur, quousque prosecturus, quantum in ipso erat, votum paternum, in Scotiam perveniret. Ceterorum vota militum memoriae non occurrunt.'*

' On the same day, after the king, surrounded by the new knights, had taken his seat at table, a great concourse of minstrels entered, carrying a drapery with manifold ornamentation, in order that they might invite and induce the new knights especially to vow some deed of arms before the device. The king himself vowed first; that he would avenge the insult offered by Robert de Bruce to God and the Church; and that when that had been accomplished, he would never again take up arms against Christians but would arrange to make his journey to the Holy Land, without (hope of) return. The king's son also vowed that he would never stay two (consecutive) nights in one place until he had fulfilled, as far as in him lay, his father's vow to arrive in Scotland. The vows of the other knights do not come to mind.'

Flores Historiarum : ' *Tunc allati sunt in pompatica gloria duo cigni vel olores ante regem, phalerati retibus aureis vel fistulis deauratis, desiderabile spectaculum intuentibus. Quibus visis, rex vovit votum Deo caeli et cignis se velle proficisci in Scotiam, sanctae Ecclesiae injuriam ac mortem Johannis Comyn et fidem laesam Scotorum vindicaturus, mortuus sive vivus. Sponderent igitur illud votum caeteri magnates fide bona asserentes se secum paratos esse in vita regis et post mortem ipsius cum filio suo principe in Scotiam proficisci, votum regium expleturos.'*

' Then two cygnets or swans, ornamented with golden nets or gilded pipings, were brought in in showy splendour before the king; an agreeable spectacle to those looking on. After he had surveyed it, the king vowed a vow to God in heaven and the cygnets (or swans) that he purposed to set out for Scotland, to avenge the injury done to Holy Church, the death of John Comyn and the broken faith of the Scots. Thereupon the other nobles bound themselves by the same oath, affirming in good faith that they were prepared to set out for Scotland with the king while he lived and, after his death, with the Prince, his son, in order to fulfil the royal vow.'

Murimuth : ' . . . *ad festum Pentecostes, rex Edwardus fecit filium suum Edwardum, dictum de Carnarvan, militem apud West-monasterium et alios fere centum*; *ubi dedit filio suo praedicto ducatum Aquitaniae*; *et vovit ad signum (crucis) quod mortem dicti Johannis Comyn vindicaret, et quod Scociam de manibus Roberti de Bruys recuperaret. Et idem votum quasi omnes unanimiter cum ipso voverunt, ad quod faciendum in anno proximo se pararunt.*'

' . . . at the feast of Pentecost king Edward made his son, Edward, styled ' of Carnarvon ', knight, and about a hundred others, at Westminster, where he gave his aforesaid son the duchy of Aquitaine, and vowed to the image (of the cross) that he would avenge the death of the said John Comyn and would recover Scotland from the hands of Robert de Bruce. And, as if with one voice, all vowed the same vow with him, toward the fulfilling of which in the following year they made themselves ready.'

The matter these extracts contain, though interesting and unique, is incomplete and inconclusive. Trevet was no stranger at Court but he wrote his *Annales* some seven or eight years after the Pentecost banquet had taken place. What he recollected about it leaves the reader with the impression that his information was first-hand but sketchy. He takes it for granted that his readers will know that he is referring to the banquet because he switches, without any warning, from an enumeration of the aspirants to ' When the king had taken his seat at table ', and, after mentioning the Prince's vow, his memory or his interest lapsed. He admits that he cannot recall the vows of the rest of the knights. There is much in his brief account which calls for discussion but it will be simpler to examine the versions in the *Flores Historiarum* and Murimuth's *Chronica* first, so that all three may be considered together.

The monk of Westminster is, if anything, even more abrupt than Trevet in his transition from the knighting ceremony to the banquet, for he moves directly from his description of the Prince taking refuge beside the altar to the circumstances of the vowing, without intimating in any way that the scene of action had changed. It will be noticed, also, that there is no mention of the personal vow made by the Prince; but the monk remembered what Trevet forgot, namely, the vows of the other knights.

Most of the manuscripts of the *Flores Historiarum* end at 1306. The additional portion, covering the period 1307 to 1325, was written by Robert of Reading and is quite different in character. Consequently, it is reasonably certain that the monk who described the knighting was giving a strictly contemporary and probably on-the-spot account of it. As such, his version may be adjudged the most valuable.

Adam of Murimuth, in the introduction to his *Chronica*, says that he collected the material for it, up to 1305, from books in the cathedral libraries of Exeter and Westminster, but that after that date, because he felt he had reached an age at which he could weigh facts for himself, he used his own experience, setting down in note form those things which seemed to him to be worth recording, but taking care to record the truth ' without praising, blaming or even remembering anyone or anything too much.' Such conscientiousness and tact are wholly commendable, although the final results of the exercise of them can be disappointingly negative, as is proven by his description of the knighting. It appears that he did not begin to write out his *Chronica* in full until after 1325, by which time his recollection of what had happened at Westminster in 1306 had become attenuated and blurred. His memory, like Trevet's, failed him with regard to the number of aspirants and he evidently considered the details of the banquet among those things not worth recording; yet his version, thin as it is, is not without a certain value. He remembers the vow to avenge the death of Comyn and to recover Scotland from Bruce, but king Edward's determination to avenge the insult offered to God and the Church are, surprisingly, passed over in silence. Again, no reference is made to any specific vow made by the Prince.

The basic similarities in the three accounts need not be dwelled upon; they are obvious. It is when we attempt to particularize that difficulties in interpretation reveal themselves—foremost among which are those relative to the circumstances of the vowing. The monk of Westminster states that two gold-ornamented swans were brought before the king, but he omits to mention who brought them. Trevet does not speak of swans at all. He says that a crowd of minstrels brought in an ornamental drapery and then goes on to describe the king making his vow ' *coram signo* '. Murimuth refers to neither swans, minstrels nor drapery, yet adds that the king made his vow ' *ad signum* '. Five out of the nine manuscripts of the *Chronica*, all dating from the mid to the late fourteenth century, have this reading. The remaining four, including the Harley MS., have ' *signum crucis* ', a very understandable error in view of the fact that Murimuth's incomplete description of the vowing gives no clue to the correct meaning of *signum* in this context.

A first reaction to the discrepancies is to assume that by *coram signo* and *ad signum* Trevet and Murimuth meant *coram cigno* and *ad cignum*, since these spellings were inter-changeable at the time. It would be a simple way out of the difficulty were it not that by adopting it we automatically ascribe to the two chroniclers an additional weakness of memory, inasmuch as their statements would now imply that there were not two swans but one. The monk of Westminster alone refers un-equivocally to swans by name, and he definitely says there were two. He was right, because there is incontrovertible evidence to that effect in the Wardrobe accounts. At the end of the roll of liveries issued to the aspirants, E101/362/20, among the extra issues of cloth for various other purposes connected with the knighting, there is this entry : ' *Galfredi cissori Regis ad cooperiendum ij Cygnos Vrnos*[4] *die Pentecostes . . . j pecia Cindonis viridis afforciati* '. ' To Geoffrey, the King's tailor, for covering two ornamented swans on Whitsunday . . . one piece of pure green silk.' This satisfactorily disposes of any argument as to the number of swans and at the same time substantiates Trevet's *amictus*. The foundation for his much embellished drapery was the length of green silk from the Wardrobe. So far, so good;

---

[4] 'ornamented' is a purely provisional rendering, because *vrnos* is otherwise un-recorded. Du Cange lists *vrna* (3), with the meaning *theca, feretrum*: ; which suggests that *vrnos* might have carried some particular meaning here, since *theca* could mean any kind of case or receptacle. In the context of *cygnos vrnos* it could possibly refer to the special stand or holder used for mounting subtle-ties. If it were given this meaning the issue of green silk for covering it would make very good sense; yet the grammatical difficulties appear to be in-surmountable. Even if *vrnus* be assumed to be an alternative to *vrna*—and change in grammatical gender was not uncommon in Mediaeval Latin—the form *cygni vrni* remains to be explained.

There is the possibility that *vrnos* may stand for a Latinized form of *aornés*, from OF. *aourner*, to decorate or ornament.

but there are further complications. Trevet's *Annales* were originally written in French for the king's daughter, Princess Mary, the nun of Amesbury. They were not translated into Latin until some time later. The question arises, did Trevet originally write *cisne* (*cygnus*) or *signe* (*signum*)? If he wrote *signe*, what does it mean? Also, if the two swans were covered with embroidered green silk, how are we to envisage this intriguing spectacle? Were the swans real? Were they alive or cooked? Were they, on the other hand, artificial? Were they for consumption or show?

If they were artificial, that is, made of sugar, gum and paste in the form of a mediaeval 'subtlety', some of the foregoing questions might be easily answered. Trevet's and Murimuth's use of *signum* becomes more intelligible. They were not referring mistakenly to one swan instead of two, but to the subtlety as a whole. *Signum*, at that time, carried the meaning, 'a device', a work of art, an image or a model. It is used in this sense by Higden to describe the statue of an ancient Roman outside the Vatican. Trevisa's English equivalent is *signe*.[5] The subtlety was, without question, the apotheosis of the mediaeval chef's culinary art. It figured at all great feasts. At the coronation banquet of Henry V, in 1413, there was one 'great swan sitting upon a green stock', surrounded by six cygnets and twenty-four other swans with mottoes in their beaks. The two swans of 1306, decked though they were in golden nets or pipings, seem amateur beside such an ornate and intricate piece of work as this.

The other detail that becomes more intelligible is the *amictus*. This drapery probably served as some kind of canopy for the whole device.

---

[5] *Est et aliud signum ante palatium domini Papae, equus aeneus et sessor ejus manu dextra quasi populo loquens, sinistraque quasi frenum regens, habens avem cuculam inter aures equi et nanum quasi moribundum sub pedibus . . . . .'* Trevisa's version runs: '*Pere is anopere signe and tokene tofore þe Popes paleys; an hors of bras and a man sittynge þeron and halt in his ri3t hand as þou3 he spake to the people, and halt his bridel in his lift hand and haþ a cukkow bytwene his hors eres and a seek dwerf vnder his hors feet . . .'* (*Polychronicon* (Rolls Ser.) Vol. I, 228.

On p. 224, at the commencement of his descriptions of the statues and images in Rome Higden has written in the margin, '*De statuis et signis Romae'*, so that there can be no doubt about the use of *signum* to mean an image, model or work of art. Trevisa's use of the English word, *signe*, confirms it. Hence, in terms of the confectioner's art, it meant a figure or device.

The fact that a great concourse of minstrels brought the two swans to the king as he sat at table might strengthen the view that they were something different from just two roast birds. One of the regular concomitants of a mediaeval banquet was the *intromissum* or *entremets*, which usually took the form of a spectacle of some kind and, according to Du Cange,[6] was staged during the middle course of the meal. The minstrels of the household were responsible for producing it and took part in its presentation. Since the Whitsuntide banquet, despite the aura of festivity surrounding it, was a preliminary to a most serious military expedition, the *intromissum* the minstrels of Edward I devised took the form of the customary knightly vowing with a difference. The grave and the gay seem to have been cleverly combined in an original and attractive device.

Why two swans were chosen to be the heart of the show is anyone's guess. Up to date no literary nor historical work in which knightly vows were made before a swan is known to have been written prior to the Pentecost feast. The well-known references to knights making vows to a roast peacock, in the *Voeux du Paon*, to a live sparrow-hawk, in the *Voeux de l'Epervier* and to a roast heron, in the *Voeux du Hairon*, are of no help because these three poems were composed after 1306. In each case there was only a single bird and that not a swan. It could be postulated that, since chivalry was so obviously the moving spirit of the Pentecost knighting, the heralds might have selected the heraldic swan as an apt motif for their spectacle, but, seeing that the hero of the hour was the Prince of Wales, why should they have opted to honour other knights whose coats of arms carried the swan, men like Humphrey de Bohun or Robert de Tony ? Although there is no evidence that the de Bohun or the de Tony swans had anything to do with the two swans of the feast, a considerable amount of speculation[7] has been generated by the idea; but the three descriptions of

---

[6] s.v. *intromissum*. See also *Mémoires sur l'ancienne chevalerie*, La Curne de Sainte-Palaye, 1759. New ed., with introd. and notes by Charles Nodier (Paris 1826), I, 208.

[7] *The Buik of Alexander*, ed. R. L. Graeme Ritchie (*Scottish Text Soc.*, Edinburgh, 1925–29), Vol. I, Introd., xxxv. ff.
   Political Songs and Poems, Edward III to Richard III, ed. Thomas Wright (Rolls Ser., 1859), 1–25.
   The Swan Badge and the Swan Knight, Anthony R. Wagner, *Archaeologia*, 97 (1959), 127 ff.

the ceremony which have been preserved are too scanty to warrant any theorizing of this nature. For Trevet, the monk of Westminster and Murimuth the device of the swans was apparently too trivial a subject upon which to waste words.

Making a vow to perform some worthy deed of arms was an integral part of the ritual of the knighting ceremony. As a rule, the newly-made knight made his vow in church or immediately after he had been dubbed. This kind of vow, irrespective of its special connection with the mediaeval crusader-knight, was age-old. It was partly an expression of early man's awareness of the power of the gods. To preserve his life or obtain a desired objective he bargained with his deity, accompanying his vow with a propitiatory sacrifice. When sacrifice was discarded something else was substituted for it, a symbol which would serve to sanctify his vow and bind him to perform it. From this habit a whole body of *gab* or boasting literature arose, and, as the vows in the *Voeux du Paon* and *Voeux du Hairon* prove, the vow of the Christian mediaeval knight frequently merged with the secular, drunken *gab*.[8] That Edward I should

The History of the Orders of Knughthood of the British Empire, Sir N. Harris Nicolas.

Ritchie believed that the vowing on the swans was the brain-child of Thièbaut, half-brother of Henry, Comte de Bar (son-in-law of Edward I), and bishop of Liège. He contends that Jaques de Longuyon composed the *Voeux du Paon* at his instance and that he also 'inspired the similar *Voeux de l'Epervier*'. Concerning the vowing of 1306, he says, 'When Edward I, who was not without some of the foibles of French chivalry, was moved to wrath by the murder of Comyn and the Coronation of the Bruce, he held a great assembly at Westminster, May 22, 1306, and the doors of the hall being opened, a seneschal entered, marshalling two attendants who bore upon a large tray two swans covered with a network of gold. Edward I, then in the last year of his life, vowed to God and the swans that he would march into Scotland and chastise the Bruce, while Edward, Prince of Wales, who had been knighted by his father that day with nearly 300 others, took a similar vow . . . . It was, no doubt, Thièbaut who suggested the strange ceremony to Edward as a local custom of Bar.' (xxxix–xl).

It is hardly necessary to refute this in detail. Ritchie stated that Trevet's *Annales* was his source, but the inaccuracies in his rendering are patent. He could not have referred to the text. He has mingled the accounts of Trevet and the monk of Westminster, although there is in neither of them any mention of the doors of the hall being opened, of a seneschal marshalling two attendants or of these last bearing the swans on a large tray. He leaves the reader with the impression that, because Thièbaut was the 'uncle' of the Dammoisele de Bar (who was married at the time of the knighting to John de Warenne) he was present at the festivities, but I can find no evidence that he was in either London or any other part of England at the time.

8 Examples are innumerable and of infinite variety. The *Histoire de Messire Bertrand du Guesclin*, written in 1387, gives some of the more ordinary ones, common among French and English soldiers alike: not to sleep in a bed, not

have vowed to avenge Bruce's insult to God and Comyn's murder before he set out for Scotland was by no means extraordinary. If it had not so happened that he made his vow before a minstrels' device of the swans there is every reason to believe that it would have been passed over without remark. There is no indication given by the monk of Westminster, the only writer who actually mentions them by name, that the swans in themselves carried any significance.[9] Nor do Trevet and Murimuth give the least hint that the *signum* was of any particular importance. R. S. Loomis, however, convinced himself that King Arthur was behind it all.[10] ' The last event of the reign ', he says, ' which had an Arthurian colouring occurred on Whitsunday, 1306.' Nothing which has survived in either contemporary chronicles or in the Exchequer records warrants such an assumption. Trevet and Murimuth, as men of the Court, could be expected to have referred to it if it had been in any way an outstanding feature of the vowing or the festivities. The sombre truth is to be found in the old king's vow,[11] which proves all too clearly that what was uppermost in his mind was something more serious than imitating Arthur and his court. He was intent on avenging Comyn's murder and was all too aware of his own approaching end.

A favourite theory is often hard to sacrifice. Although Loomis grudgingly admits that, ' in none of the Arthurian texts is there anything resembling the oath by a brace (*sic*) of swans ', he cannot bring himself to relinquish his belief that

---

to eat more than three sops of bread in wine, not to eat meat, not to undress at night, not to eat anything after supper—until the vow has been fulfilled. The *Voeux du Paon* and *Voeux du Hairon* offer more fanciful ones. One of the most colourful and arresting is that mentioned by Froissart. A party of young English knights caused quite a sensation at Valenciennes, because every one of them had one eye covered with a piece of scarlet cloth. They had made certain (unspecified) vows to their ladies at home and would not remove the eye-shades until they had fulfilled them. (Bouchon's edition, 57–8).

[9] The fact there were only two strengthens the supposition that they formed a subtlety, for swans were very common as roasts at private meals as well as at banquets. Usually about 20 were provided by the counties for a normal Christmas dinner at the royal palace.

[10] *Edward I, Arthurian Enthusiast, Speculum*, 28 (1953), 114–27.

[11] It is worth remembering that Edward I's vow not to take up arms against Christians was by no means original. The counts of Flanders and Blois had sworn the same vow in 1188: '*quod nunquam arma gestarent contra Christianos donec redierint de peregrinatione sua Jerosolimitana.*'' Hoveden, *Gesta Regis Henrici Secundi*). It is very likely that both the King's and the Prince's vows were conventional, military ones, not ones borrowed from romances.

Edward I and his son had King Arthur in mind when they made their vows, for he concludes, 'Evidently, then, the ceremonies of 1306 had an Arthurian background.' As yet I have been unable to find any evidence that this was so.[12]

The turbulent sea of surmise is not as pleasant to sail on as the calmer waters of fact. It is because their accounts are so woefully inadequate that the three chroniclers lay themselves open to dangerous speculation. They fail to satisfy natural curiosity; but it would be extremely unwise to argue from their supposed omissions. Outside London both banquet and swans went unremarked or, perhaps, to be on the safe side, we should say, unrecorded. If Arthurian ideas or motifs were present, no one thought it worthwhile to mention them. What actual records have remained are of a totally different character. In the Exchequer records there exist two veritable remnants of the banquet. They are of so prosaic a nature that flights of fancy have little chance of misrepresenting their contents. They are a bill for provisions which were being delivered to the royal kitchens immediately before the feast and a list of gratuities given to some of the minstrels who entertained the king and his guests. Both documents are clerks' accounts, set down on the spot, while the baskets of fish and carcasses of meat were coming in, and while the minstrels were crowding round for their cash. In their unromantic fashion these bits of parchment say a great deal more than the impersonal descriptions in the chronicles.

E101/370/21 is composed of three pieces, which can scarcely be dignified with the name, *rotuli*, yet they are in reality little rolls of preliminary accounts. The first membrane, roughly cut, is uneven in width, and measures 14 ins. by 4 ins. (5 ins. at the bottom). It is so badly crumpled and rubbed that a good part of the handwriting is indecipherable. The heading, however, is clear : '*Die Dominica xxij die May, videlicet die Pentecostes.*' Where the script is legible it is possible to discover what provisions were still being delivered at the palace on Whitsunday morning : 209 sides of bacon, carcasses of beef

---

[12] Some of the statements which Loomis makes are wholly without foundation. For example, he speaks of Edward 'assuming the role of King Arthur' at the banquet of 1306 (p. 121) and concludes that Edward 'evidently liked to think of himself in the rôle of Arthurus Redivivus'. (p. 126).

from the sheriffs of Oxfordshire, Buckinghamshire and Wilt-
shire, 50 odd bream, 15 salmon. Payments to Cardoill, the
King's yeoman in charge, are mingled with the items. The
food commissioned from the counties was being brought in
up to the last minute. The list appears to be a hasty one, set
down in much abbreviated clerical shorthand. Two totals are
entered at the end. Together they come to £100 3s. 10d., the
equivalent of just over £20,000 today. As this sum represents
the merest fraction of what was expended on food alone, one
begins to appreciate the cost of the whole of the knighting
ceremony.

The second membrane is in a much better state of preserva-
tion. It is a regularly cut strip of parchment, 14 ins. by 5 ins.
The items are not too abbreviated, possibly because the clerk
was not quite so rushed for time, seeing that it was only Saturday, ' *Die Sabbatici xxj die May apud Westmonasterium* '. When
baldly stated the contents do not sound very promising; they
are no more than a list of the names of the fishmongers who
were supplying the fish for the feast, together with details of the
kinds of fish supplied, how much in terms of number and weight
and what each man was paid. The amount and variety of fish
supplied are well worth mentioning : 5000 salted eels, 287 cod,
136 pike, 102 salmon, mackerel by the load, in basket after
basket, each holding the equivalent of a bushel of oats, herring
by the hundred, plaice galore, conger eels, ' great eels ', tench,
bream, dace, flounder, merling (whiting), mullet, 201 stockfish
and 4 barrels of sturgeon. The prices paid varied according to
sizes and quantities of the loads supplied by each trader. A
salmon cost between one and three shillings (£10 to £30),
150 dace, five shillings, 24 ' great eels ', fifty shillings, 6 pike,
twenty shillings; the cheapest were mackerel, 200 for a shilling
and stockfish, Shakespeare's ' poor John ', five shillings for 53.

More interesting are the names of the sellers. I have not
been able to identify all of them, but, out of forty odd, twenty-
five are to be found mentioned in the *Calendar of Letter-books of
the City of London*. There they are revealed as being not only
fishmongers but as citizens of note, prosecuting important
duties in the government of the city. In Letter-book B, which
is chiefly a record of recognizances, several of them occur as
lenders and borrowers of sizeable sums. Letter-book C is full

of miscellaneous information. The fishmongers and stock-fishmongers whose names appear in the royal clerk's list are to be found acting as jurors, mainpernors, witnesses to various deeds and auditors of the City Chamberlain's account before it was presented to the King's Treasurer. When grants in aid were made, they were responsible for collecting the City's grants; when a proclamation was issued in Christmas week to prohibit the raising of the prices of provisions, they were appointed to see that the ordinance was carried out. Others acted as overseers to ensure that there was no cheating in weights and measures. Finally, looking after the children of a deceased fellow-merchant or acting as attorney for one who could no longer do business for himself were among the acts of kindness and duties these men undertook.

The third membrane, measuring 6 ins. by 4 ins., appears to be a supplementary list to the second. It bears the same heading but contains only ten entries, eight of which list supplies of cod, eel, mackerel and salmon; the last two are payments to Cardoill.

The men whose names have been preserved in these documents were not the humble fishermen who had to bring the fish off the boats at sunrise, but reputable and wealthy city merchants. Royal banquets were part of their life-blood. Between them they netted on the Saturday before Whitsun over £6,000 in present-day money. The three creased strips of parchment upon which their names and transactions have been recorded have outlasted the aspirants' silks and satins. The identities of the new knights can be discovered with comparative ease, for they were mostly men of high or gentle birth whose deeds are writ large in the annals of the reign of Edward II. For thirteen of them the gold thread in their gorgeous cointeses barely had time to tarnish, because they were dead by 1310. John Comyn, the son of the man for whom the Pentecost ceremony was really held, was killed at Bannockburn in 1314. Forty-two others turned against the Prince when he became King. By the end of his reign at least a third of the brilliant company of new knights were dead.

There is a certain satisfaction in having rescued from the waters of Lethe twenty-five fishmongers, who belonged to the vast multitude of unremarkable men. They went about their daily business unmindful of whether time would remember them, yet their contribution to the festivities was important, not only for the guests who enjoyed their salmon, eels, pike and sturgeon, but for us. It is as if we have been allowed to go behind the arras for a few moments, to look at the back of the picture. The other manuscript relic of the banquet will take us once more into the great hall.

THE PAYROLL

Transcript of MS. E101/369/6

Recto : The Latin List
Verso : The French List

SOLUTIO FACTA DIVERSIS MENESTRALLIS DIE PENTECOSTES ANNO xxxiiij[16]

INTRAUIT   RECTO

[Rich]ard.................quietus
Mellers......quietus [par le Roy] Laisescu . ... dim. marc.
Janin de la Toure trounpour .... dim. marc.
[Guillot de] Roos vilour .... dim. marc.
v pueris Principis cuilibet ijs .... xs

Richard Le Harpour qui est oue le Conte de Gloucestre
Wauter Bracon Trounpour
Wauter Le Trounpour
Johan Le Croudere
Tegwaret Croudere
Geffrai Le Estiuour   a ceux xj
Guillot Le Taborer   por toute La
Guillot Le Vilour   Comune
Robert Le Vilour   xvij li. iiij s. viijd.
Jake de Vescy
Richard de Whetacre

Vidulatori Domine de Wake.................Vs.
Laurentio Cithariste..........................dim. marc.
Johanni du Chat cum domino J. de Barr...dim. marc.
Mellers .... Vs.
Paruo Willelmo organiste Comitisse Herefordie.........V.s.
Ricardo de Quitacre Cithariste .... dim. marc.
Ricardo de Leylond Cithariste .... dim. marc.
Carletone Harald .... Vs.
Gilloto Vidulatori Comitis Arundellie .... dim. marc.
Amckyn Cithariste Principis .... Vs.
Bolthed .... Vs.
Nagary le Crouder Principis .... Vs.

Matheo le Harpour .... Vs.
Johannes[1] le Barbor .... Vs.
ij Trumpatoribus J. de Segraue .... dim. marc.
Ricardo vidulatori Comitis Lancastrie .... Vs
Johannes[1] Waffrario Comitisse Lancastrie.............. xld.
Sagard Crouther .... xld.
Willelmo de Grymesar' Harpour .... xld.
Cithariste Comitisse Lancastrie .... xld.
ij menestrallis J. de Berwike .... xld.
Henrico de Blida .... xld.
Ricardo Cithariste .... xld.
Willelmo de Duffeld .... xld.
V Trumpatoribus Principis pueris cuilibet ijs ...... Xs. in toto.
iiij^{or} Vigilibus Regis cuilibet dim. marc. .... xxs.
Adinet le Harpour .... xld.
Peroto le Taborer .... xld.
Ade de Swylingtone Cithariste .... ijs.
Dauid le Crouther .... xijd.
Lion de Normanuille .... ijs.
Gerardo .... xijd.
Ricardo Cithariste ....ijs.
Roberto de Colcestria............ijs.
Johanni le Crouther de Salopia .... xijd.
Johanni le vilour domini J. Renaud................. xijd.
Johanni de Trenham Cithariste .... ijs.
Willelmo Woderoue Trumpatori .. .. ijs.
Johanni Cithariste J. de Clyntone .... ijs.
Waltero de Brayles .... xijd.
Roberto Cithariste Abbatis de Abbyndone ...... xijd.
Galfrido trumpatori domini R. de Monte Alto ... xijd.
Richero socio suo .... ijs.
Thome[2] le Croudere .. .. ijs.
Rogero de Corleye Trumpatori .... ijs.
Audoeno le Crouther .... xijd.
Hugoni Daa Cithariste .... ijs.
Andree vidulatori de Hor' .... ijs.
Johanni Sagard .... xijd.
Roberto de Scardeburghe .... xijd.
Guilloto le Taborer Comitis Warrewici .... iijs.
Raulin menestrallo Comitis Marescalli .... iijs.
Matheo Waffrario domini R. de Monte Alto ... ijs.
iij diuersis menestrallis cuilibet iijs. .... ixs.

Galfrido Cithariste Comitis Warrenni .... ijs.
Matilli Makeioye .... xijd.
Johanni Trumpatori domini R. Filii Pagani ... xijd.
Ade Taburrario³ domini J. Lestraunge .... xijd.
Reginaldo le Mentour menestrallo domini J. de Buteturte ...
xijd.
Perle in the Eghe .... xijd.
Gilloto Cithariste domini P. de Malo Lacu ......xs.
Roberto Gaunsille .... xld. Item .... xld.
Jacke de Vescy⁴ .... dim. marc.
Magistro Waltero Leskirmissour et fratri suo cuilibet iijs. ......
vjs.

SITIVᴚ.LSƎNƎW ILVꓷ IIᴚVNƎꓷ

VERSO

Cuilibet | Le Roy de Champaigne | par Mons. Capenny
| Le Roy Capenny |
| Le Roy Baisescu | cuilibet V marc. Summa
ij | Le Roy Marchis | ...xvj li
x marc. | Le Roy Robert | j marc.

par Phelippe de Caumbereye par Mons. Roy Capenny
Artoys ...lxs.
xxs. Summa—lxs.

cuilibet j | Robert le Boistous | par Mons. Roy Capenny
marc. | Gerard de Boloigne | cuilibet iiij marc. Summa...
| | ...cvjs. viijd.
ij marc. | | par Mons. Roy Capenny

cuilibet xs. | Bruant | cuilibet xls. Summa............iiij li.
xxs. | Northfolke |

cuilibet | Carltone | par Mons. Bruant
dim. | Maistre Adam Le | cuilibet xxs.
marc. | Boscu | Summa..............lxs.
xxs. | Deuenays |

par | Artisien | cuilibet xxxs.
Mons. | Lucat | Summa............ iiij li. xs.
Roy | Henuer |
Capenny
cuilibet
dim.
marc. xxs.

par
Mons.
Ricard
de
Haleford
cuilibet
xxs.
vj li.
xs.

Le Menestral Mons. de
  Montmaranci
Le Roy Druet
Janin Le Lutour

Guillotin Le Sautreour

Gillot de Roos—par Jacke de Vescy
Ricard de Haleford—par Mons......as⁵
Le Petit Gauteron

par Mons. Roy
Capenny

par Mons. Gauter«
le Petit.
par Mons. Guillot
harpour le Rois.
dim. marc.
cuilibet xls.
Summa......xxvj li

Baudet Le Tabourer
Ernolet—par Mons. Baudetti Le Taborer
Mahu qui est oue La Dammoisele de
Baar
Janin de Brebant
Martinet qui est oue Le Conte de
Warwike
Gauteron le Grant

par Mons.
Baudetti
Le
Taborer

xs.

le harpeur Leuesque de Duresme
Guilleme Le Harpour qui est oue
Le Patriarke
Robert de Clou
Maistre Adam de Reue
Henri le Gigour
Corraud⁶ son compaignon—par
        Mons. Henri le Gigour

Cuilibet
dim.
marc.
viij
marc.

Le tierz Gigour
Gillot Le Harpour
Johannes de Newentone
Hughethun Le Harpour lour
  compaignon
Adekin son compaignon
Adam de Werintone
Adam de Grimmeshawe–par Mons.
        Robert de Clou
Hamond Lestiuour-par Mons. Roy
        Druet
Mahuet qui est oue Mons. de

Cuilibet
ij marc.
Summa...
xxj li.
  dim.
  marc.

Tounny—par Mons. Roy Druet
Johan de Mochelneye
Janin Lorganistre
Simond Le Messager—par Mons.
               Roy Druet

par Mons.   Les ij Trumpours Mons. Thomas de
Ricard le   Brothertone
Vilour   Martinet Le Tabourer

             Richard Rounlo
             Richard Hendeleke
             Janin de La Tour   —par Mons. Johan
             Son compaignon   Le Waffrer
             Johannes Le Waffrer le Roy
             Pilke
par Mons.   Januche —Trumpours Mons. Le Prince
Guillot   Gillot
  Le
Trumpour   Le Nakarier
             Le Gitarer
             Merlin
             Thomasin vilour Mons. Le Prince —
               par Mons. Guillot Le Trumpour
Cuilibet   Raulin qui est oue le Conte le Mareschal
vjs.   Esuillie qui est oue Mons. Pierres de   Cuilibet
viijd.   Maule   j marc.
xiij li.   Grendone   Summa…
dim.   Le Taborer La Dame de Audham   xl marc.
marc.   Gaunsaillie   — par Mons. Ricard
                          Le Vilour Rounlo
             Guilleme sanz maniere
             Lambyn Clay
             Jaques Le Mascun
             Son compaignon—par Mons. Jaques Le
                           Mascoun
             Mahu du North
             Le Menestral oue les cloches
dim.   Les iij menestraus Mons. de Hastinge —
marc.   par Mons. Cosin & Markin
             Thomelin de Thounleie   —   par Mons.
                         Robert de Clou

Les ij Trumpours Le Conte de Hereforde
Perle in the eghe
Son compaignon
Janyn Le Sautreour qui est oue Mons.
  de Percy
Les ij Trumpours le Conte de Lancastre
Mellet
Henri de Nushom
Janyn Le Citoler

cuilibet	Eilliame⁷	
dim.	Fairfax — par Mons. Roy Marchis	cuilibet xxs.
marc.	Monet	Summa…iiij li.
ij marc.	Hanecocke de Blithe	

Summa totalis : Cxiiij li. xs. Et issi demoerent des CC marc. pur partir entre les autres menestraus de la commune xviij li. xvjs. viijd. Et a ceste partie faire sunt assigne Le Roy Baisescu, Le Roi Marchis, Le Roy Robert et le Roy Druet, Gauteron Le graunt, Gauteron Le petit, Martinet Le Vilour qui est oue Le Conte de Warewike et del hostiel Mons. Le Prince ij seriantz darmes [et j] clerke.

I have omitted the abbreviated *pacatus* against each entry.
¹ In these two instances the clerk has forgotten to put *Johannes* in the dative.
² ms. *Thomo.*
³ ms. *Tobrrar.*
⁴ Between the entries for *Gaunsille* & *de Vescy* there is : *Regi Capignye* ——— dim. marc., but it has been crossed out.
⁵ ms. indecipherable.
⁶ So ms., but we know from other sources that his name was *Conrad.*
⁷ Botfield has read this name as *Gilliame,* but the initial is definitely not the clerk's capital G. It can be either his capital E or capital S. I have been unable to trace the minstrel as *Gilliame, Eilliame* or *Silliame.*
  In the bottom left-hand corner of this side of the roll the following four entries have been made and crossed out:
    Les ij Trumpours Mons. Thomas de Brothertone.
    Martinet Le Taborer.
    Richard Le Vilour.
    Raulin qui est oue Le Conte Mareschal.

E101/369/6 is a parchment roll, 24 ins. by 8 ins. On one side it bears the title, *Solutio facta diversis menestrallis die Pentecostes. Anno xxxiiij*, followed by a list of 83 entries in Latin. At the foot, written upside down, indicating that it was this side of the roll that faced outwards for purposes of reference, is *Denarii dati menestrallis*. On the other side, with no heading, is a list of 86 entries, written in French, with a concluding note to the effect that the sum total paid out to the minstrels whose names figure in the list was £114-10s.-0d., and that £18-16s.-8d. remained out of 200 marks to be divided among ' the other minstrels of the company '.

Like E101/370/21, this roll is a prosaic document, no more than a record of two lists of names, with the amount of money given to each individual. Up to the present nobody has been interested in the worthy fishmongers, but the minstrels have not gone unnoticed. The Payroll, as we shall now term it for the sake of convenience, has been printed twice : in 1841 by Beriah Botfield in his *Manners and Household Expenses of England in the Thirteenth and Fifteenth Centuries*, Appendix, pp. 140-45; and in 1930 by Sir E. K. Chambers, in his *The Mediaeval Stage*, Appendix C. Chambers reprinted Botfield's version verbatim and apparently without consulting the manuscript, because no mention is made of Botfield's omissions. Botfield was concerned only with reproducing a simplified transcription, for he was using the manuscript to illustrate certain aspects of mediaeval social life. Chambers made use of it solely to exemplify the nature of mediaeval entertainment and to draw from it both general and particular conclusions from the seeming oddity of the minstrels' names. In reality it is a much more valuable document than either of them realized. As printed by them it appears to be a neat, clear piece of work, but this is because the numerous notes, additions and corrections have been left out.

The two lists have been written by different clerks. That in French, on the reverse side, although it has no heading, may well have been the first written. It probably came from the Prince's Wardrobe, for an entry in the Wardrobe book of John de Drokenesford proves that the 200 marks referred to in the list was a special gift in cash from the king and were handed to Walter Reynolds, the Keeper of the Prince's Wardrobe, for

the express purpose of distributing *largesse* to certain minstrels
in the name of the Prince :

| Money given to minstrels for the knighting of the Prince. | To King Robert and certain Kings of Heralds and also to other divers minstrels, for making their minstrelsy in the presence of the King and other nobles present at Westminster on Whitsunday of the current year; that is to say, on the day of the knighting of lord Edward, the King's son, Prince of Wales, 200 marks, by gift of the lord Prince, by order of the King. By the hand of master Walter Reynolds, Keeper of the same Prince's Wardrobe, giving and distributing the money to them in the name of the Prince. At London, 23 May (1306).' |

(E101/369/11, f.96ʳ)

The Latin list, despite the fact that it carries both the general
heading and the filing reference, has the appearance of having
been written on the back of the French one. It obviously
belongs to the King's Wardrobe. Therefore, the first interesting
fact to be noted about the manuscript is that it contains two
completely different accounts. At the head of the Latin list
there are five entries almost totally rubbed away. These are
followed by a group of 11 names bracketed together and label-
led *La Commune*. The rest of the list is a straightforward transcription of names and amounts not arranged in any recog-
nizable order; and, because there was not enough room on the
parchment to complete the list, the last eleven, with one
crossing-out, have been squashed on to the right-hand top side
of the roll.

By contrast, the French list, written in a similar although
different hand, is neatly arranged in groups bracketed according to a scale of payments. The impression gained is that it
was carefully prepared with a view to sharing out the 200 marks
in a manner which would be at once fair and satisfactory to

all concerned. The scale of payments in the Latin list is much less lavish but, since the names of some of the minstrels occur in both lists, it cannot be concluded that those in the Latin list were inferior or less important; nor were they the remnant, *les autres menestraus*, to which the note at the foot of the French list refers. The total payment in the French list comes to £115-16s.-8d. and not £114-10s.-0d. as stated by the clerk. His mistake has been made in the group which was paid 2 marks. The third *geige*-player was not originally included in the list with his two fellow-country-men, Heinrich and Conrad. No doubt this was an oversight as all three were German minstrels resident at Court but the third one had only recently arrived and would not have been well-known to the Wardrobe officials. The clerk wedged his name in under the title, *le tierz Gigour*, but forgot to add the extra 2 marks to his total. With this slip rectified, the final total is correct. If those in the Latin list had been the recipients of the remnant of the 200 marks, they would have received, all told, £18-16s.-8d. (or £17-10s.-0d. if the third *geige*-player's 2 marks be subtracted) but they did not. The total comes to £31-19s.-8d. Therefore the Latin list is a separate account and , although unquestionably connected with the Whitsunday ceremony, has nothing to do with the Prince's *largesse* of 200 marks. Both Botfield and Chambers failed to notice this and the latter seems to have misunderstood the clerk's statement about the distribution of the left-over, for he says, ' two hundred marks were distributed in smaller sums amongst the inferior minstrels, *les autres menestraus de la Commune*.' (p. 42)

With a list of this kind it is easy to slide into making false assumptions because, apart from the hidden identities of many of the minstrels, there are other pitfalls which come to light only after one has discovered who the minstrels were. Most of the names which look as though they belong to Frenchmen turn out to be Frenchified names of Englishmen. Again, what often appears to be a nickname or stage-name is found to be an ordinary English, French or Welsh surname. So much has been written about the mediaeval minstrel from a romantic point of view that an uninformed reader of E101/369/6 can be forgiven for misinterpreting a large part of it. The gulf between domestic and wandering minstrels was a wide one. It can be asserted without hesitation that none of the latter appear in these two Wardrobe lists. That there were plenty of them in London during the knighting festivities cannot be doubted, for they would have flocked to the city for pence as eagerly as the pigeons do in Trafalgar Square for the pickings thrown to them by the modern commonalty but if they had managed to get near the palace or New Temple they would have been lucky indeed. Analysis of the Payroll proves that no minstrel outside royal and knightly circles had even a sniff of the 200 marks. The largest part of that handsome sum was reserved for the cream of the minstrels belonging to the royal and aristocratic households. There was nothing for strangers.

I have not been fortunate enough to identify every single person whose name has been entered on the Payroll; perhaps that was too much to expect; but I have come to know most, some in more detail than others. On the basis of the facts about them which I have gathered together it is possible to present two analytic tables which will illustrate more clearly than any general statement can, how misleading at first sight, the Payroll can be.

TABLE 1. Classes of Minstrels

Class	No.	Class	No.
TRUMPETERS	19	GUITARISTS	1
TABORERS	6	ORGANISTS	2
NAKERERS	1	CAMPANISTS	1
ESTIVOURS	2	ACROBATS	1
BOY MINSTRELS	5	FENCERS	2
HARPERS	26	REGES HARALDORUM	6
VIELLE-PLAYERS	13	HERALDS	4
CROWDERS	9	SERGEANTS-AT-ARMS	1
GEIGE-PLAYERS	3	GROOMS	3
PSALTERY-PLAYERS	2	WAFERERS	5
LUTENISTS	1	WATCHMEN	4
CITOLE-PLAYERS	1	MESSENGERS	1

TABLE 2. Classes of People in whose Service the Minstrels were

Position in Society	Kinds and Numbers of Minstrels
KING	2 taborers, 1 nakerer, 1 estivour, 4 watchmen, 1 waferer, 1 messenger, 1 organist, 4 harpers, 2 vielle-players, 3 *geige*-players, 1 lutenist, 1 citole-player, 2 *reges haraldorum*, 4 heralds, 1 sergeant-at-arms (*balistarius*), 1 groom of the chamber (*robarius*)
QUEEN	1 psaltery-player
PRINCE OF WALES	2 trumpeters, 5 boy minstrels, 1 taborer, 1 harper, 1 vielle-player, 2 crowders, 1 guitarist, 1 waferer
OTHER ROYAL CHILDREN	2 trumpeters (Thomas of Brotherton) 1 harper (Countess Warenne) 1 harper (Lady Despenser) 1 'minstrel' (Joan de Bar) (also Countess Warenne)
BISHOPS	2 harpers (Anthony Bek, bishop of Durham)
ABBOTS	1 harper (Nicholas de Culham, abbot of Abingdon)
EARLS	2 trumpeters, 1 vielle-player (Lancaster) 2 trumpeters, 1 vielle-player (Hereford) 1 harper, 1 *rex haraldorum* (and vielle-player) (Gloucester) 1 taborer, 1 ' minstrel ' (Warwick) 1 harper (Warenne), 1 vielle-player (Arundel)
COUNTESSES	1 harper, 1 waferer (Lancaster), 1 harper (Warenne), 1 organist (Hereford), 1 waferer (Gloucester)
BARONS/ KNIGHTS	2 trumpeters (John de Segrave) 2 trumpeters, 1 waferer (Robert de Monhaut) 2 trumpeters (Henry de Beaumont) 2 trumpeters, 1 valet/minstrel (Robert fitz Payn) 1 taborer, 1 harper (John Lestrange) 1 harper (John de Clynton) 1 harper, 1 ' minstrel ' (Peter de Mauley) 1 vielle-player (Hugh le Despenser, Senior) 1 vielle-player (J. Renaud) 1 psaltery-player, 1 *rex haraldorum* (Henry de Percy) 1 ' minstrel ' (John de Bourtetourte) 1 ' minstrel ' (Jean de Montmorenci) 1 ' minstrel ' (Robert de Tony)
LADIES	1 taborer (La Dame de Audham) 1 vielle-player (La Dame de Wake) 1 ' minstrel ' (Lady Isabella de Vescy)
OFFICERS OF THE ROYAL HOUSEHOLDS	1 valet/estivour (John de Drokenesford, Keeper of the King's Wardrobe) 1 harper (Walter de Beauchamp, Steward of the King's Household) 1 ' minstrel ' (Hugh, earl of Norfolk, Earl Marshal of England) 2 ' minstrels' (John de Hastings, Steward of the Queen's Household)

Position in Society	Kinds and Numbers of Minstrels
	2 ' minstrels ' (John de Berwick, Keeper of the Queen's Gold) 1 ' minstrel ' (Leo de Normanville) squire of King's Household)
FOREIGNERS	1 *rex haraldorum* (Le Roy de Chaumpaigne) 1 vielle-player of the King of France 1 ' minstrel ' of the *envoi* of the King of France 3 *geige*-players from Germany

Although these tables do not contain the names of all the minstrels on the Payroll, they show very clearly the particular nature of the document. As a possible picture of the minstrels present at the knighting it is, to say the least, fragmentary. For example, two of the most important royal minstrels do not find a place in it, namely, John Depe and his son, the king's two personal trumpeters. The Wardrobe accounts and even the clerks' jottings on the Payroll itself prove that there were numbers of other Court minstrels present who did not happen to come in for any of the 200 marks; people like the herald, Roger Marchys, the Queen's Fool, Robert; Richard de Blida, Artoys, Cosin and Markin, Nicholas de Ranci and many others. Nor is it reasonable to think that William le Sautreour was the only minstrel present from the queen's household or that Anthony Bek and Nicholas de Culham were the only ecclesiastics there with their harpers; or that Thomas, earl of Lancaster had brought with him just two trumpeters and one vielle-player. Why the minstrels listed should have been selected to be the lucky ones cannot now be explained.

Who was responsible for the dividing and distribution of the 200 marks in the first place can only be surmised. As the gift was made expressly in the name of the Prince, it is but logical to assume that he and his officers would have had a hand in deciding who was to benefit from it. There is some evidence that a task of this nature was usually handed over to one or more of the senior minstrels of the household. In 1290, at the marriage of Princess Margaret to John de Brabant, the bride-groom made a gift of £100 (£20,000) to the 426 minstrels who had performed during the festivities. The money was given in a lump sum, ' *in grosso* ', to Walter de Stourton, one of the king's harpers; and the clerk has added the note, ' *Memorandum* :

that, concerning these £100, they were paid to the aforesaid minstrels as the minstrel (Stourton) said, ' *ut dixit menestrallus.*' (C47/4/5,f.48ʳ). Again, in 1300, when the king was keeping Christmas at Northampton, John de Drokenesford handed to Richard Rounlo, King's Vielle-player, 20 marks (approx. £5,200) for him to distribute among divers minstrels who had entertained the king and queen ' on the days of Christmas and St. Stephen'. Richard was given the cash, so says the clerk, ' to divide among the said minstrels in accordance with that which the status of each shall demand', *unicuiusque iuxta suum statum exiget.*' (Add. MSS. 7966, f.66ᵛ)

The footnote to the Payroll not only confirms the existence of this practice but adds something to our knowledge of it. No fewer than seven minstrels were appointed to make the distribution of the rather miserable left-over, the £18-16s.-8d. (approx. £3,770), among *les autres menestraus de la Commune*. Four of them were King Heralds and therefore representatives of what may be termed the most senior branches of ministrelsy. Also in attendance were two sergeants-at-arms, to act as police officers, and a clerk to note the payments on a roll. It is a great pity that this roll has not survived; it would have completed the list of those who received the 200 marks.

E101/369/6, then, is not a comprehensive account but a small domestic one, relative to only two aspects of the whole affair. Just as the bills for the fish are no more than an indication of the magnitude of the banquet, so the Payroll provides nothing but a hint of the hundreds of minstrels who thronged the palace at Westminster on Whitsunday, 1306.

In order to give the reader some idea of the purchasing power of the wages and gifts in cash given to minstrels in the fourteenth century, I have inserted, in brackets, against the sums they received approximate modern equivalents.

On the advice of the Coin Department of the British Museum I have multiplied by 200, but present-day inflation has rendered this original estimate rather low.

THE MINSTRELS

i. *Status and duties*

Before passing on to the identities of the minstrels named on the Payroll it is advisable to say something about royal domestic minstrels in general. References to them, their categories, instruments and various forms of minstrelsy, as they occur in the records, need to be amplified, otherwise many of the biographical details relevant to each individual will not be fully understood.

Members of the royal household, by which are meant those receiving wages and livery, were usually classified in three groups. In the first, representing the highest class of society under the king and the nobility, were the knights, that is, both bannerets and bachelors or ' simple knights ' as they were called, and the king's clerks, sergeants and squires. The second contained the king's falconers and huntsmen, the minstrels, the wagoners and the mounted messengers. In the third were the valets or grooms of the various officers of the household, the sumpters, the palfreteers, the ' boys ' (*garciones*) and the foot messengers.

Such a grouping is to be found, for instance, in a counter-roll of domestic payments for 1284/5, but it was not always rigidly adhered to. In theory it may have been long established but the testimony of the Wardrobe records proves that some, at any rate, of the minstrels were squires, because they received a squire's wage and were styled *Magister/Monsire*. The Payroll itself provides an example. On Whitmonday morning, when the *largesse* was being distributed, several of the minstrels collected not only their own gratuities but those of friends, and, in order to remind themselves of what money had been paid out, the clerks jotted down notes of the transactions on the French side of the roll. In every case they referred to the minstrel to whom they had handed the money as ' *Monsire* ', from which it can be inferred that they were regarded as gentlemen rather than as craftsmen or inferior servants.

The statutory wage for the minstrel and others in the second group was 4½d. per day (£3-15s.-0d.), while that of a squire of the household was 7½d. (£6-5s.0d.). The Wardrobe accounts are not consistent, for sometimes minstrels received 4½d. and at others 7½d. according to their status in the household at the time. John the organist, under Edward II, received only 4½d., which clearly puts him in the regular category but other entries prove beyond doubt that the majority of the first-class minstrels under Edward I were grouped with the squires. William le Sautreour, the Queen's psaltery-player, is definitely called 'squire of the Queen's Household' (MS Cott. Nero c viii †136ᵛ). Data of this kind suggest that the general classification was modified to suit the king's or the queen's desires, but, as far as the Household Ordinances were concerned, minstrels as a class were consistently placed in the second class. Under Edward III no minstrel received more than 4½d.

Whether the squire-minstrels under Edward I were so classed because of their social status outside Court it is impossible to say. Today it is a comparatively simple matter to get to know the social standing of the Master of the Queen's Music, but that of a gentleman like William remains a mystery, despite the fact that I have been able to discover a good deal about his wealth, property and business transactions. I know where he lived but not where he was born, nor who or what his parents were, nor what kind of upbringing he received. There is evidence that the post of court minstrel was jealously guarded in families down even to the time of Charles II. Fathers saw to it that their sons were trained to follow in their footsteps and so retain the coveted position at Court. At times father and son were at Court together, like John Depe and his son, the personal trumpeters of Edward I. There are many instances of minstrels bearing the same name and occurring in the records for years in succession but there are no means of proving that they were father and son or members of the same family, although in many cases it is highly probable that they were. To presume to place them in any particular social class would be extremely unwise. A gifted musician, like any other artist, is not and never has been the product of any one social stratum.

To be a member of the royal household did not necessarily mean that one was permanently resident at Court. The minstrels belonged to the class of servants who, in the words of

John Pecham, ' *vont et vient* '.[1] When a man was taken into
Court on wages, an annual contract with him was drawn up
and his wage was fixed at a daily, not an annual, rate. He was
then paid according to the number of days during the year on
which he had been on duty. All wages due were acknowledged
and checked before being entered in the Wardrobe accounts
but they were not always paid on the date specified nor *in toto*.
There was no system for the regular payment of wages, such
as we have now, because regular ready money was not always
available. Royal revenue from the counties came into the
Exchequer at various times and when it did arrive it had to be
apportioned to meet the multifarious claims upon it. As a
result, the wages of palace officials as well as of minstrels, were
paid piecemeal, by cash advances or imprests. No fixed period
of time elapsed between one payment and the next. The books
of prests which have survived paint a very human picture of
a sharing out of cash whenever it arrived and for as long as it
lasted. Sometimes the recipients would be fortunate and get
several payments within a matter of weeks, as Adam the King's
Harper did in November and December 1305, when he received the equivalent of £140 in less than a month.

In addition to his daily wage the minstrel, like any other
household servant, received two sets of livery a year : a winter
and summer *roba*, the long overdress of the period, and two
pairs of shoes. It is doubtful whether either the kind of material
or the weight of the shoes varied according to the seasons. All
the evidence points to the contrary. Apparently household
livery was normally issued from the Wardrobe, which held
bales of cloth and quantities of leather and furs bought by the
King's Clerks at Stamford and other fairs. In the accounts,
although some entries state the yardage issued, the issue of
livery nearly always figures as a sum of money equivalent to
the livery's cost, normally 20s. for each *roba* and 10s. for each
pair of shoes. If the minstrel did not happen to be in residence
at the time of the issue, he received nothing, unless one of his
friends kindly collected it for him. The cloth was the same in
colour, kind and quality as that issued to most of the servants,
including the squires. A book of prests for 1305[2] contains a

---

[1] *John Pecham's Jerarchie*, M. Dominica Legge, *Medium Aevum*, XI (1934), 82.
[2] E101/369/16.

list of liveries issued from the Great Wardrobe to a number of the minstrels mentioned in the Payroll. Each one was allowed 7 ells of cloth (8 yds., 2 ft., 3 ins.), divided into 3½ ells of two different colours, either blue and green or blue and striped. One lamb's fur was allowed to each for trimming. The cost was 27s. 6d. for blue and striped and 24s. 6d. for blue and green, inclusive of lamb's fur. In our terms it was a handsome and expensive outfit; its value today would be nearly £300. In 1305 the money would have purchased 2 hogsheads (108 galls.) of good beer and 300 water-pitchers, respectively.

Nothing in the records indicates that these minstrels wore any kind of distinctive dress; nor, by the way, did they have their heads and beards shaven. The portrait of William le Sautreour[3] as well as miniatures of the period prove conclusively that they were dressed in the gentlemanly garb of the time, but it is possible that this may apply only to the squire-minstrels. A distinction was drawn between trumpeters on the one hand and ' string-men ', such as harpers, lutenists and vielle-players, on the other. It is possible that the trumpeters, the 4½d. per day men, would have worn a special style of dress. There may also have been a difference in status. The Household Ordinance of Edward II, drawn up at York in 1318, lays down that trumpeters and musicians ' shall have wages and clothing each according to his status, at the discretion of the Steward and the Treasurer.'[4]

While they were on duty at Court, they had their commons provided : a morning meal, *gentaculum*; a midday one, *prandium*; and an evening one, *cena*; together with daily issues of bread and wine. (roughly 10s. each). The Household Ordinance of Edward III,[5] although somewhat later than the period with which we are concerned, gives a much more comprehensive picture of Court minstrels' liveries. Minstrels were provided with other necessaries besides clothing, wages, bread and wine; they were given lodging for themselves and their horses, firewood and candles in winter; and were allowed to bring into

---

[3] See Frontispiece.
[4] *The Place of Edward II in English History*, T. F. Tout, Appendix I, 272. See also Add. MSS. 21993, f.41.
[5] *A Collection of Ordinances and Regulations for the government of the Royal Household, Edward III to William and Mary.* (Society of Antiquaries, Lond. 1799.)

Court two honest servants to carry their instruments and a torch-bearer for winter nights, ' whyles they blowe to souper'. One can safely assume that such necessities were also automatically provided for the minstrels of Edward I. Although their clothing allowance remained unchanged, at 20s., the wages of all were reduced to 4½d. and ale instead of wine became their daily portion. Only 13 minstrels were appointed; no distinction was drawn between trumpeters and string-men and the latter had to leave court the day after they had performed at the regular festivals of the year. Compared with the kind of life the great minstrels of Edward I lived, this sounds meagre and demeaning. On the Payroll alone, which is by no means a complete list of royal servants, no fewer than 27 royal minstrels are mentioned. Evidently the high-water mark of minstrelsy had been reached and the tide of prosperity was gradually ebbing by the end of the fourteenth century.

Under Edward I all minstrels remained on duty for varying periods of time and their duties depended almost entirely upon the kinds of instruments they played. The work of the trumpeters, drummers and fifers, apart from their military duties, was to attend upon the king to support his dignity. Two personal trumpeters preceded him in his comings and goings, to announce his approach or departure, whether inside or outside the palace. When he rode abroad, with his household, the trumpeters acted as both announcers and guides. Their signals kept the company from straying, especially when in unfamiliar surroundings. Their special calls would inform the rest of the entourage where the king was. The horn-blowers, *cornours*, blew the night-watches, called everyone to meals, informed the inmates of the palace when the king was about to go riding or hunting, and raised the alarm when fire broke out. The taborers and fifers served as a danceband or accompanied the turns of acrobats and jugglers. The string-men's duties were equally varied : they played at mealtimes, like a café orchestra, entertained king, queen, princes, princesses, nobles and guests in their private rooms, sat up all night trying to soothe a bad sleeper, played to the king when he was bored with having to stay in bed after having been let blood, played a major part in all Court functions and festivities, and, with the organist, provided music for church services. These are a few of the

activities to which the Wardrobe accounts testify. It is important to remember that they were regular duties, performed at
command. In the words of the household Ordinance of York,
' they shall make their minstrelsy in the presence of the king
at all times pleasing to him.'

Their most exacting duties, ones calculated to bring to the
fore their greatest skill, were those connected with great Court
functions, such as the Christmas, Epiphany, Easter and Pentecost feasts, royal marriages, entertainment of foreign royalty
and the like. At these, all kinds of artistic shows were put on
and the minstrels would be called upon to organise them and
produce new compositions to suit the occasion. The device of
the two swans with its train of accompanying minstrels is an
admirable example.

Their duties did not end with their temporary residences in
the palace. They went to war with the king both at home and
abroad. On these occasions their wages were increased to 12d.
per day and their horses were valued by the Marshal so that
the king could, if it became necessary, compensate them for the
loss of them. The 12d. wages were shared between the Marshalcy and the Wardrobe, the former paying 7½d. with fodder and
litter also allowed, and the latter the minstrels' statutory wage
of 4½d. Whether minstrels took part in the fighting is doubtful.
There is plenty of evidence that they were on the field. In
1300 Nicholas le Blond, then King's Harper, travelled with
Edward I from London to Caerlaverock. The itinerary can be
traced in terms of wages paid to him on the journey, from
14 April to 30 August; through St. Albans, Dunstable, Pichley,
Stamford, Peterborough, Chippenham (Cambs.), Bury St.
Edmunds, Gaywood, Caisthorp, York, Carlisle, Caerlaverock,
and later, after the siege, on to Kirkcudbright and Dumfries.[6]
Altogether he received £10-2s.-7d., which, with the subtraction
of the payment owing to him for a horse that he had to purchase
on the way, amounted to the equivalent of about £2,000. In
1306 the king's four harpers, William le Sautreour and many
others set out with the king and queen for Lanercost after the
knighting.

---

[6] Add. MSS. 35291, f.158r.

On campaign a minstrel's duties would include the composition and rendering of victory *sirventois*, ' duty ' songs, to celebrate the defeat of the enemy or acclaim the deeds of the victors. One such is the poem entitled *Le Siege de Karlaverok*,[7] an eye-witness account in praise of the bannerets and other knights who took part in the siege. Their coats of arms are described in workaday couplets, but the minstrel who composed it was not only knowledgeable in heraldry; he had a shrewd, observant eye for human behaviour. Mingled with his pedestrian lists of blazons are lightning character-sketches which could have raised both ire and laughter in the tents.

Judged by present-day standards the remuneration of a royal or Court minstrel was reasonably good—approximately £1,500 to £2,300 per annum. The rate of pay was respectable but the work was not what we would call full-time. It does not seem to have been even regular, in the sense that fixed periods of attendance at Court were set. One of the most revealing documents to come to light relative to this, and of great importance, is to be found in the Exchequer accounts, E101/371/8. It is only a fragment from the Marshalcy rolls, but it happens to be an entry referring to Hugh de Naunton, one of the King's Harpers. On Thursday, 20 May 1305, when the King was at Kennington, in Surrey, Hugh arrived at Court, with two horses and a groom, to take up his duties on wages for the first time. There follows a bare list of his attendances at Court until 18 August 1307. After he arrived on 20 May he remained at Court for just under four weeks, and left on 30 June, but returned on the following Wednesday, 7 July, having been off duty for precisely one week. The Court was now at Canterbury and he remained on duty for just under six weeks, leaving it at Rawreth (Essex) on 20 August. Over two months elapsed before he put in an appearance again, on 31 October, at Westminster. There he was on duty for a week. He left again on 8 November, and did not return until 10 December. By this time Edward I was in Kingston-Lacy, where he was going to spend Christmas. As might be expected, Hugh was on duty during the Christmas and New Year festivities, but he left again on 28 January. His period of duty had lasted exactly

---

[7] *The roll of arms of the princes, barons and knights who attended Edward I at the siege of Caerlaverock*, ed. Thomas Wright (Lond. 1864).

seven weeks. From January to May he was absent, a space of almost four months, but he returned again in time for the knighting of the Prince. After the Pentecost feast was over, he remained on duty until 17 June, when he left with an advance of one mark for his wages. Seven weeks later he joined the King at Newcastle-on-Tyne. He moved with the Court to Lanercost, left on 3 February but was back again with the King at Carlisle on 25 March. Edward's life was now fast ebbing. Hugh was with him when he died and stayed with the Court until 30 July.

This fragment of manuscript establishes that royal minstrels did not attend Court at regular times or for regular periods, although they were on wages. The question arises, who dictated their movements ? Did they come and go as they pleased or were their periods of service subject to some internal household arrangement ? In either case the pattern of their work was singularly flexible, with the inevitable result that their wages, when considered in the long term, were unstable. Although they were doing what was virtually part-time work, it seems to have been far from insecure. The records prove that the majority remained in Court all their working lives : Richard Rounlo, 35 years, Richard Pilke, 26 years, John Drake, 23 years, John the lutenist, 22 years, to mention but four. The records also prove that their work was highly profitable, not so much from the point of view of wages and livery, although these provided a firm base of modest security, but on account of another source of income, *largesse*.

Despite the fact that, according to the Household Ordinance, minstrels were at the beck and call of their masters and mistresses, the Wardrobe books are full of references to *de dono* payments made to them. The occasions vary. Sometimes they were given special rewards for special ceremonies, as, for instance, at the Prince's knighting, but *largesse* was regularly dispensed at all festivals, marriage-feasts, celebrations of births and so on. Yet there are also scores of entries noting gifts of money given to both wind-men and string-men for performing at what might be called ordinary times, that is, entertaining various members of the household during the course of day or night or, as the records put it, 'making their minstrelsy in the presence of . . .'. On the evidence I have collected it would seem that *largesse* formed a part of the minstrel's legitimate expectations. For his master or mistress it constituted something in the nature of a self-imposed obligation. At the same time, it must not be forgotten that such gratuities were also a mark of genuine appreciation of the minstrels' skill; they reflected the pleasure which the hearers derived from their performances. Expressed, as they are, in mediaeval silver pennies, they do not appear very large to us, but when they are changed into modern equivalents they make a greater impact on the mind. The 5 marks handed to Robert Parvus, King of Heralds, as his portion of the 200, would be approximately £700 today. William le Sautreour and John the lutenist received the equivalent of about £500 each. These are somewhat larger gratuities than were usually given on less august occasions, but it is clear from the Wardrobe accounts that gifts to domestic minstrels were substantial at all times; so that, in terms of cost of living the king's *largesse* added considerably to his minstrels' incomes. In addition to the hundreds of pounds they received in this way they benefitted from gifts in kind. From time to time they were given horses, armour, lengths of cloth, silk cloaks, silver-gilt cups, gold clasps for their mantles, new instruments, venison from the King's forests, timber for building or repairing their houses, dead oak-stumps for winter firewood and, above all, land, property, rents and wardships. When they grew old or were no longer able to work, they were sent to some wealthy abbey or prosperous minor monastery in which to end their days.

So much, in great brief, for their lives in Court. What did they do when they were off duty ? What of their private lives ? There is enough material to hand to prove that they were well-to-do gentlemen who, like professionals at any time, did their work and, when off duty, lived lives comparable in every way to those of their fellow-citizens of similar social and economic standing. They are seen to be ordinary householders, living with their wives and children within reasonable distance of the palace. As citizens of substance they were under no necessity to add to their income by travelling during their free time from castle to castle or hall to hall ; and there is no evidence that any of them did so. This does not mean that they did not, upon occasion, visit the households of members of the royal family or of the greater nobles. Whenever there happened to be a great royal marriage or a purification feast for a princess or other noble lady, they made it their business to be present. Sometimes they were requested to stay for a time at other households connected with Court. For example, between the homes of the de Clares and the de Bohuns royal minstrels travelled freely. The differences between their visits and those of minstrels of lesser breed lies in the fact that they had right of access not solely by virtue of their craft but because they were known in person to the heads of the households concerned. I have yet to meet with an entry which proves that a royal minstrel was performing in a milieu other than that in which he was accustomed to work, namely, the circle of the nobility.

Their days must have been full. There were regular and special functions to practise for, instruments to see to, their own compositions to work at, daily practice to keep their fingers supple, their sons to train and, perhaps, other pupils as well. It is not as romantic a picture as is conventionally painted, but, since it is based on sober fact, I trust it will be the more credible.

What was true of the minstrel of the king's household was also true of the minstrel attached to the households of the nobility. On the Payroll there are the names of numbers of baronial domestic minstrels who attended their masters at the knighting. Details concerning some of them have been gleaned from Court records. It has not been possible to discover how their wages compared with those of court minstrels because reliable information on this score is lacking. It is unlikely that they received as much as $7\frac{1}{2}$d. per day, except in some of the greatest households, such as those of Thomas, earl of Lancaster and Gilbert, earl of Gloucester, which vied with the king's household in wealth, number of servants and general magnificence. In them the domestic minstrel would have enjoyed high standing. For the rest, every nobleman, every knight, every gentleman with social pretensions had his bevy of minstrels, no matter how small; his trumpeters, drummers and pipers, his harper and his waferer. These are the ones who appear most frequently in the Wardrobe accounts, because they invariably accompanied their masters when they came to Court. Land, houses, and rents were given them in the areas in which they lived; they received statutory wages and livery; they benefitted from their masters' and mistresses' *largesse*. In fact, the social and economic pattern of their lives was a replica of that of the court minstrels.

If all minstrels both at Court and in baronial hall had been professionals, the task of identifying the men and women on the Payroll might have been much easier. All were rewarded for ' making their minstrelsy ' and, since the occasion was a festive one, there is every reason to believe that ' minstrelsy ' here means entertainment of the kind usually understood when we use the word; yet analysis of the list has revealed that numbers of the people named in it were serving in the household in other capacities and received court wages for duties far removed from singing songs, playing a musical instrument or acting in plays. They were, among other things, heralds, messengers, sergeants-at-arms, grooms of the chamber, soldiers, sailors and watchmen. These were the amateurs whose numbers swelled the ranks of the professionals.

In the middle ages nearly everybody played an instrument of some kind. Among the higher classes ability to compose songs and poems and to play an instrument was taken for granted. Such accomplishments were part of a young gentleman's education and it follows that squires[8] in the royal household would be amateur musicians of one sort or another, which helps to explain the heterogeneous nature of the Payroll. Although it is ostensibly a cash account relative to ' entertainers ', it is actually a record of money given to various domestic servants, who were either professional or amateur minstrels; and they are all rightly called *menestralli* because the term covers both meanings. What is not clear is how far the amateurs were involved in regular court entertainment. Since the financial rewards they received were in the nature of *largesse*, it might be argued that what they did was done of their free will, but the structure of life at Court would seem to

---

[8] The following extract from the Black Book of Edward IV outlines clearly what part the squires played in the general social life of Court : ' Thes esquiers of household of old be accustomed, Wynter and somer, in after nonys and in evenynges, to drawe to lordez chambrez within Courte, there to kepe honest company aftyr theyre cunyng, in talkyng of cronycles of kinges and of other polycyez or in pyping or harpyng, synging, other actez marciablez, to help occupy the Court and accompany straungers tyll the tym require of departing.'
See *The Household of Edward IV, the Black Book and the Ordinance of* 1478, ed. A. C. Myers (Manchester 1959).

have given them little option. Most likely, the situation in the
royal household, with regard to both organized and private
entertainment, was fluid. A body of professionals was appointed
which formed the nucleus of wage-paid entertainment, but
there existed as well a reservoir of amateur talent that could be
and evidently was continually drawn upon. In this way the
needs of the household, particularly during the customary
festivals and family banquets, could be met from within its
own ranks. Certain types of minstrels very much in demand—
acrobats, jugglers, conjurors, tumblers, funambulists and the
like—do not figure in either of these two groups. I have come
across no minstrel of this sort serving on court wages. The one
woman minstrel on the Payroll of whose sex one can be absolutely certain was one of these. Matilda Makejoy was a *saltatrix*,
which was something more than a plain tumbler. She was an
acrobatic dancer. Only three references to her occur in the
Wardrobe accounts, yet they pose the problem of her relationship with the court. During Christmas 1296 she was making
her vaults in the presence of the Prince, then 13 years old;
her next appearance was at the knighting in 1306; four years
later she was performing on Midsummer Day before the two
boy princes, Thomas and Edmund. It is a pity that there is no
mention of her in the City records; something more about her
might have come to light. She represents a whole class of
minstrels about whom virtually nothing is known. The jugglers,
conjurors, acrobats and dancers who performed before the
king were not likely to have been common charlatans, yet they
do not appear to have been on the same footing with the
minstrels employed at Court. Matilda was known to the royal
children, was present at the Pentecost festivities, and was
obviously remembered and welcomed in the royal households
for at least 14 years. Perhaps she was one of the numerous City
minstrels who made their living by regular performances at
the many guild and other functions. Details about life on the
periphery of Court are hard to find. Somewhere in the nebulous
region between royal hall and city shop there must have
existed a collection of professionals whose ways of earning
their daily bread were as multifarious and mysterious as those
of many London-dwellers of today, among them reputable

artists who, by virtue of the patronage of the palace, regarded themselves as being almost the same as court minstrels.

ii. *Classes of minstrels represented*
(a) *Musicians*

The nearest one can ever get to catching a fleeting understanding of the quality and variety of the music which filled the London air on the day of the knighting will be a tentative appreciation of the different kinds of instruments in respect of their construction, range and timbre.

HARP. The dominant sound would have been that of the harp. Although the Payroll does not supply a complete record of the number of minstrels present, it testifies to the superiority of this ancient national instrument. The harpers outnumber all other groups of instrumentalists. Their eminence was still unassailed. No doubt this was due partly to conservatism, because the harp was the national instrument of the English, but its own nature, of course, contributed most to its long-lasting popularity.

Its scale was diatonic and consequently somewhat restricted in range, yet it seems to have been admirably suited to its two main purposes; accompanying the monophonic singing of elegies and narrative verse; and providing often by its music alone solace for the spirit. The kind of singing or chanting then in vogue was comparatively simple, its compass rarely going beyond fifths, sixths and octaves. This the diatonic scale could match. In a way the limitation of the harp-scale was its virtue, for it produced a type of music which must have possessed the quality Browning had in mind when he wrote in *Abt Vogler* of ' the C major of this life '.

What gave this ancient harp music its special timbre was the instrument's construction. Degrees of pitch were obtained chiefly by means of the unequal lengths of the strings, the tension being more or less the same in each. The player could vary the musical quality of the notes by either using a plectrum instead of the fingers (or finger-nails) or by plucking the strings at different points along their length, which, to a sensitive ear, could have produced very delicate, harmonic overtones. Much of its appeal lay in its simplicity and plangency, for the early harp was totally unlike its modern, concert descendant. It was easily portable, small, usually about two feet in height and possessing anything from six to a dozen strings.[9] The absence of accidentals rendered it musically simple but this did not mean that it could not, in the hands of a master, produce technically brilliant compositions. Up to the beginning of the fourteenth century it held pride of place in the royal household, but after Edward I died subsequent Wardrobe books provide a silent testimony to the beginning of its decline. After 1307 there are no entries which refer to a group of ' King's Harpers ' as there regularly used to be to the devoted four of the old king. Edward II followed the newer fashion. During his reign one can trace the change which was gradually coming over the musical world.

VIELLE. It was a change which had begun in the early eleventh century, when the use of the bow was introduced into Western Europe. Bowed instruments were well-known in the East, but the West does not seem to have borrowed anything except the bow. Our own instruments, such as the rote and the vielle, which were originally plucked, were retained, but musicians started playing them with a bow. The effects were far-reaching; the rote developed into the crowd or *crwth* and the vielle and gigue became the prototypes of the violin. With the use of the bow it became possible to produce sustained notes on strings without changes in pitch; and since the finger-boards of these instruments were unfretted, a new dimension in technical skill was created. Making the scale devolved upon the player, his fingering had to be executed with a precision that was wholly dependent upon a perfect ear; but these demands upon his skill, new and difficult though they were, were accompanied by measureless freedom. One has only to think of the range, resources and brilliance contained in the four strings of a violin to realise what a stupendous advance in music had been made possible by the introduction of the bow. During the twelfth and thirteenth centuries the vielle,

[9] It would be very dangerous to dogmatize about the mediaeval harp. Over the centuries it underwent considerable change in shape and size. References to it in contemporary literature indicate that it could vary from one to three or four feet in height and have anything from six to thirty-six strings. The usual type, however, seems to have conformed to the two-foot size I have mentioned, which was easily portable and wide enough in range to enable a minstrel to show off his execution. The little six-stringed one, often hung at the belt, was, apparently, solely for accompanying singing.

in particular, had developed out of recognition of its former self. It would be foolish to imagine that it had attained the purity of tone of a modern violin; the bow was still far from perfect. The hairs in the arched type depicted in contemporary miniatures and sculptures were tensed by means of the fingers, because there was neither shaft nor screw. The hair itself was weaker, there being only about 40 to 50 horsehairs in one bow as compared with the 100 to 120 in ours; and since the end of the bow was held in the whole, closed hand and not, as with us, by the tips of fingers and thumb, there could have been little flexibility in the player's wrist. Consequently, his bowing would have been rather rigid and his execution scratchy. Another factor which would have rendered his music somewhat muted was the positioning of the bow on the strings. According to the illustrations in manuscripts, the player drew it across the middle of the strings, about a third of the way up the finger-board. He also held his instrument in an awkward and tiring way, against the breast and sometimes in a peculiar horizontal position across the chest, which would have entailed vertical bowing. The number of strings varied from three to five, one of which was sometimes a bourdon off the finger-board. Finally, the neck of the vielle was probably too short to allow any change of position. It seems fairly certain that the viellist played in just one, or what we call the first, position.

These details do not give a very encouraging idea of vielle music; yet, in its day it was lauded as the best of all instruments. De Grocheo[10] declared that the vielle contained within itself and to a subtler and more delicate degree than other instruments, the power to reproduce all musical forms. Innumerable references to it in mediaeval literature echo his praise. It was an instrument that could be sweet, merry, soothing or sad; it could set the feet itching to dance or tell the grief of the heart. In other words, it was already displaying the qualities of the violin. If we could hear it now it would probably sound primitive, but the ears of those who listened to it were attuned to it and found it beautiful. Perhaps the *geige* ought to be classed with the vielle since some authorities are of the opinion that the German *Geige* was the same instrument as the *Fiedel*,

---

[10] *Die Musiklehre des Johannes de Grocheo*, von Johannes Wolf (*Sammelbände der Internationalen Musikgeschellschaft*, Leipzig 1879-1900), 65-130.

which later they equate with the vielle.[11] Conrad and Heinrich, the two *geige*-players named in the Payroll, had been living in Court for seven years; they and their instruments were well-known to the Wardrobe clerks. Had they been vielle-players we should expect the clerks to have referred to them as *vidulatores* or *vielers*, but this they never do. They invariably call them *gigatores*, *gigatores Alemannie* or *gygors*, *gigours*. Such clearly deliberate usage points to a distinction of some kind between the two instruments.

PSALTERY.   Entries in the Close and Patent Rolls alone amply prove how favoured William, the queen's psaltery-player, was. The instrument he played belonged to the lyre/harp family. Sometimes it is referred to as a kind of dulcimer but it was more in the nature of a harp laid flat, with the sound-box under the strings.   Contemporary illustrations show it in a variety of shapes, the most frequently depicted being one like a flat, triangular box, with the apex of the triangle cut off and the two sides curved in to allow the player to bring his arms round to the front of the instrument, because this type of psaltery was held against the player's breast. Its twelve or sixteen metal strings were stretched diagonally across the sound-box, with buttons to fix them on one side and tuning pegs on the other. The number of sound-holes varied from one to as many as four or five. It could be played with either the fingers (or finger-nails) or quills. The use of metal strings and quills would have rendered its tone bright, sharp and resonant, but if the strings were of silver, its music would have sounded delicately soft and sweet. In pictures and sculptures of the time it invariably found a place in the hands of some sweet-faced angel in a heavenly choir; on earth it was the ideal instrument for the intimacy of a private apartment.[12]

---

[11] *The Origins of Bowing*, Werner Bachmann. Trans. Norma Deane (Oxford 1969), 75.
In his Introduction Bachmann warns the reader that he has used ' fiddle ' (*Fiedel*) throughout his book to denominate all kinds of bowed instruments because, as he says, the various mediaeval words for them were sometimes confused even in their own day.

[12] Chaucer's word-picture of ' hende Nicholas ', the Oxford student, who was as modest as a girl and sweet as liquorice-root, beguiling the evening hours with his ' gay sautry ' in his lodging, is incomparable. (*The Miller's Tale*, 27-32). One of his favourite tunes was *Angelus ad Virginem*, which happens to be one of the wisps of melody preserved from the distant past. There is a recording of it on *His Master's Voice* Long Play Record, Side 2, Band I, of Volume III *The History of Music in Sound*. (*Ars Nova and the Renaissance*).

There is not enough information available to enable one to speculate upon the kind of repertoire that William le Sautreour had at his command. Long *chansons de gestes*, *romans* and narrative *lais* would have called for the grandeur and mellow melodic simplicity of the harp but an instrument like the psaltery was best suited to lyrics and hymns, to songs which, whether grave or gay, admitted a wider musical versatility to accompany their varied metrical forms. Whereas the harp compelled prolonged attention, the psaltery charmed by the comparative brevity of its compositions.

CROWD or CRWTH. The Prince and his friends appear to have had a particular liking for this instrument. In his Wardrobe books, when he was both Prince and King, references to harpers are virtually non-existent, but payments and gifts to crowders are frequent.

Venantius Fortunatus in his oft-quoted statement about different instruments being characteristic of different peoples, ascribed the *chrotta* to the *Britanni*. This may have been true in the sixth century, when he was writing, but the crowd was well-known throughout Europe during the middle ages. Originally it seems to have been a sort of lyre but by the thirteenth century it was being played with a bow, and therefore acquired a finger-board and a bridge. In many ways it was an odd instrument. It was rectangular in shape, with two large apertures in its top half to enable the player to hold it and at the same time insert his thumb and fingers to reach the strings. Most contemporary illustrations of it show it as having six strings, four on the finger-board and two at the left of it, to be plucked with the thumb. That it had a special appeal cannot be denied, yet it is difficult to understand what it was. There was nothing that a player could do on the crowd which could not have been done better on the vielle or the *geige*, a fact which might help to explain why it gradually fell out of favour. Perhaps its attraction lay in its suitability for accompanying singing. After the vielle had dispensed with its bourdon strings, the crowd, which retained them, was able to provide simultaneously a melody, played on the stopped strings, to match the singer's voice, and a bourdon, to furnish a low, satisfying background. Whatever it was, it appealed very much to the Prince. In later centuries, long after it had been cast aside elsewhere, it lingered in Wales, becoming a favoured, almost a national instrument of the descendants of the Britons to whom Venantius Fortunatus had ascribed it so long ago.[13]

ORGAN. The large, pneumatic organ had been an indispensable part of church equipment from very early times. The monastery at Winchester was famous in the tenth century for the phenomenally large one built by bishop Elfegus. It possessed 400 pipes in a row and two sets of bellows, ' twice six above and fourteen below ', which 70 strong men, their arms ' dank with much sweat ' worked to enable the organist to produce a sound that was shattering. The ' iron voice ' beat upon the senses like thunder; everyone who heard it covered his ears with his hands—and it could be heard all over the city.[14]

There were plenty of others of similar crudity. They did not have hinged keys; the complete slide had to be pulled out and pushed in by the organist, so that playing consisted in more or less thumping the keys with the fist. Volume was terrific. Ailred of Rievaulx, writing in the mid-twelfth century, has left a realistic account of a choir singing to the accompaniment of one such instrument : ' Why are there so many organs . . . in church ? And, I ask you, what about the horrible snorting of the bellows, sounding more like a crack of thunder than the sweetness of a musical tone ? And what about the drawing-in and the breaking-off of the singing ? . . . There are times, I am ashamed to say, when it sounds like horses whinnying . . . you will see a man with his mouth open as if he were ready not to sing but to emit a breath he has been holding back . . . the whole body is shaken about in actors' gestures, lips are distorted, shoulders roll round . . . In the meantime the poor people in the congregation, trembling and astounded, marvel at the din of the bellows . . . it is not without guffaws and laughter that they gaze at the gesticulations of the singers . . . You would think that they had assembled not in a church but in a theatre, not to pray, but to gape at a spectacle.'[15]

[13] See *Welsh Minstrels at the Courts of Edward I and Edward II*, Constance Bullock-Davies, *Transactions of the Hon. Society of Cymmrodorion*, Sessions 1972 and 1973 (Lond. 1974), 114f.
[14] *Epistola Wolstani Monachi Wentoni ad Elfegum Wentanum Episcopum*, Migne, *Pat. Lat.*, 137, 107-11.
[15] *Speculum Charitatis*, Migne, *Pat. Lat.*, 195, 570-1.

Probably it was not quite as bad as Ailred tried to make out; he was no lover of worldly ways and trifles. Chrétien de Troyes,[16] writing a little later in the same century, says it was customary for people to go to church on the great festivals, especially to hear the organ, so that there must have been some virtue in these clumsy, bellowing old mammoths. Like everything else made by human hands, they underwent improvement. Gradual development of the keyboard, as well as an increase in the number of keys, gave the player greater freedom. He was able to use his fingers instead of his fists. By 1306 the compass of the large organ was two octaves, the pipes were arranged, as now, large at the sides and small in the middle, and the use of more than one keyboard had been introduced. Concurrently two smaller types were being developed. The *positive*, so called because it could be placed wherever it was wanted, was a handy substitute for the immovable church organ. It became very popular, because its reduced volume provided softer and sweeter music; but, most popular of all, especially with singers, was the completely portable model, the *portative*. This was small enough to be slung by a strap from the shoulder. It had diminutive pipes and an in-built bellows which the player worked with one hand, while he played on the keys with the other. The tiny bellows gave light wind-pressure, which enabled the key-action to be lightly and quickly responsive. Although the player could use only one hand, his skill in fingering made up for the restriction. It was on a *portative* that the famous blind Italian organist and composer, Francesco Landini (c. 1325-97), used to play.

The two organists on the Payroll were no doubt masters of all three kinds. At the knighting, their services would have been required not only in the royal chapel but in hall and private appartments, for organ-playing was not, at that time, restricted to church-services; it was very much a part of secular entertainment.

FRETTED INSTRUMENTS : *lute, citole* and *guitar*

These instruments are poorly represented on the Payroll. There is only one player of each.

---

[16] *Le Chevalier de la Charette*, 3518-9, ed. Mario Roques (Paris, 1972. *CFMA*).

The lute of the fourteenth century was smaller than the Elizabethan type with which most people are familiar. Its distinguishing feature, then as now, was its bent back peg-box, but it did not acquire its four courses of paired strings until late in the century, so that the lute that Janin le Leutour played at the knighting would have sounded musically simpler than its descendants; yet it would have possessed the same individual beauty of tone since this was dependent upon its rounded back and the extraordinary fragility of the slats of wood which went into its composition. With so finely made a body it could pick up vibrations and overtones from anywhere. It is one of the most responsive of instruments in skilful hands and an excellent companion to the human singing voice. At the feast of 1306 it could have been regarded as one of the newer instruments still making its way to the forefront. Janin first appears in the royal records in 1285 and is the only lutenist mentioned in the Wardrobe books for the whole period to 1327. He stood supreme among royal minstrels, being highly thought of and bountifully rewarded by Edward I, Edmund Crouchback and Henry de Lacy. Perhaps he owed his early advancement to queen Eleanor of Castile, for the lute does not seem to have been introduced into Western European countries other than Spain much before the middle of the thirteenth century.

The *citole* was either fig-shaped or round, with a flat back like a banjo. References to it in contemporary poetry suggest that its tone was soft and sweet. The author of *La Clef d'Amors*[17] (c. 1280) speaks of it as being one of the instruments specially suited to women. Although its music may have been soft and sweet, it would have had as well the penetrating, clear tone of the fretted instrument, because it is the masterly placing of the fingers on the frets which contributes to the production of the characteristic, clear-cut notes. Between 1306 and 1326 only three citolers are mentioned in the Wardrobe books. Janyn appears nowhere else except on the Payroll.

The *guitar* was flat-backed, with four strings and much stronger than its near cousin, the lute. In Spain both were called guitars, but the lute, *guitarra moresca* or *saracena*, was of

---

[17] ed. Hermann Suchier (Halle 1870, *Bibliotheca Normannica*), 97.

oriental origin, while the guitar, *guitarra latima*, was, as its name implies, of indigenous, probably Roman origin. It was this European guitar that Peter, *Le Gitarier*, played. It is very unlikely that two minstrels, Janin le Leutour and Peter le Gitarier, would have been so clearly differentiated by name had they played the same instrument. One cannot help thinking that these three players on the fretted instruments represented at the knighting a group of minstrels somewhat apart from the others. While harpers, vielle-players, crowders and psaltery-players occur in great numbers throughout the reigns of Edward I and Edward II, there were only three citolers, two or three guitarists and a single lutenist. Music at that time, especially stringed music, was, in terms of historical perspective, in a state of flux. In 1306 it was still in the world of *ars antiqua*, despite the fact that a new spirit was abroad. Walter de Odington had yet to write his *De Speculatione Musicae*; Guillaume de Machaut was then but an infant. Nevertheless, the famous polyphonic *rota*, *Sumer is icumen in*, was already about fifty years old. It had heralded the coming revolution in music; *ars nova* was on the way. Viewed from this angle, the great Whitsunday feast was something in the nature of a *grand finale*. It was the last magnificent concert of Edward's reign. His days were numbered; so, too, were those of his harpers, both physically and in the world of music. Not long after the death of their master, their names drop, one by one, out of the Exchequer records. Other instruments, other music and other techniques were coming into vogue. The long, long day of the harp was practically over. It is true that it retained a place in Court until the reign of Charles II, but by that time it had ceased to occupy the pre-eminent position it had held in the royal household up to the death of Edward I. As far as I am able to judge from the evidence supplied by the Wardrobe and other accounts, no subsequent harpers ever held pride of place in the king's chamber as Edward's four had.

WIND AND PERCUSSION INSTRUMENTS. The music provided by the trumpets, drums and fifes needs to be considered separately since most of it, during the knighting and feasting, would have been either ceremonial or ancillary, although this does not preclude the possibility of its having been also appreciated in and for itself. No military music has survived from this period, but it would be dangerous to assume that it was lacking in variety and technical skill. Clerks' notes to the effect that a particular trumpeter, taborer or nakerer had been given *largesse* for performing in the royal presence intimate that the minstrels possessed individual talent and expertise.

The standard mediaeval *trumpet* was about four feet long, with a cylindrical bore and a bell-shaped mouth. Metal rings encircled the joins in the stem, because no other method of lengthening the tube was then known. Folded trumpets do not appear to have been devised before the end of the fourteenth century. Length of stem was of the utmost importance ; the longer the trumpet was the more brilliant and incisive was its tone. The originality and skill of the trumpeters at the feast can only be guessed at. No doubt the compass of their instruments was wider than we think, for range depends a good deal on tongueing. Experts like John de Catalonia, Robert Parvus, the King's *Rex Haraldorum*, would have been no strangers to the art of flurrying, which would have added immense variety to the long notes. As a rule the trumpets were brass or bronze and their music consequently grand, arresting and powerful. Stateliness in ceremonial and menace on the battlefield have always been associated with their trenchant blasts. Sometimes royal trumpeters, as now, had silver trumpets. Gillot and Januche[18] possessed them. As they preceded and announced the Prince at his knighting, their fanfares and flourishes would have had all the sweet brightness that silver trumpets give.

In addition to its use in hunting and war, the *tabor* was very much a social instrument. It was a fairly small two-skin drum played either solo or with the fife. Its sticks were wooden and unfelted. For beating time at dances it was indispensable. It also provided the quick, exciting rolls that have always been a necessary accompaniment to jugglers' and acrobats' turns. No more than six are mentioned on the Payroll, but there were probably many others present, for they would have been in great demand throughout the day.

The *nakers* were more useful on campaign than in palace entertainment. They were small kettle-drums, played in pairs

---

[18] See under *Januche*.

slung from the waist or strapped on the back of a groom while the nakerer operated the sticks independently from behind. From the point of view of sound-production they possessed greater potential than the tabor, because they could be tuned to a more exact pitch and the resonance could be varied according to whether the shell was made of wood or metal. Janin, the Prince's personal drummer, is the only nakerer mentioned in the Payroll. His duties were probably entirely ceremonial.

Estive.[19] It used to be thought that this instrument was a kind of flageolet but expert opinion now inclines to the view that it was a form of bagpipe, an instrument much more popular in the middle ages than is generally realized. A special kind which keeps on recurring in literary works is the *estive de Cornouaille*, always associated with love-songs. The melodies of the once famous *Breton lais* were played on it. If it were in truth a bagpipe, it would have been not the large cornemeuse, which was played out of doors, but a smaller kind, similar to those seen in the hands of angel-minstrels in sculptures.

Bells. The minstrel who played the bells at the feast is nameless. He could have been an expert with the hand-bells or a player of bells on the frame. Both kinds of performance were incredibly old even in the fourteenth century.

It is good to end on a note of hesitancy. So little is known about the details of mediaeval instrumental music, that caution and diffidence should be one's watchwords when venturing to say anything about it. Above all, one should beware of depreciating it. Our instruments are so sophisticated that there is a temptation to imagine that the music played on instruments six hundred odd years ago would have been simpler than and inferior to our own. The following snippet of information ought to give us pause : the Seigneur de Fontaine-Guérin, when he was imprisoned in the castle of Mesargnes by the Vicomtesse de Turenne in 1394, relieved the tedium of his days by composing a long poem on hunting, in which he described in detail the music of the hunting-horn. Every province in France had its own way of sounding it and, in the author's opinion, the

---

[19] *New Oxford Hist. of Music*, III, 495.

usage of Maine and Anjou excelled all the rest. This he proceeded to explain, first giving the musical scale used and then
all the different hunting-calls, fourteen in number. The method
he used for his explanation was perfectly clear to him, but time
and change robbed it of its meaning for those who came after
him. Three hundred years later, Lacurne de Sainte-Palaye,
after reading it, sadly concluded, ' Quoique l'auteur se vante
d'avoir mis beaucoup de clarté dans son poeme, il ne nous en a
paru plus intelligible.'[20]

(b) *Heralds*

So large a number of minstrels, all anxious to display their
various skills, could not have been allowed to clamour indis-
criminately for an audience. While it remains true that individuals would have been commanded at all hours to perform
their customary duties during attendance upon their masters
and mistresses, the knighting was an occasion upon which
organized entertainment would have been obligatory, since
the minstrels, both those of the royal households and those who
had come with the aspirants, were gathered at Westminster to
provide what could, under the circumstances, be termed
public entertainment. Some would have been detailed to
accompany the Prince and play during the dubbing ceremony;
others would have been sent to the Abbey to play while the
Prince dubbed the other young men, though it is doubtful
whether a note could have been heard above the din. The
élite of Court minstrels would have been reserved for the
ushering of the decorated swans into the great dining-hall;
scores would have been on duty to accompany the cavalcade
of the aspirants from New Temple to Westminster and to play
during the banquet. The people responsible for organizing
their activities were the heralds. As individuals they were
themselves proficient in one or another branch of minstrelsy,
but those who feature in the Exchequer records are indistinguish-
able from the king's sergeants-at-arms. At the same time, not
all king's sergeants-at-arms were heralds. The King Heralds,
Robert Parvus, Walter Marchis and Caupenny and the heralds,
Bruant, William Carleton and Thomas Norfolk, were sergeants.

---

[20] *Mémoires sur l'ancienne Chevalerie*, Jean Bapt. Lacurne de Sainte-Palaye, (1781),
tom. II, 283-4.

They were paid sergeants' wages, received sergeants' livery. Whatever duties they performed as heralds did not procure them a different status nor a different wage. They were appointed and given the title, *Haraldus* or, if they happened to be chief herald, *Rex Haraldorum*, but, as far as the Wardrobe accounts were concerned, they were sergeants-at-arms. Occasionally they occur as *balistarii*, arbalesters of the king's bodyguard, and are given their titles, but their office, as such, is never officially acknowledged. Neither *Reges Haraldorum* nor plain *Haraldi* are ever referred to in the Household Ordinances as being officers of the household, nor have I come across any reference to the issue of *cote armure* to them.[21] From such negative evidence it could be argued that they appeared to have duties but no statutory office, yet, by virtue of their duties they certainly held a special office in both royal and baronial households.

The little that is known about their early history is extremely hazy, depending on allusion rather than on definite, historical facts, but, by postulating past conditions through comparison with later developments, it is possible to infer that the office of herald, including that of *Rex Haraldorum*, was one created by the king and that his creation was accompanied by some sort of ceremony involving, for both herald and king of heralds, the presentation of a large goblet or cup and, for the king of heralds alone, the setting upon his head of a crown.[22] Both heralds and kings wore a tabard or *cote armure* and carried a baton. By these insignia they were differentiated from other sergeants.

It is generally accepted that a herald's primary duties were concerned with the tournament, but it is chiefly from literary sources that support for this contention has been derived. Heralds were sent throughout the area, province or county to proclaim when and where a tournament was to be held. At

---

[21] See under *Le Roy Robert*.

[22] No early description of this ceremony seems to have survived but the following entry in Machyn's diary serves to support the inference that a specific one certainly existed : ' The Sonday, the xxj day (of) November, the quen's grase (did) sett a crowne (on) Master Norrey's hed, kyng at armes (and) created him Clarenshus, with a cup of (wine), at Sent James, her grace's place.' (*The Diary of Henry Machyn*, 1550-63. ed. J. B. Nichols, Lond. 1848, *Camden Series*, 158). The year was 1557, the queen, Mary Tudor, and Norroy, created Clarencieux, Sir William Harvey.

the tournament itself they announced the names of the contestants, described their blazons, gave the signals to commence or cease, called out the combatants in time for their jousts and declared who were the winners. When they were attached to a particular knight, they made it their business to advertise his prowess, to urge him on during tilts or tourneys and, in every way possible, to add to the discomfiture of his opponent.

The pictures drawn by poets[23] of these men are often far from pleasant. Baudin de Condé considered the majority of them impostors and upstarts in his own profession of minstrelsy. Henri de Laon, another poet of the late thirteenth century, declared that he would like to become a herald because the life offered a marvellous opportunity for one to become an idler and a grabber; a herald did little but talked a lot. Jacques Bretel[24] was equally satirical. In his opinion—and he was describing a tournament which actually took place at Chauvency in 1285—heralds were coarse dolts, liars and hypocrites. Their chief object in life was to despoil knights. Heralds crop up continually in the course of his poem. He mentions four kings-of-arms by name and at least a dozen heralds. The descriptions of them vividly reflects his dislike. They shout raucously, like crows; one is as vicious as a watchdog; another is bald; another, weather-beaten and skinny. When they were not in the lists, they appear in a rather better light, because their duties were less pugnacious and vociferous. Indoors they acted as masters of ceremonies and call-boys, and, as Bretel takes pains to point out, one of their most important tasks was to learn the blazons of all the knights taking part in the tourney. He describes one, however, and at length, who seems to have been more like the kind of herald our Wardrobe books portray. For him he had no disparaging sneer; on the contrary, he obviously treated him with respect. This was Bruiant, who was wearing *cote armure*[25] and who told him the names and the

---

[23] *Les Contes des Hiraus*, (*Dit et Contes de Baudouin et de son fils, Jean de Condé*, ed. Aug. Scheler, Brussels 1866), I, 168ff.
  Dit des Hyraus, ed. M. A. Longfors, *Romania*, XLIII (1922), 222ff.
  See also *Heralds and Heraldry in the Middle Ages*, A. Wagner (Oxford 1939).

[24] *Le Tournoi de Chauvency*, ed. Maurice Delbouille (Liège 1932, *Bibliothèque de la faculté de philosophie et lettres de l'Université de Liège*, Fasc. XCIX).

[25] When Bretel arrived at Chauvency in the early part of October 1285, he met this herald and asked him for his help, because he realized that he did not know the names or blazons of all the guests. Together they entered the great

blazons of all the knights assembled in the hall; a very different type of person from the rough brutes who haunted the lists.

There was a radical difference between the king's sergeant-at-arms and the ragged boors despised by the aforementioned poets. The one was a trusted servant, the other a roving rogue; the one had a regular wage, the other picked up his money where and how he could; the one had an issue of cloth to make his own suit, the other wore his master's cast-offs or else went about in hessian; the one was a king's officer, the other a play-boy, a gamesman, a referee. Is it possible that these two kinds had anything in common ? In thirteenth century England, when royal permission had been granted for them to be held, tournaments were magnificent spectacles more in the nature of splendid entertainment—at any rate in theory—for the fighting was usually *à plaisance*. The combatants used blunted swords and coronals were placed on the tips of their lances. At these legitimate functions the *Reges Haraldorum* and the ordinary heralds would have had their parts to play, but if this was their sole *raison d'être* they would have had little to do, because Edward I banned all tournaments in England from 1299.[26]

If Wace can be relied on, heralds were originally something more than tournament officials. They were the descendants of the Classical ' proclaimers '[27] and interpreters, the special military messengers who combined, when necessary, the duties

hall of the castle and took a seat by one of the pillars :
> *Bruiant despoille sa garnaiche*
> *Que d'armes estoit painturée,*
> *Delez l'estache l' ruée*
> *Assis me sui et il lez moi.* (298-301)

[26] See *Heralds of England*, Sir Anthony Wagner (Lond. 1967), and *The Tournament in the Thirteenth Century*, N. Denholm-Young, in *Studies in Mediaeval History*, presented to Sir Maurice Powicke, edd. R. W. Hunt, W. A. Pantin and R. W. Southern (Oxford 1948).

[27] The Greek κῆρυξ. Instances are numerous in the *Iliad* and the *Odyssey*. See Daremberg et Saglio, *Dictionnaire des Antiquités Grecques et Romaines*. Among the duties of the Greek herald were : convening the assembly, procuring silence, giving the command to begin battle, carrying military messages, parleying with the enemy and, later, announcing the names of the winners at the Olympic games, after every event.

For the duties of English and French heralds on campaign, see *Histoire de Messire Bertrand du Guesclin*, ed. Claude Menard (Paris 1618). This biography of the famous Constable of France was written in 1387 and deals with incidents during the Hundred Years War. French and English heralds figure frequently in it and their work as military messengers is described in detail. See especially Chap. XIV, 408f.

of envoy and interpreter. Declarations of intent, strictly in relation to warfare, were the messages with which they were entrusted. When Duke William and King Harold exchanged messages before the arrival of the English army at Senlac, William sent Hugh Margot, a monk of Fécamp, to Harold, and the English king replied to his rival and enemy by sending a French-speaking herald :

> *Donc a Heraut pris un message*
> *Ki de France scut li langage* (11949-50)[28]

Whether this be truth or anachronism with regard to 1066 is immaterial. Wace was using the word *heraut* in what was to him a familiar context; which implies that, in the twelfth century, when heralds were beginning to make their appearance as uncouth officials at ordinary tournaments in France, there were already in existence heralds who were king's officers. Herein may lie the solution to the apparent discrepancy between a Robert Parvus on the one hand and the riff-raff of the French tournament world on the other. While a court herald came to include tournament duties among his older, more specifically military ones in the royal service, those who spent their days wandering the countryside in search of temporary work at any kind of tournament which happened to be taking place, were homeless adventurers, with no permanent position in any king's court or baronial castle.

According to Upton and Du Cange[29] a man could not become a herald before he had completed seven years' service in the army. It is a kind of qualification that seems to be supported by thirteenth and fourteenth century records. Robert Parvus, the most important *Rex Haraldorum* of Edward I, provides an example. Throughout the whole of his long service he remained a squire and king's sergeant-at-arms. His duties included supervision of fortifications in Scotland and elsewhere; he was, ' King Robert, minstrel and squire-at-arms ', ' King Robert, the trumpeter of the King ' and organizer of court entertainment. In all the numerous references to him there is not one single one relating to a tournament. The same

---

[28] *Le Roman de Rou*, ed. Andresen (1877).
[29] *De militari officio*, lib. I, cap. 12 ; Du Cange, s.v. *Heraldus*.

is true of all the other heralds and kings of heralds mentioned in the Wardrobe books, with one exception. On Christmas Day, 1300, Walter le Marchis, *Rex Haraldorum*, was given 40s. (£400) for proclaiming by order of the king and in the king's presence in the great hall of Northampton Castle, that *no* tournaments were to be held in England.

As far as positive evidence goes, the duties of royal heralds in relation to tournaments appear to have been at best subsidiary, but there was a definite link between these and their military duties; namely, their concern with knighthood and blazons. On active service their specialized knowledge of these matters was very important. They were responsible for drawing up the lists of knights at musters; they were the king's righthand men with regard to information about the enemy; when need arose, they were employed on military missions, as secret agents, military messengers and, if so qualified, as interpreters. King Caupenny, for instance, was ' from Scotland '. He was no mere visitor to the knighting; he had been present at the wedding festivities of the Princesses Joan and Margaret in 1290 and, soon after, had been taken into the royal household on wages. It is hardly likely that he was there solely to make minstrelsy and amuse the ladies. His knowledge of the Scottish terrain, its barons and their pedigrees, with much else besides, would have been extremely useful. That was what heralds were for. Between them the heralds at the knighting would have been able to provide the king with a knightly census of almost the whole of the country : Walter le Rey Marchis, herald of the Scottish border, Le Roy Druet of the South Wales and Gloucester areas, Caupenny of Scotland, Bruant of the Midlands and John de Monhaut, a *Rex Haraldorum* from Mold, who, although not mentioned on the Payroll, had been on wages at Court since 1297. Robert Parvus, if I interpret the indications in the records aright, was herald for the south of England.

Material relative to both royal and baronial heralds under Edward I is fragmentary, yet a kind of pattern is seen to emerge from it. They divided their time among military affairs, tournaments and minstrelsy. Concerning their duties connected with tournaments, the Wardrobe records are silent, except for the proclamation of prohibition already referred to.

Those dealing with military affairs, such as carrying of *communiqués*, conducting of prisoners, mustering of troops, drawing up of ordinaries, preparing muster-rolls and the like, are satisfactorily documented. It is their minstrel duties within the household which stand out most clearly, involving, as they do, all the ceremonial that was an integral part of everyday routine, together with the organizing of special functions and theatrical and other shows. They were directors, actor-managers and musicians. An entry in Baldock's *Journal* for 1320/21 (Add. MSS 9951, f.19ʳ) makes this perfectly clear. At the time, King Robert Parvus was still at Court, and he accompanied Edward II to France when the latter at last decided to pay his long-delayed homage for Gascony to the French king. Robert and other minstrels provided an entertainment for him at Amiens, for which they were rewarded with the splendid gift of £20 (£4,000). The entry runs : ' To Robert King of Heralds and of Royal functions and to other minstrels for making their minstrelsy at the banquet of the lord King held at Amiens, by gift of the same lord King into his own hands, at Amiens, 8 July.........£20.'

In dress they did not differ from other squires or minstrels of the household. In 1306 King Robert and King Caupenny received exactly the same livery as the king's four harpers and his waferer, yet it is certain that heralds wore a tabard with the coat of arms of their lord depicted on it. In the case of the royal heralds this *cote armure* must have been provided by the king. So was the crown, baton and cup of the *Rex Haraldorum*. A hint to this effect is to be found in the *Black Book of Edward IV* : ' (be it) alwey remembered that the cup wiche the King doth create any king of armes or harold withall, hit standith in the charge of the jewel-house and not uppon the thesauer of houshold.'[30] Which is also a further indication of the unofficial nature of the herald's work. He had neither wage nor livery for being a herald; he was clothed and paid for *as a herald* out of the privy purse.

(c) *Waferers*

In contrast to the heralds the waferers held specific office for which they were given a daily wage. Viewed from our stand-

---

[30] Myer's ed., *op. cit.*, 131-2.

point it was an odd sort of office. Although they could ' make their minstrelsy ' their primary duty in the household was simply to make wafers, but doing just that involved more than at first sight appears.

The Household Ordinance of 1318 laid down that ' there shall be a waferer who shall serve the king with wafers in hall and in his private room according to his office. And he shall take 8d. (£6-13s.-4d.) per day from the Pantry for his requirements. He shall have sugar from the Wardrobe, eggs from the Poultry and fuel from the Fueltry according to what he shall need for the King's service, after discussing it with the Steward and the Treasurer. And he shall receive as wages 7½d. per day, 2 sets of clothing per year or 40s. in cash; and, whether he be well or ill, he shall take for his daily commons one issue of bread, one gallon of beer from the kitchen and one mess of roast.' Therefore John Drake, the King's waferer, was on squire's wages, but he had an issue of wine as well. In status he was the equal of the King's Harpers, the Queen's Psaltery-player and the Kings of Heralds.

In order to fill in some of the gaps in our knowledge concerning the nature of his work, it is necessary, owing to lack of strictly contemporary information, to draw upon a later Household Ordinance, that of Edward IV,[31] which specifies in greater detail the duties of the waferer and the necessaries of his office : ' It (sc. the office of Waferer) hathe one yeoman making wafyrs and sauely and clenely to kepe them covered and under lock and by assay to be delivered for the King's mouth to the sewer . . . He taketh for the stuffe of this office . . . first, for the flower, of the sergeaunt of the bakehouse dayly or wekely as he hathe nede, by a tayle (tally) . . . and sugar of the greete spycery; towells of raygnes (Rennes), towelles of worke and of playne clothe; fyne coffyrs, small gardevyaunds and bakyng irons; and of the office, if it nede, egges . . . The statutes of noble Edward the Thirde, for certain reasons used in thoose dayes, gave this office greete wages, clothing and higher lyvery than he taketh nowe because his busynesse was muche more.'

The passage is not only informative but significant. Wafers

---

[31] Myer's ed. *op. cit.*, s.v. *Waferer*.

were made out of flour, sugar and eggs (if necessary); they were cooked in baking-irons, carefully wrapped in fine Rennes linen cloths and locked away in special boxes; and the waferer had to examine (? and taste) them before handing them to the valet who was to serve them to the king. By the time of Edward IV the King's Waferer had dropped in status from squire to yeoman and the duties of his office had become relatively unimportant. His wages had been cut, his livery was poorer, because ' his busynesse ' was much less. The making of wafers in the royal household was evidently more important in the fourteenth than in the fifteenth century. The status of John Drake and Richard Pilke in the households of Edward I and Edward II bears witness to the truth of what has been said in the above extract and the fact that waferers from other noble houses were present at the knighting festivities is additional confirmation. Had the office been of negligible importance, the countesses of Gloucester and Lancaster would not have brought their own waferers to Westminster in their trains. The Wardrobe books prove that Master John Drake accompanied Edward I wherever he went, at home or abroad, and had so much to do that he rarely took time off. When the king died and the debts of the Wardrobe were drawn up, John was owed the equivalent of about £16,000 in back wages. The reason why the office was important is that wafers used to be served with the sweet, spiced wine called Ypocras (or Hipocras), especially for the *issue de table*, the last course at dinner.[32] The custom must have been very old, because the family of Liston of Liston Overhall manor in Essex held its land by serjeanty of making wafers for the king's feast, when summoned to do so, '*facere canestellos ad summonititionem ad festum Regis*', as early as 1185. During the reign of John the notice of this serjeanty is brief, no particular royal feast being mentioned, but the omission may well be due to the nature of the entries in the *Red Book of the Exchequer*, which give only the name of the current holder and the kind of serjeanty : ' *Johannes de Liston : per serjanteriam faciendi canestellos*.'[33] Under

[32] ' all maner fruytes and wafers shall come to the bourde alwey without brede, the bourde auoyded whan wafers come with ypocras or other swete wynes.' *Ibid.*, p. 113.

[33] *Rotuli de dominabus*, ed. J. H. Round (*Pipe Roll Society*, 1913), 72. See also *Red Book of the Exchequer* (Rolls Ser.), II, 457, 506.

Henry III it was changed; Godfrey de Liston held of the king in chief by service ' of making wafers (*vafras*) when the King wears the crown; at the King's cost.'[34] In later notices relative[35] to the same serjeanty one sees the words of the author of the *Black Book* coming true. In the twelfth century the Listons were required ' to make ' the wafers; in the fourteenth, ' to make and serve ' them; and finally, as the century and the end of Edward III's reign drew to a close, they had ' to find a waffrer ' to do the service for them or, as Blount[36] has it on a different authority, ' the service of paying for, bringing in and placing of five wafers before the King as he sits at dinner upon the day of his Coronation.' Since they had to make and serve only 5 wafers for the king at rare intervals, the Listons' serjeanty was a light one. The Court Waferer had to make hundreds every day.

The word for wafer which was used in the *Rotuli de dominabus* and the *Red Book of the Exchequer* is *canestellus*, an alternative to *canistrellus*, the diminutive of *canistrum*. The form in Classical Latin is *canistellum*. Du Cange, s.v., defines it as ' a kind of bread made in the form of a *canistrum* ' which in Classical times meant either a reed basket for carrying bread, fruit or flowers, more particularly at religious festivals, or a kind of stand or mat upon which wine-cups were placed at dinner. The two meanings, ' basket ' and ' stand ' were carried into the middle ages with slight modifications : the *canistrum* became the basket[37] in which the *eulogiae* or blessed breads (not the Eucharist breads) were carried and distributed; and also the stand or

---

[34] *Calendar of Inquisitions*, I, No. 648.
[35] *Ibid.*, IV, No. 150; VII, No. 45; X, No. 473; XII, No. 151. *Testa de Nevill*, 226.
[36] *Fragmenta Antiquitatis* : *Antient Tenures of Land* etc., Thomas Blount. enlarged and corrected by J. Beckwith (Lond. 1815), 54.
 Blount, and after him Beckwith, trace the serjeanty through the reigns of Edward III, Richard II, Henry IV, James II and George III, by which time the squire of Liston Hall was William Campbell, and at the coronation of George III ' the king was pleased to appoint his son, William Henry Campbell, Esquire, to officiate as his deputy, who accordingly attended and presented the wafers to their Majesties.' (55).
[37] In his reference to John de Liston's service noted in the *Red Book of the Exchequer*, Blount (and Beckwith) rendered the Latin as ' John de Liston held the town or farm of Liston in the county of Essex by the serjeanty of making baskets for the king ', and quoted Ainsworth's *Law Latin Dictionary* as his source for the meaning of *canestellos*, but it is clear from all the other references to the serjeanty that the word meant *wafers*.

plate which was put under lamps to catch the drips of oil. From which last it may be reasonably inferred that the use of the diminutive form to denote a wafer meant that a wafer was small, flat and probably circular.

Du Cange, s.v. *Canistrellus*, quotes a very interesting passage from the Chronicle of Robert, abbot of Chartres, under the year 1176. On the summer festival of St. Martin (4 July) the monks of the abbey were accustomed to make ' certain fancy breads *(artificiales panes)* which they call ' *canistrelli* '. By using the word *artificiales* Abbot Robert was implying that these breads were not ordinary ones but ones ' contrived by art ', that is, made in a different way. If they were wafers similar to those served to our kings, and our earliest reference to wafers is only nine years later than when Robert was writing, then *artificiales* could certainly be applied to them, for wafers were made in a special way and contained ingredients never put into bread. During the reign of Henry III this old word *canestellus* was replaced by the French *gauffre*. In its Latinized form it appears as *vafra*, *wafra* and *gaufra*.

The basic ingredients were flour, sugar, water and eggs (optional), which were mixed to form a dough stiff enough to be called a paste and to be kneaded. In this wafers differed from waffles, fritters and pancakes, which are made from a loose batter. *Le Ménagier de Paris* (1393)[38] uses *gauffres* as a generic term; special names were given to the various kinds of wafers then popular, such as *supplications*, *portes*, *estriers*, *galettes* and *gros batons*. There were sweet ones, flavoured with wine, honey or powdered ginger; and savoury ones containing cheese. In shape they were, as a rule, round and thin like the *oblatae* or holy wafers, but some, like the *gros batons*, were fashioned into ' rods of like size and in like manner to chitterlings '. In England they were often coloured with saffron. All were baked in irons.

There is a certain amount of evidence that the circular ones were curled while hot and served rolled. *Le Ménagier de Paris* specifically mentions ' sugared *galettes* ', which were the ancestors of the modern French and Breton *galettes*. Laneham,[39]

---

[38] Trans. and ed. Eileen Power (Lond. 1928).
[39] *Kenilworth Festivities*, published anonymously, Warwick 1825; *Robert Laneham's Letter*, ed. F. J. Furnivall (Lond. 1890, *New Shakespeare Society*).

in his well-known description of the man dressed up to portray a harper of old time at the pageant devised by Leicester for Elizabeth I at Kenilworth in 1575, says of the ruff about his neck that ' every ruff stood up like a wafer '. The gofering-iron used for curling ruffs derived its name from *gauffre*, meaning a honey-comb as well as a wafer. A pile of curled wafers would look like the edge of an Elizabethan ruff, which itself produced a honey-comb effect.

The one detail concerning all wafers for which there is no firm evidence is their size. If the measurements of old wafering-irons and of modern French *galettes* may be taken as guides, the average size of the mediaeval wafer would have been about 4″ to 6″ in diameter. The irons[40] hardly need describing. They consisted of two circular iron plates connected by a single bent rod, rather like a gigantic sugar-tongs. The special fuel which the King's Waferer collected from the Fueltry was dry wood cut into thin spills, so that the fire should be kept bright.

---

[40] The only reference to court baking-irons I have come across is in the Prince's Wardrobe Book for 1303 (E101/363/18), f.5ʳ : ' To Reginald, the Waferer, for a pair of irons for his work, bought by him for making wafers for the said Prince ; paid into his own hands on 5 January, 13s. 4d. ' They were quite an expensive item, nearly twice the price of a cross-bow, and would cost about £140 in present-day money. The groom who manipulated them wore protective gloves. Cf. the very interesting description of how the Eucharist wafers were made in the eleventh century. Lanfranc laid down the rules in his *Decreta pro ordine Sancti Benedicti*, written c. 1087 : The responsibility for making the holy wafers rested with the sacristan. He was to select the wheat with great care, grain by grain wherever possible and after this had been done it was to be placed in a clean sack, made of good quality material and carried to the abbey's mill by a zealous servant. No dust was allowed to pollute it during the grinding. The flour was then to be carried back to the sacristan, who put it through a bolting cloth in a place surrounded by a curtain. The sacristan himself, while he carried out this operation, was to wear his alb and have his head covered with an amice. On the day on which the wafers were to be made, the monks who were to help him were to wash their hands and faces, put on their albs and wrap their heads in their amices. The only brother not required to do this was the one who would be holding the baking-irons. The flour was heaped on to a spotlessly clean table, one of the monks sprinkled water on it and kneaded it firmly with his hands until the paste was of the right consistency. It was then divided into pieces of the requisite size, shaped into flat rounds and baked; the brother holding the irons was to wear gloves. Throughout the whole process of making and baking the monks chanted psalms or the Cannonical Hours, whichever the sacristan preferred. No one was allowed to speak except the brother manipulating the irons, who could briefly give the necessary orders to the servant who was bringing in the wood for the fire. And, adds Lanfranc, with the touch of the master cook, ' the wood ought to be very dry and carefully prepared (i.e. cut into spills) several days beforehand.' Migne, *Pat. Lat.*, 150, 488.

According to *Le Ménagier de Paris* the usual number of wafers
served per person was 4, but the Liston family had to provide
the king with five, so that perhaps the allowance at Court was
five. For the 300 knights-aspirant alone, 1,500 would have
had to be made. If the king, queen, and all the other guests
are added, at least 2,000 to 3,000 wafers were cooked for the
Whitsuntide banquet.

John Drake's ordinary daily duties were not quite so onerous
but he had to serve wafers at the *issue de table* every day without
fail; and if he were absent from Court his deputy had to
officiate in his stead. No second King's Waferer is mentioned
in the Wardrobe books of this period but John, like all the
other King's Officers, must have had a groom and a boy to
serve him. To the groom would have fallen the duty of deputis-
ing for him. The Ordinance of Edward IV particularizes the
daily duty of the royal waferer. What it says may not have
been equally true of the court of Edward I, especially in view
of the author's statement that the Waferers used to have much
more to do in the time of even Edward III, but it gives some
idea of the number of people for whom John Drake would have
had to make wafers while he was on duty and helps to explain
why in some years he did not have a single day off : ' The
cotydan seruyce is to the King, to dukes, to erllys, to the
steward of the householde, thesaurer, comptroller, cofferer
and to such straungeors as they assigne for that seruyse hit
shall requier.' At the court of Edward I the range of persons
was probably not nearly so restricted, but a mere 25 diners
would have needed 135 wafers and this does not include the
duty of making wafers for individuals in their private rooms
whenever they asked for them. John's office could have been
no sinecure. In 1294, when the king was at Conway, 2 quarters
of wheat were issued to him for his office. The mind boggles
a little at the thought of the number of wafers which could be
(and apparently were) made out of 16 bushels of flour.

(d) *Watchmen*

During the latter part of the reign of Edward I there were,
according to the Wardrobe accounts, five watchmen attached
to the royal household, at the daily wage of $4\frac{1}{2}$d. ($£3$-15s.-0d.).
There is evidence that watchmen from Windsor Castle some-

times joined the king's household for special duties or for fixed periods of time. These appear to have used ' de Windsor ' as a surname. There were Alexander, Richard and Geoffrey. Richard seems to have been Prince's watchman at first and became King's watchman in 1307, after the death of the old king. In an entry for May 1306 he is expressly called ' Richard the watchman from Windsor ' because he was summoned to Byfleet (Surrey) by special command of the Prince not to act as watchman but ' to make his minstrelsy in the presence of the lord Prince and his nobles '. His *largesse* was 20s. (£200).[41] Alexander and Geoffrey occur as King's watchmen from at least 1300 but Alexander drops from the records after 1303. The other four, whose names occur regularly in the accounts from 1300 were Adam de Skyrewith, John de Staunton, Hugh de Lincoln and Robert de Fynchesley. Either Geoffrey or one of these four was the odd man out on the Payroll. Entries relative to their wages usually refer to them in two pairs, so that probably only four were on duty at any one time. The fifth may have acted as reserve. Such a provision would have been necessary, because watchmen's work was continuous and of the highest importance. There were years when Adam de Skyrewith like John the Waferer, was never absent from Court.

Calling the night-watch was one of the watchmen's primary duties. He had to blow or pipe the hour four times during winter nights, from Michaelmas to Shrove Tuesday, and three times during summer nights, which works out at approximately every three hours. In addition he had to make regular tours of inspection throughout the palace, trying every door, and keeping a sharp look-out for pick-locks and other wrong-doers. Above all, he had to be on constant guard against the ever-present danger of fire. About a month before he was summoned to Byfleet, Richard de Windsor had saved the Prince and other inmates of Windsor Castle from being burned in their beds. He and other watchmen raised the alarm, helped to extinguish the flames and ' at the same time evacuate various people ' from burning buildings. The Prince showed his personal gratitude by giving each of them 10s. (£100).[42]

---

[41] Add, MSS 22923, f.7ᵛ.
[42] *Ibid.*, f.6ᵛ.

The Household Ordinance of Edward III hints at some of the extra duties watchmen were called upon to perform on special occasions. After the institution of the Order of the Bath, the royal watchmen were required to keep guard ' at the making of Knyghtes of the Bathe, watching by nyght-tyme upon theym in the Chapell '. A similar duty probably fell upon the shoulders of watchmen in earlier reigns at ordinary knightings, long before the Order of the Bath was instituted and it was no doubt a crystallizing of what had been customary. The four watchmen of the Payroll, therefore, may have received their half-mark each (£66-13s.-4d.) for keeping guard at the Abbey while the Prince and his companions performed their vigil. On the other hand, they may have received it for ' making their minstrelsy ', because there is clear evidence that they were accustomed to entertain their royal masters in the capacity of talented amateur musicians.

Male Bouche, the watchman in the *Roman de la Rose*, took up to the battlements with him a collection of instruments: pipes, horns and trumpets to sound the hours; and Cornish bagpipes and flutes with which to amuse himself during the night hours. Being a misogynist, he sang and played only those songs which had as their theme, ' *Qu'onques ne trova fame juste.*' It is doubtful whether Richard de Windsor concentrated on the same subject when he entertained the Prince at Byfleet, but Male Bouche's way of passing the time in between calling the watch proves that watchmen were both instrumentalists and singers. In 1302 Robert de Fynchesley also made his minstrelsy in the presence of the Prince, this time at Marlborough and received the equivalent of £100 for doing so.[43] Bare as they are, these references indicate the proficiency of royal watchmen as minstrels. *Largesse* was not the only kind of reward which came their way. Like all other royal servants they received grants of land, property, rents and wardships. There is an illuminating example of the last in the Patent Rolls,[44] with regard to Adam de Skyrewith. In Dauthorp, Yorkshire, in 1303, there was a man called John de Dauthorp, who owned lands in the area and in Cumberland, (where Adam came from), but he was

---

[43] E101/363/18, f.21r.
[44] *CPR* (1301-7), 123.

quite unable to administer them because he was ' an idiot from birth '. Edward I granted the custody of the lands to Adam. In March 1303 John died; therefore, his lands had to go to his nephew, William Bucket, who was his heir. The inheritance was taken from Adam but when the king's Escheator carried out the necessary inquisition prior to handing them over, he found that William was also an idiot. The king then regranted them to Adam ' for the life of the said William or until he return to sanity '. With a wardship of this kind the custodian could reap the revenue of the estate and receive any income due to the ward, provided he administered the estate and looked after the ward in a proper manner. The grant was distinctly to Adam's advantage. It was tantamount to making him the owner.

(e) *Messengers*

Royal messengers have been a feature of human society from the earliest times. It gives one pause to realise that Darius, the great Persian king, had an organized system of postal communication in the early part of the fourth century B.C. Later on, imperial Rome had her *Cursus Publicus*, which, like the postal system of Darius, was initiated primarily for the use of the army, but the messengers who comprised it were the genuine ancestors of the mediaeval messengers and, to a certain extent, of our modern postmen, in that they were paid carriers of state letters and parcels. Both Persia and Rome, however, boasted a vehicular service, which was not instituted in this country until the nineteenth century.

The Roman *tabellarius*, as his name indicates, was the carrier of letters written on wax tablets, which were tied with a thong and the knot sealed with the writer's signet. His mediaeval counterpart carried a piece of parchment, folded or rolled and sealed with the sender's personal seal. One would think that safety and secrecy would have been ensured by the seal, but such was far from being the case. Tampering with seals and inventing modes of altering writing on parchment developed into a devious art on its own. By and large, written letters sent out by the king reached their destinations safely if only because King's Messengers were picked men, whose honesty and lives were at his mercy. If they were found to be guilty of treachery, death was their punishment; if anyone attacked or maltreated them, the king's vengeance was their protection. How weighty that vengeance could be is illustrated by the following two recorded incidents : Matthew Paris[45] relates how in 1250 Sir Walter de Clifford, one of the powerful barons of the Welsh March, dared to treat a King's messenger with contempt. He forced him to eat his royal master's missive, wax and all. Henry III was so incensed that Clifford barely escaped with his life. He was deprived of his liberty and fined 1,000 marks (approximately £15,000) and only eventually allowed to return home under pledge. In 1290 another royal messenger who was carrying a letter from the queen (Eleanor) to Scotland was intercepted, imprisoned and ill-treated by the constable of Rokesburgh Castle. Because he had been detained for nearly three months and therefore unable to execute his mission, he appealed to the king. Edward I fined the constable the equivalent of £10,000 for his contempt of the king and ordered him to pay the messenger £20,000 in damages.[46]

There does not seem to have been a fully organized postal service for the royal household much before the reign of Edward I.[47] The duty of carrying the king's letters was either entrusted to special envoys or linked to a serjeanty. For example, two men in Leicestershire, David and Baldwin of Skiffington, held land to the value of 51s. per annum (about £500) by serjeanty of ' being the mounted messenger of the lord King ' and the duty involved carrying the royal letters ' throughout England whenever summoned to do so, at his own cost, for 40 days '.[48] This was about 1250. A service of this sort was adequate up to a point but it was, at best, haphazard. Under Edward I a professional messenger service came into being. While still reserving special envoys, such as heralds and high-ranking minstrels, for diplomatic or secret business, he instituted an organization of mounted messengers, *nuncii* and runners, *cokini*. During his reign an average of 14

---

[45] *Chronica Majora* (Rolls Ser.), s.a. 1250.
[46] *Rotuli Parliamentorum*, I, 48 (No. 35).
[47] For a detailed study, see *The King's Messengers*, 1199-1377, Mary C. Hill (Lond. 1961).
[48] *Testa de Nevill*, ff.88b, 89a, 93b.

nuncii were employed in the royal household at a daily wage of 3d. (£2-10s.-0d.) and up to 40 *cokini* on an *ad hoc* basis, for these were kitchen-boys who could be called upon to run with an urgent message whenever necessary. Later on, during the reign of Edward II, when these became regular household messengers they acquired the name, *cursores*.

The Simond Le Messager of the Payroll was a *nuncius*, a Queen's and King's Messenger of long standing. The fact that he was a recipient of the Prince's *largesse* suggests that he was also an amateur minstrel. There is no valid reason for doubting that, if Waferers and Watchmen 'made their minstrelsy' at Court, Messengers would not do likewise, although, up to the present I have found no precise evidence to prove it.

(f) *Acrobats*

Since I am concerned here solely with those minstrels whose names appear on the Payroll, it will be appreciated that a number of facets of minstrel life have been neither mentioned nor discussed. Several categories of instrumentalists are not represented on the Payroll, nor are there any identifiable conjurers, mimes, jugglers, funambulists, *gestours* and fools, although there is rich evidence in the records that such took part in royal household entertainment. There may be some among those whose names give no clue to their category, but Matilda Makejoy is the only one of whom we can be absolutely certain, because her name and category are recorded in the Wardrobe books. She was a *saltatrix* or female acrobat; not on wages and therefore not a royal domestic minstrel, yet she appears to have been attached, if that is the right word, to the royal household for at least 14 years.

Her profession was one which could boast of long and honourable ancestry. Homer[49] and, later, Xenophon[50], testify to the custom of having acrobatic dancing-girls to provide entertainment during feasts and banquets. The word Homer uses is κυβιστητηρ, meaning ' one who falls forward '; Xenophon's term is 'ορχηστριδα, ' a dancing-girl '. This is the term which more nearly equates with *saltatrix*, because

---

[49] *Iliad* XVIII, 605-6; *Odyssey* IV, 17-19.
[50] *Symposium*, II, 1.

in the *Symposium*, the 'ορχηστρίδα was an acrobat as well as a dancer and the two activities were not separate. Her complicated acrobatics were performed while she danced and were therefore regarded as an essential part of her dancing. Matilda was in the direct line of descent from these earlier Classical *saltatores*, who were a sort of cross between acrobats and ballet-dancers.[51]

Some idea of what her performances could have included can be gained from the story of the tumbler of Notre Dame, written about the middle of the thirteenth century.[52] A poor acrobat turned monk found himself odd man out in the monastery because he did not know how to do anything seemly or useful as a contribution to the service of God and the Virgin. He had done nothing in his life except turn somersaults, vault, pirouette, prance on his toes and leap in the air :

> *Car n' ot vescu fors de turner*
> *Et d' espringier et de baler,*
> *Treper, saillir ice savoit*
> *Ne d' autre rien il ne savoit* (25-8)

When he had decided to offer all he had to give—his ' tumbling' —to the Virgin, he gave her the benefit of his whole repertoire, with the addition of a new ' turn ' which he evidently improvised on the instant, *Cestui ne fis jo onques mais* ' (215). He began with small, low jumps and went on to big, high ones; then he turned forward and back somersaults, followed by a

---

[51] The link between music and dance is too old to need verification by means of reference to ancient literature but Roger Bacon, writing in 1266-7, re-stated its value in terms of contemporary philosophy. In chapter 59 of his *Opus Tertium* (Rolls Ser.), when discussing the nature of earthly music, he speaks of the kind which has no sound, namely, the rhythmical motion of the body, which accommodates itself to and blends with the music of both song and instrument : ' for we see that the art of (musical) instruments, and song and measure and rhythm, does not bring the flood of full delight to the senses unless accompanied at the same time by gestures and leapings-up and bodily turnings, all which, when they are skilfully executed in harmonious proportions, bring perfect sensual delight to both ears and eyes.'

Although he may have had in mind here the natural bodily rhythm which music sets up in players and singers, as well as the specific combination of dancing to music, either vocal or instrumental, what he says does not deny but rather confirms the age-old knowledge that music and dance together produce a singularly pleasing effect upon the senses. No dancer in the middle ages would have performed without the accompaniment of music. How closely Matilda and her like approached the art of ballet would have depended upon the quality of their performances. The pirouetting and toe-dancing of the tumbler of Notre Dame and the pretty kiss-dance of the two girls in the *Roman de la Rose* exemplify ballet in its embryo stages.

[52] *Del Tumbeor Nostre Dame*, ed. E. Lommatsch (Berlin 1920, *Normanische Texte*).

series of special vaults or turns, each of which had its name :
*le tor francois, le tor Champenois, le tor d'Espaigne, les tors c'on fait
en Bretaigne, le tor Loheraine* and *le tor romain.* After he had
performed these, he placed his hand before his brow and danced
a most delicate pirouette. Next, he fell on his knees and
addressed the Virgin, telling her that his tumbling is all he
can do, and begging her not to despise him. When he started
again he did a hand-walk, with his ' feet in the air and tears
in his eyes '. Finally, after another breathing-space, in which
he again pleaded with the Virgin, he did his new turn, followed
by the Vault of Metz, and continued to dance, spin and leap
until he sank to the ground exhausted, dripping from head to
foot with sweat, ' like fat from roast meat on the spit '.

Here is a repertoire of a minimum of ten items. In it were
old favourites such as the hand-walk and the traditional Roman
Vault, combined with regular acrobatic and dance features
and a wide range of special numbers culled from France,
Britain (or Brittany) and Spain. It was a long programme,
because the tumbler went on performing during the whole
time that the other brethren were at Mass. Without his rests,
when he prayed to the Virgin, he could not have carried it out.

An acrobat's life has never been an easy one. Matilda
Makejoy's work was intricate and arduous, as may be judged
from illustrations in early manuscripts. Her most distinguished
and notorious forerunner was, as far as ecclesiastical painters
were concerned, Salome, whom they always depicted as a
saltatrix. In MS. Harley, 1527, f. 29, she is seen performing
either a hand-balance or a hand-walk. Other manuscripts
contain pictures of female tumblers doing well-known tricks;
in MS. Cott. Domitian, A2, f.7^r, one is in the act of performing
the contortion which the dancing-girl in Xenophon's *Symposium*
did, namely, bending backwards until her body will be in a
hoop, with her hands resting on the floor; another, in Royal
MSS. E iv, f. 58, is engaged in a hand-balance on the points
of two swords; while in MS. Bodley, No. 264, a girl is doing
either a hand-walk or a somersault to the accompaniment of
pipe and tabor. The monkish artists were not very good at
suggesting movement, nor were they particularly observant,
because they often depict acrobatic stances which are not only
inexact but technically impossible; they draw the set of the

shoulders too rigid and the curve of the loins in somersaults too little. Also, the women acrobats are invariably decently covered from neck to toe in the long gown of the period. Sometimes even their feet are totally wrapped up in the hem of their dress. It is unthinkable that Matilda Makejoy could have executed her vaults and turns in such a garb. There was enough mortal danger in her job without adding to it by obscuring her vision and preventing the free movement of her limbs. Male tumblers frequently acted in the nude. There is more than a hint that this was so in *Del Tumbeor Nostre Dame*. When the tumbler decided that he would indeed offer his skill to the Virgin, he took off his monk's habit but kept on his tunic-vest, so that he should not dance naked before Our Lady's statue :

' *Mais por sa char que ne soit nue*
Une cotele a retenue.' (139-40)

According to the poet's description of it, his tunic may have been his stage costume (when he wore one), for it was thin and glossy, little more than a vest or chemise :

' *Qui mout estoit tenve et alise,*
Petit vaut miex d'une chemise.' (141-2)

and before he began his performances he girded it tightly about him. There is no evidence to hand that *saltatrices* danced in the nude, but a descriptive passage in the *Roman de la Rose* provides proof that they wore short tunics or *coteles* similar to those worn by the *saltatores*. As he walked in the Garden of Desire, the Lover came across a group of minstrels entertaining Deduiz. There were singers and musicians, girl-jugglers throwing tambourines up in the air and catching them on their finger-tips, and two very slender, dainty dancing-girls ' attired in short tunics and with their hair plaited into a galloon.'[53]

---

[53] *Deus damoiseles mout mignotes*
Qui estoient en purs cotes
E treciees a une trece. (Bk. I, 759-61).
The text I have used is that edited by Langlois (Paris 1914-20, *SATF*).
Felix Leroy, in his recent edition of the poem (Paris 1966-70, *CFMA*), defines *en purs cotes* as ' vetues seulement de leur cotte, c'est a dire, sans manteau ', and *cote* as ' sorte de tunique a manches, piece essentielle du vetement, ici, toujours feminin '. Chaucer renders the passage :
Ful fetis damiselles two,
Right yonge, and fulle of semlihede,
In kirtles, and non other wede,
And faire tressed every tresse. (*The Romaunt of the Rose*, Frag. A, 776-9.)

It was this kind of sensible and obviously correct costume that Matilda wore when she ' made her vaults ' before her royal audience. Had she worn the long dress the monks put on women acrobats in their drawings, she would have met with an early death. One of the ever-present risks for all acrobats was the possibility of a broken neck, especially when making the forward somersault, which has retained to this day the name of *casse-cou* in France. Vertigo, loss of nerve, giddiness, misjudging of distances, slips, falls, even moodiness could cause sudden death.[54] Training, therefore, had to be constant and rigorous; and, in order to attain suppleness and develop the arm and chest muscles, it had to be begun in infancy. Grimaldi, a direct descendant of the mediaeval tumbler, made his first appearance at the Old Drury Lane theatre in 1780 at the age of one year and eleven months. Mayhew's description of the early training of a street acrobat in 1856 probably comes near to the truth of what went for training in earlier times. The father of the man who talked to Mayhew was himself a tumbler, and had acted with Grimaldi. ' He brought me regular up to the profession and when I first came out I wasn't above two years old, and . . . he used to take my legs and stretch them and work them round in their sockets and put them up straight by my side . . . it hurt me terrible. He put my breast to his breast and then pulled my legs up to my head and knocked 'em against my head and cheeks about a dozen times. It seems like as if your body was broken in two and all your muscles being pulled out like India rubber.'[55]

The upbringing of Matilda was, without doubt, equally painful. She would have reached the pinnacle of her profession when she was in her teens; the active life of a first-class acrobat does not extend much beyond twenty years. Like that of any modern gymnast, a mediaeval acrobat's period of peak per-

---

[54] Just about the time when Matilda was doing her turns for the boy princes, Jehanes, sire de Joinville, later Steward of Louis X, was writing his *Histoire de St. Louis*. In it he describes how, when accompanying Louis IX on crusade, he witnessed the performance of three brothers, minstrels of Armenia, who were entertaining the young Prince of Antioch and his mother. One of their tricks was turning their heads round until their faces were at their backs. The eldest brother was so afraid that he might break his neck that he crossed himself before bringing his head back to its normal position.
[55] *London Labour and the London Poor*, ed. J. D. Rosenberg (New York 1968), III, 90-1.

formance was necessarily limited. Inevitable weakening of the muscles combined with failing powers would have forced him or her off the boards. Perhaps one of the real reasons why the tumbler of Notre Dame entered the monastery was that he was past his prime. He was fortunate. Many fine acrobats in later ages, having neither monastery nor pension, ended their days as miserable beggars. The fact that reference to Matilda ceases after 1311, suggests that she had, by that time, more or less reached the end of her career. Edward II was partial to clowns, conjurers and acrobats. Had she been still attached to Court after this date it is more than likely that her services would have been called upon and her name would then have figured in the records. There were plenty of royal children to be amused, but by 1311 she had been a favoured *saltatrix* at Court for over fourteen years.

In order to appreciate her quality we ought to try to forget the solemn, wrapped-up Salomes depicted by the monks and see in our mind's eye a trim, lithe, muscular young woman in a shimmering short-skirted dress, with her hair becomingly plaited or braided and held close to her head in a snood. Thus habited she becomes a more credible ancestor of the long line of women acrobats stretching from Homer' κυβιστητηρε to the ballerinas, gymnasts and bespangled circus acrobats of our own time.

(g)　*Fencers*

Walter Leskirmisour and his brother were probably at the Westminster festivities expressly to give a display of the art of fence, yet it is unwise to place too much confidence on the evidence of their name alone. Sir Walter de Beauchamp, Steward of the King's Household, had a squire/groom called William Leskirmisour. Was he also a fencer or was the name in this case a surname only, like its modern forms *Scrimshaw*, *Scrimshire* ? Another servant, not of the household but well known to the clerks of the Wardrobe, was John Leskirmisour, master of a galley at Winchelsea and a trusted employee who shipped stores for the army to Scotland. A squire/groom and a master mariner would seem to have little in common, least of all in the art of fence, but to argue thus may be quite wrong, because the art of fence, or ' sword and buckler ' as it was then called, was a form of minstrelsy which had been popular in England long before the Normans took possession of the land. In any case, the surname originated from the holder's or his forebears' skill in the game. If Walter and his brother were, as seems most likely, professional sword and buckler men, they belonged to the same class of minstrels as Matilda Makejoy, those who lived and worked in London but who were called upon when need arose to perform at Court. Such a conclusion appears to be supported by the fact that they were paid their 3s. (£30) each, not out of the Prince's *largesse*, but from the Wardrobe. A description of their performance cannot be anything but speculative, because no account of sword and buckler play has survived. The few illustrations of it which appear in our manuscripts convey little more than an idea that it was a display of skill performed to the accompaniment of horn or pipe. Each player was armed with a sword and a round shield, the latter large enough to reach from neck to groin in Anglo-Saxon times, but in the thirteenth and fourteenth centuries no more than a small targe about a foot in diamater. This type was strapped to the left forearm and was used as an arm-guard rather than as a protective shield. Cut, thrust and parry, combined with dexterous defence must have consti tuted the major part of the entertainment. In Anglo-Saxon times it was probably appreciated in a somewhat different way from that in which it was in the time of, say, Edward I, because the gentlemanly sport from the twelfth century on-wards was tourneying, but since every man in the middle ages carried a sword of some sort, skill in the use of it would have been gratifying if only as a spectacle. In the tourney and the joust there was neither time nor opportunity for brilliant expertise with the sword. In the tilt it was only a secondary weapon and all that was expected from the combatant using it was the raining of heavy, battering blows on the armour of his adversary. Sword and buckler play as practised by pro-fessional minstrels would have been elegant by comparison; it gave scope for trained footwork, pyrotechnic display of swordsmanship and cleverly thought-out stances of defence. No doubt the pleasure which the king and his noble guests derived from watching the bouts of Walter and his brother was akin to that which enthusiasts feel nowadays when watching a fencing or boxing match. There is no evidence that gentlemen ever indulged in it themselves. Those who excelled in sword and buckler play did not belong to the knightly class. It was the sport—and more than sport—of the ordinary citizens. The king and his knights liked to watch and bet on the fighters because a contest between two skilled opponents holds perennial attraction, irrespective of class. That this held good for sword and buckler play admits no denial, for it was a traditional feature of all great banquets and festivities. It fell out of fashion and even then regretfully, only when the rapier and the Italian art of defence made their appearance in England towards the end of the sixteenth century. ' Sword and buckler fight begins to grow out of use,' says a stalwart Englishman in a comedy of 1599,'[56] I am sorry for it. I shall never see good manhood again. If it be once gone, this poking fight of rapier and dagger will come up. Then a tall man that is a courageous man and a good sword and buckler man will be spitted like a cat or a rabbit.' From this and other chance references to the height of combatants, it seems fairly certain that reach was considered a signal advantage.

Compared with rapier and dagger fencing, sword and buckler play, though skilful, was probably rough and crude. In the city of London its reputation was bad. Masters in the art opened schools in which to teach it but so many profligates and disreputable foreigners flocked to them that they were closed by royal edict in 1286; which sheds new light on Walter and his brother and their appearance at Court. According to the edict only freemen of the City were henceforth allowed to live in it. Therefore Walter and his brother were citizens of London and their reputation above suspicion. Sword and buckler play in itself was obviously not condemned. It was the misuse of it which brought upon it the rigour of the law. Anyone who kept a fencing school within the city was to be fined 40 marks (approx. £5000) for each offence and all the aldermen were to make ' thorough search in their several wards for the detecting of such offenders, in order to bring them to justice and an exemplary punishment.' In spite of the edict schools of fencing continued to be established, mostly in

---

[56] *The Two Angry Women of Abingdon.* Quoted from *Schools and Masters of Fence*, Egerton Castle (Lond. 1892).

defiance of the law but sometimes licensed under it. As the *Liber Custumarum* and the *Liber Albus*[57] prove, the ban was enforced time and again, yet the schools persisted and flourished. The main burden of complaint against them was that the undesirables who frequented them turned the tuition they received to bad account, namely, robbery with violence, well-paid, secret assassination, and open personal brawls. Honest citizens, however, sometimes objected to the schools for other reasons. In 1311 one Master Roger Le Skirmisour was brought before the mayor on a charge of ' keeping a fencing school for diverse men and for enticing thither the sons of respectable persons so as to waste and spend the property of their fathers and mothers upon bad practices.'[58] In this accusation may lie one of the reasons why William, Sir Walter de Beauchamp's valet, was called ' Leskirmisour '. Young men of his social standing were not necessarily averse to learning the ancient, if bourgeois, sword and buckler play. As for John, the master mariner, he might well have been adept at it, because he belonged to the class of sturdy men to whom it would have been a traditional sport. The weight of what evidence there is suggests that both these servants of the king could have owed their cognomina to their individual skill in the game.

Whatever its origins, sword and buckler play gradually developed into an art of fence which presented, Janus-like, two faces to mediaeval society : it was a reputable professional minstrelsy, designed to provide sporting and stimulating entertainment; it was also a potentially dangerous form of lawless duelling.

iii. *Who the minstrels on the Payroll were*

The facts I have been able to collect concerning each individual minstrel are often few and woefully inadequate when considered in relation to the fulness of their lives; even so,

---

[57] ' *Et qe nully teigne escolle deskirme ou bokeler dedynez la Citee sur peyne denprisonement.*' *Liber Albus,* I, 274. (Rolls Ser.).
' *Et ensement pur ceux qi se delitent de mesfere, vount aprendre de eskirnir de bokeler deinz le cite, de nuit et de jour, et pur ceol pluis senbaudissent de maufere—purveu est, qe nul tiegne escole ne aprise, de eskymir de bokeler deinz la cite de noit ne de jour. Et si nul face, ert la prisoun xl jours. E qe il ne resceive apprentiz de jour, sil ne soit home de bone fame et conu; et sil face, et de ces soit atteint oit mesme la peine.*' *Liber Custumarum,* II, pt. 1, 282-3 (Rolls Ser.).
[58] Castle, op. cit., 24.

there seems to be sufficient material salvaged from the past to enable at least some of them to be drawn out of the flat background of anonymity and invested with a touch of three-dimensional quality. The Wardrobe Books and Exchequer Accounts are very matter-of-fact records. Hard cash is their central theme. It is only on rare occasions that a chance entry will suddenly bring to the surface a detail of human character or experience which illuminates, if but for a second or two, the reality of life hidden behind the pounds, marks, shillings and pence. These small but telling scraps of information enrich our knowledge in often quite unexpected ways, pinpointing little characteristics of now one, now another minstrel who had, up to that moment, been no more than a name.

The details which strike one first and forcibly are those that throw into relief the more dramatic sides of human nature : John of Trentham killing his fellow-harper, Adam of Grimshaw; John the Crowder killing Richard Croft; Richard Pilke killing Stephen Fraunketon; William Sagard killing Robert Aubray. This sounds a blood-thirsty record for royal minstrels but anyone who is familiar with mediaeval historical records knows that life in thirteenth and fourteenth century England was precarious for everybody. Musicians, as well as men in other walks of life, were no exceptions when it came to homicide. Besides, because a man is a musician, he is not, *ipso facto*, a man of peace, no matter in what century he happens to be living. As always, it was a minority who gave free rein to their passions. Side by side with the quarrelling and the sword-play went the gentler, more normal habits of living. As they appear in the records, the majority of the minstrels on the Payroll will be seen to have been hard-working professionals, more often than not good friends one to another; husbands and fathers, careful about their property, making sure their sons followed in their footsteps, jealously guarding their jobs at Court and remaining at work until the time came for them to be pensioned off. When they were sick or absent from Court, they sent their wives to the Exchequer to collect their dues for them; they fulfilled all the duties of citizenship and grew prosperous by the exercise of their talents. For many of them the crunch came when they finally became unfit for work. People like William le Sautreour and John le Leutour, who seem to have husbanded their resources, were able to fall back upon their savings and retire into the comfortable life of well-to-do London citizens, as befitted their status; others, not so fortunate or perhaps not as far-seeing and thrifty, who spent freely while they earned, as many artists do, found themselves homeless and penniless in their old age. It was for these that the king requested either corrodies or shelter and maintenance in the various abbeys and monasteries, in which, it has to be acknowledged, they were by no means always welcome. The records show that numbers of monasteries tried to evade what must have been a heavy drain on their resources. Royal minstrels did not arrive at the monasteries alone; they came with servants and horses, had to be given private rooms and be maintained according to their former living-standards. It was an easy way of shifting the responsibility of looking after old servants on to the backs of others and of stemming the everlasting flow of cash from the king's privy purse. During the middle ages it was a recognized, accepted way of dealing with the old. No doubt, in many, many instances the monks gladly performed this merciful and meritorious service, but when the practice was pushed to the extreme, it became a mockery of the Christian duty it was supposed to be and an imposition by the king. Much would have depended upon the character of the individual minstrel and also, to a certain extent, upon the kind of instrument he played. Harpers, lutenists, psaltery-players, vielle-players and crowders could have found ready acceptance among the majority of the brethren, not only because they were first-class executants, who could provide rich entertainment, but also because, as professionals, they could have had a good deal in common with those members of the fraternity who were themselves specialists in music. On the other hand, trumpeters, taborers and nakerers, unless they could play other instruments as well, would not have had much to offer; like the poor tumbler of Notre Dame, they might often have felt like fish out of water. No record of how exactly retired minstrels comported themselves in their new quarters has come to hand. Probably some were arrogant and overbearing, others polite and accommodating; a number would have been too old or too infirm to do anything except occupy a sick bed; a few, like Simon le

Messager, would have been blind. They were, at any rate, not left to starve as numbers of great musicians in later centuries were. Although there existed patent injustices in this virtually enforced placing of retired royal minstrels in ecclesiastical institutions, the idea in itself was neither reprehensible nor irrational. It was a fault in the right direction.

One further detail relative to the lives and activities of minstrels named on the Payroll and in the Wardrobe accounts calls for brief, general comment. Very rarely is any specific information about their performances given by the clerks. References to these are usually entered under the blanket phrase, ' making his/their minstrelsy '. It covered a wide range of talent, which has to be interpreted, wherever possible, in the light of its context. Generally speaking, the clerks particularized only when they were entering payments made to ' stranger ' minstrels or minstrels in the service of people other than members of the royal households. The following examples will suffice to illustrate the practice :

> ' To Thomas, the harper of the earl Warenne, for playing the harp (*citharizanti*) in the presence of the King at Macclesfield . . . (E101/351/21 and C47/4/5 f. 51ᵛ) To the Fool, Martinet, of Gascony, for playing (*ludenti*) before the lord Edward, son of the King . . .(*L.Q.G.*, 166) To seven women, meeting the King on the road between Taskes and Uggehall and singing (*cantatibus*) before him as they were wont to do according to the custom obtaining at the time of lord Alexander, late King of the Scots . . . (Add. MSS. 8835, f. 42ᵛ) To Melior, the harper of John Mautravers, playing his harp (*citharizanti*) before the lord King . . . (E101/318/6, f. 21ᵛ) To John, the trumpeter of Lord Robert fitz Payn, for trumpeting (*trumpanti*) before the King on the day of Epiphany . . .(E101/368/6, f. 21ᵛ) To William the Saltimbanque and other of his companions, making their leaps (*facientibus salta*) at Surfleet (Lincs.) on the return of the King through the town . . .(E101/375/8 f. 14ᵛ) To John de Coton, a Lombard, making his minstrelsy

with snakes (*cum serpentibus*) before the King at Canterbury . . . *Ibid.*, f. 27ᵛ)
To Bernard, the Fool, and 54 of his companions coming naked before the King, with dancing revelry (*nudis. . .cum tripudio*) at Pontoise . . . Ibid., f. 32ʳ)'.
Entries of this kind, though highly gratifying, constitute a warning to any reader of the manuscripts. Unless one has corroborative evidence, it is unwise to try to guess what ' making his minstrelsy ' means.

For easy reference I have listed the minstrels in alphabetical order and not in the order in which they appear on the Payroll. The letters L and F against their names stand for Latin list and French list respectively.

A

Adam Le Boscu. F.

If *boscu* be the equivalent of *bossu*, then he was Adam the hunchbacked, but it is very unlikely that he was the same person as Adam de la Halle, the famous minstrel of Arras, who was also known as Adam le Bossu, although, as he himself protested, he was not deformed in this way. *Le Bossu* was his family surname. He died c.1285-89. (See *Romania*, 86 (1965), 10-11; and 89 (1968), 116-24.)

In Arras, according to manuscript sources, *Le Bossu* was spelt variously, *Bochu*, *Bocu*, *Bocus*, *Boceus*. The form *Boscu* appears to have been an English variant. There is a twelfth-century example of its use as a surname in the Register of Worcester Cathedral priory : ' *Winifrid Boscu* '.[1]

There is a possibility that the Adam of the Payroll was a herald. His name comes next to that of Carlton, the herald, and his *largesse* was collected for him by another herald, Bruant.

Adam de Grimmeshawe. F.

Grimmeshawe is probably Grimeshargh (Lancs.), a few miles NE of Preston. At the time of the knighting Adam had only six more years to live, because he was killed by a fellow-minstrel of the Court in 1312. See *Johannes de Trenham.*

---

[1] *The Cartulary of Worcester Cathedral Priory Register, I.,* ed. R. R. Darlington. Publications of the Pipe Roll Society, LXXXVI (1962-63), 216, No. 416.

Adam de Reue. F.

The manuscripts offer no clue as to the whereabouts of *Reue*. There was a *Rue* in Ponthieu (Somme), a *Rewe* in Devon, NNE of Exeter; *Rue* was also an alternative spelling for Routh (Yorks.) and Rhiwabon (Denbighs.). It could also be *Reve*, but I have come across no place-name with this spelling in the records.

Three men with the surname *Rue* appear in the Wardrobe accounts : Henry de Rue, Waferer of the Countess of Gloucester Gille de Rue, status and occupation unknown, and Adam the minstrel.

Adam de Swylingtone. L.

Swillington, West Riding (Yorks.)

Since minstrels frequently called themselves by the name of their masters, Adam could have been the harper of Sir Adam de Swillington, who was definitely one of the knights who went in the army to Scotland immediately after the festivities at Westminster; but there is no documentary evidence that he was at the knighting.

Adam Taburrarius domini J. Lestraunge. L.

The taborer of John(V) L'Estrange, first Lord of Knockin (Salop), who was about 53 years old at the time of the knighting. He had been King's Yeoman in 1278 and in Gascony on the king's business 1287-9. He also served in the campaigns in Wales and Scotland and was at the siege of Caerlaverock in 1300. Died 1308.

Adam de Werintone. F.

Warrington (Lancs.)

Unidentified.

Adekin. F.

Since he is described in the Payroll as being the fellow-harper of Hughethun, who is, in turn, called the fellow-harper of Johannes de Newentone and Gillot Le Harpour, Adekin is no other than Adam de Clitheroe, one of the notable harpers of Edward I.

His name occurs in the records from 1298 but he must have been appointed King's Harper before 1296, because in the April of that year, when he was with the king at Berwick-on-Tweed, he went to law about one of his swords which his boy-groom, Hugh, had stolen from him on the Friday of Easter week. The following week he happened to see a certain Gregory de Twyselton wearing it and promptly accused him of possessing his property. Gregory declared before the magistrate that he had bought it honestly in open market and was therefore acquitted. Whether Adam regained his sword is not stated but the clerk who recorded the case described him as ' Adam, the King's Harper '. (*Bain*, II, 189).

In 1297 he accompanied the king on his expedition to Flanders, and his fellow-harper on that occasion was Nicholas Le Blund. At Bures St. Mary (Suffolk) Edward I gave them 40s. (£400) between them to buy a packhorse for carrying their bedding; and in Canterbury, on 1 June, a Wardrobe clerk paid Adam 40s. in reparation for a black hackney which he had handed over to the Almonry. By 19 November the king and his entourage were at Ghent. Here Adam received 33s. (approx. £305) to cover the portion of his wages which were paid by the Marshalcy, together with 4½d. per day for the upkeep of his horse. This sum was payment for 92 days ' minus 4, on which he was paid in victuals.' At Harwich both Adam and Nicholas received the regulation 20s. each for their livery. (Add. MSS. 7965, ff. 52ʳ, 58ᵛ, 77ʳ, 126ᵛ)

On 22 February, 1298, Adam, home again with the king at Windsor, was paid 100s. (£1,000) on account, for money owing to him. (E101/357/f.14ʳ). In addition to numerous notices of payments for his winter and summer livery, the records for 1300 and 1301 contain an entry which throws a sidelight on his financial status. While at Linlithgow, in October 1301, he lent John de la More, Chaplain of John de Benstead, Controller of the Wardrobe, the equivalent of nearly £70 in ready money, under recognizance , which shows that he was not without a reasonably well-lined purse when on campaign. (Add. MSS. 7966, f.178ᵛ)

Nicholas Le Blund either retired or died by 1305 for, after that date, Adam's fellow-harpers were Johannes de Newentone, Hugh de Nauntone and Gillot de Morley. As the Payroll proves, they were all at the knighting festivities in 1306 and when the king set out for Scotland in June they went with him and remained at Lanercost priory, receiving *largesse* of 1 mark (£133-6s.-8d.) each on Christmas Eve and half a mark each on Easter Sunday. (E101/370/16, ff. 1ᵛ, 3ᵛ, 6ʳ, 9ʳ)

After the old king's death Adam's livery dues and wages were sadly in arrears. He had not received his livery dues since 1302. A Wardrobe account (E101/369/11, f.165ᵛ) records payment of £7 (£1,400) owing to him for five years, except for his winter *roba* for 1303, when he was absent from Court. His wages for the whole of 1306 had not been paid. They amounted to approximately £6-10s.-0d. (£1,300). Out of this total he had been paid on account only 20s. (£200), but the remainder was paid to him on 1 March 1307 (that is, if the entry really records payment and not statement of debt). Even this was not the final statement of money owing to him. When the debts of the Wardrobe were ultimately drawn up, a further £7-9s.-6d. (approx. £1,500) were still outstanding.

That Adam could maintain himself (and his family) under such circumstances and at the same time lend money under recognizance to the Controller's chaplain, proves how well-off he must have been.

Clitheroe (Lancs.) was the country residence of the king's cousin, Henry de Lacy, earl of Lincoln. It was a very wealthy and important town, which assumed almost royal state when the earl was there. From it he received in annual revenue the equivalent of about £12,000. Adam may have entered the king's service on his recommendation. See *Janin Le Lutour*.

Adinet Le Harpour. L.

Like Adekin, Adinet is a diminutive of Adam and may refer to Adam de Clitheroe. The clerks are often inconsistent in their use of names.

Amekyn. L.

Prince's Harper. His name does not occur in any of the Wardrobe books nor have I found a reference to him in any of the other records.

Andreas vidulator de Hor'. L.

Unidentified. Perhaps Hor' stands for Horham (Suffolk) or possibly for Oare (Sussex).

Artisien. F.

' one from Artois ' ? Since his name is bracketed with those of Lucat and Henuer, he was probably a sergeant-at-arms. See *Lucat.*

Artoys. F. (margin)

That there was a minstrel called Artoys present at the festivities is proven by a marginal note on the Payroll. Philip de Cambrai, vielle-player of the French king, was handed his *largesse* of 60s. by King Caupenny; but the clerk has added in the margin a note to the effect that he was given another 20s. ' *par Artoys* ', although this sum was not included in the clerk's total.

In all probability he was the same minstrel who is mentioned in a Wardrobe book of 1290 : ' 12 July. Paid concerning Artoys, the fool of the Count of Artoys, in respect of his coming to the wedding of the Lady Margaret, the King's daughter, and returning to his own country . . . 40s.' (C47/4/5, f.48ʳ).

Edmund Crouchback, brother of Edward I, had married Blanche, sister of Robert, count of Artois, in 1275. Thomas of Lancaster was their elder son. Edmund died in 1296, Robert in 1297 and Blanche in 1302. It would have been natural for a domestic minstrel like Artoys to have come to serve in the household of Thomas or even in the king's household.

Audham

See *Le Taborer La Dame de Audham.*

Audoenus le Crouther. L.

Owen the Crowder. One of the Welshmen at Court, but his identity is a little uncertain, because four Owens are mentioned in the accounts : Elias Owen, Owen Picot, or Pygod, Owen Seys and Owen Gogh.

The case for Elias is not very strong. Although his name occurs often, for he was a sergeant, it usually appears as Elias Audewyn (when not turned into its Latin equivalent, *Elias Audoenus*).

Owen Picot or Pygod was a squire of the royal household. Together with the three Welsh squires, Rhys Maelgwn, Gruffydd ap Maredudd and Cynan ap Maredudd, he was with the king at Lanercost in 1306/7 and was given, presumably for making his minstrelsy, 10s. on Christmas Eve. His name occurs with those of a number of well-known minstrels of the household, such as John Depe and his son, King's Trumpeters, Adam, John, Hugh and William, the King's Harpers, and the four King's Watchmen.

Owen Seys was another Welshman, who had been at Court for several years. His cognomen, *Seys*, implied that he could understand and speak English.

There remains Owen Gogh. During the reign of Edward I he was one of the King's Welshmen. Under Edward II he became a King's sergant-at-arms. (MS. Cott. Nero, Cviii, f.97^r; *CCR*, 1315, 144.) In this capacity he was sent, in 1313, with other sergeants to Thomas of Lancaster, to forbid him to hold a tournament anywhere in the kingdom. (*CCR*, 1313, 71).

Since the *crwth* was one of the favourite instruments of Welsh minstrels and of Welsh gentlemen in general, either of these Owens might have been the Owen of the Payroll. What seems to tip the scales in favour of Owen Gogh is that, in the list of the debts of the Wardrobe, his name occurs directly in company with those of other prominent minstrels of the household : (Owing to) Owen Gogh, 18d.; John the Organist, £4-6s.-3d.; John the Nakerer, £4-19s.-4d.; Baudet the Taborer, 3s.10d$\frac{1}{2}$.' (E101/357/15, f.25^r)

B

Baisescu (*Le Roy*). L. and F.

Of the six *Reges Haraldorum* whose names appear on the Payroll, King Baisescu is the only one whom I have failed to identify. He does not figure in any of the Wardrobe books or other accounts. That he was a person of importance goes without saying. The *largesse* given to him, including the extra 2 marks in the margin, amounted to the equivalent of nearly £950. Although he was one of the King Heralds deputed to supervise the sharing-out of the remainder of the 200 marks, and must have been, therefore, well-known at Court, his identity remains a mystery.

Baisescu, although originally a French nickname, had become an ordinary English surname by at least the early fourteenth century. Two instances of it have been noted in the Patent Rolls, under the form *Besescu*.[2]

Baudet le Tabourer. F.

Originally the taborer of Edward I but apparently assigned to the Prince's household by 1300.

In 1297 he was one of the large group of royal minstrels who performed before the Count and Countess of Holland on their wedding-day, and received 20s. *largesse*. (Add. MSS. 7965, f.52^r)

In January 1300, Prince Edward set out from Langley with the new queen, Margaret, to join the king at Lincoln. Three small membranes recording some of the household expenses of the journey have survived. The second contains a list of servants accompanying the Prince, and among the minstrels is ' *Baudettus Taborarius*'. (E101/360/10)

At the end of the reign, when the debts of the Wardrobe were drawn up, he is, once more, among the royal minstrels of the king's household, ' (Owing to) Baudet the taborer, 3s.10½d. (E101/357/15, f.25^r); and he continued to be a king's minstrel under Edward II. Like many professional minstrels of the time he played more than one instrument. When he was with the king on the Scottish border in 1312, he was called ' Baudet the trumpeter.' (*Bain*, III, 418.)

' *baudet* ' now means ' jackass ' but it is very doubtful whether it carried that pejorative meaning in the fourteenth century. The word for a donkey then was ' *baudouin*'. The surname *Baudet* is probably derived from OF. *baud, baldé*, meaning ' boldness ', ' sprightliness '. It has remained in English as *Baud*. There is no hint in the records as to Baudet's Christian name but in the *Testa de Nevill* (1216-1306), there is reference to a Roger Baudet, who held land in Suffolk by serjeanty of ' paying the ancient fee of 100 arrows yearly to the king '. (pp. 231, 238)

Blida, Blithe.

See *Henricus* de Blida.

---

[2] According to Weekley, *English Surnames*, 270, Baisescu is an obsolete nickname, formed from Fr. *baiser* and *écu* (a coin, a ' shield ', money) and meant ' money-kisser '. An English equivalent would be ' lickpenny '. See also *CPR* (1314), 149/50 and 246.

Boistous.
See *Robert* le Boistous.

Boloigne.
See *Gerard* de Boloigne.

Bolthed. L.
Unidentified.
Probably an ordinary surname. One similar to it occurs in a letter of Edward I to the abbot and monks of Westminster abbey; one of the brothers was called ' *Robertus le Bolthod.*' (*Foedera*, I. pt. ii, 959.)
There is a place-name, Bolt Head, off Prawle Point, Devon. Cf. also, Old Norse, *bolth*, a short, heavy man; and OE *bolt*, an arrow-head.

Bracon.
See *Wauter* Bracon.

Brayles.
See *Walterus* de Brayles.

Brebant.
See *Janin* de Brebant.

Bruant. F.
John le Boteler, or John Butler, first appears in the records as a royal herald in 1306 ; ' To John Butler, Roger Macheys and Thomas de Norfolk, heralds, 6s. 8d. each by gift of the king for the expenses of their journey between Winchester and London. Paid into their own hands at Winchester on 6 April.' (E101/369/11, f.100ᵛ) The 6 April was the Wednesday of Easter week. Six weeks later he was present at the Prince's knighting, together with Thomas de Norfolk and another herald, William Carlton; and since it was he who collected Carlton's *largesse* for him on Whitmonday morning, he could not have been a stranger to the Wardrobe clerks; yet on the Payroll he is styled ' Bruant '.
It would be easy to jump to the conclusion that he had adopted *Bruant* as an heraldic name, for OF *bruiant* means a

torrent or cataract, from which the adjective, *bruyant, bruiant,* meaning ' booming ' and ' resounding ' was formed. ' The boomer ' would have been a very suitable name for a herald; one is reminded of the Bull in the *Roman de Renart,* whose name was *Sire Bruians*; but Bruant as well as Butler was used as this herald's surname.

At the tournament held at Chauvency in 1285, the herald who so kindly described the blazons of the guests for Jacques Bretel was called Bruiant. The Bodleian manuscript of the poem (MS. Douce 308) has the Anglicized form of the name, *Bruant.* Was he the same person as John Butler ? It is not impossible, for, had he been a young man of about 20 when he was at Chauvency, he would have been around 40 at the time of the Prince's knighting and 60 odd when last heard of in 1325. The indisputable evidence of the Exchequer accounts points to his having been a herald in the royal household under the name of Butler. Why, for instance, was he John le Boteler at Easter and Bruant at Whitsun ? Had he recently assumed the second or was it a long-standing alternative title ?

Under Edward I he was no more than a herald but some time during the reign of Edward II he was promoted to the office of *Rex Haraldorum.* When exactly the promotion took place is unknown, because his name does not appear in the records after 1306 until 1322, when he was taken prisoner after the battle of Boroughbridge. From references in the *Parliamentary Writs* and the *Foedera* something of his history can be pieced together. He was styled Le Roy Bruant and was fighting on the side of Thomas of Lancaster; he owned property in Pontefract, the chief residence of Earl Thomas; and felt the weight of Edward II's hatred and revenge; which suggests that he had transferred his loyalty to the Earl of Lancaster and had become his *Rex Haraldorum.*

After the battle was over, a list was drawn up of those who had been executed, slain, hanged and imprisoned or who had fled overseas. It was a survey in retrospect, for it was compiled in 1327. Among those imprisoned was ' le rey Bruant ' (MS. Cott. Cleop., D. ix, ff.83ʳ-85ʳ; *PW.,* II, div. 3, 604), but before he was incarcerated, his property in Pontefract was confiscated and given to someone who had once been his friend and fellow-minstrel in the royal household, William de Morley, the

Gillot le Harpour of the Payroll, now *Rex Haraldorum* of Edward II: ' On 28 October (1322) the king gave to William de Morley, called *Roi du North*, King's minstrel, those houses in the town of Pontefract, with their appurtenances, which had belonged to John le Boteler, called *Roi Bruaunt*, lately an enemy of the king; and which, by forfeiture, came into the king's hands '. (*Foedera*, II, pt. i, 498, See also *CPR*, 1321-4, 210.)

The author of the *Vita Edwardi Secundi*, describing the situation after Gaveston's execution, reveals how bitter the animosity between the households of the king and of Thomas of Lancaster was : ' If anything pleases the lord King, the household servants of the earl strive to subvert it, and if anything pleases the earl, the household servants of the King say it is the work of traitors.'[3] Something of this personal hatred and enmity seems to breathe in the statements just quoted from the *Foedera* and the rolls. Boroughbridge was the king's hour of triumph. William de Morley had remained true to his old master's wayward son; Bruant had defected to Lancaster. In the transference of the latter's property to the former there is something more than the giving of a minstrel's property to another minstrel; there is a hint of malice in the action. The subsequent behaviour of Edward II was unmistakeably vicious. Bruant was the only minstrel relentlessly pursued by his vengeance. He ordered an inquisition to be held at Marston (? Long Marston, about 12 miles west of York) where Bruant was captured. He had escaped thus far, in the company of six other soldiers. On 14 April, after the prisoners had been led away, the commissioners found the last sorry remnants of Bruant's and his companions' freedom : their seven horses, four haketons, four habergeons, three bacinets, two pairs of metal gauntlets, two pairs of cuisses, one pair of leg-guards, one doublet (*joupell*), one *roba*, one pair of shoes, four swords, three lances, two pikes and a silver spoon which had belonged to Geoffrey the cook (*le Keu*), one of the seven. (*Cal. of Inquisitions*, II, 134.)

Bruant was taken first to York and then on to the castle of Berkhamsted, where he remained until the autumn of 1325. On 28 October of that year the king sent three of his sergeants-

---

[3] *Vita Edwardi Secundi* ed. N. Denholm-Young (Nelson 1957), 75.

at-arms to conduct John Bruant and John de Monemouth to the castle of Berkeley for safe custody. (*CPR.*, 153.) This was the time when Edward II was retreating to the West Country and it looks as though he was determined, whatever his own troubles, not to let some of his hated prisoners out of his clutches. For some reason or other his order was not obeyed, because on 6 November he issued a further writ : ' To the sheriff of Berkshire. Order to go to Berkhamstede Castle, laying aside all other matters, and to receive by indenture from the sergeants-at-arms, John Bruant, John de Monemouth (and others), who are imprisoned in that castle and to cause John Bruant and John de Monemouth to be conducted to Berkeley castle . . . at the king's cost, there to be delivered to the constable . . . and to cause them to be kept in the castle until otherwise ordered'. (*CCR*, 424) On 10 November yet another writ was issued to the same effect. Edward was prepared to pay for Bruant's transference to Berkeley out of his own pocket; the sheriff of Berkshire had been commanded to drop everything in order to carry out the king's order on the instant; and that order had been insistent. Plainly there was little hope of remission for Bruant and his companion, John de Monemouth. No one can tell now what activated this implacable vengeance on the king's part but if Bruant were still alive in Berkeley castle in 1327, when Edward II was brought into it, himself now a prisoner, he might have pondered on the irony of Fate.

Two other Bruants occur in the records. A Thomas Bruant, who might have been a son of John, was also taken prisoner at Boroughbridge and committed to York castle with the de Berkeley brothers, Thomas and Maurice. (*PW.*, II, div. 3, 604; *CCR*, 580); and Oudinus Bruant, King's Yeoman, whom Edward II sent to the convent of Holynges in 1318, to receive maintenance for life. (*CCR*, 596)

C

Capenny (*Le Roy*). F.
James de Cowpen, harper.
He first appears in the Wardrobe accounts in 1290, when he took part in the wedding festivities of Princess Joan and

Gilbert de Clare. Another King of Heralds was present, King Grey of England, the then *Rex Haraldorum* of Edward I. When entering the payment of the *largesse* given to them both, the clerk took care to point out that Caupenny was from Scotland and the wording of the entry implies that he was not, at that time, a member of the royal household : ' Thursday, 1 May 1290 . . . . . to King Caupenny *de Scotia*, who came (to Westminster) to the feast of the aforesaid nuptials . . . 50s. (£500) by gift of the king.' (C47/4/5, f.45ᵛ; E101/352/21 (fragments))

In 1296, when Princess Elizabeth was married to the Count of Holland, Caupenny was again present, but under a different name : ' . . . to Druet, Monhaut and Jakettus de Scotia, Kings (of Heralds), 40s. (£400) each.' (Add. MSS. 7965, f.52ʳ; and 8934, a copy of the preceding.) Jaket is the diminutive of Jacke, the diminutive of Jacques, Jacobus; so that his Christian name was James, and he was evidently known, by this time, to the courtiers and clerks, as ' Jamie from Scotland ' or ' Jamie Caupenny '. A fragment of manuscript from an account book of the King's Chamber, of uncertain date but probably of between 1300 and 1307, refers to him as ' Roy *de* Copiny, harpour ' (E101/371/8, No. 152), thus proving that Caupenny was a place-name,[4] and that as well as being a *Rex Haraldorum*, he was a harper. The variety of ways in which his surname was spelt argues his familiarity with the clerks and his long residence at Court. When he first went to Westminster as a visitor the clerks got his name almost correct but throughout the following years they lapsed into their customary happy inconsistency : he became Monsire Capenny, Capigny, Capainy, Capini, Capyn, Copiny and Copyn.

Whose King of Heralds he had been in the first place is unknown. The most plausible supposition would be that he had belonged to the royal house of Scotland. Alexander III died in 1286, and, by 1296, Balliol had abdicated. It is from 1296 that Caupenny became a member of Edward I's household. There are numerous entries in the Wardrobe accounts relative to the payment of his wages and the issue of his livery.

---

[4] The locality from which he appears to have taken his name is now *Cowpen*, but the only one I know of is not in Scotland but in South Northumberland, about 9 miles from Morpeth.

After his abdication Balliol and his young son were brought to Hertford, where Edward allowed them to live in freedom until Wallace rose against the king in Balliol's name. This was in 1297 and Edward was constrained to transfer them to the Tower. It seems reasonable to suppose that Caupenny would then have found a welcome in the royal household; as herald, he would have been of great use to Edward in his campaign against Bruce. He was certainly taken into the king's favour. In 1305, on 30 September, when the Court was at Sheen (Surrey), the king made him a handsome present : ' a golden clasp worth £4-10s.-0d. (£900) given by the king to King Copyn, herald . . . ' (E101/369/11, f.172ʳ). In the following year, while the army was on its way to Scotland, the king gave him the price of a bay horse, bought from one of the brothers of Grantham Abbey. (E101/369/11, f.113ᵛ)

At the Prince's knighting he was one of the élite among the minstrels. He received the equivalent of £950 and it was he who collected the *largesse* for two of the most distinguished minstrel guests, Philip de Cambrai and Le Roy de Champagne. After the festivities were over he travelled north with the king and, during Edward's enforced stay at Lanercost, was prominent in entertaining the court, now helping to organize and stage plays to amuse the queen, now taking his turn with the other minstrels in easing the king's long hours of pain. (E101/370/16). The last notice of him is on Tuesday, 13 June, at Carlisle, where he received 20s. (£200) on account for his wages. (E101/370/16, f.15ʳ)

Carleton Harald. L. and F.

William de Carleton, King's Herald and sergeant-at-arms.

There is a Carleton in Leics., Northants., and Yorks.

In 1305 he and another sergeant, Robert Foun, conveyed armour and money to the Prince of Wales and his troops at Carlisle. (E101/369/11, f.67ᵛ)

In 1307, just after the death of Edward I, he was sent from London to Carlisle, this time on his own, with £40 (£8,000) in cash, to meet some of the expenses of the new king's household. (E101/373/15, f.9ʳ)

In neither of these entries is he specifically referred as being a herald, but he was then engaged not in herald's but in sergeant's duties.

Caumbereye
See *Phelippe* de Caumbereye.

Champaigne (Le Roy de). F.
Edmund Crouchback, who had married Blanche, the widow of the Count of Champagne, administered the *comté* until his death in 1296. Consequently, relations between the English court and Champagne were close. When the two princesses, Joan and Margaret, were married in 1290, Povret, the minstrel of the Marshal of Champagne, came to London to take part in the festivities. He made his minstrelsy in the presence of the king and, upon his leaving Court to return to France, was given *largesse* of 20s. (£200) by gift of the king. (C47/4/5, f.47ʳ)

This was in July. In November Queen Eleanor died and in her will she left a gold cup to a certain minstrel from Champagne. As it stands, the entry, quoted by Botfield, p. 110, is ambiguous. It says : ' *pro uno cypho empto, cum pede, de auro et dato per executores Reginae, cuidam menestrallo Regis Campanie, qui venit cum nunciis Francie . . . xxxixs.*' If *Regis* should have been *Regi*, then the ' certain minstrel ' would have been ' Le Roy de Champagne '. Entries in the records provide plenty of proof that Kings and Heralds were often used as special envoys. The stemmed goblet was no mean gift,; it was worth about £400 in present-day currency. Perhaps the ' certain minstrel ' was Povret.

Chat.
See *Johannes* du Chat.

Citharista Comitisse Lancastrie. L.
Unidentified.
The Countess, Alice, was not only the king's niece by marriage, but the daughter of one of his most trusted friends and counsellors, Henry de Lacy, earl of Lincoln. She married Thomas of Lancaster in 1294, when she was 13 and he about 16. After Gaveston's death, John Warenne abducted her to spite and show his contempt for Earl Thomas. She went to

live with and later married Sir Ebles L'Estrange, who died in 1335. Her third husband was Sir Hugh de Frene. She outlived him, too. She had no children by any of her three husbands and died in 1342, at the age of 61.

It seems a little odd that the royal clerks did not know the name of her harper. They knew John, her Waferer.

Clay.
See *Lambyn* Clay.

Clou.
See *Robert* de Clou.

Colcestria.
See *Robertus* de Colcestria.

Corleye.
See *Rogerus* de Corleye Trumpator.

Corraud.
See *Henri le Gigour.*

Cosin. F.
John de Cussin or Cosyn, Court minstrel from 1297 to 1312.

He was not one of the minstrels who received a portion of the Prince's *largesse* but collected that allocated to the three anonymous minstrels of Sir Robert Hastang or Hastings.

Cosin is first mentioned in 1297, when he was one of a group of minstrels performing at the wedding festivities of Princess Elizabeth : ' . . . to two minstrels of the Earl Marshal, Hamon L'estiuour, Lambin Clay and John de Cussin . . . 20s. each.' (Add. MSS. 7965, f.52^r) He had probably been a court minstrel for some time and was still a member of the royal household under Edward II. In 1312 he was with the king at Berwick-on-Tweed, riding a black horse and collecting wages for a fellow-minstrel by the name of Grillo. In this entry he is called explicitly ' Cusin the minstrel '. (MS. Cott. Nero. Cviii, f.3^r)

On 9 July his black horse was valued at Linlithgow. It was a noble creature, worth 5 marks (nearly £670).

D

Daa.
    See *Hugo* Daa.

Dauid le Crouther. L.
    Probably a Welshman, since David was an uncommon
Christian name in England in the fourteenth century.

Among the many Welshmen at Court there were four
Davids who figure fairly prominently in the records between
1299 and 1315: David Gogh, David ap Rees, David Gronow
and David de Percy. The only one of these definitely known
to have been a royal minstrel was David ap Rees. In 1302
he was, with David Gogh and David Gronow, a member of
the Prince's household (E101/363/18), and when the Prince
became king, he was a member of the royal household as one
of four of the king's Welsh trumpeters. (Add. MSS. 35093, f.1ʳ)

The other three were ' King's Welshmen ' which means
that they were squires, sergeants and/or archers. David Gogh,
a squire/archer, was a very well-known member of the household. He was already in the service of Edward I in 1299 and
remained in that of Edward II until he and his compatriot,
Ednyfed Gogh, were old enough to be pensioned off by the
king. For his long and faithful service, lasting more than
20 years, he was sent to Maenan Abbey in Conway to receive
maintenance for life and was granted a pension of 60s. per
annum (£600) from the revenues of Caernarvon.

David de Percy, a sergeant, also served in the households
of both Edward I and Edward II. With his companion,
Llewelin Treblerth, he was responsible, in 1305, for going
into Wales to select foot-soldiers for the army in Scotland.
One of his fellow-sergeants was Thomas le Crouthere, who
collected his own and Llewelin's wages in 1306, just after the
knighting festivities (E101/370/16). All three were with the
king on his last journey to Scotland and the Welshmen were
sent into their homeland to find more soldiers for the Prince's
contingents.

Of David Gronow nothing is known except that he was a
member of the Prince's household in 1302/3.

The David le Crouther of the Payroll could have been one of these four, inasmuch as they were gentlemen of the royal households and therefore certain to have been amateur musicians. Also, the fact that David ap Rees was or became King's Trumpeter, did not then preclude the possibility of his being a crowder as well; but in all the entries relating to them the four Davids are given their full names, so that, if, for example, we were to suggest that David le Crouther was David Gogh, we should be hard put to it to explain why the clerks, who knew him intimately and always called him David Gogh, should suddenly refer to him as David le Crouther. The same would be true of the other three, yet, David le Crouther was certain to have been a minstrel belonging to either the royal households or to the household of one of the guests.

Deuenays. F.
' Devonian ' or ' of Devon '. The name remains in English as the surname *Devonish, Devenish.*

Several men of this name appear in the records from the reign of Henry III : William le Devenays, King's Clerk; Gervase le Devenays, King's Messenger (*nuncius*); Richard le Devenays, sumpter of the money-chests; another Richard, valet of the Pantry; and Thomas, sumpter of the King's clothing and bedding.

It is this last who seems to have been the Devenays of the Payroll. His name appears regularly in the Wardrobe books from 1294 to 1307. Three days before the king's death he was paid half a mark either as part of his wages or, more likely, as a gift from his sick master. Thereafter, the records are silent concerning him. Like so many of the servants of Edward I, he retired, or was dismissed, from Court. Since his work was of so personal a nature, it is probable that he lost his post because the Prince would have had his own groom of the Chamber and would have raised him, on his accession, to Thomas's office.

As was appropriate, Thomas seems to have begun his career at Court as *subcissor Regis*. (E36/202, f.6ʳ) Both he and Richard, *sometarius coffrorum argenti*, were employed in the king's household at the same time, 1294/5. If Richard happened to be Thomas's father, the way could have been paved for Thomas to be promoted from being assistant tailor to being *sometarius robarum Regis*. As groom of the King's Chamber his wages were 4½d. per day (£3-15s.-0d.) The Wardrobe books and books of prests are full of notices concerning the payment of his wages and payment for the transport of the king's clothes, but now and again an entry reveals Thomas in a more individual, intimate light. To the clerks he was not always *Le Devenays, Thomas le Devenays* or *Thomas Devenays*; when the mood took them they would enter the payment of his wages under the heading, ' Tommy Devenish ' (*Thomelo Deuenish*, Add. MSS. 7965, f.78ᵛ). In 1305, when Edward I was ill and scarcely able to sit on horseback, Thomas was not absent from duty for a single day (E101/368/27, f.21ᵛ); in the same year he bought a backgammon board and counters ' for the king's use ' at Durham (E101/369/11, f.36ᵛ); at Lanercost, on a bleak Tuesday at the end of November, 1306, he supervised the work and paid the wages of ten tailors who were sewing furs for two days in order to make the king's bedroom more comfortable. (E101/370/16, f.1ᵛ)

Drake.
   See *Johannes Waffrarius*.

Druet (Le Roy).   F.
   Druet is a well-known English surname. Modern forms are : Drewitt, Drewett, Drewatt, Druett, Drouet. It is the diminutive of another, equally well-known surname, *Drew*, which derived from OF. *dru*, ' vigorous ', ' lively '.
   Monsire Druet was a king of Heralds from at least 1297 and a player on the vielle. Evidence concerning him is fragmentary but he seems to have been a *Rex Haraldorum* in one of the royal households. In 1297 he was present, with two other Kings of Heralds, John de Monhaut and King Caupenny, at the wedding of Princess Elizabeth. (See *Capenny*) In 1303 he was with the king at Burstwick, entertaining Lady Mary, the king's daughter. (Add. MSS. 8835, f.44ᵛ)
   According to the Household Ordinance of 1279, one of the king's two butlers was a man called Druet, so that King Druet may have had a father or other relative holding office in the royal household. In 1311 he was definitely a minstrel (and,

presumably, King of Heralds as well) in the household of the old king's grandson, the earl of Gloucester : ' To King Druet, vielle-player, and John Perle (Purley), trumpeter, minstrels of the lord earl of Gloucester, for making their minstrelsy in the presence of the two (young princes, Thomas and Edmund), 13s. 4d. (£133-6s.-8d.) as a gift from them . . . on the last day of December, at Striguil Castle '. (E101/374/19, f.8ʳ)

Duffeld.
See *Willelmus* de Duffeld.

E

(E)illiame. F.
Unidentified. See p. 6, n. 7.

Ernolet. F.
A court vielle-player, one of the minstrels entertaining the Lady Mary at Burstwick in 1303 : ' To King Druett, John de Monhaut, *Arnulett* the vielle-player, John de Swansea, James le Mazon and other minstrels making their minstrelsies in the presence of the Lady Mary . . . xxxs.' (£300) (Add. MSS., 8835, f.44ᵛ)

Esuillie, qui est oue Monsire Pierres de Maule. F.
' who is with Monsire Peter de Mauley.'
The de Mauleys were a baronial family living in Yorkshire. Their ancestor, Peter de Mauley, a Poitevin, became a member of King John's household.
The Peter who brought Esuillie to the knighting was one of the aspirants and the son of the first baron de Mauley. He was 26 years old.
See *Gillot, citharista domini P. de Malo Lacu.*

F

Fairfax. F.
Two men with this surname are mentioned in the records and both were in the army. John Fairfax occurs between 1295 and 1298, and William Fairfax in 1319.

In August 1295 John obtained a commission of oyer and terminer to enquire into his complaint against four men who had entered his holding and home at Walton by Thorpe Arches (Yorks.) while he was on the king's service in Gascony and had stolen his cattle and other animals, and had driven them to Salgrave, in Bucks. (*CPR*, 164) From this it can be legitimately concluded that he was a serving soldier, probably a sergeant, a view which is further substantiated by the fact that in 1298, the year of the battle of Falkirk, he was given letters of protection to go with the army in Scotland.

There is only one entry referring to William Fairfax, but it proves beyond doubt that he, too, was a serving soldier and sergeant. In 1319, the year of the fall of Berwick, he was paid sergeant's/squire's wages and his horse was valued, according to army regulations, ' in the war in Scotland.' (E101/378/14, f.25ʳ)

Frater.
See *Walter Leskirmissour.*

G

Galfridus Citharista Comitis Warrenni.   L.
Geoffrey, the harper of Earl Warenne.
At the time of the knighting, John de Warenne, seventh earl of Surrey, was a minor, about 19 years old, but Edward I granted him seisin of his grandfather's lands on 7 April (1306), because he had decided to offer him his young grand-daughter, Joan, La Dammoisele de Bar, in marriage. According to E101/369/11, f.96ʳ, the marriage took place on 20 May, and, two days later, John was knighted by the Prince.

There exists in the Public Record Office an Ordinance which was issued for him when he became a member of the royal household. (E101/371/3). It illustrates the size and cost of an aristocratic knight's retinue. He was allowed to have, at the king's expense, 2 valets and a boy to carve before him at table, 2 sets of clothing a year, and 2 sets of clothing for his three aforesaid servants. In addition he was to have a chamberlain, a valet of the Pantry, and Butlery, a valet of the Kitchen,

2 palfreys and 2 palefreteers, 3 sumpter horses and 3 sumpter grooms, 5 horses for his 3 squires, and 3 horses, on wages. There was an allowance of 2s. 6d. (£25) per day for his 10 horses, and 2d. (£1-13s.-4d.) per day for his grooms, making a total daily allowance for horses and grooms of the equivalent of nearly £40. For dinner, he was allowed 3 pennyworth of bread (£2-10s.), 3 messes (of meat etc.) from the Kitchen, one jug of wine and 2 jugs of beer. For supper, 4 pennyworth of bread, 2 jugs of wine, 3 jugs of beer and 3 messes from the Kitchen. After dark, he was provided with a torch ' for as long as it will last ', 2 candles, 3 perchers, (tall candles) and 2 torets. All in all, this young man was attended by 14 servants at a cost, to the king, of about £300 per week.

His later life was chequered, like his family coat.[5] At first he was a bitter opponent of Gaveston but after Warwick and Lancaster stole Gaveston from his keepers and had him beheaded, Warenne, because he had pledged his lands and his honour to ensure Gaveston's safety, suddenly found himself in danger of losing everything he possessed, as well as his life. He changed sides and for the rest of his life supported Edward II although he refused to go to Scotland in the year of Bannockburn and failed to attack Thomas of Lancaster in 1317. He abducted Lancaster's wife, not for his own pleasure but to humiliate Lancaster. By this time he was tired of Joan de Bar and was having an affair with a married woman, Maud de Nerford. He tried his hardest to get a divorce from Joan, even going to the length of declaring that before his marriage (i.e. when he was a minor) he had had carnal knowledge of Mary, sister of Princess Eleanor, his wife's mother; in other words, the Lady Mary, the nun of Amesbury.

Time passed; he lived apart from his wife, but Edward II made him pay *him* £200 (£40,000) a year for her maintenance. She was his niece and of the blood royal. Maud died. Warenne then bestowed his affections on Isabel de Holand, ex wedlock. He never obtained his divorce. On 29 June 1347, when he was in his early sixties, he died, leaving no legitimate heir. Joan out-lived him by 14 years. She died in 1361, a matron of 61.

---

[5] ' *De or e de asur eschequeré* '; checky, gold and azure.

One cannot help wondering whether, as Geoffrey the harper watched his master's life unfold, he composed any songs about some of the incidents in it. He had plenty of interesting material to hand.

Galfridus, trumpator domini R. de Monte Alto. L.
and *Richerus, socius suus.* L.
Geoffrey and Richer, the two personal trumpeters of Lord Robert de Monhaut.

Lord Robert de Monhaut (Mold, Denbighshire) was 52 years old in 1306. He became baron by writ in 1298. His alternative title was Lord of Hawarden.

His presence at the Prince's knighting is readily accounted for by the fact that he was one of the king's trusted veteran knights. He had served frequently against the Scots. The author of *Le Siege de Karlaverok* describes him as one who strove mightily to gain military renown.

The minstrel called John de Monhaut, who was attached to Court, came from Mold but there is no evidence that he was connected in any way with Sir Robert. (See *Capenny*)

Gaunsille, Gaunsillie.
See *Robertus* Gaunsille.

Gauteron le Grant. F.
Unidentified. His name does not appear in the Wardrobe accounts, yet he was evidently a minstrel or officer of some importance, because he was one of those appointed to divide the remains of the 200 marks among the anonymous minstrels.

Gauteron le Petit. F.
So styled in the note at the end of the French list, but in the list itself he is called *Le Petit Gauteron*.

Identity uncertain. There are numerous references in the Wardrobe books to a Walterus Parvus, a foot-messenger (*cokinus*) in the royal household. There is also a Walterus Parvus, *sub-ianitor Regis*. Walter the foot-messenger occurs from 1290. Again, there is a Walterus Parvus de Woodstock, who may or may not be the same person as Walter the messenger, resident in Court at the same time, carrying letters from

the king and doing such odd jobs as a little fishing for the royal
kitchen at Worcester, when William, the king's *Piscator*, was
ill, (1294) and repairing ditches and making fences around
Lanercost Priory (1306/7). In no instance is he referred to as
being a minstrel, yet, in the book of prests for 1294/5 (f.21ᵛ),
in which he was paid 6s. 8d. (£66-13s.-4d.) ' for his expenses
for going out of Court to fish ', his name comes immediately
after that of Simon Lowys, the late Queen Eleanor's messenger,
who was also at the festivities and who appears on the Payroll.
(See *Simond Le Messager*)

Geffrai Le Estiuour. L.
   One of *La Commune* and therefore, in all probability, a
bagpiper belonging to one of the royal households.

Gerard. L.
   Gerard may be either a Christian or a surname.
   There were three Gerards in the royal household : Gerard
de Comont, King's sergeant-at-arms; Gerard Dorum, King's
Yeoman; and Robert Gerrard, probably a sergeant, for in
c.1300 he was responsible for taking a load of wax (for seals)
for the king from London to York. (E101/371/8, No. 113)
   The name of Gerard Dorum occurs regularly in the Wardrobe records from 1296 to 1318/9. Under Edward I he was
groom of the King's Chamber (Add. MSS., 7965, f.123ᵛ) He
was with the king at the siege of Caerlaverock and remained
with him at Lanercost (E101/370/16, f.10ʳ). After the king's
death he continued to be King's Yeoman, for his name appears
very often in the Wardrobe book of Edward II for 1318/9.
(Soc. of Antiq. MS. 121, f.128ᵛ and *passim*) He could well have
been the Gerard of the Payroll, but in the records he is never
referred to as simply, Gerard. He is always given his full
name. The same is true of Gerard de Comont.

Gerard de Boloigne. F.
   Since he received the handsome reward of 4 marks
(£533-6s.-8d.) he was a minstrel of some importance. The

Count of Bologne was a kinsman of the king, so that Gerard may have been a distinguished guest from France.[6]

Gigour.
See *Henri* le Gigour.

Gillot Le Harpour. F.
William de Morley, one of the four King's Harpers. A squire of the royal household. (E101/368/27, f.22^r)

The Exchequer accounts are full of references to his being paid his wages, either in full or in part. One entry of this nature is especially valuable. He was on campaign with the king in Scotland during 1299/1300 for a period of 52 days, commencing on 14 July and finishing on 4 September, ' the first day included but not the last '. These words prove conclusively that he arrived at Caerlaverock castle on the very day it surrendered. The other King's Harper, who is known to have been present at the siege is Nicholas Le Blund.

There are five places in England called Morley : a parish in Devon, a borough and parish in Yorkshire, SW of Leeds, a village and parish NE of Derby, a hamlet in Durham, WSW of Bishop Auckland, and a village in Cheshire, NW of Wilmslow.

I have found no clear evidence to indicate from which of these William took his name, but, since he was, in later life, styled *Roi du North*, the chances are that he hailed from one of the Morleys north of Trent. Sir William de Morley, a well-known knight in the time of Edward I, held land in Normanby, in the borough and parish of the Morley near Leeds.

William the harper is first mentioned in the records in 1299 and his name disappears from them in 1326. He was King's Harper for about seven years and *Rex Haraldorum* for just under twenty. After the battle of Boroughbridge he was given the property of Le Roy Bruant (See *Bruant*). His heraldic title, *Roi du North*, seems to imply that the area over which his

---

[6] He may, alternatively, have been the minstrel of Brankalo de Boloigne, one of the aspirants. Sir Brankalo accompanied the king to Scotland after the knighting; 'Safe conduct, until the Purification, for Brancaleo de Audalo de Boloigne, returning home after coming to the king in Scotland.' (*CPR* (1306), 462. dated 4 November at Lanercost.)

jurisdiction as herald extended was co-extensive with that allotted to the King's Escheator North of Trent.[7]

His loyalty to both Edward I and Edward II was unquestioned; he was with the old king at Lanercost and remained true to Edward II to the end of the reign.

In the Wardrobe accounts, he was usually called William or Gillot de Morley, *Citharista Regis*; sometimes, Gillot de Morle, *harpour*; in contexts in which he could not possibly be mistaken for William de Morley, knight, he is plain William de Morley. Finally, in the last entry I have found concerning him he is Willelme, *Roi des Heraux*. (Soc. Antiq. MS. 122, f.64ᵛ)

Gillot, Citharista domini P. de Malo Lacu. L.

The harper of Lord Peter de Mauley, the father of Monsire Peter (See *Esuillie*).

Lord Peter, the first baron de Mauley was 57 in 1306. He was at the knighting not only to see his son dubbed. He was one of the king's veteran soldiers, who had fought in Wales, Gascony and Scotland. It must never be forgotten that the Prince's knighting was the prologue to the campaign against Bruce.

Gillot de Roos. F. *Guillot Le Vilour, Guillot de Roos, Vilour.* L.

William de Roos, King's Vielle-player.

There are indications in the records that by 1306 he was an elderly man. In the counter-roll of domestic payments of 1285 his name appears among those of the royal minstrels. In 1293/4 Edward I granted him an annual fee of 100s. (£1000) from the Wardrobe and on 6 December 1296 he was granted exemption for life from being put on assizes, juries or recognizances, and was made quit for life ' from any custody of the maritime parts due from him by reason of his lands.' (*CPR*, 223.) In this entry he is called ' William de Ros, the king's minstrel ', and it is expressly stated that these privileges were bestowed upon him ' for his long service.' Although not explicitly on wages, he still attended Court during 1296-1306. He was one

---

[7] Such a division of the country for heraldic purposes was not new. There had been a Peter, ' *Rex hyraudorum citra aquam de Trente ex parte borialis* ', in 1276. See *Glossarium Archaiologicum*, Henricus Spelmann (Lond. 1687), s.v. *Heraldus*; *Heralds and Heraldry in the Middle Ages*, Sir Anthony Wagner (Oxford 1956), 39-40.

of the minstrels who played before Princess Elizabeth and her husband at their wedding (Add. MSS., 7965, f.52^r), and one of *La Commune* at the Prince's knighting.

Sometime between 1297 and 1299 he was robbed by a man called Wyot de Keu, who was arrested in Cambridge, with William's goods on him, and who was subsequently hanged. (*CCR*, (1299), 262, 351)   The value of the stolen property amounted to the equivalent of nearly £900, which is additional proof of the good, financial standing of royal minstrels.

Gillot lived, apparently, on his pension from 1293, because after that date there are no entries relating to payment of his wages.   Edward I did not usually grant these ' fees ', as they were called.   The recipients of them, few in number, were special cases and, in every instance, valued old servants of the king or the queen.   William de Roos was one such and the last entry which refers to his annual pension is dated 8 December 1305, when he was given half a mark (£66-13s.-4d.) on account at Bamford (Derbys.) (E101/368/6, f.8^r).

The place from which he took his name is not easy to identify. There are a number of Roos, Roose, Ros, Ross and Rhos -es in Britain.   Perhaps, if the exemption from the ' custody of maritime parts ' noted above referred to the area in which he held his lands, then the Roos in Yorkshire may have been his native town, for it is situated 7 miles east of Hedon and therefore only two or three miles from the coast.

Gillot, Trumpour Monsire Le Prince.   F.

Gillot was really King's Trumpeter (Add. MSS., 35291, f.159^v) but in 1300 he began to be lent to the Prince, as an entry in the Wardrobe book for that year proves : ' To Gillot the trumpeter, on account, in money paid to him by R(oger) de Chisulle, for his wages for certain days when he was out of Court in the entourage of the Lord Edward, the King's son, in the month of January . . . 4s. (£40) by the hand of Master Roger, on 19 February, at Lincoln.' (Add. MSS., 7966, f.178^r). This entry refers to the journey the Prince and Queen Margaret made to Lincoln in January 1301.   On the roll which contains the names of the servants who went with them, Gillot's name, together with that of his fellow-trumpeter, Januche, appear, but the clerk has given both of them their proper names

William (*Willelmus*) and John (*Johannes*). (E101/360/10, mem.1)
With only ' William the trumpeter ' to go upon, it is well-nigh impossible to trace him . At the end of the reign, in the list of the debts of the Wardrobe, he is called ' William the trumpeter ' and unquestionably a minstrel of the royal household. (E101/357/15, f.13ʳ) In 1307, under Edward II, he was with the king from July to October. (E101/373/15, f.5ʳ), and in the same Wardrobe book, on f.19ʳ, there is an entry concerning payment of £4 (£800) to a group of minstrels, who performed in the king's and Gaveston's presence, at Dumfries in August, which possibly uncovers William's identity : ' King's minstrels. To William of the Queenhithe, Janin the trumpeter, Januche, the nakerer, Janin the organist, the king's minstrels, making their minstrelsy in the king's presence at Dumfries, 10 August, 20s. to each of them, by hand of the said Willelm'. Some years later, c.1315, Margery, the wife of ' Willelm trumpeter ', saw to it that the usual annual contract for her husband's employment at Court had been drawn up with the royal clerks at Westminster, so that William was consequently able to collect his wages for the 122 days on which he had been on duty and away from the City. (E101/374/15, f.34ᵛ) In this entry he is not called William of Queenhithe, but, since his wife was resident in or near London, it may well be that Gillot was, in fact, the same trumpeter as William ' *de la Quenheth* '.

The last reference to him that I have found is in the *Parliamentary Writs*, (Vol. II, div. 2, 127) in which the name ' William the trumpeter ' appears in a list of those who were pardoned for rebellious behaviour re the Despensers in 1317/8. Names of other, authenticated minstrels of the royal household are also in the list, among them two of Edward I's watchmen, Hugh the harper and the sergeant-at-arms, Richard Foun. It looks as though Gillot, like many of the minstrels of the old king, objected to the new favourites of Edward II and showed it in no uncertain manner; for which he seems to have paid the price, for thereafter his name is not found in the household accounts.

Gillot, Vidulator Comitis Arundellie. L.
William, the vielle-player of the Earl of Arundel.

Edmund fitz Alan, earl of Arundel, was another of the aristocratic aspirants.

He was just over 21 when he was knighted by the Prince. According to Peter de Langtoft (*Chronicle*, Vol. II, 369, Rolls Ser.) he married John de Warenne's sister, Alice, at the time of the knighting, but *The Complete Peerage* states that he married her in 1305/6 while he was still a minor.

During the reign of Edward II he was, at first, in opposition to the king, because he hated Gaveston, who had beaten him in tournament; but in 1321 he changed sides, married his eldest son to a daughter of Hugh le Despenser, and from then on was one of the diminishing number of nobles who remained loyal to Edward II. When the king fled to the west country in 1326, he went with him but was captured in Shropshire by the queen's forces and beheaded, without trial, at Hereford on 17 November. He was in his forty-second year.

Gitarier (*Le*). F.

Two entries in a Wardrobe book of the Prince of Wales provide a little more information about this minstrel. His name was Peter, and, after the knighting, he and Henry de Blida took up residence in the Prince's household for nearly two months. On 12/14 June Edward I, in fulfilment of his vow, set out for Scotland, but the Prince remained at Lambeth, where Peter the Guitarist went and entertained him and his nobles. For his performance he was given, as a gift from the Prince, 23s. (£230) to buy himself a suit of clothes. A little later on, perhaps as a result of his June visit, he and Henry de Blida, who was also present at the knighting, were commanded to stay in the household, ' making their minstrelsy in his (the Prince's) presence by turns ', for which they received 4½d. per day for the specified period of 52 days, by the end of which time they were all in Scotland sharing in the initial triumph over Bruce and his followers. Peter and Henry had been taken into the Prince's household to accompany him on his journey north. They are called ' Prince's minstrels ' by the clerk. (Add. MSS., 22923 and MS. Harley 5001 (a copy), ff.10ʳ, 44ᵛ,48ʳ)

Grendone. F.

John de Grendon, minstrel of Anthony Bek, bishop of Durham. (See *Guilleme le Harpour qui est oue Le Patriarke*)

On 25 October 1304, when the king was at Burstwick, John came to court and made his minstrelsy in the presence of the king, for which he received *largesse* of 40s. (£400); and a silver-gilt cup worth 76s. 8d. (£750), (Add. MSS., 8835, ff44ʳ, 121ᵛ)

There is a village of Grendon, south of Wellingborough (Northants.), a hamlet of the same name NW of Atherstone (Warwicks.) and a Grendon Bishop NW of Bromyard (Heref.)

Grymesar'.

See *Willelmus* de Grymesar'.

Guilleme Le Harpour qui est oue Le Patriarke. F.

'William the harper who is with the Patriarch.'

The Patriarch was Anthony Bek and the reason why he was so styled is worthy of explanation. He was one of the richest, most magnificent and most colourful lords in England. Until 1298 he was a favourite with Edward I. It is possible to say of him that he was a perfect example of the Church Militant in its literal sense. He not only kept a personal retinue of 140 knights but led his men himself into battle. In 1296 he was at the head of 500 cavalry and 1000 foot in the offensive against Balliol, and, in 1298, at Falkirk, he commanded the second division of the king's army. Between then and 1300 (he sent a contingent to Caerlaverock but did not turn up himself) he lost the king's favour over a petty quarrel at Hoton convent (Leics.), whose Prior-elect, Richard, fearing that his election would be quashed, refused to allow the bishop to enter the convent if he were accompanied by his retinue. Such an affront to such a man, aristocratic and haughty in the extreme, was not to be tolerated. Henceforth it was war to the knife between him and the prior, who happened to be a man with as much strength of will as the bishop himself. The king arbitrated in the quarrel and declared that the one who disobeyed his orders should feel the weight of his anger. He decided in favour of the prior. Bek ignored his ruling and thus forfeited the king's friendship. The prior, whom Bek had removed, was re-instated but the bishop, persisting in his defiance of the king, left England for Rome, without seeking royal permission; for his impertinence his extensive estates were sequestered. At Rome, however, the sumptuousness of his entourage, his cool, autocratic behaviour—he played with the falcon on his wrist even in his interviews with the Pope (Boniface VIII)—swept all before him. The Pope dismissed Prior Richard and his complaints, and Bek returned to England triumphant. Only one thing rankled; Richard was still Prior, which was something the bishop's pride could not stomach. When Boniface died, he accused Richard once more to Benedict VI, but Benedict died before he could come to any decision. Bek then took his case to his successor, Clement V, who deprived Richard of his office and, as a mark of special Papal favour, created the bishop nominal Patriarch of Jerusalem. This was in 1305. The presence of his minstrels at the Prince's knighting implies that the king had, in some measure, accepted the situation, but Richard, nothing daunted, collected a thousand marks (approx. £14,000) and set off for Rome again, where he obtained a reversal of the Pope's sentence of dismissal. He, now, was the victor—or was he ? He died in Rome when he was about to start for home. The Pope promptly purloined his thousand marks and all his possessions for the Papal treasury.

As might be expected, Edward II, who took delight in doing everything his father would have objected to, restored bishop Bek to the royal favour and granted him, in 1307, the sovereignty of the Isle of Man. Bolstered once more with royal friendship, Bek went to the convent at Hoton, in 1308, and suspended for ten years all those monks who had supported Prior Richard.

It is not a pretty picture of human nature, more particularly of ecclesiastical human nature, yet it has its humorous side. Two years later, on 3 March 1310, the great bishop went to meet his Maker, in sufficient odour of sanctity to be allowed burial in Durham cathedral, but he had to use a side door to get to his grave, out of deference to St. Cuthbert.

I have come across only one reference to his harper, William, or Gillot, as he is called in the Wardrobe book for 1304. In its way the entry carries the flavour of Bek's character and at the same time throws a little extra light on that of Edward I. Fierce in anger the king may have been, but he was not one to bear a grudge indefinitely. ' To Gillot, the harper of the lord bishop of Durham, 5s. (£50) for bringing a goshawk to the king as a present from his master; and for looking after the bird during the time that he was coming to the king.' (Add. MSS., 8835, f.44ʳ) The clerk has not dated the entry, but Edward was at Beverly from 17 to 20 October.

Guilleme sanz maniere. F.

The waferer of Princess Joan, countess of Gloucester. He was appointed to the office sometime between 1291 and 1306, because, when she paid a visit to her father in Herefordshire in 1290, shortly after her marriage to Earl Gilbert, she took her waferer with her and his name was Henry de Rue. (C47/4/5 f.52ᵛ)

William's name does not appear in the records before 1306 but this is surely fortuitous. In February 1307 he visited the Prince's court at Wetheral (Cumberland) and was given 20s. to cover his expenses for his return from Wetheral to his lady mistress. (Add. MSS. 22923, f.14ᵛ and MS. Harley 5001, f.36ᵛ)

Countess Joan died suddenly on 23 April (1307). The title of Earl of Gloucester and the estates passed to her son by Earl Gilbert. William must have remained in the service of the new young earl, Gilbert, then 16 years old, for, although he was at Lanercost with the old king in June, making his minstrelsy and receiving *largesse* of 40s. (£400), he is called ' the earl of Gloucester's minstrel.' (E101/370/16, f.16ᵛ)

On the Payroll he is ' *sanz maniere* '; in the Prince's Wardrobe book, ' *saunz manoir* '; and in the Lanercost Journal, ' *sanz manere* '. All three forms are general in OF. (*manier, manoir, manere* or *maner.*) The type of surname was common in both France and England in the Middle Ages : *Sanshelme, Sanssurnom, Sansgonele, Sansterre*; Hoodless, Landless, Sorrowless, Bookless, Careless, Lawless, Loveless, Faultless, Peerless, etc.

Guillot de Roos.

See *Gillot* de Roos.

Guillot Le Taborer. L.

One of *La Commune.* As a member of this consortium, he was almost certain to have been a minstrel in one of the royal households, but it is imporssible to identify him on the slender evidence I have collected.

A William de Gayton, taborer, who was living in London in 1310/11, lent, under recognizance, the sum of 50 marks (roughly £7,000) to a fellow-citizen. (*CLL.*, B.22) There is nothing to prove that this William was a royal minstrel, yet the sum he lent was the kind of loan a royal minstrel was able to lend.

After the battle of Boroughbridge, Edward II granted to John le Scot (one of the boy-minstrels, now grown up) 8 acres of land and one acre of meadow in Pontefract and Friston which had belonged to ' William le Tabourer, a rebel, which have come into the king's hands by forfeiture.' (*CPR.* (1325), 161) Perhaps this was Guillot Le Taborer, a minstrel of Thomas of Lancaster, who, like Le Roy Bruant, had been a king's minstrel and had ultimately thrown in his lot with Earl Thomas.

Guillot, le Taborer Comitis Warrewici.   L.

Guy de Beauchamp, ninth earl of Warwick, was in his mid or late thirties at the time of the knighting. He himself had been knighted by Edward I in 1296. As an experienced soldier —he had fought at Falkirk and Caerlaverock and had served in the Scots wars 1298-1304—as a close and trusted friend of the king, and as Chamberlain of the Exchequer, he would have been one of the most important people at the Whitsuntide ceremony. Gaveston coined several insulting names for him, among them, ' black dog of Arden '. He is said to have remarked on hearing it, ' If I am a dog, I shall bite, when opportunity offers.' Which he did, in 1312, a fatal bite for Gaveston.

Another of his minstrels at the feast was Martinet, his vielle-player.

Guillotin Le Sautreour.   F.

William Le Sautreour. One of the wealthiest and most elegant of the royal minstrels. He was psaltery-player to three queens.

His first appearance in the records is in 1298, when three of his servants robbed him. On or about the 1 August they broke into his house by night and carried away goods and chattels to the value of £100 (£20,000). He was then living in Thames Street, in the parish of All Hallows the Less but at the time of the robbery was probably in Stirling with the king and queen. (*Cal. of Inquisitions*, Vol. II, 44, No. 186 and C. 145/74/No. 29)

Queen Eleanor died on 28 November 1290 and, although Edward I did not marry Margaret of France until 4 September 1299, William remained at Court as Queen's Minstrel, as is proven by an entry in the Wardrobe book for 1299/1300. The Treasurer of the Queen's Wardrobe returned to the King's Wardrobe the sum of 27s. 11d. (approx. £279-3s.-4d.) which had been subtracted ' from the wages of Guillot le Psalterion, minstrel of the *said queen* (sc. Eleanor) ' because this money had been allowed for ' in the Marshal's Roll *in the time of the said Queen*, by which he received a gift of hay and oats from the King's Marshalcy.' (*LQG.*, 7.)

After Edward's second marriage, William became Queen's Minstrel to Margaret and when, in 1308, she ceased to be Queen Regnant, he became the minstrel of Edward II's queen, Isabella.

His surname, if he had one, has been either lost or accidentally not recorded. When his wife, Juliana, died c.1314/15, an enrolment of general release of her lands and property, dated 18 March 1315, at London, was issued to ' Guillot le Sautreor, minstrel, and to John le Grey, his son.' (*CCR.*, 311/12.)

His status at Court is clearly and fully documented. From before 1298 he was a squire in the Queen's household receiving his wages of 7½d. per day and his winter and summer livery. Hints that he was a favoured minstrel are to be found many times in the records. In April 1300, when travelling with the court, one of his horses, a bay hackney with a white star on its forehead, was returned to the Almonry; for it he received the regular compensation, in this case, 40s. (£400). He then bought another horse for himself from Robert de Cotyngham, Controller of the King's Wardrobe, and paid ' more than 40s.' for it out of his own pocket, whereupon the king made him a gift of 20s. toward the extra cost. (*LQG.*, 111-2)

His horses were regarded as part of the royal establishment and were moved from place to place at the king's expense :

' (payment for) 55 horses on 28 June (at Carlisle 1300), on which day there came 5 palfreys of the Lord Edward, the King's son and 3 horses of Guillot, the Queen's minstrel, by order of the King.' (*Ibid.*, 95.)   In 1302, ' at the instance of Margaret, Queen of England ', the king made a grant in fee simple to ' Guillotus the Sautriour, her minstrel, of the houses in London, late of John de Butterlye, deceased, in the king's hands by reason of his debts.' (*CPR.*, 48.) and later in the reign Edward ' conferred on Guylot le Sautreour ' a rent amounting to one mark (£133-6s.-8d.) per annum, ' issuing out of a tenement in the city of London, which once belonged to Reymund de Burdeus.' (*Cal. of Inquisitions*, Vol. II, 16, No. 55) When he passed from the service of Queen Margaret to that of Queen Isabella, he was not only the queen's favoured minstrel but ' the king's well-beloved Guillot le Sautreour '.   (*Cal. Chancery Warrants*, (1310), 314.)

As both squire and minstrel of the Queen's Household he accompanied her on her travels both at home and abroad. When, in January 1301, she was instructed to join the king at Lincoln and to travel in the company of her stepson, Prince Edward, William was one of the squires who was issued cloth for a new winter livery so that he could accompany his royal mistress in garments that befitted her and the Prince's estate. (E101/360/10, mem.1.)   On the occasion of Edward II's marriage in 1308, which was solemnized at Boulogne, William went with Queen Margaret to the ceremony.   It is interesting to note that the person who signed his letters of protection, enabling him to travel abroad, was Piers Gaveston, who had been made Keeper of the Realm while the king was away. (*CPR.*, 44.)   From the beginning of the reign William was, so to speak, at the heart of the contention which was to arise over Gaveston's presence and influence in England.   He remained loyal to the king until 1319 (the last reference to him).

In 1309 he was sent abroad, presumably as a special envoy, ' on the king's service ' but his business is not specified. (*CPR.*, 147.)   In 1313 he went to France once more, this time with the king and queen shortly after Gaveston's execution. Queen Isabella was escorted by Aymer de Valence and it was in his entourage that William travelled.   (*CPR.*, 581, and *Foedera*, Vol. II, pt. 1, 212.)

Unfortunately, there is never any reference to the precise nature of William's work as a musician. That his principal duty was to entertain the queen in her private apartments can be taken for granted; there can also be no doubt that he took part in the general concerts and entertainments organized in Court by the Kings of Heralds. When King Caupenny organized the production of miracle-plays for Queen Margaret at Carlisle in 1307, it was to ' Guillot le Psalterion ' that the king's *largesse* was given to be divided among all those who had taken part, himself included. (E101/370/16, f.13ᵛ)

Outside Court he was, like Janin le Leutour, a wealthy and respected citizen of London. Documentary evidence from various sources points to his being remarkably well-to-do. Sometime before 1301 he had been lending money under recognizance to a person or persons connected with the Wardrobe. He had also acquired a piece of land in Shropshire, which the Priory of (Much) Wenlock wanted to obtain, probably because it adjoined its own acres. On Easter Monday 1301 some agreement between the king, the prior of Wenlock and William was concluded which resulted in the following quitclaim :

' Let it be known by these presents that I, Gillot, minstrel of the Lady (Margaret), Queen of England, have received from Master John de Drokenesford, Keeper of the Wardrobe of the Lord Edward, illustrious King of England, 20 pounds in sterling, by the hand of the Prior of Wenlock, given to me for quittance of a piece of land to him, under the seal of the said Master John, for money owing to me in the said Wardrobe for divers recognizances. In witness whereof my seal, appended to these presents, is given at Feckenham (Worcs.) on 3 April.'

This quitclaim, written on a small piece of parchment (E101/684/62., No. 3) has unique value. In addition to identifying William and testifying to his prosperity—he received the equivalent of £4,000—it provides us with his portrait. The seal, although very small, is intact. See *Frontispiece*.

William owned other property, chiefly in London. In 1298 he was living in what is now known as Upper Thames Street but he had other property in Martin Lane (off Cannon Street) and Swan Lane, which, in his time, was called Ebbegate. As a citizen of London he entered into recognizance, often for quite sizeable sums. For example, on 12 November 1302, Sir John Sudeley borrowed £20 from him on security of his lands and chattels in Gloucestershire. He repaid the loan, otherwise William might have become a landowner in the west country. John de Lung, a London goldsmith who borrowed £40 (£8,000) from him was not so lucky. On 29 September 1304 the Sheriffs of the City were ordered ' to take the body of John de Lung and safeguard the same until he shall have paid to William le Sautreour, minstrel to the Lady Margaret, Queen of England, the sum of £40 due under a recognizance.' Which they did, and committed John to Newgate while an extent and valuation of his property was made. It then transpired that he also owed money to a Canon of St. Paul's, and, as he could not or would not satisfy either of his creditors, he was kept in Newgate while a second extent and valuation of his property was undertaken. He languished in prison for over six months until it was ruled that part of his property, comprising two messuages and ten shops were to be handed over to William in lieu of the debt or until the debt be paid. What the final outcome was has not been recorded; probably William never regained his £8,000 but became the owner of the messuages and shops in Cripplegate instead. (*CLL.*, C., 213, 244.)

Further light is shed upon his activities and character as a business man by the long quarrel and lawsuit he had over the messuage and four shops in London (situation not specified) which the king had granted to him at the instance of the queen in 1302. John de Butterlye, whose property it had been and who had died in the king's debt, had been the Keeper of the King's Forest at Havering-atte-Bower (3 miles N of Romford, Essex). In some way which the surviving records do not clarify, Jordan Moraunt, one of the King's Clerks, seems to have been related to or had special connections with the Butterlye family, and immediately contested the grant, because William had been precipitate and had taken possession of the property when, so Jordan argued, he could be granted lawfully only the ' debt '. He brought an action of novel disseisin against William, which the king not only could not but did not wish to ignore. He ordered both William and Jordan to appear before him on the morning of 3 June 1303, ' there to shew what right pertains to each party in this matter.' By this time William evidently realized that he had made a mistake. ' Guillot, wishing to avoid the damages he might have incurred if Jordan had recovered the tenements (by law), rendered the tenements to Jordan before the Council, renouncing all his rights saving to him 20s. yearly only, to be received from the tenements (in rents) until he should be satisfied for the debts in which John (de Butterlye) was bound to the King at the Exchequer at his death.' (CCR., 108.) One of Jordan's most telling thrusts was that the king's original grant could have prejudiced the rights of John's heir, and, although this important part of the enquiry has not been explicitly recorded, it did take place. In the meantime William was not getting his legitimate rent, because the sheriffs were taking an unconscionable time in levying the extent of the property. William complained to the king, no doubt through the queen. On 12 March, while the court was in Scotland, the king sent a letter (from St. Andrews), to the Chancellor, Treasurer and barons of Exchequer, pointing out that ' the sheriffs of London have not levied (the extent) as they might well have done and so Gilotyn is delayed.' (Cal. of Chancery Warrants, 1304, 206.) and he issued a mandate to them ' to put all possible counsel and diligence to the levying of the extent to the profit of Gilotyn.' (Ibid.)

Two years later William triumphed over Jordan. John de Butterlye's nephew and heir went before the king and quitclaimed to the king all right to his uncle's property, whereupon the king granted it again in fee simple to William. (CPR., (1306), 420). According to law and the king's grant, the messuage and shops were now well and truly William's, and he took possession of them once more but he reckoned without Jordan, who professed to have found a legal flaw in the assize of novel disseisin, and he declared that while he was in Gascony on the king's service, (the king by this time being Edward II) Gillot le Sautreour had wrongfully obtained possession of the property. (CPR., (1307), 41.) From then on it developed into a bitter tug-of-war between Queen's Minstrel and King's Clerk. Time and again the king appointed commissioners to ' examine and correct an alleged error ' in the assize; time and again the commissioners did not meet or else failed to reach a decision.

By 1310 William seems to have had the king openly on his side, despite the fact that Jordan was one of the king's right-hand men. Edward issued a mandate ' to command the sheriffs and coroners of London to put the more loyal and better people of the city, both aldermen near the tenements and others who will know the truth, on the assize . . . arraimed against the king's well-beloved Guillot le Sautreour about some tenements in London.' (*Cal. of Chancery Warrants*, (1310), 314.) Nine years later the king was still appointing commission-ers ' to examine the record and process . . . and correct any error ' in the case. How it ended is unknown. The first to fade from the scene was William; after 1319 his name no longer appears in the records but Jordan flourished until after 1323, getting himself disliked and even hated by laymen and clergy alike. He was an astute, litigous and ruthless king's servant. William put up a good fight against him until the winner of all contests, death, put an end to the game.

By 1319 William had lost his wife and his erstwhile employer, Queen Margaret, who died in 1318. He had been a royal minstrel for nearly 25 years and must have been in his fifties, at least, when the last troubles of the reign of Edward II were brewing. His position when Queen Isabella took up arms against her husband would have been very difficult, that is, if he were still alive.

During his years in the Queen's Household he travelled the length and breadth of England. From Cumberland he went into Scotland; from London he crossed the Channel to France. As befitted a gentleman of his standing, he travelled in style, with his horses, servants and grooms, among whom there was certain to be one whose special duty it would have been to carry his psaltery, carefully packed in its leather bag, with its plectra and a supply of extra strings.

H

Haleford.
    See *Ricard* de Haleford.

Hamond Lestiuour. F.
    In the Wardrobe books he is called Hamon Lestiuour. *Hamond, Hammond* was and is an ordinary English surname.

Hamond the estive-player was a valet of John de Drokenes-ford. At the time of the knighting he had already been in Court for 10 years or more.

In 1296, in his capacity as groom of the Wardrobe, he was paid 10s. (£100) for ' carrying, with the utmost haste, letters of the Treasurer to the lord bishop of Coventry and Lichfield on the King's business, concerning money paid by him for his passage by water between London and Gravesend, when conveying divers hackneys for his journey on horseback and for his expenses in going to Dover and returning in the month of February.' (Add. MSS. 7965, f.15^r); also, another £10 for ' a bay horse bought for him by Ralph de Manton (Cofferer of the Wardrobe) at Westminster in the month of April and given to Willelm le Fissher for draught work in the long cart which belonged to the Duchess of Brabant (Princess Margaret), and which was assigned to the Wardrobe for carrying the King's jewels and other harness of the Wardrobe.' (*Ibid.*, f.17^r) In the same year, in his capacity as amateur minstrel, he was given 20s. (£200) for performing at the wedding of Princess Elizabeth.

Hanecocke de Blithe.
See *Henricus de Blida.*

Hendeleke.
See *Richard* Hendeleke.

Henricus de Blida. L. *Hanecocke de Blithe.* F.
King's Minstrel.
There is a Blyth in Notts., Staffs., and Suffolk, and two in Northumberland. In view of the spellings *Blide* and *Blida* which occur in the Wardrobe books as well as the *Blida* and *Blithe* of the Payroll, Henry probably took his name from the locality known as *Blythe, Blithe*, in the rural district of Meriden, Warwicks.

To the clerks of the Wardrobe he was Henry (*Henricus*) but in Court he was *Hancock*, a pet form of Henry.

Up to at least 1303 he was a minstrel of Edward I but the only two entries concerning him which I have come across suggest that he was a favourite with the Prince. In the Prince's

Wardrobe book for 1303 he is called *menestrallus senioris Regis*, an odd title for Edward I, because it was never given to a reigning monarch unless his son and heir had been crowned during his lifetime. It strikes a significant note, as though the *familiares* of the Prince's household were in the habit of calling the king, among themselves, ' the old man ', and mentally hastening the accession of the Prince. Henry de Blythe was with the king at Newcastle-upon-Tyne; the Prince was also there, and, since it was only a matter of sauntering from one household to the other, he went (or was summoned) to entertain the Prince on 8 May : ' To Henry de Blythe, the old king's minstrel, 6s. 8d. (£66-13s.-4d.) by gift of the Prince to buy himself a tunic (*tunica*). For entertaining the Prince at Newcastle-upon-Tyne.' (E101/363/18, f.22^r).

The second reference to him is to be found in another of the Prince's Wardrobe books, but for 1306/7, He and Peter the Guitarist were commanded to join the Prince's household for 52 days. (See *Gitarier, Le*)

There were other Blythes at Court, notably Richard de Blythe, King's Trumpeter; John de Blythe, valet of the Prince's (and later Edward II's) household; Master Adam de Blythe, one of the clerks of the Earl Marshal; Collard de Blythe (position unknown), a squire of Sir John de Cromwell. The Henry of the Payroll may have been related to one or more of them.

Harpeur Leuesque de Duresme (Le). F.

On the Payroll this entry has been squashed in immediately preceding the one referring to *Gilleme . . . qui est oue Le Patriarke*, and the 10s. given to him has been entered on the left hand side. He was another harper of bishop Bek.

Henri le Gigour. F.
   Corraud son compaignon. F.
   Le tierz Gigour. F.

Heinrich, the *geige*-player, with his companion, Conrad and ' the third *geige*-player.'

Heinrich and Conrad were resident at Court and classed as King's minstrels. The first reference to them appears in the rolls of daily issues of bread and wine for April 1299, (E101/

356/13). Although the clerk has entered only the one word, *Gygors*, it is safe to assume that Heinrich and Conrad are meant, because no other *gigours* at court are mentioned in any of the manuscripts I have read. Heinrich's name was easy to convert to its French equivalent but the clerks experienced difficulty with that of Conrad. From time to time he appears variously as Girard, Cunrad, Corraud, and even Sconrad but there are enough entries with the correct spelling to prove that his name was, in fact, Conrad.

A book of prests for 1305/6 proves that they were on court wages (E101/368/27, ff.46^v, 47^v.), yet the majority of the entries in the Wardrobe books are relative to the many gifts which Edward I made them. They illustrate the care he took of them and, by inference, how much he enjoyed their music. Sometimes the gifts took the form of simple *largesse* : ' To Henry and Girard (sic), *geige*-players from Germany, minstrels of the King, 13s. 4d. (£133-6s.-8d.) to each of them, by gift of the King, on Saturday, 29 April (1306) at Kempsey (Worcs.). Paid into their own hands.' (Add. MSS., 7966, f.66^v); ' To the two German *geige*-players, 2 marks (£266-13s-4d.), by gift of the King on Sunday, 30 April, at Kempsey.' (*Ibid*.); ' To the two *geige*-players, 2 marks on Sunday, 16 July (1301) at Berwick-on-Tweed.' (E101/359/5, ff.3^v, 8^v); ' To the two *geige*-players, half a mark each on Thursday, 17 October (1302), at Dundee.' (Add. MSS., 35292, f.12^r). On other occasions money was given to them to buy things; for example, a saddle and girth for their pack-horse, firewood for their rooms, clothes for themselves, litter for their horses and straw for their beds and for other ' certain necessaries '. (Add. MSS., 7966, ff.67^r, 69^r; E101/364/13, f.32^v; E101/368/6, ff.8^r, 21^r ; E101/369/11, f.102^v).

While they were in England they must have met with some unexpected experiences. French was the language of Court but, as the rolls of the issues of bread and wine indicate, when they ate in hall they met Englishmen, Frenchmen, Welshmen, Flemings and Brabançons, all talking Anglo-French, but all, no doubt, reverting at times to their native tongues. At the end of seven years' residence, Heinrich and Conrad, unless they were singularly unlike their modern compatriots, would have returned to Germany with a smattering or more of several new languages, as well as with some tunes and songs peculiar to England and Wales. In like manner the King's Harpers and the Welsh squires would have added some German music and song to their repertoires. Incidentally, the two Germans would have seen a great deal of Britain while they were here. They played to the king from London to Perth.

The third *geige*-player, although not given a name on the Payroll, was another Conrad, ' a certain *geige*-player, Conrad le Pefer, from Germany, who came to the King by command of the King of Germany and stayed in England for a certain time during the months of March and April.' (E101/369/11, f.100ᵛ) This was in 1306. He should have gone home in the middle of April, because the clerk recorded a gift to him from the king, of 60s. (£600) to cover his expenses while he was here and for his return journey home. The king had granted him licence to leave by 10 April but by that time the Prince's knighting had been decided upon and Heinrich and Conrad were also due to go home after it; so Conrad le Pefer stayed on for another six weeks; hence the appearance of ' *le tierz Gigour* ' on the Payroll, an unexpected addition which has been squeezed in after the names of Heinrich and Conrad.

When the festivities were over, all three returned to Germany. Not only do their names vanish from the accounts but John de Drokenesford, when making up the books in 1306 stated in a roundabout way that the German minstrels' long sojourn at the English court had come to an end. In his *Receipts and Expenses of the Wardrobe* for 1305/6 he totted up how much had been spent on them : ' To Henry and Conrad, King's *geige*-players, minstrels from Germany, staying in Court by the King's command, making their minstrelsy at the King's wish, £12-18s.-8d. (approx. £2,600); by gift of the King, for them to buy certain necessaries for themselves; in cash, given to the same from time to time by order of the King during the 30th, 31st, 32nd, 33rd and 34th years of his reign.' (1300-1306) (E101/369/11, f.102ᵛ) After this there were no more entries concerning them; and there is no evidence that they accompanied the king to Scotland after the knighting.

Henri de Nushom.   F.

Elsewhere in the accounts, his name is spelt *Neusom, Newsom,* so that it is not certain whether he was Henry de Newsham or Henry de Newsome.

There are six Newshams : two in Durham, one each in Northumberland, Lancs., Yorks., and Lincs. Newsome is in Yorks., an ecclesiastical district SE of Huddersfield.

Henry was a harper. In 1306 he was probably one of the Prince's minstrels, because later on, under Edward II, he was one of the king's harpers. His name never appears in the Wardrobe books of Edward I. The earliest reference to him, other than that in the Payroll, is dated 1322/3 : ' To Henry de Neusom, harper, 20s. for his winter clothing.' (Stowe MSS. 553.) In 1325 he was one of the king's minstrels being issued new livery to accompany the king on his flight to France. (E101/381/11, Frag.) He remained loyal to Edward II to the end. He is last heard of on Thursday, 30 January 1326, playing to the king and the Countess of Norfolk, Thomas of Brotherton's wife, at Hevingham (Norfolk): 'Paid to Henry Newsom, harper of the king, and to Richardyn, citole-player of the king, who made their minstrelsies in the presence of the King and the Countess Marshal, who had dined with the king on that day, 20s. each.' (Soc. Antiq. MS. 121, *Accounts of the King's Chamber*, f.49ᵛ or p. 50).

Henuer. F.

Unidentified. Perhaps a sergeant-at-arms. See *Lucat.*

Hughethun Le Harpour. F.

Hughethun represents an older form of *Huggin*, the diminutive of Hugh or Hugo. Today, perhaps, he would be called *Hughie.*

On the Payroll he is described as being the ' *compaignon* ' or fellow-harper of William de Morley and John de Newentone, while Adam de Clitheroe is called the ' *compaignon* ' of Hughethun. All four were styled King's Harpers.

There were two musicians at Court who were called ' Hugh the harper ' : one was Hugh de la Rose, whose surname appears to have been taken from Castle de la Rose, 7 miles SW of Carlisle; the other was Hugh de Naunton, who hailed, in all probability, from the tiny Cotswold village of Naunton, 5 miles W of Stow-on-the-Wold. Both were in court at the time of the knighting; both were at Lanercost during the king's last illness.

The weight of evidence supplied by the Wardrobe accounts and other records favours the view that the Hughethun of the Payroll was Hugh de la Rose. In a Wardrobe journal of 1304/5 he is definitely called *Citharista Regis* and, as such, received part of his wages, together with the other three : ' King's Harpers. To Gillot de Morle, Johann de Newenton, Hugo de la Rose, Adam de Clyderowe, 20s. each, on account, for their wages; by the hand of Master Gillot, on Saturday, 8 January. (At Kingston-Lacy, where the king had been keeping Christmas.) This entry proves that Hugh de la Rose was one of the quartet holding the title ' King's Harpers.' Hugh de Naunton, although he entered court on wages on 20 May 1304, was never called King's Harper, in so many words. Another proof that Hugh de la Rose had been King's Harper for a long time before 1304 appears in the *Fine Rolls*, which prints a grant under Privy Seal which Edward I made to Hugh le Harpour ' for good service in parts of Scotland and elsewhere.' This Hugh could not have been Hugh de Naunton, who had only just entered court on wages. The grant was a piece of land ' of 12 acres and a rood of waste in Inglewode Forest . . . in the place called ' Rawebankes ' It was therefore right in the part of the country from which Hugh came. He was allowed to enclose it, bring it back to cultivation and hold it in perpetuity for a yearly rent of 12s. 3d. ($£122$-10s.) (Vol. I, 515, 523).

A book of prests for 1305/6 testifies to his being on duty with the king at Lanercost : ' To Hugo de la Rose, King's Harper, 10s., on account, for his wages; paid into his own hands on Tuesday, 1 November, at Lanercost.' (E101/368,/27, f.65[r]). In the same year, in company with King Caupenny, King Robert, Adam de Clitheroe, John de Newentone and John Drake, he received his 27s. 6d., on account, to cover the cost of his blue and striped cloth and lamb's fur for his *roba*. Until he is lost sight of at the end of the reign, he remained in his distinguished position as *Citharista Regis*.

Hugo Daa, citharista.   L.

Huw Da, ' Good Hugh '; a Welsh harper, who probably came to the knighting in the train of the L'Estrange family. Sir John L'Estrange was there with his taborer.

John, second Lord Strange of Knockin (Salop.) held 536½

assarts in the manor of Ellesmere, including Colmere and Hampton, and, in a commission to arrent the wastes there and ' to deliver the same to the tenants thereof ', a list of these tenants is given, among whom, with several others bearing Welsh names, is a *Hugo Da* (*CPR.* 1319, 372.) John of Knockin died in 1311 but his son, another John, was a minor in the king's ward in 1318. Later on, when he came of age, he led a troop of Knockin soldiers to join the forces of Thomas of Lancaster. He was taken prisoner at Boroughbridge and died in the following year, 1323.

During the reign of Edward I the member of the L'Estrange family who would have been most well-known to courtiers and clerks was Roger L'Estrange of Ellesmere. He had been often summoned to serve in the army, had been sent to Rome on the king's business, was Justice of the Forest South of Trent and was one of the barons who appended his seal to the famous letter to the Pope in 1300/1301.

If the Hugo Da, who was one of the L'Estrange's tenants, was the harper who came to the Prince's knighting, he would have been well-known; the clerks would not have bothered to put down ' *Hugo Daa, citharista domini R.* (*or Sir J.*) *L'Estrange*; ' *Hugo Daa, citharista* ' would have been sufficient.

J.

Jake de Vescy. L.
James de Vescy. His name occurs also in the French list but only in a clerk's note to the effect that he collected a half-mark *largesse* for Gillot de Roos. In this instance his name is spelt *Jacke*.

He was one of *La Commune*. His name suggests that he was a minstrel of Lady Isabella de Vescy, widow of Sir John de Vescy of Alnwick (Northumb.). Sir John had been the king's *Secretarius* (confidential adviser) and one of his closest friends. It was he who had negotiated the marriages of the three princesses, Margaret, Eleanor and Elizabeth. Lady Isabella was his second wife, a kinswoman of Queen Eleanor and sister of Henry de Beaumont. In 1288 Sir John died, aged 44 and *sine prole*. The king took care of his friend's widow, granting her many favours, among them, in 1305, the custody of Bamborough

Castle. Her brother, Henry de Beaumont, was also looked after. At the time of the Prince's knighting he was a member of the Prince's household. (See *Janin de la Toure*.)

It goes without saying that Sir John and Lady Isabella were closely connected with Court. After her husband had negotiated the marriage of Princess Margaret in 1290, Lady Isabella accompanied the fifteen-year-old bride to Brabant and remained there with her for nine months. Later, as widow and dowager, she became chaperone and friend of her namesake, Isabella, Edward II's girl-queen. Some entries in a household roll of Prince Edward, when he was eight years old (1292), gives an insight into her position as intimate guest of the royal family : ' On this feast of Pentecost, there were, with the Lord Prince, Edward (Balliol), son of the King of Scotland, Lady Agnes de Valence, the Prior of Merton, Master John de Lacy . . . and Lady de Vescy . . . On this (Whit) Monday came the Castellan de Bergles and with him three knights . . . On the same day Lady de Valence and Lady de Vescy and the son of the King of Scotland departed after breakfast.' (*Issue Rolls*, 109.)

Both Isabella and her brother exercised such influence over Edward II and his household that the Lords Ordainers banished them from court in 1310 but their absence was short-lived. As soon as Gaveston had been beheaded, they were back and, when Edward and his queen went to France in 1313, Lady Isabella was one of the company who travelled with the queen. (*Foedera*, 212.)

If, as seems most likely, Jake de Vescy were her minstrel, his presence in *La Commune* is readily accounted for.

Janin de Brebant.   F.

One of the few foreign minstrels other than the visitors. He was the vielle-player of Lord Hugh le Despenser, the Elder, whose son, Hugh, the Younger, was knighted by the Prince.

John, the young Duke of Brabant, had lived in England for five years before he married Princess Margaret. He had his own household and Brabantines would have been numerous in it. Also, the fact that the Duke of Brabant was the King of England's son-in-law would have been more than sufficient to open the way for minstrels from Brabant to seek their fortunes in English baronial households. The Despensers, although not yet the prime favourites of the Prince, were on the way to becoming so. The only reference to Janin de Brabant that I have come across, in the Prince's Wardrobe book for 1306/7, proved that they were welcome visitors to his household : ' To John of Brebant, vielle-player of Lord Hugh le Despenser, coming to the Prince's court in the train of his master and making his minstrelsy there in the presence of the Lord Prince and other noblemen, in the month of February, 40s. (£400) by gift of the Prince, the money being given him by Master W. de Boudon; at Wetheral (Cumb.)' (Add MSS. 22923 and MS. Harley 5001. f.37ʳ).

Janin Le Lutour. F.

John, the king's lutenist; a man of importance and substance. He is described in the Patent and Close Rolls as a citizen of London but they do not happen to mention where in the city he lived. According to Stowe, the Guildhall Chapel was built c. 1299 and Newcourt (*History of the Diocese of London*, Vol. I, 361) says it was founded for five chaplains, ' whereof one of them was to be Custos, to celebrate therein divine Offices for the Souls of (among others) *John Luter and Isabel his wife.*' If this John were Janin, it would go to prove that, like most of the royal minstrels, he lived in the area between Cheapside and Thames Street.

My earliest reference to him occurs in the counter-roll of domestic payments, 1285, where he appears as Johann Le Leutour, in the list of the king's minstrels. Thereafter he appears regularly in the Wardrobe accounts, receiving his squire's wages and his issues of summer and winter clothing. He seems to have had some special relationship with the king's brother, Edmund, earl of Lancaster, and Henry de Lacy, earl of Lincoln, because both were instrumental in getting the king to relieve him of all the taxes and burdens which went with being a king's subject and a citizen of London. This was in 1295, when he had been King's Lutenist for ten years or more : ' 26 August 1295, at Westminster. Exemption for life, at the instance of Edmund, the king's brother and of Henry de Lacy, earl of Lincoln, and with the assent of the commonalty of the city of London, to John le Leutur, citizen of London, from all tallages, aids, watches and contributions whatsoever, which might be exacted from him by the king or his ministers, by reason of the said John's lands, tenements, rents and other things, or merchandize within the said city or without; and from being put on assizes, juries or recognizances, or from being made mayor, sheriff, escheator, coroner, reeve, alderman or any other minister there against his will.' (*CPR.* (1295), 144.) In modern terms this means that he paid no taxes at all and was excused all civic duties. A truly splendid gift. He took good care, and who would not, to see that the taxmen made no mistakes. In 1304 the Sergeant of the Guildhall and the bailiffs of the city tried to force him to pay the aid of one-fifteenth, which Parliament had voted the king. John promptly got out his charter, marched to the Guildhall in protest, and also sent a letter of complaint to the king. Edward I, then with the army in Scotland, wrote immediately to the city's assessors of tallage and ordered that ' John le Leutur, citizen of that city ' be acquitted of the tax and released from ' any distress that they may have levied for it.' (*CCR.* (1304), 135.) In the Guildhall it was found that the clerks had forgotten to cross John's name off the tax-roll. ' It was thereupon ordered that his name should be removed from the Roll and that he should not in future be assessed.' (*CLL. C.*, 138) Henceforth all was peace and no tax.

Whatever the nature of the connection between him and the two earls was, it lasted throughout the reign, for in 1300 and 1305 he accompanied the earl of Lincoln (Edmund of Lancaster had died in 1296) to France ' on the king's service.' (*CPR.* (1300), 542; (1305), 380.)

With his old friends and colleagues, Ricard Rounlo, Gillot de Roos, King Nicholas Morel and Thomas, the Court Fool, he made his minstrelsy in the presence of the Count and Countess of Holland on their wedding-day in 1296. (Add. MSS. 7965, f.52^r), receiving as *largesse* the equivalent of £500. In 1303 the young Prince of Wales made him a gift of £10 (£2,000) ' as a help toward building his house in London.' (E101/363/18, f.23^v) Although he had no need to lend money under recognizance, he did so out of choice. In the winter of 1302/3 he lent £50 (£10,000) to two fellow-citizens, who were probably his personal friends, because one of them, John de Triple, used to act as his attorney when he was out of the country. (*CLL.* B. 122.) What a respected standing he had in the city can be inferred from another entry in London's letter-books; he received pledges, sealed with the seal of the attorney of a certain tailor, Adam, which were sent to him ' for safe custody '. (*CLL.* B. 135.)

When he was not in London he was either abroad on the king's service or else accompanying the king himself. He was in Scotland in the year of the great victory at Falkirk, 1298, and was riding on a ' pommely grey rouncy ' (dapple-grey hackney), a fine mount, for it was valued at 8 marks (well over £1,000).

At the time of Edward I's death John had been a royal minstrel for more than 22 years. The fact that he was building a house for himself in London in 1303 might imply that he was contemplating retiring when the reign of his old master should come to an end. Details in the accounts relative to his wages and livery help to strengthen the conjecture. In 1306/7 he was on duty at court for only 50 days out of the 365, and he received no livery for winter and summer *robae*, because he did not attend the Christmas and Midsummer festivals to collect it. (E101/364/13, f.22ᵛ). Many, perhaps all, of those 50 days were spent with the dying king at Lanercost. After 1307 his name disappears from the Wardrobe books.

Janin Lorganistre. F.

Although all entries concerning him date from 1307, John must have been the minstrel of Edward I before he became that of his son, because his name appears in the list of debts of the Wardrobe drawn up at the end of the reign. There were £4-6s.-3d. (£862-10s.) owing to him which represented back-wages for a considerable period of time, since, unlike the great string-men squires of court, he received only the minstrel's regulation wage of 4½d. per day. (E101/357/15, f.25ʳ).

For the next seven years his name appears regularly in the Wardrobe accounts, as receiving wages and livery, although his actual attendances do not seem to have been of long dura-tion. For example, in 1309 he was in Court for only 87 days and in 1310/11 for 81. (MS. Cott. Nero C viii, f.5ʳ; E101/374/5, f.29^r). In the August of 1307, however, when the newly-recalled Gaveston gave a banquet for Edward II near Dumfries, John was there, performing with his friends and colleagues, William of Queenhithe, Janin le Trompour and Januche le Nakerer, and receiving the customary *largesse* of 20s. (£200). (E101/373/15, f.19^r).

His identity is uncertain, because in one entry he is called John *Gallicus* and this immediately raises a doubt as to whether this organist is the same person with whom the records have been dealing before that date, which is 1311. The epithet seems to suggest that John Gallicus was the organist of the new queen, Isabella of France, and that the John of the earlier records was a different person.

The most interesting facts about John *Gallicus* which have come to light are those concerning the training of a little orphan boy, Tommy Scot, on whom Queen Isabella took pity sometime between 1309 and 1310, when she herself was only 15 or 16 years old. She found him either at Berwick-on-Tweed or somewhere in the lowlands of Scotland, and brought him with her to York : ' To little Thomelin the Scot, an orphan boy, to whom the Queen, moved by compassion and love, has granted food and clothing out of her Almonry, the price of 4 ells (5 yards) of blanket and a quilt, bought for the bed of the same Thomelin through John of Stepney, merchant of London . . .6s. 6d. (£65).' ' To the same, from the Queen's Almonry, the price of 4 ells of mixed cloth, for a gown to be made for him . . .8s. 2d. (£81-13s.-4d.) ' For an *alphabeticus* for teaching little Tommy, 3d. (£2-10s.). Paid into his own hands at York, on 20 January. (MS. Cott. Nero. C. viii, ff.135^r, 157^v).

By 1311 he had been sent to London to be brought up by John the Organist's wife : ' To the same (Thomelin), sent to London to stay with Agnes, the wife of John *Gallicus*, the organist, to learn his letters from her . . .40s. (£400), for the expenses of his wife from the Feast of St. Michael (29 September) of the present, fifth year (1311), up to the same feast the following year. And for little necessaries bought for his use, together with a plaster for putting on the scab on his head, 12s. 8d. (£126-14s.-4d.) from the Queen's Almonry; by the hand of the said Agnes, who received the money in the Queen's

Wardrobe on 17 August of the sixth year (1312) at Eltham.'
(*Ibid.*, f.140ʳ)

What happened to Tommy in the years which followed is
not recorded. He may have been trained by John to be a
chorister/musician or have been taken into the household of his
benefactress as a valet.

After 1312 John's name disappears from the records. There
is no further mention of either John the Organist or John
Gallicus, the Organist. 1312 was the year in which Gaveston
was beheaded, and Edward II and Isabella went to France.
Two years later, at the court of one of Edward I's dearest
allies and friends, James II, King of Arragon, a John the
Organist, *Anglicus*, obtained permission from King James to
travel through his kingdom, under his protection, playing the
organ and, by his express command, giving lessons to Catalon-
ian organists.[8] One wonders whether this may have been the
John the Organist of the Payroll, the minstrel of Edward I,
who, foreseeing the miserable state into which England was
about to fall under its wayward, incorrigible monarch, had
betaken himself to a safer, more peaceful and at the same time
highly cultured court, where minstrels of all nations were
warmly welcomed. If he were, he would have been assured of
the patronage of his old master's friend, the kind of patronage
which was generously afforded to John *Anglicus*.

Janin de la Toure, trounpour. L. *Janin de La Tour.* F.
                                      son Compaignon. F.

Janin was one of the trumpeters of Henry de Beaumont. His
name appears only once in the records of 1307—1327; in
1310, on 14 July; ' To Johann de la Tour, trumpeter of Lord
Henry de Beaumont, 20s. (£200) into his own hands, by gift
of the king.' (E101/373/10, f.7ᵛ). His fellow-trumpeter remains nameless.

Henry de Beaumont was the younger son of Louis de Brienne,
Vicomte de Beaumont. Louis' father was John de Brienne,
King of Jerusalem and Emperor of Constantinople. His mother
was Berengaria, daughter of Alfonso IX, King of Léon.

---

[8] *Cantors und Ministrers in den Diensten der Könige von Katalonien-Arragonien im
14 Jahrhundert*, Von H. Angles, (Leipsig 1925) s. 57.

Alfonso's son was Ferdinand III, King of Castile, and Ferdinand was the father of Eleanor of Castile, queen of Edward I. This is why both Henry and his sister, Isabella, were called kinsman and kinswoman of the Queen. It also explains why Henry was brought up as a squire in the household of the Prince of Wales. Although favoured by Edward II, he turned against his royal cousin and it is said that he was one of the people who prevented the planned escape of Edward II from Berkeley Castle. (See *Jake de Vescy*.)

Januche, Trumpour Monsire Le Prince.   F.
    For his fellow-trumpeter, see *Gillot*.
    It is by no means easy to identify Januche, because he appears in the records as *Johann* and *Janin* as well as *Januche* and *Janoche*. Where references to the Prince's trumpeters by name, *Johann* and *Willelm*, are explicit, (E101/360/10, mem. 1.) it is fairly safe to conclude that these two were the *Januche* and *Gillot* of the Payroll, but further than that one dares not go, because the Wardrobe books prove that *Januche* and *Gillot* could have been different Johns and Williams at different times.
    In the counter-roll of domestic payments, 1285, there occurs, under the heading ' King's Minstrels ', ' *Janin* the minstrel of the Lord Edward.' At that time the Prince was about twelve months old, which suggests that Janin was his ceremonial trumpeter. In 1302, when he was 18 years old, the Prince had two Johns as his trumpeters : *John Garsie*, a Londoner, and *John de Catalonia*, a Spaniard. It is uncertain which of these would have been the Januche of the Payroll. An earlier entry in a fragment of the Wardrobe journal for 1300/1301 does not help, since it merely records : ' To Johann the trumpeter of Edward, the King's son, 6s. 8d., on account, for his wages.' (E101/359/5, f.2^r). Again, although John Garsie and John de Catalonia appear together in the Prince's Wardrobe book for 1302/3, neither of them is expressly called Januche : ' To Thomasin, the vielle-player, John Garsie, John de Catalonia, trumpeters, and John le Nakerer, the Prince's minstrels, making their minstrelsy in his presence at Newbattle (Edinburgh) on Trinity Sunday, 2 June, 12s. each (£122-10s.) by gift of the lord Prince to buy black silk cloaks for themselves.' (E101/363/18, f.21^v). Further references to them in the same Wardrobe

book are tantalizing; at one moment the clerk gives them no names : ' for the making of four penoncelles of beaten gold, with the Prince's arms on them, for his trumpeters; and for painting and fringes, 26s. (£260).'; at the next, he is calling one of them *Janoche* : ' To John le Nakerer and Janoche the Trumpeter of the Prince, making their minstrelsy in the presence of the lord Prince at Newcastle-upon-Tyne, on Monday, 6 May, 8s. (£80) each, by gift of the Prince, to buy two haketons for themselves. Paid by the hand of Robert de Durham there.' (f.22ʳ). On the verso of the same folio John de Catalonia becomes *Janin* : ' To Janin de Catalonia, Prince's trumpeter, 13s. 4d. (£133-6s.-8d.) by gift of the Prince, to buy a brass trumpet for himself.' Finally, they are given their full names once more and it is now John le Nakerer who becomes *Janot* : ' To Master John Garsie and John de Catalonia, trumpeters (and) Janot le Nakerer, the Prince's minstrels, 33s. (£330) (being) the cost of 3 habergeons and 3 iron collarettes, bought from Richard the habergeon-maker and given to them in January, at Dunfermline.' (f.23ʳ). In another of the Prince's Wardrobe books for 1303/4 they appear like Tweedledum and Tweedledee : ' . . . 2 silver trumpets, bought at the same time by the Prince and given, by his order, to *Janin* and *Januche*, his trumpeters, for their good service to him in the Scottish war . . . ' (Add. MSS. 8835, f.130ᵛ (*Jocalia*)). On the Payroll only Januche appears, yet in 1307, Janin appears again, from 29 July to 20 October, that is, after the death of Edward I. (E101/373/15, f.5ᵛ). Which John was he ? Sometime in 1307 John Garsie died, leaving a little boy of eight years old, also called John, who was given into the custody of a London skinner, William de Pountfreyt, together with 20 marks (approx. £2,800) which his father had left for his upbringing. (*CLL. C.*, 208).

After 1307 Janin and Januche are lost sight of in the accounts but years later, in 1323, when Edward II, flushed with his triumph over Thomas of Lancaster, was handing over the lands and property of his hated uncle's minstrels to his own, he made a grant ' to John le Trumpour, for good service, of the houses and lands late of William le Tabourer in Pontefract and Friston, at the yearly rent of as much as William used to render for the same.' (*Cal. Fine Rolls*, III, 250).

Janyn Le Citoler. F.
Unidentified.
Edward II had two citole-players, other than or after the
time of Janyn : Thomas Dynys, or Thomas Citoler; and Jiron
Vala, or Yomi Vala. They occur 1312-1325 and were ' *com-
paignons* '. (MS. Cott. Nero. C. viii, f.195^v; E101/375/8, f.29^v;
E101/381/11. frag.)

Janyn Le Sautreour, qui est oue Monsire de Percy. F.
Sir Henry or Lord Percy, for he was made baron by writ in
1298, was one of Edward I's veteran knights. He was about
33 years old at the time of the knighting. In 1294 he had been
summoned for military service in Gascony but when the king
had to postpone his expedition to France on account of the
rising of the Welsh, he accompanied him on his march into
Wales. In the following year he served in Scotland and was
knighted by Edward I after the capture of Berwick. He fought
at Dunbar, was made Warden of Galloway and Ayrshire,
was Justice in Dumfries, and Regent during the king's absence
in Flanders in 1297.
After the death of Edward I, he joined in the opposition to
Edward II and was with Thomas of Lancaster at Newcastle
when the king only just evaded capture. He was also with the
earls of Pembroke and Surrey when Gaveston was caught at
Scarborough but he did not live to see the miserable outcome
of Edward's subsequent behaviour, for he died in October 1314.

Jaques Le Mascun. F.
A court minstrel. He was one of the select group of musicians
who entertained Princess Mary at Burstwick in 1304. (See
Druet, Ernolet.)
His name, in English, would have been James Mason. The
surname, *le Mascun, le Mazon,* was common in France and
England.

Johan de Mochelneye. F.
The abbey of Muchelney (Somerset) was a Benedictine
house of ' large and fine structure '. (*Monasticon*, II, 356) In
1306 the abbot was John de Hentone but I have found no
evidence that he was present at the knighting, in which case

John might have been his minstrel. Like most other wealthy abbeys, Muchelney was frequently called upon to provide food and lodging for royal servants no longer fit for duty. In 1309 Richard Devenays, valet of the Pantry, ' who long served the late king ' was sent there ' for the necessaries of his life in food and clothing for himself and a groom, and for a chamber to dwell in.' (*CCR.* (1309), 232). Again, in 1317 Thomas Prest, ' who long served the king, is sent to the abbot and convent of Muchelneye, to receive the same allowance as Peter le Messager deceased, had in that house.' (*Ibid.*, (1317), 452)

Johannes, Citharista J. de Clyntone. L.
The domestic harper of Sir John de Clynton.
Sir John was about 46 years old in 1306. His presence at the knighting needs no explanation, for, like Lord Percy, and many others there, he was a veteran knight of Edward I. He served in both the Scottish and French wars, and, in 1298, led a contingent of Welshmen to Carlisle. In 1300 he was made knight of the shire and, immediately after the knighting of the Prince, was sent to Ponthieu on the Prince's business.
Edward II gave him posts of great responsibility. He was made Constable of Wallingford Castle in 1308, and Seneschal of Ponthieu at the same time or soon after. Unfortunately, he did not live long to enjoy his honours. He died in January 1311. His residence and estates were in Warwickshire.

Johannes, Trumpator domini R. Filii Pagani. L.
Lord Robert fitz Payn was another veteran of the Scottish wars. He was King's banneret in 1297 and was at the siege of Caerlaverock in the company of Earl Warenne. In the same year he was made baron by writ. In 1304 he was made Constable of Corfe Castle. Since he had had livery of his father's lands in 1281, he was probably between 40 and 50 at the time of the feast and had come to Westminster not only to be at the king's service, but to see his 21-year-old son and heir, Robert, knighted by the Prince.
Under Edward II he became Steward of the King's Household, Constable of Winchester Castle, Justice of the Forest South of Trent and, in 1313, after Gaveston's death, accompanied the king and queen to France. He saw the end of Gaveston

but did not live to witness the king's folly with regard to the Despensers. He died on 30 August 1315.

John, his trumpeter, is mentioned once in the Wardrobe books. On Thursday, 6 January, 1305/6, when the court was at Kingston-Lacy, he gave a virtuoso performance before Edward I : ' To John the trumpeter of Lord Robert fitz Payn, playing his trumpet in the presence of the King, on the day of the Epiphany of the Lord, 20s. (£200) by gift of the King, into his own hands.' (E101/369/11, f.99ᵛ)

Johannes, le vilour domini J. Renaud. L.

The vielle-player of Lord John Renaud (fitz Reginald), a veteran of the Welsh wars and aged about 50. He served overseas in 1297 and was summoned to serve against the Scots in 1298, 1301 and 1306. Hence his attendance at Westminster. He died when the troubles of Edward II's reign were just beginning, in June 1310.

Johannes, Waffrarius Comitisse Lancastrie. L.

John, the waferer of the Countess of Lancaster. See *Citharista Comitisse Lancastrie*.

Johannes le Barbor. L.

Le Barbor, le Barber, was a fairly common surname. Thomas le Barbor was one of Henry III's sergeants; Robert le Barber was a valet of Sir Hugh le Despenser, the Elder, and Roger le Barbor was one of Edward I's sergeants-at-arms.

The John le Barbor of the Payroll was a royal squire. In the *Gascon Rolls* (ff.489-90), in a mandate from Edward I to Gilbert Pecche, Constable of Bordeaux, concerning valuation and compensation for the horses of his knights and squires, both John le Barbor and another minstrel, John de Cressy, are mentioned : ' one iron-grey horse for John le Barbor, valued at 8 marks, and one Powis horse for John de Cressy, valued at 8 marks.' John de Cressy was one of the minstrels who staged the miracle-plays for Queen Margaret at Lanercost in 1307. Some ten years later, John, if he be the same John le Barbor, was a groom of the King's Chamber. His name appears in a list of the officers of Edward II's household ; ' To John le Barbor (and) Adam le Waffrer, 4s. 8d.

(£46-13s.-4d.) each for their shoes for the whole year.' (MS. Soc. Antiq., 120, 69ʳ).

Johannes du Chat, cum domino J. de Barr.. L.

Perhaps a minstrel of Sir John de Barres, special envoy of King Philip of France. In 1300 Sir John had been sent to England with Peter de Mouncy, King's Clerk and Canon of Angers, to beg Edward to grant a truce to the Scots. In a letter of Edward I to King Philip, in which he acceded to the latter's request, the two envoys are referred to as ' Mestre Pierre ' and ' *Monsire John de Barres, dist Piau de Chat, Chivaler.*' (*Foedera*, II, pt. 1, 924/5).[9]

Before they returned to France, Master Peter and Sir John Catskin were given two silver cups each by King Edward and Queen Margaret. (*LQG.*, 335/6).

There is no incontrovertible evidence that Sir John came over again for the Prince's knighting but there is every possibility that he did, seeing that Edward was about to launch another campaign against the Scots.

Johannes Le Croudere. L.

One of *La Commune* and therefore probably attached to one of the royal households. The following entry may refer to him : ' Sunday, 23 August 1304, at Jedburgh (Roxburghshire). Pardon to John de le (*sic*) Crouther for the death of Richard del Croft and for (other) homicides.' (*CPR.*, 254). Cf. *John de Trenham* and *Thomas le Crouther.*

Johannes Le Crouther de Salopia. L.

John, the *vintenarius*, soldier-minstrel from Shropshire.

An entry in the Wardrobe book for 1300 will help to explain why he was at the knighting festivities : ' To John le Crouder, *vintenarius*, for his wages and those of the 20 archers-on-foot, first taken on wages on 11 July; from that day up to the 15th day of the same month, both days included; that is, for 5 days, 18s. 4d. (£183-6s.-8d.) The dates prove that this little band was enlisted for the siege of Caerlaverock Castle. The author

[9] In the *Foedera Piau* has been either misread or misprinted as *Pian*. See *CPR* (1300) 541; *CCR* (1303) 106.

of *Le Siege de Karlaverok* pays tribute to the infantry-bowmen, one of whom was so excellent a marksman that, when one of the Scots was pushing out the flag of surrender, he shot an arrow through his hand and into his cheek. John le Crouther was a valuable man to the king; he could recruit a company of archers at need and was, no doubt, as skilled himself at shooting as he was at playing the *crwth*.

Johannes de Newentone. F.

King's Harper. There are at least a dozen Newingtons in Britain, from London to outside Edinburgh. Fortunately for us but not for him, John had his houses robbed in 1304 while he was with the king in Scotland, and the commission set up to enquire into the case solves the problem : ' A commission of oyer and terminer to Ralph de Sandwych and Robert de Burghersh, to enquire into a case of robbery in which some persons . . . by night broke into the houses of John le Harpur of Newenton, at Newenton, in the county of Kent.' (*CPR.*, 283.) The modern parish and village of Newington is situated NW of Sittingbourne.

From c. 1298 to 1300 the four King's Harpers were: Walter de Stourton, Nicholas le Blund (or, Blond), Adam de Clitheroe and William de Morley. Sometime between these two dates Walter died. A man called Henry de Grey owed Walter's wife, Maud, £100 (£20,000) and he acknowledged the debt under recognizance on 1 April 1299. In this acknowledgement Maud is referred to as being ' late the wife of Walter de Sturton.' (*CCR.*, 299.)

Walter, therefore, had died before April 1299 and John de Newentone was appointed King's Harper in his stead. The Wardrobe accounts supply a wealth of evidence concerning him from 1300 onwards. By means of the numerous entries relating to the payment of his wages, his movements can be traced and the names of his fellow-harpers discovered. For example, in 1302/3, from December to October, he was with the king at Hungerford (Berks.), Odiham (Hants.), London, Brechin (Forfarshire), Roxburgh, Perth, Dundee and Dunfermline. Up to 1303 his fellow-harpers were Adam, William and Nicholas, Adam and Willian constituting the first pair and Nicholas and himself the second, but toward the end of 1303

Nicholas either retired from service or died, because on 8 January 1304, when the king was keeping Christmas at Kingston-Lacy, the four King's Harpers are named in the Wardrobe accounts as being ' Gillot de Morle, Johann de Newenton, Hugo de la Rose, Adam de Clyderowe.' (E101/368/6, f.13ʳ).

How much Edward I liked John and appreciated his minstrelsy may be judged from the costliness of a gift he gave him while they were staying at Dunfermline in the winter of 1303/4 : ' A gold clasp, worth 8 marks (£966-13s.-4d.), given by the King to Johann de Newentone, the harper, on Tuesday, 4 February, at Dunfermline.' (Add. MSS. 8835, f.122ᵛ).

The Exchequer accounts do not provide much significant detail concerning him other than to indicate where he went and how often he was paid his wages, yet, somehow, he seems to have come alive, if only because of the ordinariness of the clerks' statements. Like so many of the king's intimate servants, he appears so often and so regularly that he impresses himself upon the mind of the reader and acquires a genuine, if vague, personality. In 1306/7 he was dressed in blue and green and blue and striped, with lamb's fur trimming. (E101/369/16, ff.9ᵛ, 10ᵛ).

All four harpers were, at some time or other, at Lanercost, soothing the pain of the old king but it was John—at least, according to the records that have survived—who was with him at Burgh-upon-Sands and who received the last 10s. of his wages on 6 July, the day before the king died.

After that John de Newenton's name disappears from the records. There is, however, an entry in the *Fine Rolls*, dated 20 July 1342, recording an order to the escheator in the county of Kent ' to take into the king's (Edward III's) hands the lands late of John of Newenton.' (Vol. V., 288). If this were John the harper it would indicate that he had retired to his home and died there. If he had entered the king's service in his twenties, he would have been about 70 at the time of his death.

Johannes Sagard. L.
    Unidentified. See *Sagard Crouther.*

Johannes de Trenham, Citharista. L.
    Trenham is Trentham (Staffs.)
    What position he held in the royal household in 1306 is not

clear. His name does not appear in the Wardrobe books. He and Adam de Grimshaw, whom he later killed, may have been attached to the Prince's household. Neither of them were King's Harpers under Edward I but the few records of them that are extant make it clear that Adam was dead by 1312 while John lived to become a royal harper until 1328.

It is pointless to speculate on the reasons for Adam's murder. Short tempers and ready knives so often settled disputes in those days. The king's pardon was granted to ' John le Harper of Trentham ' at the instance of his kinsman, one James Daudely, King's Yeoman. (*CPR.* (1312), 494.)

John became a royal harper in the households of both Edward II and Edward III. In 1328, by which time he had been in the royal service for over 20 years, Edward III sought to provide him with the usual safe retreat in a monastery. The one chosen was the abbey of Muchelney. On 24 February the king sent his messenger to the abbot and convent with a letter requesting that they should admit into their house John de Trentham, the king's harper, ' who had long served the king and his father, and that they will grant him, by letters patent, the same allowance as John le Foughlere, deceased, had therein by the late king's request.' (*CCR.*, 365.) And the abbot was asked to give his answer to the bearer. The answer was ' No '. Six months later the king tried the priory at Bath. John was sent with the messenger—an old trick, often played when the heads of religious houses were trying to avoid taking in yet another royal pensioner. The Prior and convent were asked to ' write back by the bearer hereof an account of their proceedings in this matter.' (*Ibid.*, 567.) The ruse appears to have succeeded, because no further requests on John's behalf have been recorded.

Johannes Le Waffrer le Roy.   L.

Master John Drake, King's Waferer.

In the counter-roll of domestic payments, 1285, the King's Waferer was Peter, who must have died shortly after, because an entry in a Wardrobe book for 1290 records indirectly the appointment of John : ' To John Drake, King's Waferer, who is in place of Peter the Waferer, deceased, 20s. for his winter *roba*. Thursday, 26 January, at Westminster.' (C47/4/5, f.37^r).

It is possible that behind the phrase ' *qui est loco Perotti Waffrarii*', lies the fact that John had been Peter's groom and deputy and that, on his master's death, he had been promoted in office. There is record of a John the Waferer living in Hart Street, in the parish of St. Olave in 1267/8. In that year the Prior and convent of Holy Trinity, Aldgate, granted a piece of land, with houses on it, to ' John le Waffrer ', for which he was to pay 9s. (£90) per annum in rent and was to undertake to maintain the buildings in good repair. Since his name still appears on the convent's rent-roll, for the same parish, in 1307, and 1311,[10] it does not seem unreasonable to suppose that this John and John Drake were the same person, especially in view of the fact that all trace of both is lost after 1313/16.

As King's Waferer, John served under Edward I for 17 years and under Edward II for 6. The Wardrobe books are full of references to him, mostly recording payment of his wages and issue of his winter and summer clothing. There were some years during which he was never absent from Court. (E36/202/ ff.7ᵛ, 9ʳ, E101/364/13, f.24ᵛ). In 1294, at Conway, Peter de Chichester, Clerk of the Pantry, issued to him 2 quarters of wheat, presumably for his ' office ', namely, making wafers. (E36/202/f.55ᵛ).

As an amateur minstrel he was one of the great concourse who performed at the wedding of Princess Elizabeth in 1296, receiving the customary *largesse* of 20s. (£200) (Add. MSS. 7965, f.52ʳ). Later in the same year he was with the king at Ghent. Because he was rarely absent from Court, his travels, which tally with the king's itinerary, were extensive. The aroma of his wafers was wafted from London to Flanders, from Wales to Scotland, from England to France. After the knighting, when Edward I set out for Scotland on 10 June, John went with him, making his wafers every day as the Court moved from Westminster, through Thrapston, Grantham, Lasingby and Thirlwall to Lanercost, a painful four-month journey for the king. On Easter Sunday, 26 March, 1307, when Edward, with that odd access of faith and energy which sometimes comes just before the end, had risen from his sick-bed and had made his way to Carlisle, the Bishop of Carlisle gave a mark

---

[10] *The Cartulary of Holy Trinity, Aldgate. London Record Society* 1971. Nos. 134, 135.

(£133-6s.-8d.) to ' Master John Drake ' (E101/370/16, f.9ʳ), but for what reason is not stated. On 4 July, again at Carlisle, he received another mark, but by whose gift and for what service is unknown. Nor does the Journal say that he accompanied the king to Burgh-upon-Sands. He probably did ; it was only three more days of service for him.

When the debts of the Wardrobe were drawn up, John's back-wages were found to amount to well over the equivalent of £17,000.

What his position was under Edward II is not clear. Richard Pilke was the new King's Waferer; yet, after Gaveston's death, letters of protection were issued to all those ' who will be going overseas with the king '. (*Foedera*, II, pt. I, 212). Among them was ' John Drake '. After this his name no longer appears in the Wardrobe accounts.

On 20 March, 1316, Edward II sent one Gaven le Corder, on account of his service to the King and Queen, to the Prior and convent of Christ Church, Canterbury, to receive the same allowance as ' John Drak ', deceased, had in that house. (*CCR.*, 329). If this were John le Waferer, then he ended his days between 1313 and 1316.

L.

Lambyn Clay.   L.

King's minstrel.   According to entries in the Wardrobe accounts for 1328 and 1330, he was a taborer.

His name is curious.   F. *lambin* means a slow-coach or dawdler but the Christian name, *Lambyn*, is more likely to have been a pet form of *Lambard*, *Lambert*.   His surname is spelt variously, *Clay*, *Clays*, *Cley*, *Cleys* and *Claye*. If *Clay* be the correct form, it could derive from either French or English. F. *Claie* is very old and of Celtic origin.   It equates with Old Irish *cliath* and Welsh *clwyd*, meaning, as it does in modern French, a wattle hurdle or fence.   If it is derived from an English place-name, e.g. *Clay* (Essex) and *Cleye* (Sussex), we should expect the usual form, *de Clay*. (OE. *clæg*, clay-soil).   In modern England *Clay* is a regular surname.

As far back as 1281 a Lambard Cleys of London was acting as mainpernor for one John Squirret. (*CLL.*, B., 6).   Of this form of the surname I can offer no explanation, nor is there any evidence, at present, to prove that he was the Lambyn Clay of the Payroll, but the latter definitely appears in the Wardrobe for 1297, as a royal minstrel performing with many of his fellow-minstrels at the wedding of Princess Elizabeth. (Add. MSS. 7965, f.52ʳ). In 1299 his name occurs in the list of London citizens who tided the king over his debts to Gascon merchants. The war in Gascony had pretty well emptied the king's coffers. He was up to his ears in debt to Gascons who had provided him with cash and supplies with which to prosecute the war. After it was over, these loans had to be repaid. The sum owing was colossal. Edward's ' beloved Mayor, aldermen and sheriffs and other citizens of London ' undertook to pay the bills of ' certain Gascons ', namely, those living in London, on condition that the *ferm* of the city should be used to reimburse them. London's bill alone amounted to £1049-13s.-11d. (approx. £210,000). In the list of citizens drawn up by the taxmen for the purpose of reimbursement, there appears : ' Arnald Guillim de Mauveysin, debtor to Lambin Clay and his wife.' (*CLL.*, C. 47.) which proves that Lambin and his wife, like most royal minstrels, were well enough off to be included among the London citizens called upon to do their civic duty at the king's need.

Although King's minstrel, he seems to have been a favourite with the Prince. Toward the end of 1305 he fell ill and had to remain at home when the court moved into Hampshire and Dorset for Christmas. The Prince did not forget him : ' To Lambin Claye, Minstrel, ill in London, 5s. (£50) by gift of the Prince, as a help toward his upkeep during the said illness. Paid into his own hands. Received from Ringwood on 21 December.' (MS. Harley. 5001, f.32ᵛ). He was up and about in the following May, by which time he seems to have been transferred to the Prince's household, as the following entry in the Prince's Wardrobe book implies : ' To Lambin Claye and Richard, the vielle-player, Prince's minstrels, travelling in the entourage of the said Prince, between London and Dover, in May, 6s. 8d. (£66-13s.-4d.), by gift of the Prince himself, as a contribution toward two hackneys conveying them between the aforesaid places. The money was paid to them by the hand of Robert de Hurley, in the same month.'

(Add. MSS. 22923., f.7ᵛ ; MS. Harley, 5001, f.43ʳ). Either before or after this little journey, Lambin was at the Prince's knighting on 22 May.

Shortly after the death of Edward I, he fell ill again. He was now ' King's minstrel ' but he was constrained to stay at home while the court moved north. Again his master remembered him : ' On 18 July (1307), 13s. 4d. (£133-6s. 8d.) to Lambin Clay, king's minstrel, who is ill in London and is staying there after the departure of the king thence. By gift of the king himself, as a help toward his expenses for having to stay behind. Paid into his own hands.' (E101/373/15, f.21ᵛ.)

Nothing more is heard of him until the first year of the reign of Edward III, when his name appears among those of minstrels receiving the king's livery : ' Clays Le Taburer'. (E101/383/10.) Two years later, in 1330, he is again among those to whom winter clothing was issued : ' Cley le Taborer.' (E101/385/4.) If this Clay be the same person as the Lambin of the Payroll, then it can be assumed that he was loyal to Edward II throughout the reign and was taken into the household of Edward III. By 1330 he had been in the royal service over 30 years.

Laurentius Citharista. L.

A court minstrel, who, by 1306, had been a royal harper for 10 years or more, for he, too, was at the wedding of Princess Elizabeth in 1296 : ' To the Waferer of the king's son, to 4 watchmen of the king, to 2 harpers of the earl of Oxford and Lord Thomas de Multon, to Henry the harper, *Laurence the harper* and Martinet the taborer, 10s. (£100) each.' (Add. MSS. 7965, f.52ʳ).

Leylond.
See *Ricard* de Leylond.

Leskirmissour.
See *Walterus* Leskirmissour.

Lion de Normanville. L.

There was a squire called Leo de Normanville in the household of Edward II in 1312 : ' Leo de Normanville has a dark, iron-grey horse.' (*Bain*, III, 428. *Roll of Horses of Squires in the King's Army.*)

Thomas de Normanville was one of Edward I's officers; he was King's Steward in 1280, Escheator beyond Trent, 1288-c.1295, and also Constable of Bamborough Castle, 1292. Leo may have been his son or kinsman.

Lucat. F.

John de Lucca, John de Luca, John de Luke, John de Lucke, John de Lucy, John de Luka, Jaket de Luke, Jakinet de Luke.
King's sergeant-at-arms. The numerous entries concerning him give no inkling as to his abilities as a minstrel but they provide a vivid picture of the busy, responsible, even colourful life of a king's sergeant.

He was certainly in the king's service before 1294, because in that year he was sent to Gascony : ' To John de Luke, 100s. (£1,000) by the hand of William de Melton, on 24 August, for his going to Gascony.' (E36/202, p. 160). In 1299 he was transferred to duty on the fortifications around Dumfries and Lochmaben castles. (Add. MSS. 35291, f.92^r.) Nine months later, in July 1300, he was once more on sergeant's duty in the army, going with the king into Galloway after the surrender of Caerlaverock Castle.

As sergeant-at-arms of the royal household he was also a *balistarius,* one of a special company of king's cross-bowmen, and from 1300 until the end of the reign entries in the Exchequer accounts relative to his wages and livery prove that he was continually on duty in the army. (E101/359/5, f.3^v ; E101/359/6, f.10^v ; E101/364/13, f.70^v ; Add. MSS. 8835, ff.61^r, 113^r, 118.) At the end of the reign he was owed a considerable sum, £10-5s.-8d. (£2,060 approx.)

Under Edward II his position was unchanged. He was busier than ever. In 1309 he and another sergeant went to Flanders escorting two English sailors, against whom ' certain people of Flanders ' had committed ' divers trespasses.' The king sent a letter to the Count of Flanders and to the Mayor and Commonalty of Bruges, protesting at the treatment his sailors had received, and asking them to send the offenders to him. John de Luke and his fellow-sergeant accompanied the two sailors, who were being sent to name and, presumably, to identify the culprits. (*Cal. Chancery Warrants* (1309), 291.) In the following year John was given the job of looking after and repairing Odiham Castle (Hants.) (E101/373/26, f.48ʳ.) Incidentally, it was in this year, more than twelve months after he had made his journey to Flanders with the sailors that he was paid his expenses for it. They amounted to 15s. 4d. (£153-6s.-8d.) In 1311 he was in Berwick-on-Tweed, seeing to the fortifications there. In 1312 he was back in Odiham Castle. When Edward II eventually decided to march against the Scots in the fateful year of Bannockburn, John was entrusted with the highly responsible task of transporting arms and armour from London to Berwick. The indenture, drawn up between ' the Mayor and Sheriffs of London on the one part and John de Luke, the King's Esquire, on the other ' is worthy of reference because of the excellent and detailed picture it gives of the transaction. The city furnished 120 cross-bowmen, with armour, weapons and missiles. These were delivered to John, together with a statement of the cost of them : 120 aketons, at 6s. 9½d. each; 120 bacinets with iron collarets, 5s. 1d. each; 120 crossbows, 3s. 5d. each; 120 baldrics, 12d. each; 120 quivers, 4s. each; 4,000 quarrels, 20s. per thousand. In addition, £57-8s.-0d. were handed over to John to cover 28 days' pay for the men at 4d. per day for the ordinary bowmen and 6d. per day for the *vintenarii*. Sacks and casks for packing came to 24s. Carriage, comprising 3 carts, 6 carters for 18 days' travelling from London to Berwick, pay for the men, provender and shoeing for the horses, added up to 117s. The sum total came to £167-18s.-4d. (approx. £33,600). To convey a company of men across the length of England and deliver them and their accoutrements safely at their destination was no light task in fourteenth-century conditions.

When Edward II tried to flee the country in 1325/6, ' Jaket de Luke ' was one of the squires to whom new clothing was issued preparatory to accompanying the king to France. (E101/381/11). It is only in 1328 that an entry gives the merest hint that he was also an amateur minstrel or a squire minstrel. In a list of household officers receiving issues of clothing, ' Jakinet de Luke ' occurs among the squire/minstrels of the new king's household. He was still alive and in the royal household in 1330. (E101/383/4 and 385/4.)

If all the entries referred to here concern the same person (one can never be absolutely certain), then John faithfully served father, son and grandson over a period of more than 30 years.

M.

Mahu, qui est oue La Dammoisele de Baar. F.

Princess Eleanor, eldest child and daughter of Edward I and Queen Eleanor, was married in 1293, to Henry (III), Duke of Bar, at Bristol. Joan, their daughter, *La Dammoisele de Baar*, was born in 1295. Both her parents died while she was still a child; her mother in 1298 and her father in 1302. She returned to England in March 1305, to live at court with her grandfather. Shortly after she had arrived the king offered her in marriage to John de Warenne, and John ' willingly accepted the marriage '. (*CCR.*, 321) (See *Galfridus, citharista Comitis Warenni* and *Ricard de Leylond.*)

Mahu is modern *Mayhew*, a form of *Matthew*.

Mahu du North. F.

The King's Constable of Dumfries Castle was Sir Maheu de Redman, an active member of the king's forces in Scotland. In the records, especially in the Close and Patent Rolls, he is variously referred to as Sir *Maheu* de Redman, Monsire *Maheu* de Redeman, *Matheu* de Redman, Monsire *Mattheu* de Redeman; so that *Mahu du North*, ' Mayhew of the North ' may have been Sir Maheu's minstrel, come with his master to Westminster, for it is clear from evidence so far collected that Edward I had summoned to the knighting not only a body of young men to be made knights but numbers of his veteran ones as well, to assist him in his forthcoming onslaught upon Bruce and his followers. After the festivities were over and the king had moved north with his forces, he issued a mandate to ' Matheu de Redman, to levy with the Sheriff of Westmoreland 300 good footmen . . . to pursue Robert de Brus and his accomplices who are lurking in the moors and marshes of Scotland.' (*Bain*, II, 509.)

Mahuet, qui est oue Monsire de Tounny. F.

Apparently *Mahuet*[11] is another variation of *Mahu* but I have not met with the form in any other document.

---

[11] If *Mahuet* stands for *Mahaut*, the minstrel would have been a woman. *Mahaut* was a common form of *Maud, Matilda*. See, for example, Jean Renart's *Galeran de Bretagne*, 4188, 4264, 4288, in which Frêne, when she disguises herself as a minstrel, calls herself *Mahaus, Mahault, Mahaut*.

Sir Robert de Tony, son and heir of Sir Ralph de Tony. was 28 years old at the time of the knighting. He had been a ward of the king and later a banneret in the royal household. He had already served in the army in both Flanders and Scotland. At the siege of Caerlaverock he was a member of the Prince's division, and must have looked resplendent, because he was dressed all in white—white habergeon, white ailettes on his shoulders, a white shield and a white banner with a red maunch on it; all, according to the poet, signifying that he ' descended from the Knight of the Swan '; but his snowy garments covered the same kind of lawless spirit as was so often displayed in the characters of his fellow-knights. In 1301 he was accused of breaking into the property of a man in Suffolk, stealing his goods and beating his servants; in 1302 he had been arrested for jousting in defiance of the king's orders; in 1306, on his way to Scotland after the knighting, he deserted from the army. He lived to attend the coronation of Edward II in 1308 but died on 28 November 1309, just 31 years old.

Marchis (Le Roy). F.

Otherwise, *Walter le Rey, Walter le Rey Marchis, Walterus Le Marchis Rex, menestrallus,* and *Walterus Le Marchi(s) Rex Haraldorum.*

Marchis, which can derive from OF. *marchois,* ' a frontier border ', or *marchis,* ' flat, open fenland ', was a fairly common surname in mediaeval England. Families carrying it were to be found in Norfolk, Lincolnshire and Huntingdonshire as well as along the borders or Marches of Wales and Scotland. The original form seems to have been *du Marchis,* but where it occurs as *le Marchis* it appears to have been the equivalent of the mediaeval Latin *marcisius,* ' one who dwells on the March.' Walter is one whose surname falls into this group. The simple form, *Marchis,* which has become the modern surname, *March,* was also current in the fourteenth century.

Walter was a King of Heralds but it is difficult to determine to whose household he belonged. In 1298 letters of protection were issued to him and Roger de Cheyny, because they were going to set out for Scotland with Lord Henry de Percy : ' *Walterus le Rey et Rogerus de Cheyny, qui cum Henrico de Percy profecturi sunt . . .* ' This could mean either that he was Percy's herald or that he was the king's herald being deputed to go to Scotland in Percy's retinue. Again, on Christmas Day, 1301, he was with the king at Northampton and was given 40s. (£400) for making the proclamation prohibiting the holding of tournaments in England. (Add. MSS. 7966, f.66ʳ), which seems to imply that he was *Rex Haraldorum* of the king. On 8 July of the same year, when Edward initiated a fresh campaign in Scotland, and had arrived at Berwick-on-Tweed, ' *Walter le Marchis Rex, menestrallus*' joined the king's army there on the squire's usual military wage of 12d. per day, and served with the king until 9 October, leaving Dumfries a week or so before Edward retired to Linlithgow for the winter. (*Ibid.*, f.102ᵛ.) Since he was paid his full wages, £4-8s.-0d. (£880), on the spot, it looks as though he was not at that time a regular member of the royal household. As far as it is possible to draw any conclusion from such scanty information, it would appear that, as he joined the army at Berwick for special duty in Scotland, he was ' Walter, dweller in the Berwick March ',[12] the stretch of flat country in Berwickshire now called *Merse*, and a herald of the North. More than that one dares not hazard.

His presence at the Prince's knighting needs no explanation. At the same time, it is obvious that he was well-known at Court and to the Prince's household, because he was one of the Kings of Heralds appointed to supervise the distribution of the remainder of the 200 marks.

The four other men by the name of *Marchis* who were in the royal household were : Roger Ma(r)chys, herald, 1305/6; Robert and Ralph Marchys, squires, 1312; William Marchis, king's minstrel, 1335.

Markin. F.

Monsire Markin was not one of the minstrels receiving the Prince's *largesse* but he and Monsire Cosin were responsible for collecting that allotted to the three anonymous minstrels of Sir John de Hastings.

---

[12] It is worth remembering that Patrick, earl of Dunbar, King's Lieutenant in Scotland and Earl of March, was overlord of precisely this part of the country, the title ' Earl of *March* ' meaning ' earl of the *Merse*'.

Martinet, qui est oue le Conte de Warwike. F.
Another minstrel who had come with the Earl of Warwick.
See *Gillot le Taborer.*

Martinet Le Taborour. F.
He first appears in the records as king's minstrel in 1296,
when he performed at the wedding of Princess Elizabeth.
(Add. MSS. 7965, f.52ʳ.) Again, in 1300/1301, when the king
and queen were at Lincoln, Martinet, John de Cressy and
Janin, the Earl Warenne's organist, ' made their minstrelsies
in turn in the presence of the King and Queen.' (Add. MSS.
7966, f.66ᵛ.)

Between 1301 and 1302, after the two young princes, Thomas
and Edmund, had been born, Martinet was transferred to
their household, where he and the baby boys had an uproarious
time beating drums until the parchment split. They were
joined, in 1303, by Margaret, daughter of the Countess of
Hereford. She had been born at Tynemouth but was sent to
Windsor Castle to be brought up with her infant uncles. The
royal children were often sent to royal residences, such as
Ludgershall (Bucks.) and Framlingham (Norfolk) for varying
periods of time, but Windsor Castle seems to have been the
major nursery. Here Martinet went to live and play with the
children. At first, when they were very tiny, they played with
his drum—and broke it. ' To Martinet the minstrel, making
his minstrelsy in the presence of Thomas and Edmund (4 and
3 years old), the two sons of the King; and for repairing his
tabor, broken by them, 2s. (£20) from the Almonry. 12 July,
1305, at Ludgershall.' (Add. MSS. 3766, f.1ʳ). And after
baby Margaret arrived, 'To Martinet the Taborer, making his
minstrelsy in the presence of the Lords Thomas and Edmund,
the King's sons, and the Lady Margaret (2 years old), the
daughter of Elizabeth, Countess of Hereford; and for repairing
his tabor, broken by them, 7s. (£70).' (*Green*, Vol. III, 40)[13]
It needs no effort of the imagination to visualize the scene and
hear the row. The 7s. covered Martinet's reward as well as
the cost of the new skin for his tabor. A year later, in 1305/6,
they were old enough to have their own drums and burst them

---

[13] *Lives of the princesses of England from the Conquest,* Mary Anne Everett Green,
6 vols. (1846).

to their hearts' content : ' To Martinet the Taborer, for repairing the little drums of the King's sons; and for money paid by him for parchment for covering the said drums, at Windsor, on 18 November, 11d.' (£9-3s.-4d.) The change to toy drums was of great benefit to the household economy, if nothing else. When Christmas came, that is, the Christmas before the knighting, the king and queen were at Kingston-Lacy but the children remained at Windsor, where they enjoyed their own favourite kind of minstrelsy—drums and trumpets : ' To Martinet the Taborer, William and John, the trumpeters, minstrels of the two young princes, 20s. (£200) for making their minstrelsy in their presence on Wednesday and Thursday, 5 and 6 of January, the eve and feast of Epiphany, by gift of the aforesaid (young) lords, at Windsor Castle.' (E101/368/12, f.4ᵛ). The young lords were now five and four years old. In the following May, Prince Thomas was considered old enough to attend his step-brother's grand dubbing. That is one of the reasons why Martinet, William and John, were among the minstrels receiving *largesse* at Westminster.

Mascun.
   See *Janyn le Mascun.*

Matheus le Harpour. L.
   Unidentified. Since his name comes immediately after that of the Prince's crowder, Nagary, it is possible that he may have been a minstrel in the Prince's household.
   The Prince had a crowder called Matthew. Minstrels often played more than one instrument, so that Matthew the harper might be Matthew the crowder under another guise, yet the clerks rarely made mistakes of this nature.

Matheus Waffrarius domini R. de Monte Alto. L.
   The waferer of Lord Robert de Monhaut.
   See *Galfridus trumpator.*

Matillis Makejoye. L.
   Matilda Makejoy, dancer and acrobat.
   Although it is very apt for her profession, Matilda's surname is not a stage-name. It belongs to a special group of English surnames : e.g. *Makefare, Makehayt, Makebotere, Makepeace,* etc.

Unfortunately, there are only two entries concerning her in the Wardrobe books but they cover a span of 14 years. In 1296 when the king was keeping Christmas at Ipswich, she gave a performance before Prince Edward, then a boy of 13 : ' To Matilda Makejoy, acrobat, making her vaults in the presence of Lord Edward, the King's son, in the King's Hall, at Ipswich, 2s. (£20), by gift of the Lord Edward ; by the hand of Nicholas Artaud (one of the king's sergeants-at-arms), on 27 December.' (Add. MSS. 7965, f.52ʳ) In 1311 she was delighting another youthful audience, the boy princes, Thomas and Edmund, now 11 and 10 years old respectively : ' To Matilda Makejoy, acrobat, making her minstrelsy in the presence of the two (young princes), Thomas and Edmund, 2s. by gift of both on the order of Lord Thomas, at Framlingham, on 24 June.' (E101/374/19, f.8ᵛ).

See pp. 55-60.

Mellers. L.
Unidentified.
An ordinary English surname.

Mellet. F.
Unidentified.
A surname of French origin. Attested 1293 : ' Safe conduct to . . . John Mellet, merchant of Abbevill, going to various ports and elsewhere in the realm to view wines and other goods . . . ' (*CPR.*, 20.)

Le Menestrel Monsire de Montmaranci. F.
Monsieur de Montmorency was a kinsman of the king. Simon de Montfort, who had married the sister of Henry III, was the son of Simon IV, Comte de Montfort and his wife, Alix, daughter of Bouchard V, Sire de Montmorenci.

The Monsire de Montmaranci of the Payroll was Jean I, who had succeeded his brother, Mathieu V, ' toward the middle of 1306,'¹⁴ Like Bishop Bek, he was one of the magnificoes of the time, vying with the royal houses of France in splendour and force of arms. As a soldier, he served under

¹⁴ *L'Art de verifier les Dates.*, tomes xi, 481f. and xii, 25f.

four French kings in succession : Philippe le Bel, Louis X, Philippe V and Charles le Bel. He died in June 1325.

His minstrel, who received 40s. (£400), is bracketed with distinguished minstrels of the English court, and King Caupenny collected the money for him.

Menestralli J. de Ber(wike), (*ij*). L.

Two unnamed minstrels of Sir John de Berwick, who, during Queen Eleanor's lifetime, had been Keeper of the Queen's Gold. He was also King's Clerk, Justice in Eyre, Keeper of the abbey of Bury St. Edmunds and Keeper of the bishopric of Lincoln. In the early part of the reign he was a very important Court officer and, when Queen Eleanor died (1290), was appointed one of the executors of her will.

He was probably coming on in years in 1306 and did not live long after the old king, his master. He must have died shortly before 1312, because in that year Edward II granted the prebend of Blebury, in the diocese of Salisbury, which John had held, to one of his clerks and also granted to Oliver de Burgedala, his yeoman, ' those houses in the city of London in the street which is called Sevyng (?Seething) Lane, which John de Berewic had held for his life by grant of Queen Eleanor, the king's mother.' (*CPR.*, 481.)

Menestralli (iij diuersi). L.

Perhaps minstrels of one or more of the guests, unknown to the clerks.

Menestraus Monsire de Hastings (Les iij). F.

Sir John Hastings or Hastang of Abergavenny was Steward of Queen Margaret's household. It seems strange that the clerks did not enter the names of these minstrels. for they would certainly have known them.

Sir John died in 1313.

Menestral oue les Cloches (Le). F.

This description is so stark that both man and bells fade into irretrievable anonymity.

Merlin.   F.

Three Merlins appear in the records between 1307 and 1330. The first, who figures in them most prominently and frequently, was John Merlyn, a squire of Lord Aymer de Valence. Shortly after the death of Edward I he was with the earl in Dumfries, delivering to the Wardrobe the equivalent of about £7,000 for the upkeep of 60 men-at-arms in Scotland. (Add. MSS. 35093, f.3ʳ.) When the general storm over Gaveston blew up in 1310-12, the earl, with Thomas of Lancaster and other barons, opposed the king. So did his squire. John Merlyn's name appears on the list of those who were rebels (*Foedera*, II, pt. 2, 231) but he was pardoned because his master changed sides after the beheading of the troublesome favourite. Pembroke, whose life and lands had been put in jeopardy by the smart tactics of Lancaster and Warwick, remained a supporter of Edward II until he died in 1325. When the king and queen went to France in 1313, John Merlyn went also, in the train of the earl, and on 28 May, at St. Richer, he performed the peaceful and civilized task of handing *largesse* to one of the king's minstrels : ' To Jakemin de Mokenor, king's minstrel, making his minstrelsy in the presence of the king, £7-3s.-1d. (£1,430-16s.-8d.), by gift of the king, by the hand of John Merlyn, valet of Lord Aymer de Valence, earl of Pembroke. Paid to him in cash, by order of the king.' (E101/375/8,f.30ʳ).

In 1320 and 1321 John was again in France with the earl, on the king's service. (*CPR*, (1320), 520, 521; (1321), 589, 591.)

The second Merlin was a King's Yeoman. The only indisputable reference to him is to be found in the Patent Rolls for 1313 (*CPR.*, 554). He was delivering, on behalf of John de Sandale, King's Treasurer, to Walter Reynolds, the Chancellor, a schedule of horses received from Sir Robert de Clifford and Thomas of Lancaster.[15]

The third was a minstrel, the vielle-player of John of Brittany, earl of Richmond, but the only references I have concerning him are late. This does not by any means preclude the possi-

---

[15] Other references to a John Merlyn who is unidentified are to be found in *CPR* (1319) 396; *CCR* (1325) 381, 513.

bility of his being the earl's minstrel in 1306 nor of his being present at the Prince's knighting, because John of Brittany was an intimate at Court all his life. He was a nephew of Edward I and had come to live in England, when he was a child, in preference to staying in his own home and country. Merlin, his minstrel, entertained Edward II in 1320 : ' To Merlin, the vielle-player of the lord Earl of Richmond, making his minstrelsy in the presence of the lord King, 20s. (£200), by gift of the lord King, into his own hands, at Westminster, on 12 May.' (Add. MSS. 9951, f.21ʳ.)

Unless there was yet another Merlin, minstrel in the royal household, the last-mentioned seems to have become a minstrel on wages in both the king's and the queen's households at later dates : ' Merlyn le Vieler ' was issued winter clothing in 1330. (E101/385/4., *sub. Menestralli*) and c. 1330-1333, ' *Merlin vidulator menestrallus* ' was issued from Queen Isabella's household 6½ ells of yellow cloth and striped silk and a lamb's fur to make a summer *roba* for himself. (MS. Cott. Galba, E. iii, f.187ʳ.)

Mochelneye.
See *Johan* de Mochelneye.

Monet. F.
John Monet, squire and minstrel of Lord Robert fitz Payn. (See *Johannes Trumpator domini R. Filii Pagani.*)
The only two entries relating to him are interesting. In the first he is called a squire or valet : ' To John Monet, valet of Lord Robert fitz Payn, making his minstrelsy in the presence of the king, 60s. (£600), by gift of the king, into his own hands, on Thursday, 6 January 1305, at Wimborne.' (E101/368/6, f.21ʳ). In the second he is called a minstrel : ' To John Monet, minstrel of Lord Robert fitz Payn, making his minstrelsy in the presence of the king on the day of the Epiphany of the Lord, 60s., by gift of the king, into his own hands, on 6 January at Wimborne.' (E101/369/11, f.99ᵛ). Both entries, from different accounts, refer to the same occasion. Like other men of his class, he was a squire/minstrel. He provides a parallel with the squire/minstrels of the royal households.

N.

Nagary, le Crouder Principis.   L.

The Prince's crowder was either a Breton or a Frenchman of Breton extraction, because the surname *Nagary*, *Nagard*, *Naggar*, still common in France, derives from Breton *an hagar*, by aphaeresis.   It means ' le bon.'[16]   The Welsh equivalent would be *yr hygar*, ' the well-beloved '.

Nothing is known of him because his name does not occur in any of the Wardrobe books or other accounts.

Nakarier (Le).   F.

John, the Prince's nakerer, variously referred to in the records as *Johannes*, *Janin*, *Janyn*, *Janot* and *Januche*.

He falls into the category of veteran minstrels, for he served in the royal households for over 20 years.   He is first met with on Christmas Eve, 1302, when the Prince bought from Hugh de Naunton, the harper, a sorrel hack ' as a mount for John the Nakerer, the minstrel of the lord Prince.'   (E101/363/18, f.17^r).   Later on, when the Prince went to Scotland, he was given 3s. (£30) ' by gift of the lord Prince for him to buy a skin to cover and repair his nakers.'   (*Ibid.*, f.21^v); and on Trinity Sunday, 2 June 1303, when he and Thomasin, the vielle-player, and the two trumpeters, John Garsie and John de Catalonia, made their minstrelsy in the Prince's presence at Newbattle, each of them received *largesse* wherewith to buy themselves silk cloaks (*Ibid.*, f.21^v).   Further gifts to the three Johns included aketons, habergeons and iron collarets.   (See *Januche Trompour Monsire le Prince.*)

Although he was, at this time, attached to the Prince's household, John was officially king's minstrel up to the end of the reign.   The money owing to him in back-wages in 1307, £4-19s.-4d. (£993-6s.-8d.) was the debt of the king's not the prince's wardrobe.   (E101/357/15, f.25^r).

Immediately on the accession of Edward II, he became King's Nakerer and as such was in attendance upon the new king at Carlin and Nottingham.   (E101/373/15, f.5^v) and in

---

[16] I am greatly indebted to **Professor Lewis Thorpe**, who traced the French surname, *Nagary*, for me.

August he was with Edward II in Scotland when the latter was enjoying himself with the newly-recalled Gaveston. (*Ibid.*, f.19ʳ). (See *Gillot, Trompour Monsire Le Prince.*)

The next reference to John is in 1311. The king, staying at Swineshead Priory (Lincs.), was having a little private entertainment, and John was deputed to give the *largesse* to the entertainer : ' To Janin le Tregettour (Conjuror), making his minstrelsy in the presence of the king in his private room in Swineshead Priory, 20s. (£200), by gift of the king, by the hand of Janin le Nakerer, on 7 July, at Swineshead.' (MS. Cott. Nero. c.viii, f.86ᵛ). It is a quaint picture : the King of England, 27 years of age, enjoying watching conjuring tricks on a summer's day (or evening), in a private room in a monastery.

Up to 1320 John continued in his office, receiving *largesse* for himself for performing before the king (1312); being given advances on his wages and livery (1314) returning his bay horse to the Almonry and being compensated for it (1319); and being issued his winter and summer clothing (1320). By 1323 he was growing old and unfit for service. Edward then sought to place him in a monastery : ' 2 February, at York. A request from the king, addressed to the abbot and convent of Burton-on-Trent that they will grant to *Janyn nostre Nakerer,* who has long served the king, such maintenance for life in their house as John le Triour, deceased, had therein . . . '. (*CCR.* (1323) 694.) Edward chose well. The abbot and convent of Burton-on-Trent were not at all in his good books. They would have been very unwise to refuse to accede to his request. In 1310 (Edward had a long memory for those who crossed him) he had asked them to admit Sir Thomas Banbury, an indigent knight, and to ' find him the necessaries of life in food, drink, etc., and a suitable chamber to dwell in according to his estate during his life.' (*CCR.*, 335). The abbot and brothers replied that they would gladly do so if they had the means, but theirs was ' the poorest and smallest abbey of their order (Benedictine) in England ' and was ' more heavily charged in proportion to its means.' Edward had the financial affairs of the abbey looked into and wrote to the abbot to tell him that he had learned from ' trustworthy evidence ' that the excuses he offered deviated ' in many ways from the truth ' and that the abbot and convent could quite well fulfill his request. The excuse of poverty was ' wholly insufficient '. In 1311 Sir Thomas, with a royal mandate in his hand, arrived at the abbey. The abbot, as he was ordered, admitted him without delay, because the king considered his excuses ' frivolous, untruthful and inacceptable.'

John le Treour or Triour, who arrived there on 2 December 1318, was a valet of the Queen's Butlery. He burdened the abbot and monks with his presence for five years; and then John the Nakerer took his place. Being an expert at playing the side-drums would not have been much of a recommendation to the brethren; nevertheless he was admitted without a murmur.

Northfolke.   F.

Thomas de Norfolk, King's Herald.

He was with Edward I in Scotland in 1303, receiving some of his wages at Perth, Fyvie (Aberdeen), Dundee and Dunfermline. (E101/364/13, f.97ᵛ). Six weeks before the Prince's knighting, he and other heralds were prosecuting special business, probably connected with the forthcoming ceremonies, for the king. Each of them was given half a mark to cover their travelling expenses between London and Winchester.

See *Bruant.*

P.

Parvus Willelmus, organista Comitisse Herefordie.   L.

The Countess of Hereford was Princess Elizabeth. Because she was born in Rhuddlan Castle, she was called by her contemporaries, ' The Welshwoman.' When she was only 15 she was given in marriage to John, Count of Holland and, at their wedding at Ipswich, in 1297, many of the minstrels whose names appear on the Payroll were present. The young bride, when the time came for her to leave with her 16-year-old husband, found she did not want to go. A furious family squabble ensued, during which her father irritably snatched the coronet she was wearing from her head and threw it in the fire. Someone quickly retrieved it and it was sent to Adam, the King's goldsmith for renovation. At a cost of 40s. (£400) he reset in it a large ruby and a large emerald. (Add. MSS. 7965, f.13ᵛ).

In spite of his hectic tempers, Edward I was a very good and fond parent. After he had calmed down he showed that he understood his daughter's reluctance to leave her family and England at so young an age; he allowed her to stay home with him until 1298, when he himself took her overseas to her husband. Within a year she was back in England, her husband having died of dysentry. When she arrived, in August 1300, she found that her father was in Scotland and that she had acquired a stepmother, the new Queen Margaret, who was then in York. It was to her that the young widow went and they became fast friends. It is in a Wardrobe account for this same year that the only reference to Parvus Willelmus occurs. His name appears in a list of the officers and servants in the Countess' household, under the heading *Camerarii, Sometarii et Palefridarii* : ' Parvus Willelmus, with his groom, eats in the hall.' (Add. MSS. 7966, f.187ʳ). The entry implies that he was a groom of her Chamber and that he had been in her service for some time.

In 1302, when she was 20, she was given in marriage to Humphrey de Bohun, earl of Hereford and High Constable of England, then a young man of 20 or 21. From 1303 until the year of her death, 1316, she must have been almost perpetually pregnant, because she died in childbirth of her tenth child.

As the Payroll proves, Parvus Willelmus went into her husband's household with her.

Perle in the Eghe. L.
Perle in the eghe (et) Son compaignon. F.
' Pearl in the eye.'

His seemingly curious name, because it is in English, comes across the welter of Janins and Gillots like a breath of cold air entering a scented room. It serves to remind one sharply of the native culture existing outside the life of the court. As has been seen in relation to most of the royal minstrels, the court itself, for all its overlay of French, was sturdily English. ' Pearl in the eye ' was (and still is) a homely name for cataract. In Latin it was usually called *albugo oculorum* or *albuginarium malum*.

He was a blind or purblind minstrel and his ' compaignon ' was his guide. Since he was given the equivalent of £10 from the Wardrobe and another £133-6s.-8d. *largesse* from the Prince, it would seem that he was well-known and favoured in the royal households. His guide and companion was probably a minstrel too, for he was given the same *largesse* by the Prince. His name does not appear in the Wardrobe books. Like Matilda Makejoy, he may have been a London professional minstrel who had ready access to Court.

Perotus le Taborer.   L.
    Unidentified.
    Probably a taborer belonging to one of the royal households since his name occurs in the Latin list close to those of the King's Watchmen and the Prince's boy-trumpeters.

Phelippe de Caumbereye.   F.
    Philip of Cambrai, vielle-player of the King of France, Philip IV, brother of Queen Margaret. As was to be expected, he was given very special treatment. In addition to the 60s. (£600) from the Prince, he received a personal gift from the king : ' To Philip of Cambrai, vielle-player, of the King of France, at the time when the Lord Edward, the King's son, was dubbed knight, at Pentecost, at Westminster, 10 marks (£1,333-6s. -8d.) by gift of the King. Paid into his own hands, at Westminster, 28 May 1306.' (E101/369/11, f.101^r).

Pilke.   F.
    Richard Pilke, Court Waferer; later King's Waferer under Edward II.
    His precise status at court during the reign of Edward I is difficult to determine. He was never called King's Waferer. He was not the Queen's Waferer, the name of whom was Gilbert; nor was he Prince's Waferer, who was Reginald; yet the Wardrobe books prove beyond doubt that he was a waferer on court wages as early as 1301 when he was in Scotland with the king : ' To Ricard the Waferer, on account, for his wages, 2s. (£20) into his own hands on Saturday, the last day of September, at Dunipace (Stirlings.); 13s. 4d. (£133-6s.-8d.) into his own hands on Wednesday, 12 October, at the same place.' (E101/359/6, f.14^r).

The possibility is that he was, at first, John Drake's groom and deputy. There was a Richard Pilke who had served with the king in Gascony sometime during 1287-89 and who had, like so many of the men in the king's service, committed homicide. In 1295 Edward I granted him pardon, ' on account of his services in Gascony . . . on condition that he stand his trial on his return.' (*CPR.* (1295), 158.)

When Edward II ascended the throne, Reginald became King's Waferer but Richard was also still at court and on court wages. On 30 July, three weeks after the old king's death, Elena, Richard's wife, collected some of his wages for him, while they were both with the king at Carlin and, later, he himself collected them at Westminster. (E101/373/15, f.5^v). By 1310 he had been appointed King's Waferer and was receiving the squire's wage of 7½d. per day. (E101/374/5, f.34^r).

In 1311 he and his wife were sent to Framlingham to make wafers for the royal children and entertain them in other ways : ' To (Ricard) Pilke, King's Waferer and Elena, his wife, minstrels, serving their wafers at the tables of the two young princes, Thomas and Edmund, and their household, and making their minstrelsy in the presence of the said two princes, and taking their leave to go to the lord King, who was in northern parts, 20s. (£200) by gift of the two princes, by Master John de Weston, on 24 June, at Framlingham.' (E101/374/19, f.8^v).

From 1309 to 1320 entries relating to payment of his wages and to issue of summer and winter clothing are frequent. There are also a number of others, ' *super officio suo* ', that is, with regard to his actual work. These, although not detailed, provide, by implication, some interesting information. In the first place, he is the only royal minstrel I have met with whose wife accompanied him and shared his work. After leaving the royal children at Framlingham, Richard and Elena travelled north to join the king at Berwick, where Elena received from the Clerk of the Pantry the money assigned to her husband for his work : ' By the hand of Ricard Pilke, with regard to his office, 20s. in cash, given to Ricard's wife, Elena, on 14 October (1311) at Berwick-upon-Tweed.' (E101/373/26, f.2^r). In the second place, it is possible to estimate how much money was spent on the making of wafers during the years in which Gaveston was in unassailed ascendancy. Cash from the Treasury flowed out like another Pactolus : ' To Ricard Pylke King's Waferer, for money owing to him, with regard to his office (1309-10), £7-10s.-0d. (£1,500); to the same for the same (1310-11), 117s.-7d. (£1,175-16s.-8d.) (MS. Cott. Nero. C. viii, f.30ᵛ); ' By the hand of Ricard Pilke, with regard to his office, 30s. (£300); by the hand of Ricard Pilke, King's Waferer, receiving in cash, 13s.-4d. (£133-6s.-8d.), with regard to his office; by the hand of Ricard Pilke, with regard to his office, 20s. (£200); to Ricard Pilke, King's Waferer, with regard to his office, 4s. (£40) at Windsor, 5s. (£50) at York.' (E101/ 373/26, ff.2ʳ, 2ᵛ, 3ʳ, 4ᵛ), making a grand total of £16-19s.-11d. (£3,399-3s.-4d.) for ingredients (and, perhaps, some other necessaries). There appears to have been no restraint placed upon Richard's calls upon the Pantry, at least while Edward and Gaveston were enjoying themselves; and there is no reason to suppose that matters were any different when the Despensers took Gaveston's place.

Richard was still in office in 1320. The last entry concerning him occurs on 14 November of that year, when he was given 40s. (£400) in compensation for a black horse of his, which he had returned to the Almonry. (Add. MSS. 9951, f.22ʳ).

Under an extravagant king any minstrel could have lined his pockets. It comes as no surprise to learn that Richard, as citizen of London, was able to lend, under recognizance, quite sizeable sums. In 1324 Benedict de Shorne, a fishmonger, acknowledged that he owed ' to Richard Pilke, Waferer, of London, 10 marks ' (£1,333-6s.-8d.); and in the following year, John de Wroxhale acknowledged that he owed to 'Richard Pilk, citizen of London, £10 (£2,000). (*CCR.*, 154, 354.)

Pueri Principis (v)   ⎫
Trumpatores Principis pueri (v)   ⎬ L.
                          ⎭

The five boy-minstrels of the Prince. An entry in the Prince's Wardrobe Book for 1305/6 gives their names : ' The Boy Minstrels : To *Ricard le Rimour, Master Andrew, Janin Scot, Franceskin* and *Roger de Forde*, boy-minstrels of the Prince's household, 12d. (£10) each by gift of the Prince to pay for the making of their gowns for Christmas Day. Paid into their own hands on 21 December,' (MS. Harley 5001, f.32ᵛ).

In the Payroll they are called boy trumpeters, an *ad hoc* description, because, as other entries in the accounts prove, they were, first and foremost, choristers. In 1303 Robert de Newentone, one of the King's mounted messengers, was sent to fetch them from Windsor Castle to sing in church on Christmas Day : ' To Robert de Newentone, *nuncius*, sent, on one occasion, from London, and, on another, from Odiham, to Windsor to the Constable of the Castle there for the purpose of fetching the five boys to Court at Warnborough, to serve in the Prince's Chapel on Christmas Day, 8s. (£80) for five hackneys to carry them, as well as for their other expenses between those places. Paid into his own hands on 24 December at Warnborough.' (E101/363/18, f.5ʳ). As they were all under 12 or 13 years of age at the time, they would have proved a lively handful on horseback for Robert to manage, which may be why he had to make two journeys to Windsor to fetch them.

Young as they were they were very versatile. Three of them, Janin, Roger and Franceskin, were destined to become king's minstrels under Edward II. An attractive letter from Edward, when he was Prince of Wales, has been preserved, which illustrates not only the interest he took in their training but the way in which such training was carried out. Writing to Walter Reynolds, then his Clerk of the Wardrobe, he says, ' We bid you to buy in London, for our little trumpeters, a pair of trumpets which are good and strong for packing ; and a pair of little nakers for Franceskyn, our nakerer . . . '[17] In all probability, the Prince's trumpeters and nakerer, Gillot, Januche and Janin, were their teachers. Ricard le Rimour, if his cognomen means anything, was already showing promise as a versifier, and early expressed a desire to learn to play an instrument which would provide musical accompaniment to his compositions—the *crwth*. Again the Prince took a personal interest in the boy's training. Having heard that there was an expert crowder in the abbey of Shrewsbury, he wrote to the abbot, requesting him to give board and lodging to Ricard and ' to order your crowder to teach the said Ricard

---

[17] *Letters of the First Prince of Wales*, ed. N. Hone, *The Antiquary*, Vol. 31, 209.

his minstrelsy.'[18]   Which was done.   Ricard remained in the abbey from September to April 1305/6 and was back at Westminster in time to show off his newly-acquired skill at his master's splendid knighting feast.   When he had returned to Windsor Castle, five weeks earlier, the Prince had given him 3s. (£30) ' for his expenses on his return.'   After the knighting, nothing more is heard of Ricard.   The Prince was fond of crowders, yet, among the many references to them in his Wardrobe books, Ricard's name never appears.

The two trumpeters and nakerers, however, occur regularly in the records.   Janin Scot can be traced right through the reign of Edward II into that of Edward III.   He was King's Trumpeter all his life, despite his temporary desertion of the king in 1318, when, like many other minstrels of the household, he found he could not stomach the high-handedness of the Despensers.   (*PW*., II, div. 2, 127), but he was pardoned and received back into the king's favour and stayed by his side to the end.   After Boroughbridge he was well rewarded for his loyalty. Edward granted him for life and ' without rendering anything to the king ', a messuage, 8 acres of land and an acre of meadow ' in the town of Pontefract, which had been the property of Thomas of Lancaster's minstrel, William le Tabourer, a rebel.'[19] He was one of those chosen to accompany the king to France when Edward was trying to flee the country in 1325.   (E101/ 381/11, frag. and *Foedera*, II, div. 1, 606).   Immediately after Edward's abdication and death, he became King's Trumpeter under Edward III and served in that capacity until at least 1334.   His career, as far as I have been able to trace it, ran closely parallel to those of the faithful servants of Edward I. He entered the royal service as a boy and remained in it for over 30 years.

Of Roger's identity one cannot be so sure.   In all the entries referring to ' Roger le Trumpour ', he is never called Roger de Forde but, insofar as the two trumpeters who were pardoned for their rebellious behaviour with regard to the Despensers were called simply ' John Scot ' and ' Roger le Trumpour ', it is not unreasonable to suppose that this Roger was Roger de Forde.   If he were, he did not fare as fortunately as Janin Scot,

---

[18] *Letters of Edward, Prince of Wales*, ed. Hilda Johnstone, p. 14.
[19] *CPR* (1325), 161; *Cal. Fine Rolls* (1325), III, 250.

because, although he received the king's pardon, he does not seem to have been taken back into service.

Fransceskin was King's Nakerer by 1310/11 (E101/373/10, ff.3ᵛ, 5ᵛ ; E101/374/5, f.91ʳ) but his name disappears from the accounts after this date. In an entry in the Prince's Wardrobe Book for 1306 he is referred to as Franciskin Tartarensis i.e. Nakerer (Add. MSS. 22923, f.7ʳ). Perhaps he was, like John de Catalonia, a foreigner.

Master Andrew was singled out for distinction. To be styled ' master ' at so young an age bespeaks some kind of social status. I have found no reference to him in the Wardrobe accounts until c.1319, when an Andrew Noreys, King of Heralds, was given money ' owing to him for wages during the war, and his clothing.' (MS. Cott. Nero. C. viii, f.195ʳ). In 1319 Master Andrew would have been a young man in his mid-twenties. If he be the same person as Andrew Noreys, who was still King of Heralds in 1338, then he, too, like his fellow-minstrel, Janin Scot, lived to be a veteran servant in the royal household.

It would be a hopeless task to try to identify him in terms of his surname. There were scores of families called *Noreys* or *Le Noreys*, scattered over the country, in the Isle of Wight, Essex, Yorks., Lincs., Devon, Salop and Ireland; some of them ruffians, others merchants, others landed gentry. One stands out—Richard le Noreys, a squire in the household of Eleanor of Provence. In 1278 he was given letters of protection to accompany ' Eleanor, the King's mother,' on a visit to France. (*CPR*. (1275), 79.) His is the sort of family to whom Master Andrew might have belonged. His path from royal chorister/ boy-minstrel to herald and *Rex Haraldorum* would have been an easy one, seeing that his kin were or had been in the Queen's service.

There was also a Robert Noreys, one of Edward II's highly trusted servants (probably a sergeant-at-arms). In 1324, when Edward was preparing for flight, he was given the delicate and urgent task of conveying, with two sergeants-at-arms to help him, ' certain of the king's goods from the city of London to the Wardrobe.' (*CPR*, 435). Whoever he was, Robert was close to the king. While it would be useless to speculate upon the possible relationship between Andrew and these two men of the court, their presence there may serve to make ' Master Andrew ' something less of an enigma.

At the knighting the five boys were turning into budding minstrels. In three or four years their voices were to break and they would cease to be choristers. Instead of going to Oxford or Cambridge to become clerics, four of them chose to remain at court as minstrels.

Q.

Quitacre.
See *Ricardus* de Quitacre.

R.

Raulin, menestrallus Comitis Marescalli.   L.
Raulin, qui est oue le Conte le Mareschal.   F.
Raoul, the Earl Marshal's minstrel.

The Earl Marshal was Roger Bigod, earl of Norfolk. He is the Bigod of whom the story is told that, when, according to his feudal rights, he refused to go to fight in Gascony in 1297 unless the king in person led his army, Edward, enraged, exclaimed, ' By God, sir, you shall go or hang.' The earl replied, ' By God, sir, I shall neither go nor hang.' Nor did he, because he had right on his side and the king was a just man. If the story is true, it offers a nice piece of evidence that Edward and Roger knew how to use English. Roger was restored to favour and given the kiss of peace. The king could not afford to lose so staunch a man and so excellent a soldier.[20]

In 1302, when deep in financial troubles, Roger was extricated by the king, though not without some characteristic shrewdness on Edward's part. Because he had no heir, Roger surrendered both his earldom and his right to the office of Marshal to the king, together with all his estates, on condition that they should be regranted to him for the rest of his life. It so fell out that he did not have much life left. He died in late November or early December 1306. The earldom of

---

[20] According to the *Parliamentary Writs* he ' took part in almost every action of his time.'

Norfolk was then granted to the boy prince, Thomas of Brotherton.

Reginaldus le Mentour, menestrallus domini J. de Buteturte. L.

Le Mentour may be no more than a surname, yet, from Classical times, *mentiri* carried the meaning ' to feign ', ' to invent poetical fiction ' ; so that Reginald could have been a fabulist or story-teller.

Lord John de Buteturte of Mendlesham (Wilts.) was, according to *The Complete Peerage*, ' of unknown parentage ', but he was said to have been an illegitimate son of Edward I. At the time of the knighting he was about 42 years old and had held many important posts, among them Justiciar of Galloway, Annan and the Valley of the Nith, in 1302, and ' Admiral ' of the king's fleet in the north. While in this last post he had a beautiful galley of 120 oars built, at his own expense, by craftsmen of Lynn, for Edward I's use. Many years later Edward II reimbursed him. (*CCR.* (1312) 415).

When he was nearly 60, he fought against the king at Boroughbridge and Edward's surprise victory placed him in jeopardy. To save his life and his lands, he purchased the king's pardon with a fine of £1,000 (£200,000). Two years later, on 25 November 1324, he died.

Reue.
See *Adam* de Reue.

Ricardus Citharista. L.

Two harpers of this name are listed in the Latin section of the Payroll, one receiving 40d. (£33-6s.-8d.) and the other 2s. (£20). One was a minstrel in the king's household and was with the king at Lanercost (E101/370/16, f.11ʳ) ; the other may have been the harper of Sir Walter de Beauchamp, Steward of the King's Household from 1289 to 1303. He is mentioned in a Roll of Horses in 1298 : ' Richard the Harper, valet (sc. Sir Walter de Beauchamp), has a sorrel rouncy (hackney) valued at £10 (£2,000).'[21] In a later Roll of Horses, dated 1312, two Richards (perhaps the two of the Payroll) occur : ' Ricard le

---

[21] *Scotland in* 1298, H. Gough, p. 184.

Harpour has a bright bay, valued at 6 marks (£800) ; Ricard le Harpour has a chestnut bay, valued at 10 marks. (£1,333-6s.-8d.) ' (*Bain*, III, 414, 421.)

Ricard de Haleford.   F.
Unidentified.

He may have been in the train of Guy, earl of Warwick, because Haleford, modern Halford, N of Shipston-on-Stour, was part of the earl's estate and, in 1267, was held of the earl by ' the heirs of Richard de Haleford ' by service of a quarter of a knight's fee. (*Cal. Inquis.* I, 213, No. 679.)

Ricardus de Leylond, Citharista.   L.
Leylond is modern Leyland, S of Preston (Lancs.), now the home of Leyland Motors.

Harper of either Joan de Bar or Eleanor de Clare : ' Money given to the minstrels of the lady Countess Warenne and the Lady de Despenser. To Ricard de Quitacre, Ricard de Leylond harpers, and other divers minstrels, making their minstrelsies in the presence of the king and of the nobles with him, at Westminster, on the wedding-days of Joan, the daughter of the Comte de Baar and of Eleanor, the daughter of the Earl of Gloucester; that is to say, on 20 May, on which day the Lady Joan was married to John, Earl Warenne, and 26 May, on which day the said Eleanor was married to Sir Hugh le Despenser, the younger, in the king's Chapel at Westminster; in the house of Sir Otto de Grandison, in cash distributed and given at various times and by the hands of different persons; at London, at the end of May, £37-4s.-0d. (£7,440)'. (E101/369/11, f.96ʳ.)

Ricardus de Quitacre, Citharista.   L.
See *Richard de Whetacre* and *Ricardus de Leylond.*

Ricardus vidulator Comitis Lancastrie.   L.
Richard, the vielle-player of Thomas, earl of Lancaster.

Thomas was c. 38 at the time of the knighting. There seems to have been something strange about him; no contemporary was willing to speak openly about his character. The poet of *Le Siège de Karlaverok*, who has something pleasant, witty or even critical to say about all the other nobles and knights who took part in the engagement, simply describes his coat of arms. His silence is more eloquent than words. The Prince of Wales, as later events were to prove, hated him; his wife allowed herself to be abducted by John de Warenne, to humiliate him; sometimes his servants and followers played him false. It seems ironical that in his private, conspiratorial correspondence with the Scots he should have used the pseudonym, ' King Arthur.'

Richard Le Harpour qui est oue le Conte de Gloucestre. L.

Richard, harper of the Earl of Gloucester; and one of *La Commune.*

At the time of the knighting the earl of Gloucester was Ralph de Monthermer, a quondam squire in Earl Gilbert's household, with whom Joan, Gilbert's widow, fell in love and married secretly, without her father's permission, in 1297. When he came to hear of it the king was furious, because he was making arrangements to marry Joan to his cousin, Amadeus, Count of Savoy. Monthermer was thrown into prison but on the advice of friends and counsellors, Edward released him and soon grew to like him very much. He allowed him to use the style and title of ' Earl of Gloucester ' until Princess Joan died in April 1307. The title then reverted to Gilbert, Joan's son by her former husband.

Richard Le Harpour was not Monthermer's minstrel. He was the harper of Earl Gilbert and had been one of his household from before 1290. A few months before Queen Eleanor died, Roger Bigod, the Earl Marshal, married his second wife, Alice, daughter of the Count of Hainault. It was a Saturday and Midsummer Day. Where they were married is not known, although it was almost certain to have been somewhere in London. The king, queen and court were staying in the royal hunting-lodge of Havering-atte-Bower, in Essex. Most of the court minstrels, eager for extra *largesse*, went to the Earl Marshal's wedding. Three decided to remain with the king and queen and they did as well for themselves as if they had gone with the rest : ' 26 June. To Janin, the minstrel of the Earl of Albemarle, who stayed with the Lord King in Court while other minstrels were at the wedding festivities of the Earl Marshal, 40s. (£400), by gift of the king. On the same day

40s. each to Ricard, the harper of the Earl of Gloucester and Juglett (or, Iuglett) the minstrel of the Marshal of Champagne, who were staying with the Lord King in the same way.' (C47/4/5, f.47ᵛ). Queen Eleanor did not forget them either. She borrowed 60s. (£600) from the Wardrobe in order to give the three 20s. each ' because they were staying with the King and were not at the wedding feast of the Earl Marshal . . . on St. John the Baptist's day.' (E101/352/12, f.17ʳ; E101/352/21, roll.)

When Earl Gilbert and his Countess went to Ireland in 1293, Richard the Harper went with them. (*CPR.* 19, 20) and after the earl died he remained in the household under Monther mer. He had special cause to attend the knighting because the son of his old master was one of the élite aspirants. Gilbert, the only son of Earl Gilbert and Princess Joan, was no more than 15 years old at the time. He was knighted by his uncle, the Prince and, after the festivities were over, accompanied him to Scotland. Unhappily, he was one of the group of new knights (including Gaveston) who apparently became bored with the campaign and deserted. His grandfather promptly confiscated all his lands and goods and did not restore them to him until he (and the others) had come to heel. At the age of 17 he married the daughter of the Earl of Ulster. Six years later, when he was only 23, he was killed at Bannockburn.

Richard Hendeleke.   F.
    Unidentified.
    Hendeleke may be from *hendelaik*, northern dialect form of ME *hendeliche*, ' courteous '.

Richard Rounlo.   F.
    King's Vielle-player. Also styled, ' *Monsire Ricard le Vilour* ' and '*Monsire Ricard le Vilour Rounlo.*'
    Only on the Payroll has Richard's surname, *Rounlo*, been recorded. In the Wardrobe accounts he is referred to as : *Ricardus Vidulator* or *Vidulator Regis*, *Ricard le Vielour* and, occasionally, *Ricardin*.
    Entries concerning him extend over the period 1290 to 1325/6. When he entered the royal service is unknown, but from 1290 onwards he was on squire's wages and in regular

receipt of summer and winter *robae*. (C47/4/4, ff.17^r, 33^v ; C47/4/5, f.40^r ; E101/352/24.) His mounts were no miserable hacks. One, an iron grey, which he sold to the Wardrobe ' for draught work in the long cart . . . for Pantry duty ' was evidently a shire and he received 10 marks (£1,333-6s.-8d.) for it. (Add. MSS. 7965, f.20^r.)

In July 1297 he, like all the other court minstrels, took part in the wedding festivities of Princess Elizabeth. Some idea of his importance may be gathered from the names of the minstrels with whom his was grouped : Nicholas Morel, King of Heralds; Janin, the King's Lutenist ; Gillot de Roos, the King's other Vielle-player and Thomas, the Court Fool. Each of them received 50s. (£500) (Add. MSS. 7965, f.52^r). In August of the same year the king set out for Flanders. Richard, of course, accompanied him. His horse was valued, his campaign wages fixed and on 19 August the whole court embarked at Winchelsea, arriving at Ghent in the first week in September. Here the king was to stay for the next six months. On Saturday, 7 September, the day after the court had settled in, another vielle-player, Richard de Sandwich, made his minstrelsy in the presence of the king. *Largesse* of 20s. (£200) was handed to him by ' Richard the King's Vielle-player.' (*Ibid.*, f.57^r). Two months later, on 8 November, a much more important minstrel arrived at court, Adenet le Roi, the famous minstrel of Gui de Dampierre, Count of Flanders. The clerk has not specified the reason for his visit, whether it was to deliver a special message from his master or to entertain the king or, most likely, both combined, but he has given details of how the king rewarded him, in the manner customarily reserved for minstrels/envoys of high standing : ' A gold clasp, valued at 60s. (£600), given by order of the King and in the King's name, by the hand of Ricard, the King's Vielle-player, to King Adam, the minstrel of the Count of Flanders.' (*Ibid.*, f.139^r).

A further instance of what might be termed the incidental duties of a senior royal minstrel, such as Richard was, is to be found in an entry concerning payments made to minstrels who crowded the court at Christmas time. In 1301 Edward and his new queen, Margaret, kept Christmas at Northampton. How large a concourse of minstrels thronged the castle hall can be gauged from the *largesse* distributed among them—

20 marks (£2,666-13s.-4d.).   The task of dividing it among them was allotted to Richard. (See p. 13.)

A few details relative to his life outside court have come to light. On 2 February 1306, the Mayor of London issued a warrant for the arrest of one of his aldermen, Ralph de Honilane, who was in debt to the deputy-mayor and who had conveniently disappeared. Even after a second search for him had been instituted and orders given to evaluate his property, he could not be found. No one could find any of his goods and chattels upon which the debt could be levied. Eventually it was discovered that he had ' in the Vintry, in the parish of St. James, two messuages of the yearly value of £18, from which must be subtracted 100s. (£1,000) annual rent owing to Richard le Vielour.' (*CLL.* C., 245.) That he was receiving £1,000 a year in rent from property in the Vintry speaks well for Richard's financial state. There are further proofs that he was moneyed. In 1311 he lent 20 marks (£2,666-13s.-5d.), under recognizance, to a London skinner, Philip Lenfant, and in 1312 a further 10 marks to the same man and a fellow-skinner. (*CLL.* B., 47.)

By 1316/7 however, he seems to have fallen on evil times or found himself in reduced circumstances, for Edward II made him a gift of 40s. (£400) : ' To Ricard, the vielle-player, 40s. by gift of the lord king, as an aid in support of his wife and children. Paid into his own hands on 13 June, at Westminster.' (Soc. Antiq. MS. 120, f.100ᵛ.)

He is last heard of in 1325/6. In a collection of fragments, consisting chiefly of mandates for issues of knights' liveries, there is a list of the names of household servants who were being issued new clothing to go overseas with Edward II in his final effort to escape the grievous consequences of his own past follies. Numbered among the loyal minstrels who went with him was ' Ricard le Vieler '. (E101/381/11). He had been in the royal service for over 35 years.

Richard de Whetacre.   L.
Ricardus de Quitacre, Citharista.   L.
Whitacre, now *Nether* and *Over Whitacre*, NE of Coleshill. (Warwicks.)

One of *La Commune* and harper of either Joan de Bar or Eleanor de Clare.
See *Ricardus de Leylond.*

Richerus, socius suus. L.
Fellow-trumpeter of Geoffrey, trumpeter of Lord Robert de Monhaut.
See *Galfridus trumpator domini R. de Monte Alto.*

Robertus Gaunsille. L.
Gaunsaillie. F.
He is mentioned in the Prince's Wardrobe Book for 1302/3 :
' On the first day of December, 4s. (£40) to Robert Gaunsille, minstrel, making his minstrelsy in the presence of the Prince. By gift of the lord (Prince), by Master Thomas de Burton, who gave the money to him.' (E101/363/18, f.21ʳ.)
Richard Rounlo collected his *largesse* for him on Whitmonday.
In OF the word *ganse* meant a kind of piquant sauce. A line in the thirteenth century *chanson de geste, Doon de Mayence,* speaks of purees of fruit ' *au lait et a la gansaillie* ', ' laced with milk and a sharp sauce ' (v. 10515). The word appears in Scots dialect as *gansell,* but carries the extended meaning, ' a scolding ' or ' a severe rebuke '. It appears in English as an ordinary surname. (*CPR.* (1253), 178; (1262), 197.)

Robertus de Scardeburghe. L.
Unidentified.
Perhaps one of the minstrels from the royal castle of Scarborough, which figures dramatically in the reign of Edward II. It was in that fortress that Gaveston was captured.

Rogerus de Corleye, Trumpator. L.
Unidentified.
Corley is in Warwicks., a few miles NW of Coventry.

Robert (Le Roy). F.
Robert Parvus. In English, *Robert Petit* or *Robert Little.*
Variously styled *King Robert the Minstrel; Robert Parvus, King of Heralds; Parvus Rex Robertus; Robert, King of Heralds; Robert, King of Minstrels* and *King Robert, the Herald.*

Although his name figures largely in the accounts, his identity is somewhat blurred, partly because there were other men of the same name at court, notably Robert Parvus, King's Messenger. As a rule the clerks took care to differentiate between them but there are times when an entry referring simply to ' Robert Parvus ' can prove completely indeterminate.

Robert must have entered the royal service very early in the reign of Edward I, because he was already a king minstrel in 1277 : ' To King Robert the Minstrel, squire-at-arms, who is remaining on king's wages in the fortress at Berwick-upon-Tweed . . . he shall take 12d. (£10) per day.' (MS. Cott. Vesp., C. xvi, f.3.) In 1286 he was styled ' Robert Parvus, King of Heralds.' (Additional Roll, 6170). It is not known how many Kings of Heralds Edward I employed but an entry in a Household account for 1290 implies that there were two. In a list of minstrels of the royal household to whom winter and summer clothing was issued Robert Parvus appears as *Rex Haraldorum* and Nicholas Morel as *alter Rex Haraldorum*. (E101/352/24.)

There can be no doubt that Robert's duties as king's squire (i.e. sergeant-at-arms) constituted the most important part of his work. In 1293 he was in Bar, receiving his wages ' on the march ' (E36/202, 164); in 1300, with the king at Cambusnethan, Bothwell, Donipace and Linlithgow; in 1303 at Dunfermline; in 1307 with the king at Lanercost. Under Edward II he was, once again, ' remaining in the fortress of Berwick ' (*Bain*, III, 399.); yet, side by side with this soldierly activity ran his career as a minstrel.

It would be misleading to think of his minstrelsy as consisting solely of his ability to play musical instruments. There are, it is true, references to him as ' King's Trumpeter ' (E101/359/6, f.11^v; Add. MSS. 7966, f.178^r) and ' King Robert the Taborer ' (E101/374/16, f.4), which suggest that his particular form of minstrelsy was much in keeping with his work as herald and sergeant-at-arms; but other entries indicate that his court duties were much wider. He organized, as well as took part in, the regular ceremonial functions, as, for example, those at the Prince's knighting in 1306 and at the King's banquet at Amiens in 1320. (Add. MSS. 9951, f.19^r. See p. 44.) He was also responsible for providing entertainment, both in person and as a leader of the other minstrels, on ordinary festivals and family rejoicings. In 1304 he was given 40s. (£400) for making his minstrelsy in the presence of the king, on the Feast of the Circumcision (1 January), at Dunfermline. (Add. MSS. 8835, f.42ʳ); on 11 October of the same year he organized entertainment on a larger scale to celebrate the churching of Princess Elizabeth, Countess of Hereford : ' To King Robert and 15 of his fellow-minstrels, making their minstrelsies in the presence of the Countess and other of the nobility, on the day on which the Countess was churched, 6 marks (£800), by gift of the Countess, at Knaresborough.' (E101/365, 20. roll.) Eight years later, he was doing exactly the same to celebrate the churching of Gaveston's wife, but the *largesse* was infinitely greater : ' To King Robert and other divers minstrels, making their minstrelsies in the presence of the King and other nobles staying in the house of the Friars Minor at York, on the day of the churching of the lady Margaret, Countess of Cornwall, 40 marks (£5,333-6s.-8d.), by gift of the King, by the hand of the said King Robert, who received the money for dividing out between them, on 20 February (1312) at York.' (MS. Cott. Nero, C. viii, f.84ᵛ.) In entries of this nature the King of Heralds, who organized the entertainment and distributed the *largesse*, was always mentioned by name first.

The entries relating to him in the Wardrobe accounts are so numerous and diverse that they offer excellent proof of the dual nature of the herald's office at that time. It must have been an arduous life. Robert fell ill in 1316. He petitioned the king for help and was given 70s. (£700) ' by gift of the King, nominally for his wages and the taking (away) of his two horses.' (Soc. Antiq. MS. 120, f.104ᵛ). He remained in York for a twelvemonth : ' To King Robert, the Herald, who is ill at York, 40s.-10d. (£408-6s.-8d.) by gift of the lord King, nominally for his expenses and those of his two grooms and their horses. Paid to him in cash by the hand of the Sheriff and by order of the King . . . . ' (Soc. Antiq. MS. 121, f.39ʳ.) He appears to have recovered by 1319, because in the summer of 1320 he was busy organizing the banquet entertainment for the King at Amiens.

One has no inkling of how he looked at the Prince's knighting but the following entry gives some indication of the expensiveness of his attire : ' To King Robert the Minstrel, 33s.-2½d.

(£332-1s.-8d.), by gift of the lord King, to have a robe with three ' garnitures ' made for himself; being the cost of 4½ ells (approx. 16 yds.) of coloured cloth and 4¼ ells of striped cloth, given to him by Master Robert de Riston, against the Feast of Pentecost of the current year (1320) . . . and the cost of 2 budge furs for the over-dress (*supertunica*), given to him by the same for the said robe.' (Add. MSS. 17632, f.33ᵛ.) It seems strange that in so specific an entry as this no mention is made of the herald's *cote armure*. Perhaps the three ' garnitures ' (*de tribus garniamnentis*) hide a reference to it. The French word, *garnaiche*, was used in *Le Tournoi de Chauvency* to indicate the *cote armure* of Bruiant. (See p. 40 n. 25.)

Robert was King of Heralds for about 40 years, yet I have come across no reference to him in respect of his private life; no hint of where he lived; no grants to him by the king of lands, property or rents; no mention of his retirement nor of his death. The only odd little personal detail I have gleaned from the records is that, when he went to Berwick in 1312, he was riding a dapple sorrel horse.

Robert le Boistous.   F.

Robert the Lame.   OF. *boistous*, modern *boiteux*.

His name is bracketed on the Payroll with that of Gerard de Boloigne.   Since the *largesse* he received was 4 marks (£533-6s.-8d.) and was collected for him by King Caupenny, he was probably an important guest-minstrel from France.

Robert de Clou.   F.

Robert of Clough.   *Clough*, OE. *cloh*, ' a deep valley'. There are districts with this name in Lincs., Lancs., and Yorks. and a hamlet in the West Riding a few miles WSW of Huddersfield.   *Clough* is a well-known surname.

Robert, whose surname is variously spelt *Clou*, *Clogh* and *Clough* in the Wardrobe books, was a court harper. Although I have, at present, no evidence to prove it, he was probably a harper in the Prince's household because, when the Prince succeeded to the throne, Robert was styled ' Master Robert de Clough, harper of the lord King.' (E101/373/15, f.20ᵛ.)

References to him are very few and occur between 1307 and 1312. He was with the new king in Scotland in August

1307 and followed the court to Nottingham in October. (*Ibid.*, f.6ᵛ.) While at Nottingham he received 20s. (£200) for making his minstrelsy in the presence of the king (*per unam noctem* '. (*Ibid.*, 20ᵛ.)

Entries relating to him in 1311/1312 are solely for issues of winter and summer clothing and payment of 40s. (£400) compensation for a lost horse. (E101/373/26, f.93ᵛ; MS. Cott. Nero. C. viii, ff.115ᵛ, 121ʳ.)

Robert Le Vilour. L.
Unidentified.
Probably a vielle-player attached to one of the royal households, since he was one of *La Commune*.

Robertus, Citharista Abbatis de Abbyndone. L.
The abbot was Nicholas de Culham.

Robertus de Colcestria. L.
Unidentified.
He may have been a minstrel of the abbot of Colchester, Robert de Grimstead (or Grinstead). When Princess Elizabeth was married in 1296, Abbot Robert was one of the guests specially invited to the wedding. (*CCR.* (1296), 75.)

Roos.
See *Gillot* de Roos.

Rounlo.
See *Richard* Rounlo.

S.

Sagard Crouther. L.
Johannes Sagard. L.
These were two different minstrels. Concerning John Sagard I have found nothing at all but Sagard Crouther was William Sagard, a soldier/minstrel, who, with his fellow-crowder, John, the *vintenarius* of Salop., served in the army in Scotland. On 10 November 1303, at Dunfermline, Edward I granted him pardon, ' in consideration of his good service in Scotland ',

for the death of Robert Aubray. (*CPR.* 167.) Pardon for homicide was always granted on condition that the accused would stand his trial before the justices, because the indictment carried the penalty of being outlawed. In 1307, when the king was at Lanercost, William was consequently brought before the justices but he was pardoned his outlawry ' He having been pardoned on 10 November 1303. (*Ibid.* (1307), 496.)

He is mentioned in the Prince's Wardrobe Book for 1306, solely in his capacity as minstrel. On 17 April, just over a month before the knighting, he went to the Prince's court, then at Windsor Castle, and made his minstrelsy in the presence of the Prince and his entourage, and was given, ' on his departure ', 13s.-4d. (£133-6s.-8d.). (Add. MSS. 22923, f.6ᵛ; MS. Harley 5001, f.40ᵛ.) Where he came from and whence he departed is not recorded; but his surname might provide a clue.

After the conquest of Wales, Edward I gave Queen Eleanor some lands and properties in North-east Wales, including Hope and its castle, Overton, Glyndyfyrdwy and Sycharth (Denbighs.) When she died in 1290 they were again taken into the king's hands and Edward ordered Reginald de Grey, the justice of Chester, to appoint trustworthy persons to administer them for him. In the Fine Rolls,[22] where the record of this mandate is to be found, the clerks encountered difficulty in spelling the Welsh place-names ; Glyndyfyrdwy becomes Glendoverdy and Sycharth, *Saghard.* In this latter they were not as far from accuracy as might, at first, be thought, because there is documentary evidence that the Welsh form of this place-name was spelt *Syghard,* even up to the mid-sixteenth century; so that the Anglicized form *Sagard* or *Saghard* is understandable. As a surname *Sagar* still exists in the Chester area.

A William Sagard was resident in Chester Castle in 1301. At that time the Earl of Chester was the Prince of Wales, and in the Chamberlain's account for 1301 there occurs the following item : ' From William Sagard, 12s. (£120) for fruit from the garden of Chester Castle during the current year.'[23] The

---

[22] *Cal. Fine Rolls,* I, 286.
[23] *Cheshire in the Pipe Rolls,* edd. M. H. Mills and R. Stewart Brown. *Record Soc. of Lancashire and Cheshire. Appendix,* 195.

fruit from the castle garden was regularly sold to provide revenue. It would be hazardous to conclude that this William was the soldier/minstrel of the Payroll, yet if he had been a soldier stationed at the castle there would have been nothing extraordinary about his being allotted the task of carrying the proceeds of the sale of the fruit to the Chamberlain's clerks. However that may be, it is possible that a person with the surname Sagard could have come from Sycharth. The crowder William, if he came from there, would have been living in what had been the queen's demesne and in that way might have found favour in her son's household. He was known to the Prince, as the entry concerning his visit to Windsor Castle proves. The fact that he attended the knighting is additional confirmation. Finally, his name (as well as that of John Sagard) appears on the Latin list, which emphasizes that he was no stranger to the king and no newcomer to Court.

Salopia.
See *Johannes* le Crouther de Salopia.

Scardeburghe.
See *Robertus* de Scardeburghe.

Simond Le Messager. F.
Simon Lowys or Leuwys, the mounted messenger of Queen Eleanor.

He was in the royal service for more than 27 years. As an old and trusted servant of the king and the late queen, he would have qualified for preferential treatment at the Prince's knighting.

Reference to his ' going with letters of the Queen ' date from 1289 (Add. MSS. 35294, ff.5ᵛ, 6ᵛ.) In 1294 the king granted him a subsidy of 3d. (£2-10s.-0d.) per day for life, ' for his long service as messenger of the king and of Eleanor, the late queen consort.' (*CPR.*, 81.) This did not mean that he was too old for work. Far from it. In the summer of 1295 he was sent to London to look after the dean of Guernsey and his party who had come over to see the king on a private matter of some importance. The chantry at Blaunchelaunde in Guernsey, which had been founded for the souls of the king's progenitors, had been despoiled of its tithes and rents by French invaders, and Edward had ordered the dean to look into the matter and report to him. He was still in Wales when the party arrived in London but he sent Simon, now King's Messenger, forward to take charge of them until he himself should return to the capital. Part of Simon's duty was to pay the bills for their food and lodging. (*CCR.* (1295), 428; *Issue Rolls*, 95; E36/202, f.21ᵛ.) He seems to have been so busy and away from home so much in 1295 that it was his wife, Constance, who collected his 3d. per day subsidy from the Exchequer.²⁴

During the following years he was definitely acting as King's Messenger, because his name appears regularly in the Wardrobe books in the list of household servants receiving summer and winter clothing. (Add. MSS. 7965, ff.107ᵛ—131ᵛ.)

In 1298 he was with the king in Scotland, riding his streaked, apple-fallow rouncy; and in the same year he surrendered his subsidy in exchange for the custody of the manor and park of Guildford. Once again, in making the gift, the king referred to ' his long service to the late queen.' (*CPR*, 372.)

It was not only the king who favoured him. In the year Queen Eleanor died, Henry de Lacy, who owned a wood called Asheridge (Bucks.), had allowed him to fell six oaks in it, ' fit for timber ', but since Asheridge wood was within the bounds of Windsor Forest the king's permission to fell them had first to be obtained. This was readily granted. Edward issued an order to the Constable of Windsor Castle to allow ' Simon, the envoi of Queen Eleanor ', to fell the oaks and take them ' whither he will,' free of toll. Behind this generous gift lie details of Simon's private life at which one can only guess. Oaks ' fit for timber ' were ones which were suitable for either building and repairing houses or making furniture.

The last record of his carrying letters is dated 14 December 1305, when he was paid 4s. (£40) to cover his expenses when carrying missives from the king to the earl and countess of Gloucester. (E101/368/6, f.22ʳ.) His wages were the regulation 4½d. per day but his expenses were extra, and would have included provision of post-horses, fodder and litter for them,

²⁴ Hill, op. cit., 86.

his own food and lodging on the way and similar expenses for his groom.

Although he was clearly acting as King's Messenger from 1290 onwards, he seems always to have been regarded by both king and people at Court as Queen Eleanor's special messenger. All referred to him as ' *Simon qui fuit nuncius Regine* '. Even at the end of the reign, in the list of the debts of the Wardrobe, the entry concerning him was worded : ' To Simon who was the Queen's Messenger, £8-4s.-6d. (£1,645). (E101/357/15, f.2ʳ.)

Old age was creeping on him and his sight was beginning to fail when Edward II became king. In 1311 he was living in a house in the parish of All Hallows Barking, his landlords being the prior and convent of Holy Trinity, Aldgate.[25] Sometime between 1311 and 1313 his sight went completely and the king wrote to the prior and brethren asking them to grant ' to Simon the Messenger, who long served the late king and (who) is now blind, suitable maintenance for himself and a groom, in food and clothing to be received by him whether staying within or without their said house.' (*CCR.* (1313), 69.) Which he chose to do is not known but two days before Christmas 1316, justices were appointed to enquire into a case of robbery : some thieves had ' carried away the goods of Simon Le Messager at London.' (*CPR.* (1316), 601.) It was a sad end for one who, bright-eyed, had travelled the length and breadth of the country.

Swylingtone.
See *Adam* de Swylingtone.

T.

Le Taborer La Dame de Audham. F.

The identity of La Dame de Audham is uncertain. There were two ladies living during the reign of Edward I, who could have carried the title : Isabella, the widow of Sir Thomas de Audham (Aldham, Kent.) and Nicholaa, the widow of their son, Baldwin. Both Sir Thomas and Baldwin had been

---

[25] *Cartulary*, op. cit., No. 184.

tenants-in-chief. After Sir Thomas died, the king granted Isabella's remarriage to Queen Eleanor. (*CPR.* (1277), 197.)

Tegwaret Croudere.   L.

One of *La Commune*, and a member of the Prince's household. He was a soldier/minstrel. In the Prince's Wardrobe Book for 1303 his name occurs in a list of Welsh archers belonging to the household : ' To Teguareth le Crouther, 10s. (£100) for his shoes for the year.' (E101/363/18, f.18ʳ.)

Tegwared or *Tegwaret* was a name well-known throughout the whole of Wales, but there existed in the North a particular family to whom this name was attached. This was the tribe descended from *Tegwared y Bais Wen*, ' Tegwaret Whitegown ', the natural son of Llewelyn the Great. Among the Welsh soldiers who served with the king in Flanders in 1297 was one from North Wales called Tegwaret ap Llewelyn. A safe conduct was issued to him in 1298 for him to return to England. (*CPR.* (1298), 335.) Perhaps he was the Tegwaret who entered the Prince's household.

Thomas le Croudere.   L.

Whether Thomas was, like Tegwaret, a Welsh soldier/ minstrel is uncertain; his name does not provide the same satisfactory evidence, yet there can be no doubt that he was connected with Wales in a very positive way. Entries in the records prove that he was a yeoman/archer attached to the royal household; hence his presence at the knighting; but when, in 1294, the king granted him some land, it was demised to him by Robert Tibetot, King's Justice of West Wales, and it was situated in Dryslwyn, a little town a few miles west of Llandilo, in the Crown lands of Carmarthenshire. (*Cal. Fine Rolls*, I., 345.) Again, in 1304 he was sent to the earl of Pembroke, then campaigning for the king in Lothian, and was given the duty of ' bearing the standard of the company of 157 archers-on-foot, in the train of Lord Aymer de Valence . . . from 6 to 23 July.' For this duty he received 4d. (£3-6s.-8d.) per day. (Add. MSS. 8835, f.80ᵛ.) After the Prince's knighting he was with the king once more, because he was at Lanercost and was given orders to proceed into Scotland to join the train of Lord John de Bourtetourte, Admiral of the King's Fleet, and then to go with two Welshmen, David de Percy and Llewelyn Treblerth, into Wales to select foot-soldiers for the army. (E101/369/16, f.17ᵛ; E101/370/16, f.13ᵛ.)

There was another Thomas le Crouther in the king's army, who was outlawed for homicide in 1304 but pardoned in 1307 ' in consideration of his service in Scotland.' (*CPR.* (1304), 256; (1307), 492, 531.) This man, however, is always called ' Thomas le Crouther of Whitchurch ' (Salop.) and may not have been the Thomas of the Payroll, for the clerks usually took care to differentiate between people of the same surnames.

Thomasin, Vilour Monsire Le Prince. F.

Although *Thomasin* was an ordinary English surname, it seems to have been used here as a pet name for *Thomas*, because entries concerning this vielle-player refer to him as both *Thomas* and *Thomasin*.

He was already a member of the Prince's household in 1300. ' Thomas le Vilur ' was one of the household minstrels who accompanied him on his journey to join the king at Lincoln. (E101/360/10.) In 1303, when the Prince was in Scotland, Thomasin was one of the four minstrels to whom the Prince gave money to buy themselves silk cloaks. (E101/363/18, f.21ᵛ.) See also, *Januche*.

During the first year of Edward II's reign, he was with the court at Nottingham and Lambeth, receiving his wages as king's minstrel. (E101/373/15, ff.7ʳ, 7ᵛ.) He is then lost sight of until the very end of the reign but he was evidently at court for the whole of the intervening period because, when his name appears once more in the records, it is in the list of intimate household servants who were being issued fresh clothing to accompany Edward II on his intended flight to France in 1325/6. (E101/381/11.) At the beginning of the reign of Edward III his name again appears in a list of household minstrels receiving livery. (E101/383/10.)

As has been seen, Edward III retained several of his father's faithful minstrels, most of whom must have been, by that time, middle-aged and elderly men. Thomasin had been at Court for nearly 30 years.

Thomelin de Thounleie.   F.

Thomelin occurs as a surname in the fourteenth century.[26] It is difficult to decide whether it is such here or whether it is a pet name for *Thomas.*

The Thomelin of the Payroll was a vielle-player. He had performed at the wedding-feast of Princess Elizabeth in 1297. (Add. MSS. 7965, f.52ʳ.) There is a possibility that he was attached to the household of the earl of Hereford. Humphrey de Bohun, the father of the Humphrey whom Princess Elizabeth later married as her second husband, was Constable of England at the time of her first marriage and would have been present at the wedding by virtue of his office, if for no other reason. He died in 1298 and his son succeeded to both the earldom and the office of Constable. Therefore, if Thomelin were his vielle-player, one would expect him to be at the Prince's knighting, because, by this time, Earl Humphrey was not only Constable but the king's son-in-law. Also, the place from which Thomelin came (or took his name) was *Tunly,* a few miles east of Stroud. (Glos.)

Trenham.

See *Johannes* de Trenham.

Trumpatores J. de Segrave (ij).   L.

Lord John de Segrave was one of the king's veteran commanders. He was made baron by writ in 1296. At the siege of Caerlaverock his standard, together with those of St. George, St. Edward, St. Edmund, Humphrey de Bohun and Robert de Clifford, was ordered to be flown from the tower of the captured castle. At the time of the knighting he was about 50 years old.

Trumpatores Principis pueri (V).   L.

See *Pueri Principis* (V).

Trumpours Monsire Thomas de Brothertone, (Les ij).   F.

William and John, who, with Martinet le Taborer, were attached to the household of the two boy princes. (E101/368/12, ff.4ᵛ, 8ʳ.) See *Martinet le Taborer.*

---

[26] ' Geoffrey Thomlyn ' (*Cal. Inquis. Misc.,* II, No. 1520); ' Margery Tomelyn ' (*Cal. Ancient Deeds,* I, No. 859).

Trumpours Le Conte de Hereforde (Les ij).   F.

The Constable's two trumpeters would have been much in evidence at the knighting, because Humphrey de Bohun was one of the two distinguished persons who fastened on the Prince's spurs during the *adoubement* ceremony.   Henry de Lacy was the other.

Trumpours le Conte de Lancastre (Les ij).   F.

The two trumpeters of Thomas, earl of Lancaster.
See *Ricardus Vidulator Comitis Lancastrie.*

<h1 style="text-align:center">V.</h1>

Vescy.
See *Jake* de Vescy.

Vidulator Domine de Wake.   L.

It is odd that the name of this vielle-player was not recorded, because Lady de Wake was, like the Lady de Vescy, one of the dowagers at Court.   Some say that she was the daughter of Sir John fitz Barnard of Kingsdown (Kent); others that her father was a Count of Spain, William de Fenes by name.   In the Patent Rolls she is referred to as being a ' kinswoman of the King ' (i.e. of Edward II). (*CPR.* (1307), 16.)

Her husband, Sir John de Wake, had been an active knight in the army.   He had served in Gascony with Edmund, the king's brother and in Scotland with the king himself.   He died in 1300 and his widow, Joan, was favoured at Court.   In 1308, when Edward II went to France to fetch his bride, Joan was in his train.   She must have died soon after, for, on 26 October 1309, Edward gave her lands to Gaveston.

Vigiles Regis (iiij^{or}).   L.

When the king set out for Scotland after the knighting, five of his watchmen accompanied him, namely Adam de Skyrewith, Hugh de Lincoln, Geoffrey de Windsor, Robert de Fynchesley and John de Staunton.   It is, therefore, highly probable that the four anonymous ones on the Payroll were four out of these five.

Because of the intimate nature of their work their names occur very frequently in all the household accounts. The majority of the entries record only payment of their wages and issue of their winter and summer livery; on a few occasions there are references to their being given *largesse* for making their minstrelsy in the presence of the king or the prince. (See p. 52, n. 43.)

The five remained with the old king until he died but under Edward II only John de Staunton's name continues to appear in the accounts. In 1311/12 he was paid his wages at Burstwick. (E101/373/26, f.71ᵛ); in 1313 he went overseas with the king, in the company of Hugh le Despenser, the Elder (*Foedera*, II, pt. 2., 212); in 1319 he was absent from court for only 11 days (E101/373/26, f.27ʳ); and he was still in service in 1320 : ' To John de Staunton, Watchman, 20s. (£200) for his clothing for the whole year.' (MS. Cott. Nero. C. viii, f.116ʳ.)

W.

Walterus de Brayles.   L.
   Unidentified.
   Walter may have been attached to the household of Guy, earl of Warwick, because the place from which he took his name, now the hamlet of Brailes, a few miles ESE of Shipston-on-Stour, was in the possession of the earls of Warwick until 1488, when it lapsed to the Crown. The fact that Walter's name occurs in the Latin list adds weight to the suggestion.

Walterus Leskirmissour (Magister) [et] Frater suus.   L.
   The two sword and buckler men.
   See pp. 60-63.

Wauter Bracon, Trounpour.   L.
   Unidentified.
   Since he was one of *La Commune*, Walter was either a court trumpeter or one who belonged to the household of a member of the royal family.
   The surname, *Bracon*, is a fairly common one, deriving from *braconarius*, OF. *braconier*, a huntsman, one who looked after the hounds or brachets.

Wauter Le Trounpour. L.
  Unidentified.
  Another member of *La Commune*; perhaps a fellow-trumpeter
of Walter Bracon.

Werintone.
  See *Adam* de Werintone.

Whetacre.
  See *Richard* de Whetacre.

Willelmus de Grymesar', Harpour. L.
  Unidentified.
  Grymesar' probably stands for *Grimsargh*, a few miles NE of
Preston (Lancs.).

Willelmus de Duffeld. L.
  Unidentified.
  Duffeld or *Duffield* is a few miles N of Derby.

Willelmus Woderove, Trumpator. L.
  Unidentified.
  The surname survives as Woodruff.

EPILOGUE

Office hours were early in those days. According to a memorandum roll of 1304/5, it was decreed at Lincoln, on 4 January, that henceforth all payments and liveries in the King's Household would be made every day ' before prime or thereabouts ', and that no payments would be paid after that time without the special permission of the King's Steward or Treasurer or whoever was acting as their deputy. This meant that, after a gruelling day on Whitsunday, the minstrels had to be up just after sunrise on Whitmonday morning to collect their *largesse*; which may help to explain why some of them had theirs kindly collected for them by their friends and ' hosts '. If they happened to be feeling a little disgruntled at having to get up so early, they would have found some consolation in the fact that later in the week there was more *largesse* to come; not, perhaps, on so generous a scale as that which they were now waiting for, but still something to look forward to. On Thursday, 26 May, Eleanor de Clare, the king's grand-daughter, was to be married to the young, newly-knighted Hugh le Despenser, the Younger. Therefore, there would be another round of festivities, another programme of entertainment to be organized and another distribution of ready money; but, when that was over, there was to be a general exodus from Westminster. The real and stern reason for the knighting would come to the fore. The king's, the prince's and the knights' vows were now awaiting fulfilment; the affront to God and Holy Church had to be avenged, the murderers of John Comyn punished and Robert Bruce captured. ' King Hobbe ', as Edward and his soldiers derisively called Bruce, had to be liquidated.

The following fortnight was spent in final preparation for the march north. The meeting-place for the military forces, both the new knights and all others who had been summoned for service, was to be Carlisle. Aymer de Valence, the king's appointed Guardian of Scotland, was already on the track of Bruce. On 19/20 June, some weeks before either the prince or the king arrived in Scotland, he routed Bruce's small force at Methven, some seven or eight miles west of Perth, although Bruce himself managed to escape.

Among the many captives were the prime plotters, the bishops of Glasgow and St. Andrews and the abbot of Scone. They were immediately fettered and sent to Porchester, Winchester and Mere castles, respectively, to be kept in irons. Christopher Seton, who had struck down Sir Robert Comyn when he had tried to beat off his nephew's murderers, was executed at Dumfries. Twelve other knights were hanged at Berwick-on-Tweed, and the Earl of Athol and Sir Simon Fraser were sent to London to meet a gruesome fate. Fraser had once been a loyal subject of the king but had turned Scottish patriot, which, in Edward's eyes, meant traitor. He was doomed by the King's Justices to be drawn, hanged and disembowelled. A popular song[1] describing his arrival and execution still survives. The words are stark and often sickening, because they paint so vivid a picture of the incident. They also convey the temper of the time; they express the high-pitched, angry emotion which Bruce's behaviour had engendered in the London populace. After the hideous sentence had been carried out on Fraser, his head was fixed on London Bridge, beside that of Wallace, and his mangled trunk, hanging on the gallows, was encased in iron clasps and guarded day and night by two dozen men.

This was a foretaste of what Bruce and his remaining supporters might expect and a beginning of the fulfilment of the oaths sworn on Whitsunday :

> ' *Sir Edward of Carnarvon, Jhesu him save ant see,*
> *Sir Emer de Valence, gentil knyht and free,*
> *Habbeth y-suore huere oht, par la grace Dee,*
> *He wollith ous delyvren of that false contree,*
> *zef hii conne.*'

So sang a contemporary poet[2], with more hope than faith. It was not the Prince nor Sir Aymer in whom the people put their trust; it was Edward Longshanks, the old and dying king. As long as he was alive they believed the Scots could never prevail. The last stanza in the same poem voices their fierce yet tremulous confidence :

---

[1] *Political Songs of England*, ed. Thomas Wright (Lond. 1839). *Song on the Execution of Sir Simon Fraser*, p. 213.
[2] *Ibid.*

> ' *Tprot* ! *Scot, for thi strif.*
> *Hang up thyn hatchet ant thi knyf,*
> *Whil him lasteth the lyf*
>   *With the longe shankes* !'

As it turned out, nothing could have been more prophetic.

Everyone who knew him in the flesh acknowledged that Prince Edward was a fine figure of a man : *elegans, viribus praestans,*[3] debonair and of outstanding physical strength.' He was handsome, of ready speech, bountiful to the point of extravagance in his wining and dining, versatile in conversation, extremely generous and, as has been seen, thoughtful for his old or sick servants; a great lover of plays and minstrelsy, especially of the *crwth*, and much given to the pleasure and hilarious fun that could be provided by acrobats, conjurors and buffoons. In respect of his constitution he was a worthy son of his father. With his undeniable social graces, his attractive features and his fine physique, he must have looked remarkably well in his stately knight's robes. There can be no doubt that, as far as these attributes went, he was popular and acceptable, both as just himself and as heir to the throne; yet, mingled with the openly-expressed admiration, there always seemed to be a hinted reservation. In 1300, when he was a youth of seventeen, leading the fourth division of the king's army in the assault on Caerlaverock Castle, the poet, who was describing him as he rode into Scotland, found him good-looking, well-proportioned, courteous and well-bred, eager to find an opportunity to prove his strength and an excellent horseman. The coat of arms he carried was that of ' the good king, his father.' ' Now ', adds the poet, as if suddenly assailed by a possible, momentary doubt, ' may God give him grace to appear as valiant and no less.' It could be read as a non-committal statement because, if taken solely at its face value, it could mean no more than a pious, platitudinous hope that the boy will turn out to be as good a man as his father; but the author of *Le Siege de Karlaverok*, whoever he was, knew in person the men he was describing. There is every reason to believe that behind his guarded remarks there lay a shrewd

---

[3] *Gesta Edwardi de Carnarvon*, (Rolls, Ser.) ; *Chronicles of the Reigns of Edward I and Edward II*, II, 91.

knowledge of the Prince's character; it was this which raised
the disguised doubt in his mind. A similar note of uncertainty
is struck in another poem,[4] written immediately after the old
king's death ;

> ' *Le jeofne Edward d'Engletere*
> *Rey est enoint e corouné* :
> *Dieu le doint teil conseil trere,*
> *Ki le pais seit gouverné* ;
> *E la coroune si garder,*
> *Qe la tere seit entere,*
> *E lui crestre en bounté,*
> *Car prodhome i fust son pere.*'

' The young Edward of England has now been anointed
and crowned. God grant that he will follow such counsel
that the land may be so governed and the crown so
guarded that the country may be kept in unity ; and that
he himself will grow in worthiness, for his father was an
excellent man.'

With the benefit of hindsight, one can realise what the reservation in people's minds was and how well-founded it proved
to be.

Everyone has come to know that the Prince's tastes were
hardly those which his subjects considered becoming to a
monarch. He preferred digging and boating to the aristocratic
sport of tourneying; but it was not these ungentlemanly
pursuits nor even his over-indulgence in drink and sleep which
brought about his downfall. There were more serious flaws
in his character. Two of the most outstanding, which are
pertinent in the context of the knighting, were his viciousness
and faithlessness. The Canon of Bridlington and Ralph
Higden[5] each have some phrases in their delineations of his
character which flash light upon the first : ' *in domesticos
efferatus*; *astantes ex levi causa percutiens.*' The use of the word
efferatus is revealing; it is such a strong one to use when describing a man's annoyance with members of his household. Evident-

---

[4] *Political Songs of England, op. cit. supra,* 244-5.
[5] *Op. cit. supra,* n. 3. and Higden's *Polychronicon,* VIII, 298.

ly, the Prince, despite his social charm, was guilty of savage outbursts, striking those standing near him on slight pretext. Rishanger[6] shows up this nasty trait in much graver circumstances : ' Edward, the king's son, when he reached Carlisle, and the newly-made knights with him, who had all vowed to avenge the death of John Comyn, preceded his father into Scotland . . . and took such great vengeance that he spared neither sex nor age. Wherever he went he consigned towns and homesteads to the flames and laid them waste without pity.' The inevitable result of this indiscriminate cruelty was, as Rishanger goes on to point out, that the wealthy scattered in flight leaving the helpless commoners to suffer the punishment which should have been inflicted upon their guilty superiors. When the king came to hear of it he was greatly angered, ' exclaiming loudly against his son ', and gave orders that mercy should always be shown to the poor and to those who had been forced unwillingly into rebellion.

There was no fiercer fighter than Edward I, as his summary punishment of his prisoners after Methven proves, yet he did not believe in wantonly butchering the innocent commons, women, children and the old and helpless.[7] His son believed otherwise. Later on in his reign this culpable weakness was to find fuller expression. In his treatment of the nobles after Boroughbridge and in the humiliating circumstances surrounding the execution of his cousin, Thomas of Lancaster, there came to the surface not only the wreaking of a long-nurtured, closely-hugged vengeance but a display of the same cruelty which had appeared in his treatment of the poor Scottish householders.

As a breaker of oaths he was, in the long run, contemptible. Apart from the fact that he did not attempt to fulfill the vows he had made at the feast, his behaviour in Scotland, not only

---

[6] *Chronica*, W. Rishanger (Rolls Ser.), p. 230.
[7] A further example of Edward I's attitude is to be found in the following mandate issued from Carlisle on 13 March 1307: 'The king to Aymer de Valence, guardian, and his lieutenant in Scotland. As some persons, he understands, interpret his late ordinance for settling Scotland as too harsh and rigorous, which was not his intention, he commands him to proclaim throughout Scotland that all who have been compelled by the abettors of Robert de Brus to rise against the king in war or re-set Robert, innocently, by his sudden coming among them, shall be quit of all manner of punishment.' (*Bain*, II, 508.)

immediately after the knighting but progressively throughout his reign, provides a sorry record of broken promises. People at the time believed that Gaveston had bewitched[8] him, because he was so blatantly prepared to sacrifice everything to have him by his side. If bewitchment produces paralysis of judgement, then they were right. It is unnecessary to cite examples of the many occasions on which he repeatedly went back on his word; one last, grievous one will serve to show to what depths he could sink. It is recorded by the author of the *Vita Edwardi Secundi*.[9] In 1311, after recalling Gaveston for the

---

[8] How profoundly Gaveston was loathed may be sensed in two surviving popular songs which were composed shortly after his death. They are parodies of hymns well-known at the time, so that everyone would be familiar with the tunes to which the songs were set. They are too long to quote here but a few of the most trenchant lines from each will illustrate their quality:

> '*Beata manus jugulans* !
>   *beatus jubens jugulum* !
> *Beatum ferrum feriens*
>   *quem ferre nollet saeculum* !'

It is impossible to bring over the force of the Latin into English; every line is a sword-cut; but the following is a free rendering ;

> 'Blessed be the hand that cut his throat !
> Blessed the one who ordered his head to be cut off !
> Blessed be the sword which struck down
>   him whom the world could no longer tolerate ! '

The second song is equally vitriolic but in a different way. The poet not only reviles Gaveston for his arrogance and cruelty but hurls abuse at the inmates of the Dominican convent (cautiously named 'the other place') who took in Gaveston's corpse after the Earl of Warwick, Gaveston's 'black dog of Arden', had refused to allow it to pass through his castle-gates :

> *Rite corpus perforatur cujus cor sic tumuit*:
> *Terra, pontus, astra, mundus, plaudant quod hic corruit.*
>   *Trux, crudelis inter omnes, nunc a pompis abstinet;*
> *Jam non ultra sicut comes, vel ut rex, se continet;*
> . . . .
> *Sit prophanus alter locus, sit et in dedecore,*
> *Quem foedus cruor foedavit fusus Petri corpore.*
>   *Gloria sit Creatori* ! *gloria comitibus*
> *Qui fecerunt Petrum mori cum suis carminibus* !
> *A modo sit pax et plausus in Anglorum finibus.*

> 'Rightly was the body of him who was so puffed-up punctured.
> Land, sea, stars and the whole inhabited world clap their hands at his fall.
> Savage and cruel among all, he now refrains from ostentation.
> Now he no longer bears himself like an earl — or a king.
> . . . .
> Let that other place, which the filthy blood of Peter's corpse defiled, cease to be sacred ; let it be held in dishonour.
>   Glory be to the Creator ! Glory to the earls
> who caused Peter, with his spells, to die !
> Now may there be peace and the clapping of hands
> within the confines of the English.'

[9] *Op. cit.*, p. 22.

third time, in spite of his oath to the Lords Ordainers not to do so, he sent a message to Robert Bruce, promising him the kingdom of Scotland for ever if he, in return, would allow Gaveston to live there. Bruce's alleged reply would have shamed any man other than our besotted king : ' How could the King of England keep a covenant with me, when he does not keep his promises, even when bound by oath, with his own liegemen, whose loyalty and homage he has accepted and with whom it is taken for granted that loyalty to one another is mutual? No faith is to be placed in a man so untrustworthy.' At the end of his reign, when his subjects decided they could no longer put up with him, the mayor, aldermen and citizens of London wrote to the nobles, asking them whether they would swear with them to support Queen Isabella and her son and ' depose his father for his frequent offences against his oath and his crown.'[10]

So much for Prince Edward's solemn vows before the swans. He never fulfilled them. So much, too, for the vows of some of the new knights. Sixteen of them, Gilbert de Clare, Humphrey de Bohun, Piers Gaveston and Roger Mortimer among them, deserted from the army in October 1306 and had their lands and goods temporarily confiscated by the exasperated old king. Most of them could plead their youth as an excuse. The probability was that everyone was growing rather tired of the perpetual campaigns in Scotland; everyone, that is, except the king. He was the only one truly steadfast in his vows.

He set out from Westminster on 9 June, a day after the Prince, but, on account of his illness, he did not arrive at Carlisle until 30 September. The following day he took up residence in Lanercost Priory, intending to remain there only a matter of days; instead, his stay lasted five months. The Priory never recovered from the vast expense this long sojourn entailed, for the Court consisted of about two to three hundred people.[11]

The Exchequer accounts for this period, especially E101/ 370/16, the daybook, extending from 20 November 1306 to 17 July 1307, make it clear that, at Lanercost, life went on as

---

[10] *Calendar of Plea and Manorial Rolls of the City of London*, 1323-64., 11-12.
[11] See *Edward I at Lanercost Priory*, 1306-7, J. R. R. Moorman, *Eng. Hist. Rev.*, 67 (1952), 161–74.

usual as far as was possible. The business and formalities of royal household routine did not falter. John Depe and his son, the king's personal trumpeters, were in attendance to perform their daily duties; John Drake made the dinner wafers; King Robert and King Caupenny organized plays and other functions; William le Sautreour had travelled north in the queen's retinue; the four royal harpers were there to entertain and solace their master—but Edward, although full as ever of courage and determination, was fatally ill. A bill[12] for some of the medicines for him which were sent from London, while it does not help anyone to make a definite diagnosis of his disease, testifies to the pain he was enduring. There was an astringent ointment containing Socotra aloes ' for the king's legs ', another containing balsam; aromatic herbs for ordinary baths and special herbs for *stuffae*, hot, sweating baths. There was wheat oil, oil of ash and oil of bay; distilled oil of turpentine; a plaster containing laudanum and oriental amber ' for the king's neck '. Another group of medicaments were provided to counteract the general physical distress which accompanies the final breakdown of the whole system; lozenges and drinks to clean the tongue and ease the throat; soothing suckets made of resin, ' sharpened with powdered pearls and coral ', rose-water of Damascus and ' wine ' made out of the spirit of pomegranate juice; and lastly, a comforting electuary containing ' amber and musk and pearls and jacinths and gold and pure silver.' It does not sound very attractive, as medicine, and it is difficult to believe that it would have been very effective, but as far as its ingredients and cost were concerned, it was fit for a king; 8 lb. were sent, costing 8 marks (£1,066-13s.-4d. or £133-6s.-8d. per lb.)

His strength of will staved off the end for some months. Believing or forcing himself to believe that he was recovering, he left Lanercost and moved to Carlisle on 5 March 1307, but he lingered there until, in early May, something happened which roused him. Bruce, who had foiled all attempts to discover his hiding-place, suddenly reappeared in Ayrshire and forced Aymer de Valence and his troops to retreat at Loudon. An anonymous letter, preserved among the national manu-

---

[12] E101/368/30.

scripts of Scotland,[13] draws what is probably the last living picture of the indomitable old king. The writer tells his correspondent that ' the king and queen are well, but the king is much enraged that the Guardian and his forces have retreated before King Hobbe.' The letter was written on Whitmonday 1307. Perhaps the memory of the Prince's knighting the year before was in Edward's mind, for he seemed to be filled with renewed energy and optimism. ' He intends going to Dumfries,' the writer goes on to say, ' but not till after Midsummer. He has sent to London for his tents . . . yesterday, on Pentecost, he made his troops ride decked with leaves, about 400 of them, and watched them himself and was much pleased and merry.'

It was only a temporary triumph of mind over matter. Midsummer came and went; he was still at Carlisle. Toward the end of June, still convincing himself that he was getting better, he offered up his litter to God, in thanksgiving, in Carlisle Cathedral. On Thursday, 8 July he arrived at Burgh-upon-Sands, remained there the night, and died the following morning. The last items in the chemist's bill speak for themselves :

' $6\frac{1}{2}$ ozs. of balsam, for anointing the Lord King's body; aromatic powder of aloes, frankincense and myrrh, for placing in the king's body; 3 ozs. of musk, for placing in the king's nostrils.'

Many of his old, faithful servants and minstrels were with him at the end; his trumpeters, his *Reges Haraldorum*, his watchmen and his harpers; John Drake, his waferer, Tommy Devenish, his *robarius*, Gerard Dorum, his yeoman, and Rhys Maelgwn, Gruffydd ap Maredudd and Cynan ap Maredudd, his Welsh squires. These are the ones whose names occur regularly in E101/370/16; but there were others, too, with whom we have become familiar : Thomas le Croudere, Walter de Wodestoke, John de Cressy, Elias Audoenus and Guilleme sanz maniere.

Edward had willed that his heart should be taken to the Holy Land, and that his bones should not be buried but carried in the army until the vows he had made at Westminster had been fulfilled. Nobody paid any attention to these wishes.

---

[13] *Bain,* II, 526. No. 1979.

His body was taken to London via Richmond (Yorks.) and Waltham Abbey, in which latter place it lay for over two months. At last, on 27 October, it was laid to rest in Westminster Abbey :

> ' *Ore si gist soun cors en tere,*
> *Si va la siecle en decline.*'[14]

Once again a contemporary voice proved to be prophetic. Prince Edward, now the new king, after receiving homage at Carlisle from some of his nobles, moved into Scotland, ostensibly to carry on the war against Bruce, but he had already laid his own plans. Piers Gaveston was immediately recalled and, on 6 August, created Earl of Cornwall and promised Margaret de Clare of the royal house of Gloucester, to wife. To celebrate his return and his new honours, he held a banquet for the king on 17 August.

Long before the old king's body was buried, the usual plundering of dead man's goods had begun. No neater comment on the situation can be made than the following mandates :[15]

18 July 1307. Aymer de Valence commands Sir James Dalileye, the king's receiver at Ayr, ' to deliver to Sir Emori la Souche, the Seneschal of his household, and Henri, his butler, 8 tuns of wine.'

24 July 1307, Aymer de Valence commands Sir James Daliley ' to give, with all haste, a *tonel* of the king's wine to Sir Ingram de Umfraville and Sir Alexander de Balliol, that they may better do the king's business on the enemy.'

1 August 1307. ' The king commands the keeper of his late father's stores at Newcastle to deliver all the wines there to William de Brichull, his vallet.'

The Scottish campaign was abandoned. The brilliant knighting ceremony at Westminster had been to no purpose. The vows made before the swans were forgotten and remained unfulfilled. The multitude of minstrels began tuning their instruments in readiness for a new, grimmer entertainment. Piers Gaveston was back. The ' tragedy of Edward II ' had begun.

---

[14] *Political Songs, op. cit. Lament on the death of Edward I,* p. 242.
[15] *Bain,* II, 520 ; III, 1.

APPENDIX

The New Knights.

Robertus Achard.
Gerardus de Aillesford.
Edmundus de Arundel.
Egidius de Asteley.
Gilbertus de Aton.
Radulphus Bagot.
Edwardus de Balliol.
Thomas Bardolf.
Radulphus Basset.
Johannes de Bassyngbourn.
Humfridus de Bassyngbourn.
Warinus de Bassyngbourn.
Willelmus de Bassyngge.
Rogerus de Baufou (de Bello Fago, Beaufoy)
Rogerus de Bavent.
Willelmus de Bayouse (or Bayous)
Johannes de Bello Campo.
Henricus Beaufuiz. (Beaufou)
Thomas de Bechum.
Ingelramus Belet.
Johannes de Belhous.
Walterus de Berkyngham.
Ricardus de Berley.
Henricus de Bermyngham.
Ricardus de Bermyngham.
Willelmus de Bermigeham (or Bermyngham)
Willelmus Bernak.
Thomas de Berthum.
Henricus de Bery (or Biry)
Johannes le Blound.
Johannes de Boillande.
Brankalo de Boloigne (Shaw: Brankalo de Boloigne (Drantaleon de Ordalo or Endalo de B.))
Radulphus de Botteturte.
Humfridus de Boune. (Bohun)
Johannes de Boyvill.
Thomas de Boyvill.
Petrus de Bozoun.
Willelmus Brabazon.
Hugo Braiboef. (or Braboef)
Egidius de Breheus. (Breos)
Ricardus de Breheus.
Thomas de Brompton.
Petrus de Burgate.
Stephanus de Burghash. (Burwash)
Rogerus de Burton.
Johannes de Bykebury.
Georgius de Chastel.
Johannes Chaundos.
Rogerus de Chaundos.

Thomas filius domini Thomae de Chaworth.
Rogerus de Chedele. (Cheadle)
Gilbertus de Clare.
Gilbertus de Clare filius domini Thomae de Clare.
Rogerus Clavis.
Johannes de Clivedon.
Stephanus de Cobeham. (or Cobbeham)
Galfridus de Coleville.
Baldwinus de Colne.
Johannes Comyn.
Henricus filius Conani.
Robertus le Conestable.
Johannes Conquest.
Rogerus filius domini Thomae Corbet.
Thomas Corbet.
Willelmus Corbet.
Edmundus de Cornubia.
Willelmus de Cosyngton.
Philippus de Curtenay.
Ricardus Daniel.
Johannes de Daventre.
Willelmus Dautre. (or Dautrie)
Henricus de Deen. (or Den)
Walterus de Derlyngham.
Johannes Denre.
Hugo filius domini Hugonis le Despenser.
Hugo de Ditton.
Radulphus de Driby. (or Dryby)
Ricardus Druel.
Ricardus de Echebaston. (Edgbaston)
Dominus Edwardus Princeps Walliae
Bartholomeus de Enfeud (Enfeld)
Henricus de Erdyngton.
Petrus de Evere. (Ashmole and Shaw: de Evercy)
Adam de Everyngham.
Walterus Faucumberge. (Fauconberg)
Robertus de Faudon.
Thomas de Ferrers.
Ricardus Folyot.
Amaricus de Fosad. (Fossard)
Johannes de Foxley.
Johannes de Foyle.
Johannes de Frevill. (or Frivill)
Walterus de Freygne.
Rogerus de Gardeston.
Petrus de Gavaston.

Nicholaus de Genevile.
Robertus de Godemanston.
Willelmus de Goldington.
Thomas de Greillye.
Thomas de Grey.
Petrus de Gresle. (Gresley)
Rogerus de Grymeston.
Robertus filius Guidonis.
Johannes de Guyse.
Walterus Hakelut.
Johannes de Hants.
Johannes Harcourt.
Willelmus de Harden.
Johannes de Harpefeld.
Johannes de Haulo. (son of Richard
   de H. of Bucks.)
Johannes de Haulo. (son of Sir
   John de H. of Kent)
Johannes de Haverington.
Aungerus filius Henrici.
Hugo filius Henrici.
Johannes de Heryoz. (or Heriz)
Willelmus de Herperden. (or Har-
   peden.)
Robertus de Hilledeyard.
Willelmus de Holande.
Laurentius de Hollebeche.
Willelmus de Hondesacre.
Robertus de Hoo.
Hugo Hosy.
Hugo Howel
Walterus filius Humfridi.
Walterus de Hugerford. (or Huge-
   ford.)
Willelmus de Huntyngfeud.
Ricardus Huwys. (or Hewys,
   Hywysh)
Johannes de Hynton.
Rogerus de Ingefeld. (Ashmole and
   Shaw: Ingelfeld)
Johannes de Insula. (de L'Isle)
Walterus filius domini Johannis
   de Insula.
Rethericus de Ispania.
Radulphus de Kameys. (or Kamoys)
Radulphus de Kele.
Robertus de Kendale.
Rogerus de Kerdeston.
Johannes de Knoville.
Nicholaus Krvell. (Crioll)
Walterus de Kyngeshevede.
Johannes de Kyrkby.
Johannes de Lacy. (1)
Johannes de Lacy. (2)
Robertus de Lacy.
Jacobus de Lamborn.
Johannes de Langeton.
Johannes de Launeye.
Petrus de Lekebourne. (Legborn)
Thomas de Leukenore.

Willelmus Littebon.
Thomas de Lodelawe. (Ludlow)
Willelmus de Lodelawe.
Philippus de Lou.
Ricardus Lovel.
Robertus Lovel.
Thomas de Lucy.
Willelmus de Lucy.
Johannes de Lungevill.
Johannes de Lyngeyne.
Hugo de Mailby.
Nicholaus Malemeyns.
Thomas Malore. (Malory)
Willelmus de Manneby.
Johannes Mansel.
Johannes de la Mare.
Robertus de la Mare.
Willelmus Marmyon.
Johannes Marteyn.
Johannes Maudyt. (or Mauduit)
Johannes Maulevere. (or Mauleverer)
Petrus filius domini Petri de Mauley.
Johannes de Mautravers.
Johannes filius Johannis Mautravers.
Godefridus de Meaux.
Willelmus de Menymrate. (or
   Monymrate)
Morganus ap Mereduke.
Johannes de Meryeth.
Henricus le Moigne.
Walterus de Molesworth.
Johannes de Mombrey. (Ashmole
   and Shaw: Moubray)
Willelmus de Montacute.
Willelmus de Montegomeri. (Ash-
   mole and Shaw: Walterus de M.)
Thomas Mordac. (Murdak)
Willelmus de la More.
Johannes de Morteyn.
Rogerus filius domini Rogeri de
   Mortimer.
Rogerus de Mortuomari. (Son of
   Sir Edmund de M. of Wigmore.)
Johannes de Morton. (or Mortone)
(......) de Morevill.
Willelmus de la Mote.
Willelmus de Motouny. (or Motoun)
Johannes de Mouteney.
Johannes de Multon.
Thomas de Multon.
Jacobus de Nadw.....
Johannes de Neubourgh.
Johannes de Nevill.
Jacobus de Norton.
Jacobus de Nortwode. (Northwode)
Johannes de Pabenham.
Robertus filius Roberti filii Pagani.
Edmundus Pecche.
Johannes de Penbrigge. (or Penbrug)
Johannes de la Penne.

Nicholaus Pershet. (or Pershots)
Johannes de Plescis. (Plescy)
Edmundus de Plescys.
Alanus Plockenet.
Walterus le Poeure. (or Poure)
Johannes de la Poille.
Griffinus filius Griffini de la Pole.
Thomas de Ponynges.
Ricardus de Porteseie.
Rogerus Pychard.
Johannes Pykard.
Hugo de Pykeworth.
Willelmus Pyrot.
Radulphus de Rolleston.
Willelmus de Romeseie. (or Romeseye. Ashmole and Shaw: Walterus de R.)
Robertus de Roos.
Johannes le Rous.
Philippus le Rous.
Johannes de Ruda.
Willelmus Russel. (Ashmole and Shaw: Rosel)
Henricus de Rybeford. (Ashmole and Shaw: Rypsford). (Ribbesford, Worcs.)
Nicholaus de Rye.
Johannes de Ryson.
Ricardus de Ryvers.
Andreas de Sakeville.
Johannes de Salesbury. (Ashmole and Shaw: Salsbiri.)
Urianus de Sancto Petro. (de St. Pierre)
Thomas de Sandwyz. (Ashmole: de Sanwico)
Johannes de Sanwic. (Sandwich. Kent.)
Willelmus de Sauston.
Johannes Sauvage.
Robertus de Scales.
Warinus de Scargil.
Ricardus de Sculton. (or Schulton)
Galfridus de Seye.
Nicholaus de Sheldon.
Walterus de Skydemore.
Willelmus de Somercotes.
Johannes de Somere. (Somery)
Nicholaus de Somerville. (Ashmole and Shaw; Rogerus de S.)

Willelmus la Souche. (Ashmole and Shaw: de la Zouche.)
Johannes de Stauntone.
Walterus de Stirkelande.
Willelmus de Stopham.
Robertus de Strale. (or Scrale)
Johannes filius domini Johannis de Sullie.
Gregorius de Thornton. (Ashmole: Georgius de T. Shaw: Georgius (Gregory) de T.)
Johannes de Thouthorp.
Willelmus Tracy.
Johannes Treiagu.
Willelmus Trussel.
Johannes de Twyford.
Gerardus de Usflet.
Thomas de Ver filius comitis Oxonie. (Ashmole and Shaw: de Veer)
Thomas de Verdon.
Philippus de Verley. (Ashmole and Shaw: de Vyreley)
Johannes de Wachesham.
Humfridus de Walden.
Rogerus Waleis. (or Waleys)
Johannes de Walkyngham.
Adam Walran (Walerand)
Adam de Walton.
Adam de Wanneville. (Ashmole and Shaw: de Wanerville)
Johannes la Ware. (Ashmole: de la Ware)
Johannes de Warenne.
Fulcius filius Warini.
Johannes filius Warini.
Robertus de Watervill.
Radulphus de Wedon.
Thomas de Wedon.
Johannes de Weston.
Willelmus de Weylonde.
Eustachius de Whiteneye.
Willelmus de Wrotesle.
Johannes filius Johannis de Wygeton (Ashmole and Shaw: de Wegetone)
Robertus de Wykham.
Edmundus de Wylyngton.
Robertus de Wyvill.
Thomas de Yedesen. (or Zedesen)

The above list has been compiled from the one printed by Ashmole in 1672 (reproduced by Shaw in 1906) and the two which are to be found in the Exchequer records : E101/362/20 and E101/369/4.

The amount of extant material relative to the new knights would fill a very large volume. Most of them were active soldiers all their lives; a few seem to have more or less vegetated as country squires; nearly all were, at some time or another, Knights of the Shire, Justices, Commissioners of Array, Conservators of the Peace and Leaders of Levies. In the thirteenth and fourteenth centuries robbery, assault and homicide were common; abduction and rape equally so. The great lords were as culpable as their lesser brethren; both barons and knights were breakers of their neighbours' parks, stealers of the king's deer, robbers of parsons' cattle, pigs and chickens, illicit reapers of other men's crops, and abductors and ravishers of their neighbours' wives and daughters. Over and over again one meets in the records with situations in which the very knight who, as Justice or Conservator of the Peace, meted out condign punishment to a fellow-knight for offences of the kind mentioned above, was himself hauled before the Justice— often the man he had previously convicted—on a similar charge.

They were fierce, ruffianly men, sturdy, fearless, choleric and possessed of an irrepressible spirit of independence. They did not hesitate to attack the man who had conferred knighthood on them because he acted contrary to their own and the country's interests, although, it has to be acknowledged, self-interest frequently clouded their judgement and laid some of the greatest among them open to the charge brought against them by the author of the *Vita Edwardi Secundi* : ' *Amor magnatum quasi ludus in alea et uota diuitium pennis simillima*.' ' The favour of noblemen is like a game of dice and the vows of the wealthy most like unto feathers.' Much of the chaotic misery which descended upon the country during the twenty years of Edward II's reign was caused by the turbulent behaviour of some of the most influential earls, who, in order to preserve their estates, drifted now to the barons now to the king like feathers in the wind.

Set against the rich, spectacular backdrop of the Whitsuntide knighting, the new knights appear like future players in a black drama about to begin. A number of them did not live long enough to take part in more than the first scene; sickness, old age or the chances of war took them early off the boards; all the rest, with their minstrels, were, within a matter of a decade, to find themselves actors on a blood-stained stage which extended from Bannockburn to Berkeley Castle.